THE MAN WHO KNEW TOO MUCH

Robert Sito was leaning over the table, his arms creating abstract figures in the air, helping articulate his thoughts as he spoke. Stan Penskie sat back in his chair, breathless, his eyes locked on Robert's lips. The information Sito related was a revelation, stunning beyond anything Stan could have expected. If all this were indeed true, the world was on the brink of a disaster. The powers this UOP officer was describing were unimaginable; so much so that they had to be a figment of a hallucination, or one of the most ingenious and vivid conspiracy theories ever to come across Penskie's hands. Surely Sito had been exaggerating. Deep down Penskie knew Sito may have been overworked but he was not crazy. But was *this* possible? Penskie shrugged and shook his head. Somewhere in Robert's theory had to be a flaw. If he were to put all the facts together, the immediate conclusions had to be discarded as far-fetched, or insane, for the lack of a better word.

Robert was wrong. He had to be.

A sudden blast filled the room. . . .

JACK KING

THE FIFTH INTERNATIONALE

LEISURE BOOKS NEW YORK CITY

For Ela

A LEISURE BOOK®

April 2004

Published by

Dorchester Publishing Co., Inc.
200 Madison Avenue
New York, NY 10016

ISBN 0-8439-5337-3

Printed in the United States of America.

THE FIFTH INTERNATIONALE

Prologue

Warsaw, August 1991

Tall and lush trees covered the westerly façade of the Soviet Embassy, effectively obstructing the view of anyone interested in the historic building. Here and there a patch of gray stucco wall could be seen if anyone wanted to peruse closer, but anyone persistent enough to loiter about the nine-foot cast-iron fence surrounding the property would be ushered away either by the frequent sentry rounds of the uniformed and armed guards on the inside of the fence or the gray-uniformed police patrols on the outside. The man standing in one of the five windows of the second floor knew that not even the station of the Polish counterintelligence office located directly across the street in a six-story building would be able to discover his presence. Still, the unit assigned to monitor the embassy was dispached from their post for this one day. No one was to find out the identity of the man. No one was to know about his presence. His name was Col. Alexy Borisovich Rybkin, a commanding officer of *Shturm,* an ultrasecret unit of Spetsnaz. His presence in Poland, away from the events that drew tanks to Moscow's White House and kept the world at watch, was caused by an even more important circumstance.

Summoned to the nondescript office on the second floor were three men who arrived simultaneously in black Volga limousines driven by *Shturm* soldiers. The youngest of the three men was an economics professor at the University of Warsaw, a brilliant mind whose only obstacle on the path to high government office in these days of uncertainty and freedom was his communist past. Prior to 1989, the year that would forever mark the end of an era in history books throughout the world, he was an adviser to the minister of finance, a man he despised for his lack of independence and narrow-minded leadership dictated by obsolete party directions. The second man had traveled a much farther distance to attend the meeting. Officially serving the post of Polish military attaché to Bulgaria, he devoted much of his time away from Sofia to a reclusive mountain estate built for a reason known only to a handful of people in the Eastern Bloc. The last one to enter the embassy compound was the Bulgarian ambassador to Poland, for whom today's meeting would have a decisive meaning, as his post was likely to end shortly due to recent political developments in his home country.

The three men were escorted to the second floor.

Without waiting for the doors to close behind them, the military attaché rushed toward the lonely figure standing in the window.

"You were supposed to pay your dues, *not* finance your own political agenda!" he shouted, his fervent gesticulation adding a comical appearance to his stocky, balding, and unmilitary posture, so contrary to his rank of general of the *Nadwiślańskie Jednostki Wojskowe,* a formation under the command of the minister of interior.

"I admit, Colonel, the general has a point. The coup d'état puts the mission in jeopardy. While no one suggests you participated in the events for your personal gain"—the professor shot a long look to the general—"some of our members have expressed their deepest concern over your agency's intentions. Need I remind you, Colonel, that these people control significant assets, the lack of which can ruin years of preparation and cost hundreds of lives, not excluding their own?"

"Gentlemen." The silhouetted figure of Colonel Rybkin moved away from the window. "I assure you our forces in Mother Russia had no part in the coup other than—"

"Oh, please!" the general cut in, his face red in exasperation. "The KGB doesn't call the shots anymore, and especially not here! You can no longer suppress the flow of information. *Na rany Chrystusa,* have you watched television lately? Moscow is crawling with *Shturm* troops! Now the question everyone wants an answer to is, What is the foreign operations unit doing alongside the Alpha forces?"

"The *Spetsgruppa Shturm* is assigned to the first chief directorate," the colonel declared reticently. "As you undoubtedly know, Comrade General, we are subordinate to Maj. Gen. Victor Chernyakov, who is a man of political goals. To question his orders—"

"There were commanders who refused to follow Chernyakov's orders!" the general broke in.

"My, my, General, you do keep abreast! I don't believe that news has made it to CNN yet!" The Russian always suspected the general, who once headed the second department of the Polish Ministry of the Interior, responsible for the counterintelligence of having active contacts in Moscow. But he also knew the man lacked political finesse. The general had high aspirations not backed by talent. He was a good soldier, no doubt about it—his devotion to the cause was the best testimony—but his days with the organization were numbered. "As I was saying, to question Chernyakov at this stage of our development would be foolish. It would bring attention and scrutiny very much undesired, and could, as the professor pointed out, cost years of hard work, not to mention the lives of our comrades."

"If you had only paid your debt in time we wouldn't have to worry about it now, would we? Professor, I warned the board about collaborating with the Russians! History has taught us only one thing about them: It's either under their heel or at their throats."

"Now, that's enough!" The Russian slammed his hand on the table, rage in his eyes. "You have been nothing but a whining, melodramatic fool! Yes, the coup may have foiled our plans; yes, it may have cost our lives even, but there is no time like the time of turmoil, when one can attain the biggest gains. Surely a man in your position and with your background should know that." The Russian fixed his gaze on the general's face. "Now, if you'll sit down, I'll explain."

There was a time when a military general of a "friendly" nation would have stood at attention in front of a KGB colonel and spoken only when spoken to, but those times were gone forever. Or so it would seem. There was already talk of Poland joining NATO, and a Polish general had nothing to fear anymore. Yet fear was a major factor in making the general as defiant as he was. A man who was afraid panicked and lost the ability to think rationally. The general was afraid. For years now his main duty was not to serve his country but to serve the organization. The organization meant Rybkin. Fear intensified the anger.

"What's to explain? I'll bet you, Professor." The general was losing ground and needed support. "I'll bet you he's here to ladle out from the treasury!" He turned abruptly toward the Russian. "But you don't control the purse strings, Colonel. . . ."

"Sit down, General," the Russian demanded, his voice a hiss, his eyes cold and intense, a trait that had earned him the name Snake among his men.

For a moment the general wrestled with the gaze, but then he slowly retreated to his seat, a beaten soldier stripped of everything, including honor.

"As I said before, I've called this emergency meeting to *discuss* with you a change of plans and . . ." It took only a glance to halt the general's last attempt to rise. "And to remit our share. Moscow events were just as surprising to me as they were to the rest of you, I assure you. True, they may've wrecked years of preparation, but instead they provided our cause with an opportunity undreamed of before." The Russian reached down for a dark leather briefcase, turned the combination lock, and took out a manila file strapped with an elastic band. He pulled out several sheets of paper, laid them on the table, and continued, "Now, General, as the treasurer, would you care to run by us the state of the assets gathered by our comrades, up-to-date and guarded by you so closely?"

The general glanced at the professor and the Bulgarian.

Both men were too lenient. Typical civilians. Where would the organization be today if it weren't for people like him and others of military background? To follow the layout and be ready to stand up and fight! When Rybkin announced the meeting, the general knew what it was going to be about. Two years prior, when he was appointed military attaché, but more importantly assigned to guard the treasury, and had to relinquish his command of the second department of the Ministry of the Interior, he made sure not to leave his office without planting loyal contacts, both from within and outside of the organization. A decade such as the eighties in Poland produced strong ties within the department he headed, and his years in the Soviet military academy left him with some good friends who went to high places in the Kremlin and Lubyanka. His contacts in the Eastern Bloc's intelligence agencies kept him up-to-date with the changes in the community. Yes, he knew what was happening in Moscow. But he also knew better than to push Rybkin too far, and especially here, on his turf, inside the Soviet Embassy.

He swallowed his pride and read from a document he had prepared for the meeting; "In alphabetical order: Bulgaria . . ."

"The total for the bloc will suffice."

"Not including the Soviet Union"—the general could not refrain the satisfaction of pointing it out; it was his little victory—"hard currency, banks, businesses, corporations, and assets formed and owned by the bloc's agencies in the West, gold reserves, and objects of art held in Bulgaria and private estates in the West, at today's market values would cash in at approximately . . . one hundred to one hundred and five billion dollars."

"Good God!" The professor and the Bulgarian gasped simultaneously. They were well aware that the treasure had to be substantial—the collection had been going on for years—but neither had expected it to reach such a level.

The Russian pushed his papers across the desk toward the general.

"While the politicians were squabbling over seats in the White House, troops loyal to our cause were able to visit the Kremlin vaults, as well as some of the party members' dachas, and access their Swiss accounts." He paused for effect and to wait out the murmur of his interlocutors. "The figures you see are only rough estimates I prepared on the way from Moscow. As you can imagine, there was little time to prepare a full assessment. Later on you'll receive a detailed breakdown of our contribution. Read it aloud, will you?"

As the general glanced through the handwritten pages his hands began to tremble, anxiety growing in his voice.

"Gold bars . . . hard currencies . . . truckloads of objects of art, private and Hermitage . . . bank accounts, businesses set up and controlled by the Komitet . . . that's . . . that's . . ." He looked up from one man to another. "Roughly speaking, that's forty . . . maybe forty-five billion!"

The air in the room stood still. The men were processing the information. The professor was leaning over the general's shoulder, scanning the notes. One hundred and fifty billion dollars! That kind of an amount, when compared to, say, Poland's international debt of some forty-odd billion, was a fortune of unthinkable proportions.

"Where is it all? How do you plan to transport it?" The ambassador spoke with worry in his voice. It was his task to assure safe passage to and from Bulgaria. The changing political scene in his country could hinder his influence anytime. "I mean, good God, five hundred tonnes of gold . . ."

"Do not be concerned about it." Rybḳin glanced at his wristwatch. "The convoy should reach the Polish border in a matter of hours."

"Polish border? Have you gone mad?" A perplexed voice shouted.

The Russian disregarded the concern.

"Which brings me to another reason for our little get-together." He paused for effect. "It is time to move the treasury out of Bulgaria."

"Out of Bulgaria?" The ambassador gasped, a trace of relief in his voice.

"It is the safest place; we established it years ago!" The general sensed that the transfer would also mean changes, perhaps even termination of his position as the treasurer. Being in charge of billions of dollars' worth of goods, being able to see, to touch all those riches, the gold, the jewels, even those paintings, the masterpieces some collectors would be willing to shell out millions for, was a position he loved. It made him feel important and in control: It was his prerogative to assess the danger of possible seizure of the treasury and destroy it if necessary.

"It may have been the safest place to store the assets, but the times are changing, something our leaders failed to notice. As you all know the situation in Bulgaria, you can understand that in putting such sums to work, conducting grandiose financial operations out of a country that's having trouble feeding its own people would bring undesired attention in the West."

The men weighed the announcement in silence. The uncertainty, years of covert activities, illegal transfers, coverups, and the use of undue authority were finally going to reap rich rewards. There would be plenty of the one hundred and fifty billion green ones to provide peace of mind and protection for all those comrades who fought for their ideals, repeatedly jeopardizing their lives and health in the name of the ideology that failed them. Countless armies of nameless officers of the state security and intelligence services were stranded in enemy territory, even in their own countries, afraid to admit to what they did, not knowing what the next day would bring; the party members were now being persecuted for their political beliefs, the very fundamental right the new democratic system was supposed to provide and guarantee. Instead it was freedom and democracy for the chosen.

"Of course," Rybkin continued, "to achieve our goals, certain changes are necessary. Our intelligence indicates, and any avid observer will concur, that the current Polish administration will fold within weeks."

The Poles were taken aback. Rybkin's statement could not have been merely drawn out of observation. True, the political scene in Poland resembled a street marketplace, with politicians trading lucrative appointments and bickering over bills and responsibilities, and the people growing angry over closures, layoffs, and hyperinflation. But to say the government was about to fold required more than ample observation. It meant that Rybkin was better informed than both Poles would like to see. Partnership in conspiracy aside, it was a matter of national honor and pride. Unless, of course, Rybkin's sources consisted of the members of the organization they had all fathered, which would bear great testimony to its efficiency.

The Russian was a keen observer of human emotions and was quick to dispel any doubts.

"Years of careful planning are reaping their rewards. Our organization's reach is deep-rooted in all the bloc's governments," he continued when the agitation subsided. "The situation opens new perspectives for you personally as well as for the organization as a whole. Poles are disillusioned with the new system, which was meant to bring them prosperity, but seemingly brought only rising prices and unemployment. It is safe to predict that the new government will steer to the left, but it will be even more essential that the adopted policies of free market economy and democratization continue. We will need your expertise and dedication to the cause in the new administration. . . ."

Excitement followed his words. The men savored the new possibilities, the sweet taste of vindication, feelings that lingered in the last years of uncertainty and growing fear of retribution and expected trials of the former communist regime's officials.

"General." The Russian stood up; the officer followed. "I am pleased to inform you that you will receive a task worthy of a military officer. As defense minister you will be personally responsible for safe passage of the treasury onto Polish soil and its subsequent safety within your country." Rybkin noticed the general stroking his chest, as if looking for medals, his eyes adrift. That self-possessed buffoon was a mistake from the start, the Russian thought. "And you, Minister." He turned toward the professor. "You will make sure our funds are securely invested and managed."

"Minister . . ." The professor was flustered. His dreams were coming to life. "But you cannot seriously expect Poland to launder a hundred and fifty billion dollars!" he said.

"Arrangements have been made for your nomination as minister of finance in the new government, and similar positions will be filled with our people from other countries associated with our organization." He nodded toward the Bulgarian ambassador. "Of course, you won't be drifting alone in the open seas. Our people will seize other strategic positions within the government; their sole purpose will be to provide you with enough freedom in your decisions.

"Poland is already experiencing the boom of the new reality. The amount of Western capital pouring into the country is the highest in the region. Your country's eagerness to continue and sustain the open-market economy is exactly what we need to safely invest and multiply our assets. Poland's wide-open doors to the West will help us achieve what our ideologists and military could not. One day you will join the European Community, perhaps even NATO. We have to be prepared. We shall activate the corporations and sleepers our agencies have placed all over the Western hemisphere. There isn't a government department, a major financial institution, or a corporation in which we won't have an asset or a hook in someone. In the years to come the West will be ecstatic with the transitions in the former bloc. The world is watching; the world wants a democratic Russia, and the coup could not come at a better time to prove the Evil Empire is crumbling. The Soviet people want democracy, prosperity, and freedom. Our squabbling politicians, the breaking off of the satellite countries, and the loosened grip on certain Soviet republics are providing the world with exactly what it wants to see. The illusion of the tyranny ending and of the West's victory is uncanny. The West wants to believe it and shall have it.

"Gentlemen," the Russian finished triumphantly, "the West, and indeed the world, will be won with the only weapon and argument it understands and fears: money, the one ideology our fathers and predecessors dismissed."

Jack King

Moscow, September 1991

"The government resigns. The president concedes and appoints a new prime minister." This and similar headlines dominated the front pages of Poland's biggest daily newspapers. The reader was shuffling through a stack of freshly arrived papers until he found the one he was most interested in. He scanned the feature article and the paragraph that brought a smile to his face: Gazeta *learned from its sources that the new premier has already chosen his cabinet. . . . Jerzy Konieczny, a professor of economy at the University of Warsaw, will head the ministry of finance. . . .* Farther down the page a brief note read: *On a sad note, Poland's military attaché to Bulgaria died from cardiac arrest upon receiving his appointment to the post of the minister of defense.*

The reader put down the paper and looked out the window. Yes, to survive and thrive, the organization had to be restructured. Fewer soldiers was the first step in the reform. More hotheads would have to fall to make room for professionals: economists, lawyers, financial planners, and bankers—strategists who would build an empire based on a corporate model, not on guns.

He chuckled at the comparison and leaned on the windowsill.

The sky was unusually blue over Moscow.

Chapter One

Warsaw, Monday, December 2002

It was a dreary winter day for the embassy staff. Christmas was around the corner, the shopping craze already circulating in bloodstreams and nervous systems, bringing everyone's work chores to a standstill. What could be more important than the prospect of a long awaited holiday, a chance to see family, to finally have an opportunity to sightsee? Working overseas was supposed to be fun: See new places, experience strange customs, eat exotic foods, and somewhere in between put in a few hours to earn a paycheck. Instead, employees were expected to do the job of three or four; the diplomatic corps was notoriously understaffed; the combination of a lack of knowledge of the local language and strange cultural customs added to a stressful and disappointing experience. The lure of the foreign land quickly subsided, giving way to everyday drudgery, broken up on the rare occasions such as holidays. But once holidays were near they took over the whole body and mind. No matter what the project, there was a time when one's senses stopped responding to the boss's spur. One lived for holidays.

Stan Penskie was sitting at a café, a stack of freshly arrived newspapers from home lying unopened in front of him on the small round table. A second cup of cappuccino was reaching the bottom of the mug, and he pondered ordering another one. The large window cast a view over Three Crosses Square; small drops of rain were forming long streaks on the glass; the day was cold, dark, and wet, a typical winter day in Warsaw. A thought crossed his mind to return to the embassy before the weather changed for the worse, since he had left his cellular phone and jacket in the office, but he had not moved. The café was only a short stroll from the embassy's compound, and in any case, there was no point in rushing back; everybody at the office being on edge before the holidays, people were agitated and unwittingly aloof. He took the last sip and made eye contact with the waitress. Another tall cappuccino.

He stretched back in the chair and looked about the room. The café was filled with faces he vaguely recognized. Attachés from neighboring diplomatic missions would normally lunch at the Sheraton hotel just across the street, but as it became too popular, some of them, particularly those who preferred local cuisine or being surrounded by locals, withdrew to the Wilanowska Café, small and forgotten, but once a popular place on the corner of Ujazdowskie and Three Crosses Square. True, Wilanowska had seen better days; before the Sheraton opened, it was the only place in the area where one could get a decent cup of coffee, and even today there was something authentic about it, something that let the occasional shot of *Żubrówka*, a bison grass-flavored vodka, flow more smoothly down one's throat than it would in the clinical environment of the hotel.

Penskie was thinking about the holidays: Christmas Eve with father and Margaret and Robert, and the long-awaited trip to the mountains. To his surprise he found the latter more desirable. The majestic splendor of the snowcapped mountains, free of tourists and far from the city, was alluring. He was not an unsociable person—far from it: He was young, eligible and enthusiastic, good company at any event, and not surprisingly was invited to and attended most that were organized by colleagues from the embassy. But that was before. Last year took its toll on Penskie's emotional life, so much so that he'd been asked to take time off. That, however, proved to be easier said than done. The legal attachés' office was one of the busiest sections of the embassy, and with a staff of only three, their tasks overlapped as one case ended only to be replaced with another, usually a more demanding one. Penskie was a deputy legal attaché, or, in plain language, an officer of the Federal Bureau of Investigation, known in the diplomatic lingo as a legat. The legal attachés' office in Warsaw, along with numerous others in different cities around the world, was created in response to the growing threat to American and global security. The legats were there to ease and provide the exchange of information and cooperation between police departments of the countries or geographical regions in which they were established, and the United States. Some of them were considered cushy jobs, like the offices in London or Rome, but the ones in Warsaw and Moscow were something else. Stepping on Polish or Russian crime bosses' toes, in countries where hired assassins were skilled, cheap, and plentiful, presented dangerous working conditions and somewhat of a headache when it came to work relations inside the diplomatic mission. In the legats' line of duty, leaving the embassy compound could result in a dagger in the back, and injury or death of embassy personnel was a big concern of the deputy chief of mission, or DCM. The DCM was a pain in the neck from the day the FBI officers had moved in, always concerned with the whereabouts of the legats, who, in his opinion always stuck their noses where they did not belong, and making their job too constrained for the requirements. To be effective in this region of the world one had to know the criminal element: the way it thought and operated. Courtroom drama was for pencil pushers, and legats were not sent to Poland to attend to the DCM's vision of tuxedoed diplomats. They were cops who had a job to do, a job tougher than any of them had anticipated, and a meddling DCM did not make things easier.

Stan Penskie started his career with the Chicago field office, where the Bureau was investigating organized Eastern European gangs. From car thefts and car smuggling in Poland and former Soviet Republics, the cases grew to include human trafficking of mostly young girls lured to the United States by job prospects who often ended up as prostitutes, and to alcohol, arms, and amphetamine distribution and trade. Most cases Penskie worked on were controlled by Poles and had Russian Mafia connections, not a surprising turn of events, considering that nothing could bypass Poland on its way to the bottomless pit that was Russia. For centuries Poland was the gate between Western Europe and

Asia, and today, being an aspiring member of the European Union, Poland was the most important operations ground for the Russian Mafia outside of Russia.

Human, drug, and arms trafficking, being the three most profitable and best developed of all underground activities, prompted the Bureau to seek help from its overseas counterpart. Penskie was teamed up with Robert Sito, one of the first Polish officers to come to Quantico to study modern techniques of organized crime fighting. Sito, an officer of the Organized Crime Unit of police headquarters, proved to be the starting point in breaking up and seriously hindering the mob's activities in Chicago and indeed the entire Great Lakes region.

Little else could build as strong a bond between two men as the experience of living fast and on the edge, such as the undercover work in an unscrupulous and hostile environment where one could expect never to see the light of day again. Penskie and Sito became friends. Stan, temperamental, often in hot water with his superiors, but an excellent field agent, and Robert, analytic and reticent, lent their team a much-needed touch with reality that kept them out of trouble and culminated in a successful breakup of the mob. This first case left little doubt in Stan's mind that his part in the success of the investigation was only a coincidence. His work came on a wave of enormous emotional involvement. He could not work otherwise. At times Robert's cold, analytical approach would drive Stan out of his skin. The case taught him that his place was where the action was: He was born to work in the field, to become a part of the game, and to gather the necessary intelligence, which others analyzed and planned a strategy around. There were doers and there were thinkers. Penskie was a doer, a man of action gliding in the slow world of office clock-watchers and policy makers whose guidelines he was forced to follow. He lost his passion for the job.

The joint success intensified the link between the two countries and resulted in even closer relations when the FBI's legal attachés' office opened in Warsaw in 1997. Sito, now working with the *Urząd Ochrony Państwa,* the State Security Office, and having had the American experience, became the acting liaison between the UOP and the legal attachés. Stan, speaking fluent Polish, was posted to Warsaw as the deputy legal attaché, his temper playing a large role in the assignment to such a hot spot.

The change of scenery restored his failing interest in the job. The assignment proved to be what his mind and body longed for. Eastern Europe was where the action was.

Once again he worked closely with Sito. Their friendship continued, and over the years an even stronger bond developed between Penskie and Sito. Having once run into each other on the slopes of Giewont Mountain in the High Tatras, they discovered a shared passion for mountains, and their friendship moved to a new level. Leaving their professional duties behind, they hiked and climbed together the peaks of Poland's highest mountain range every opportunity they had. An unspoken rule of not discussing their jobs on each and all occasions prevailed. During one such trip Stan brought along his sister. She worked as a history teacher at an American high school in Kraków, a temporary job she got on a whim while visiting Stan and traveling through Poland.

Margaret and Robert fell in love.

Penskie never mentioned to his superiors his sister's relationship with an officer of Poland's premier intelligence agency. Quite frankly the thought never occurred to him, and in his mind it was nobody's business anyway. While befriending a foreign national was not a reason for security concern, even in these days of Poland's being a member of NATO and considered a friendly nation by the United States government, it would nevertheless become an opportunity for the likes of the DCM to make it a living hell for any employee of the embassy with an off-duty relationship with a state security officer. Stan drew the line between his duties and private life deliberately and firmly: It was nobody's business what he did in his spare time, and his conscience was clear. He knew Sito professionally and personally; their relationship was based on friendship and mutual respect, and he knew Sito felt the same way.

Penskie occupied a table at the rear in a somewhat isolated part of the café on a raised platform separated from the rest of the room by a waist-high partition. He was thinking about his friend and sister when a figure appeared in the narrow entrance foyer. The man scrutinized the room, visibly out of breath, as if he had run a long distance before entering the café. He scanned the room once more and wove his way between the tables to the raised platform.

"Thought I might find you here," the man said in a low voice.

"Robert!" The man's sudden appearance startled Penskie. He was at a loss for words and was gazing at his friend, speechless.

Water dripping down his nylon coat, his wet mane straight and flush against his forehead, Robert Sito took the seat across the table. Barely visible light gray steam rose off his shoulders; the café was notoriously overheated. He unbuttoned the coat, withdrew a folded newspaper from the inside pocket, and placed it on the table.

* * *

Cold December rain intensified and was streaming down the window, like a filter distorting the view and making patrons unaware of the life outside the café. Had the rain been lighter Penskie probably would have noticed a dark SUV pull to the curb directly across the street from Wilanowska. He would have perhaps realized the car had stopped at an illegal place, right at an intersection, and perhaps noticed the peculiar interest with which the men had scanned the Wilanowska Café. Still, he would have disregarded it as an ordinary occurrence—thousands of cars parked illegally on the streets of Warsaw every day. The number of cars had outgrown the number of available parking spaces.

"Unit One to Control," the driver said in Polish to a microphone attached to a headset, a trace of a Russian accent in his voice. The second man, who occupied the backseat, controlled a portable electronic surveillance unit resting on a small tripod mounted to the window and directed at the café. The man adjusted the controls and, apparently satisfied, signaled the driver.

"We're in position. The subject has made contact with . . ." The driver paused uncomfortably.

"Repeat that, Unit One."

"The subject has made contact with . . . the FBI man."

There was a brief silence before the voice responded. It was quiet but firm.

"Continue surveillance and stand by for further instructions, Unit One."

The driver and his companion exchanged disconcerted looks.

Chapter Two

Robert Sito was very anxious as he leaned over the table and murmured, "I'm in deep trouble, Stan. I mean . . . I don't know what to make of this anymore."

He quickly looked around and pushed the newspaper across the table.

Stan opened the paper, still surprised by the coincidence of his friend's arrival, and gasped. There was a light brown folder inside the newspaper. Large print on the cover read, *Tajne Specjalnego Znaczenia,* with *Urząd Ochrony Państwa*'s seal underneath.

"What the hell is this?"

"It means 'top secret . . .' "

"I know what it means, Rob." Penskie nervously scanned the room, his voice a hissing whisper: "We can both end up in crap even at the suspicion of my ever being in the proximity of something like this!"

"Believe me, we already are in it so deep we can only hope we're not going to drown!"

Penskie leaned back, his eyes darting back and forth between Robert and the folder, as if weighing the implications of his involvement in what appeared to be state security affairs. Something was wrong. Robert knew Stan's position when it came to mixing business with pleasure, and was too smart to make such a shallow attempt to turn him over. The thought was brief, as Stan shook his head, realizing his friend deserved more than superficial accusation. Still, Sito should have followed proper procedures if it was a matter of business—but the fact that he brought it out at these circumstances suggested otherwise.

"You know I would not have done it this way if the circumstances weren't extraordinary. It has little to do with the *Urząd*. . . ."

"Then what *does* it have to do with?" Penskie pointed to the UOP's seal.

"Well, yes, but it goes far beyond it! I'm not sure I should be talking to you as an officer because when you hear it you'll have every right to take me for a lunatic. I'm here because I need a friend."

He knew he should say no immediately and walk away, but innate curiosity took over.

"Shit. You have five minutes."

Robert appeared relieved. He loosened the scarf around his neck.

"I'm guessing you know about Andrzej Borysewicz's murder?"

"The prime minister? Would be hard to miss it on the news."

"Same one, only, what's more important in this case, he

was also the chief of the *Służba Bezpieczeństwa*, UOP's predecessor, in the eighties."

"And?" Stan was perplexed.

"The media is suggesting robbery. The guy was loaded, you know, like many other apparatchiks of those days. But between you and me, people like Borysewicz do not just get robbed," Sito paused for a moment to wave off the waitress. "They die in accidents, or of cardiac arrest," he continued quietly. "Every high-ranking party official in communist Poland had a permanent, often lifetime security agent assigned for his protection. A whole army of slacking off, paunch-growing, coffee-sipping agents were employed full-time by the state. They worked and lived on the premises of the protected individual, and in most cases, apart from checking incoming parcels and doing crossword puzzles, had little else to do."

"Robert!"

"Just a minute; I'm just trying to paint the full picture for you. After the collapse of the regime and cuts to the budget, most of these privileges were withdrawn and things started to happen." Sito opened his hand, bending each finger as his recited: "A former minister of finance died in a car crash, as did the head of counterintelligence; a former party secretary broke his neck while skiing; someone else drowned in his pool, and so on. Sixteen of the once-highest officials of the former regime died suddenly in the past five years alone!"

"Payback for the *Proces Szesnastu?*" Penskie recognized the similarity to one of the biggest kidnapping-and-assassination cases in Polish political history.

"What?" Sito looked confused.

"The sixteen right-wing government leaders killed by the commies back in the forties."

"I see what you mean," Sito said. "Alas, there is no connection. I'm talking about some of the biggest *skurwysyny* dropping dead in less than believable circumstances. So when more sudden deaths occurred, those being accidents and all, other bastards, like Borysewicz, moved out of their state-owned apartments on Aleja Róż, and into high-fenced, state-of-the-art-security-systems-and-round-the clock-sentry villas outside the city. They employed the services of very exclusive protection agencies, or maintained their own private armies, most staffed by ex–Secret Service agents. Borysewicz's was one of such estates, an impenetrable fortress, but—"

"But it *was* penetrated! You've got the suspects, haven't you?" Penskie pointed to the front page of the newspaper Sito had brought.

"Sure, caught as they were fleeing the neighborhood," Robert answered with sarcasm. "Three small-time crooks in uniforms of the security agency and, if you permit the American expression, scared brainless."

"Shitless," Stan corrected.

Sito did not respond. He looked at Stan, awaiting the next, obvious question.

"And there is more to it than meets the eye." Penskie raised his eyebrow. "You have got to be kidding me!"

"I'm afraid not. There *is* an American connection." Sito opened the folder and pulled out a sheet of paper. "Does the name Economic Development and Cooperation Agency mean anything to you?" He studied Penskie's eyes. When no answer followed he continued, "The agency is involved in some pretty suspicious activities. First, two of its employees were logged in as visitors at Borysewicz's estate three weeks ago, and one of them on the day of his murder.

The same day the first visit took place, one of the Americans, Norman Bray, disappeared. He was murdered three weeks ago. His body was found this last weekend in the woods near . . ." Sito stopped, noticing a sudden change come over Penskie's face.

"Murdered?" Penskie asked rhetorically, and continued quickly to cover his unease, "Why didn't you notify the embassy?"

"It's only Monday, Stan. Besides, I was ordered to drop the case."

"What?"

"The entry logbook from Borysewicz's estate was confiscated; however, I managed to save a copy of the pages where the two EDECA employees' names were entered, just a habit I've developed lately. Anyway, I understand you were interested in the agency as well?" He pushed a sheet of paper across the table.

Penskie scanned the document. It was an ordinary sheet of paper, with vertical lines drawn by the keeper; hours in and out of the estate were entered next to various names.

"It must be a coincidence," he muttered.

"What?"

Penskie looked into his friend's eyes. There was no deception in Robert's at bringing this up. There could not be; Sito was just as concerned and taken aback as he was. Stan decided to disclose the legats' interest in the Economic Development and Cooperation Agency. He knew he would not be disclosing any confidential information by the sheer fact that he was not in possession of any.

The agency was on the legal attachés' task list since its CEO's sudden and somewhat baffling disappearance. Just over three weeks before, Norman Bray resigned as the chief executive officer, officially on the basis of family affairs. Nothing suspicious in itself; however, EDECA was a government organization with additional sponsorship from various companies interested in the development of business relations between the United States and Eastern Europe, or, to put it another way, it was created to boost American interests in competition with aggressive Western European economies entering the emerging region. EDECA provided financial and legal support for those companies who wanted to trade with America. It eased the process of forming joint ventures and helped those manufacturers seeking access for their products into the USA, and, more important, found new markets for American products and services in absorbent Eastern Europe. As part of a standard practice the American diplomatic mission acted as a watchdog, particularly in such cases where communications or other sensitive technologies were involved, as these were especially susceptible to industrial espionage.

The Economic Development and Cooperation Agency dealt with millions of dollars and a long list of sensitive technologies. The chief executive officer's sudden resignation was naturally recorded with the embassy, but no action was taken, at least not until the CEO's wife filed a complaint of his not arriving at home. She was more concerned about a skipped alimony payment than his well-being, but the episode brought the EDECA to the legats' attention. Further inquiry revealed that Norman Bray never made it to his home in Virginia; in fact, all traces of his whereabouts ended the very day he signed his resignation. Bray's successor found a cleaned office, with no indication of what might have happened.

The previous Friday, the embassy received a message

from Washington to drop the case, as apparently the wife had finally received her child support, a bank error being blamed for the delay. The paperwork that accompanied the order to close the case included a copy of the check Norman Bray signed only a week earlier.

That was the reason for Stan Penskie's concern. While it was true that banks made errors more often than customers would like to see, he had learned that in his profession, where there were too many coincidences, there must be doubts. One did not have to be an FBI agent to realize the universally known fact that dead men did not pay debts and they definitely did not sign checks.

Penskie grew tense. If Bray died three weeks ago, then whose signature was on the alimony check signed last week? Stan was now more than willing to give his friend the necessary attention and to listen to everything he had to say. The case touched him personally. Someone had either made a mistake or had very bluntly tried to stall the Federal Bureau of Investigation's effort to find the truth.

"EDECA has been under UOP's observation for some time now," Sito continued. "The agency had a curious inclination for dealings with—how can I put it?—let's just say companies that operated on a very thin line between legitimacy and crime. Some of these companies' presidents are under investigations dating as far back as the beginning of the last decade. Either nothing can be proven, or charges are dismissed when highly placed officials intervene. Yes, I'm afraid it's a recurring problem in Poland: Business and politics are so intertwined."

"Are you talking about corruption? It may be a number one problem across the region, but EDECA doesn't have to resort to such measures."

"It's not a measure of EDECA's business ethics. The problem lies deeper and cannot be eradicated by law enforcement. It's in people's psyches: If you want to achieve something you must give. . . ."

"So Bray was receiving kickbacks? Is that it?"

"Stan, you know why so many Western businesses are failing in Poland? It isn't that people do not want or need their products or services; it's that their Western ways of approaching clients are out of place, way ahead of the times. You know: When in Rome . . ."

"Why don't you cut to the chase? Say what you mean." Penskie detested his friend's irritating taste for lecturing. Sito, however unwittingly, treated others the way a professor treated his students. How Margaret ever found him interesting was beyond Penskie's comprehension. The man lived in his own world of inner thought, while Margaret was outgoing in the extreme. What was on her mind could rarely be contained. She was like a child who spoke out loud her deepest feelings, a kid who listened intently to others as if what they had to say was most interesting and innovative. Maybe that was it: She let Sito talk, just the way she let her students open up. Did Sito talk to Margaret about his work?

"What I mean is, you have to be from here to understand the way things work. It's a process you have to grow up with. You have to be a part of that process to appreciate it. I've come to you because you might just be the only one in the Bureau to grasp it. Now, I know you weren't here in the eighties, but because of your family history you have some of the necessary background. A teenage mind sees the universe twice as perceptibly as an old one does; no matter how commonplace, everything seems new and fresh and is devoured with unwavering passion. Look, it has been a hell of a decade: a leap from a communist bastion to the structures of NATO. I can still remember the euphoria of 1989, the slogans 'Your President—Our Premier.' I mean, if you look at it, it really is a miracle, don't you think? One day they arrest people by the hundreds, people disappear in mysterious circumstances; and the next day they say, 'You want free election? You want democracy? Well, look no further, here it is!' And, bang, here we have it: free elections, market economy, we're free to travel and free to express ourselves. Except that *we* can hardly make both ends meet, while the same people are still at the steering wheel. Did you know that eight out of every ten biggest fortunes in Poland have their origins in the communist cookie jar? And I don't mean just the former elites: It seems every party member or employee of the all powerful ministry of the interior have their hands in today's till, and they are back, stronger than ever. Do you honestly think that anything really changed? Same old stuff: same people and same ideology—power. Only the way to get it differs: money." Sito paused, anger bordering on fury in his eyes. "This file"—he pointed to the folder—"contains details of the investigation into Borysewicz's murder, but it goes beyond it, too. The investigation is a sham and will be closed today or tomorrow. They 'found' the culprits and the whole thing is being wrapped up. I've been officially suspended, but I'll be damned if I let them bury it."

Stan was briefed about situations such as this one: A disillusioned officer who felt betrayed was a prime subject and needed to be reported to Dan Loomis, the station chief of the Central Intelligence Agency. The need for interdepartmental cooperation was hyped after September eleventh, and the anecdotal competition between the FBI and the CIA was a thing of the past. That is, it was that way in the briefings—or in the motivational speeches, as they were quickly dubbed—but what related to both agencies' relations could not be transferred as easily to human interaction. Dan Loomis was the second-biggest SOB at the embassy, after the DCM, and Penskie would hesitate before handing over anyone, especially Robert Sito. Damn it, Penskie realized the relationship with Robert *was* impacting his judgment and work, and he cursed himself.

"Stan, I need your help. . . ."

"Look, I don't think the legats can engage." Penskie was weary. His friend sounded sincerely concerned, but Penskie sensed he was too involved emotionally. It was becoming clear to him that Sito exhibited signs of a classic scenario among police officers around the world. For one reason or another Robert had gotten sucked into the case emotionally and could not come to terms with certain issues that arose in the course of the investigation. Maybe it was the case that outgrew his investigative abilities, or perhaps problems in his personal life affected his judgment. Penskie recalled Sito's parents dying in a car crash while traveling in the Swiss Alps and how devastated his friend was, but that was ten months ago. Whatever the reason, Robert needed a break. In an unnerving job, such as his was, holidays were mandatory. There was just one flaw in Penskie's thinking, just one thing that stopped him from ending the conversation: Sito's case was obviously going fine; the perpetrators were caught. And the pain of his personal loss was receding too; the weekends in the mountains helped a great deal. All things considered, Stan remained in his seat.

Sito, sensing Penskie's growing impatience, spoke

quickly: "The suspects we caught were close associates of one Małpa, or 'Monkey,' a pseudonym of one of the most notorious arms dealers in the Polish underground. And Małpa was, or *is*, if he's still alive, an operative of your government, with very close ties to EDECA, which, in turn, is a front for the Central Intelligence Agency. But that's not all. I think the embassy . . . the FBI . . . the UOP . . . both governments . . . they're all involved in it!"

The allegation pushed Stan to the edge of his seat. Dan Loomis, the economic attaché of the American Embassy, the station chief of the Central Intelligence Agency, was behind the murder of a former Polish prime minister? Absurd! Unthinkable! But was it? If the CIA had stakes in EDECA it would explain the sudden termination of the legats' inquiries. It would also shed some light on Norman Bray's death. But a murder? No, not possible!

But why not? After all, the CIA was back in the business of assassinations. Nine-eleven turned the world upside down, the CIA and other agencies enjoyed privileges undreamed of before. On top of that, one could not judge the CIA's actions by the FBI's standards.

"You'd bloody well better have solid proof, Robert!" Penskie gnashed out.

"Unit One to Control! Did you get the transmission?"

"Loud and clear, Unit One." There was a long pause before a firm voice continued with a trace of determination, "You must terminate the subject and retrieve the property immediately!"

"What about Penskie?"

"No names, damn it! That's a negative."

The driver and his companion glanced at each other.

"Can you repeat that, Control?"

"Not the American! Is that understood?" The voice was loud and definite. The two men looked at each other again and shrugged.

"Understood."

Sito was leaning over the table, his arms creating abstract figures in the air, helping him articulate his thoughts as he spoke. Penskie sat back in his chair, breathless, his eyes locked on Robert's lips. The information Sito related was a revelation, it was stunning and beyond anything Stan could have expected. If all this were indeed true, the world was on the brink of a disaster. The powers this UOP officer was describing were unimaginable; so much so that they had to be a figment of a hallucination, or one of the most ingenious and vivid conspiracy theories ever to come across Penskie's hands. Surely Sito had to be exaggerating—perhaps to make it more appealing, and to ensnare Penskie in this illusionary roller coaster of a plot.

Deep down Penskie knew Sito might have been overworked, but he was not crazy. Together they had been through such intricate webs of deception, corruption, terror, and murder that nothing seemed improbable anymore. It was a side effect of a cop's job: You got used to the dark side of life, not surprised by the next, more elaborate, more violent and ingenious crime. You expected it. But was *this* possible? Penskie shrugged and shook his head. Somewhere in Robert's theory was a flaw; there had to be. If he were to put all the facts together, the immediate conclusions had to be discarded as far-fetched, or insane, for lack of a better word.

Robert was wrong. He had to be.

A sudden blast filled the room.

Penskie watched with astonishment as the glass of the large window shattered into a myriad of sparkling little pieces, cold wind and rain blowing in his face. Seconds later a scream from a nearby table diverted his attention to a woman who was staring and pointing in his direction, terror in her eyes. He followed the path of her attention. The picture in front of him was paralyzing. Robert's upper body lay on the table, a portion of his head missing, blood splattered on the white tablecloth, the coffee cups, and the papers. It took several seconds before the magnitude of what had happened dawned on him. When it did, he immediately ducked under the table. Panic arose in the room when more patrons realized what had happened. Screaming and knocking down chairs, breaking glasses and cups, people rushed toward the exit doors. Penskie watched the commotion as he tried to come to his senses. It was a shot! It came through the window! The killer—or the killers—could not be far. Penskie needed a gun, but his Glock was at the embassy. He crawled toward Sito and reached under his jacket, where he knew he would find a Makarov. Yes! He had a weapon! He ducked back to the floor, scanning the room from underneath the tables. The disorganized crowd was still pushing through the door, where two large thugs dressed in rugged green coats punched and elbowed their way through the living obstacle.

Penskie quickly assessed the situation: He could not shoot without injuring innocent bystanders. He could not remain in place either; only seconds separated his temporary shelter from the killers. In between the overturned tables and chairs he could see the crowd diminishing and the two men approaching cautiously. To his left was a swinging door to the kitchen, perhaps ten feet away across an open space, his only route to survival. Penskie rose to his knees and crept toward the door, rolled over the open space, and continued crawling. He was about to push through the door when he remembered the file, and in the split second that brought him to a halt he heard a buzz and a thump on the wall, only inches from his head. He fell on the door and raced past shocked employees to the back of the kitchen. Outside was a large courtyard with an arched gate leading to Mokotowska Street. Halfway through the gate Penskie heard the doors to the kitchen slam open, but he did not turn to look back. He reached the sidewalk and turned left. Ahead were perhaps five hundred meters to Ulica Piękna and an additional one hundred meters to the embassy compound. He realized the distance was too great—he would not be able to outrun the bullets. He left the sidewalk and continued along the middle of the narrow street, a barricade of tightly parked cars obstructing the line of fire, the shots that should be heard any minute. . . . Nearing Ulica Piękna he noticed a gate similar to the one that led to Wilanowska's courtyard. It was a corner building. He darted in. As he was crossing the sidewalk he realized he had not been followed. The killers must have given up on the chase, or . . . *oh, God!* They must have anticipated his move; they knew who he was and had taken the shorter way on the intercept to the embassy: the Ujazdowskie Boulevard. Sprinting through the courtyard of the corner building, he shot out to Ulica Piękna. To his right was a bus stop with a small crowd awaiting a bus, and to his left was an empty sidewalk, a driveway to the embassy visible in the distance. Penskie could see busy traffic on Ujazdowskie, but no killers in sight. He ran on his last breath and reached the tall black iron gate of the driveway to the embassy's underground parking.

"Open the gate!" he screamed, waving his arms at the watch booth.

There was no one inside. *Goddamnit!* He could die three times before someone noticed him. He had given up on the driveway gate and was contemplating climbing over the fence, or continuing to the main entrance off Ujazdowskie, where he would undoubtedly find himself in the line of fire, when he noticed a guard with a portable metal detector watching him quizzically from a distance of some twenty feet. The visa section! He had forgotten about it.

"Open up!" he shouted, and ran past the flabbergasted guard.

Chapter Three

Washington, one hour later

"Not the American! Is that understood?" . . . "Understood." The tape player stopped.

Four men sat quietly at a conference table of an obscure law firm located in Arlington, Virginia, the significance of the intercepted surveillance team's message not yet clear to them. The fifth man, who operated the tape player, was standing over the oval end of the table. His gray eyes were smiling through the thin, antiglare-coated glasses.

"Gentlemen, we have been given a significant opportunity. The young Penskie—"

"Should we be using names?" asked one of the four men, his meek posture not representative of the agency he headed.

"I assure you, Director, this room is safer than your Langley office."

"Excuse me, Chairman, but this intercept only makes me feel insecure. It's as if there are no secrets anymore. Who knows who may be eavesdropping on us?"

"I assure you there is no reason for concern. There is probably no safer place in America right now, but let us follow the procedures. . . . As I was saying, with proper use of this intercept we can gain enough time to forestall Alpha's plans."

"Is it wise to stand against Alpha? His election seems eminent, and if we fail to stop him we will put ourselves and our families' lives in danger."

"Balcer—our leader has strong support among the council members. It is his leadership that brought the organization to its current position. We must not forget that each one of us owes his rank and office to our leader. The changes Alpha wants to implement are too great for us to stand idle and watch as our world crumbles in front of our eyes. By all means, do think about your families, your wives and children. . . . But, gentlemen, this is the decisive moment. We must openly choose sides."

The speaker examined his audience. These four men held some of the most powerful offices in the nation, but at the sheer mention of Alpha's name they trembled like schoolboys. The director of Central Intelligence was biting his nails, a nervous wreck oblivious of the presence of others around him. And the attorney general's perspiring forehead precipitated the constant wiping of his glasses. The others, they were all followers; no independent thought had ever crossed their minds. If the winds should suddenly change they would follow suit. There was no doubt in his mind: Should Alpha win the majority of the council members' votes they would follow him like obedient dogs. Human nature feared immediate power more than distant. Alpha being overseas, these four would follow orders from their closer authority, from him, the leader's deputy for the East Coast: the director of the National Security Agency.

"The intercept will be delivered to the young . . . to the FBI officer. I trust this will be sufficient to lead him to Alpha, and the imminent confrontation will ensure that the cards are turned in our favor. Control of the organization must remain in the hands of our leader."

The blank expressions confirmed his opinion of the men at the table: weaklings ready to "go with the flow." They would be replaced the moment the leadership race was over. What they could not yet realize was that they were history regardless of which way the council set its votes and support. There was no place for wavering cowards within the organization.

"What about the president?"

"You have sworn your allegiance to our organization first and foremost. Do not forget this."

"It is the organization I am concerned about! The president is on a militant streak, and if his pupil, Alpha, fails to gain control over the organization there is no telling what the president might do."

"The president will not dare raise his hand against the organization. This is why we have seized key positions in this nation and elsewhere: to assure that no one can thwart our existence. We are the legislature, the policing, and the army, and, for all intents and purposes, we are the president, too."

"One aspect we seem to be overlooking is that the president has the support of the population."

"It is temporary, and not as decisive as the White House likes to paint it. The population did not elect the president. Should he fail to recognize who did . . . he will have to go."

"Go?"

"He will have to step down."

Disconcerted looks were all that followed. The reminder of the organization's power could not be put more bluntly.

Marvin Cleft replaced the phone and addressed the panel of five: "We're on THREATCON Three, just as a precaution." He noted the puzzled look on the deputy chief of mission's face. Cleft had been posted to the embassy directly from the naval intelligence office attached to NATO headquarters in Brussels only six months ago and was still adjusting to the civilian setting. "The visa section has been closed, the applicants escorted out, and all exits are now sealed and manned. The ambassador is attending a function at the Zachęta Gallery, where a display of American art is being exhibited, and his security detail has been informed of the . . . emergency status. He should be arriving shortly. Now, would anyone care to explain what's happened? What are we dealing with?"

"We all would like to know what the hell just happened, Stan." Hank Russell, the deputy chief of mission, fixed his gaze on Penskie.

The legal attaché was sitting at the long conference table, water dripping off his drenched suit onto the soft carpet.

"As I already told Hank, just about a quarter of an hour ago I was having lunch at the Wilanowska with officer Robert Sito, our liaison with the *Urząd Ochrony Państwa.*" Penskie paused. He realized he should divulge his relationship with Robert before it was found out, but something was holding him back, and was telling him to withhold this information. He knew anything sounding unclear would have been blamed on the shock caused by the terrible event that almost cost him his life. In all fairness he really was shaken and had not yet come to terms with what had happened. "Officer Sito was . . . was . . ."

"Was?" David O'Brien, the assistant legal attaché, could not bear the ambiguity of Penskie's answer. THREATCON was the most exciting event he had seen since the Piastów mob breakup. The impatience was tearing his young mind apart.

"Sito was killed, shot right in front of my eyes."

Incredulity followed by concern were shown in the questions that followed Penskie's announcement, but the overall clamor prevented him from answering or even understanding particular words. One worry prevailed in everyone's mind: Did the killing have anything to do with any of the joint operations conducted by the legal attachés and the UOP? If the killing was in retaliation then any one of them could be the next target.

"Gentlemen!" The DCM raised his hand. "Gentlemen, calm down! Let Stan finish and we'll all have a chance to ask questions in a moment."

All eyes fixed on him, Penskie considered the right approach, Sito's words still ringing in his head: *I think the embassy . . . the FBI . . . the UOP . . . both governments . . . they're all involved in it.* He glanced at his colleagues and could not help but think that one of them, if only unwittingly, might have been responsible for his friend's death. What sounded preposterous at the café now, after the killing, took on a different light. However absurd Sito's revelations were, they were the cause of his death. His brother-in-law-to-be was dead. The tragedy was slowly dawning on him. He would have to tell Margaret. *Oh, God! Poor Margaret!*

"Stan . . . Stan!" The words came to him as if from the fog, muted and distant. The deputy chief of mission raised his voice: "Why did you meet with Officer Sito?"

"Robert . . . Officer Sito had information concerning an American citizen, Norman Bray."

"Bray, as in Economic Development and Cooperation Agency Bray?" asked Ed Powell, the legal attaché, and Stan's immediate superior.

"Yes. Apparently, Bray's body was found in the woods outside of Warsaw last Friday."

"Jeez." Powell dropped his pencil on the table and pushed back in his chair.

"Something we should know about?" Hank Russell asked.

Powell briefly explained the legats' interest in EDECA.

"If Bray was found last week, how come the cops didn't contact the embassy?" Dan Loomis asked.

Penskie looked over the table into Loomis's eyes. They were bland and blunt, as if none of the news stirred any emotion. Loomis was either very skilled at covering his feelings, or, Penskie caught himself thinking, he knew and anticipated the events. Penskie realized his suspicion was largely based on Sito's unconfirmed accusation of EDECA being somehow tied to the Central Intelligence Agency, but once the seed of mistrust and suspicion was planted, he became wary of the surroundings. His mind raced, sifting through multiple scenarios and possibilities. Once again,

Sito's death lent an aura of likelihood to his crazed suspicions.

"They had problems identifying the body," he replied after consideration. It was true.

"So the cops find a body of an American citizen and, instead of using protocol channels, an investigating officer seeks a private meeting with one of our legal attachés?" Hank Russell asked. "How do you explain that, Agent Penskie?"

Here we go, Stan thought, *Hank the Plank is in his element.* He considered the options and decided it would be better to keep his personal relationship with Sito aside. EDECA, on the other hand, would have to be dealt with, now that its chief executive officer had turned out to be paying his child support from beyond the grave. He also wanted to see Loomis's reaction to Robert's allegations. He had to know.

"Officer Sito thought it would be better to keep it low, what with the press leaks and all. According to the *Urząd Ochrony Państwa,* EDECA has an agenda of its own, or rather it follows an agenda of the United States government's agency. . . ."

"It is a government sponsored program, for Chrissake!"

Penskie was not looking at Russell, his gaze now fixed on the station chief of the Central Intelligence Agency.

"Specifically," he continued, "that of the CIA."

"Holy cow!" Powell gasped.

"That's great! It's . . . it's exactly what I need!" The deputy chief of mission stood up, started toward the window, and stopped abruptly. "Dan? I don't care what the agency is up to—I never ask and I don't want to know now either—but I do want a straight answer." Russell pressed his knuckles on the table, his face purple. "Is it true? Does it have anything to do with the agency's operations? Do we have a diplomatic incident on our hands?"

"If we do, it is only due to the Feds' noncompliance with the protocol," Loomis answered coolly, playing to the deputy chief of mission's tune. "Had they followed the protocol, we wouldn't have had to worry about it."

"Answer my question, Dan."

"Off the top of my head, I am not aware of any operations conducted in conjunction with EDECA."

Powell cleared his throat, bringing Loomis to a halt. The legal attaché did not like the direction in which the conversation was steering.

"The CIA's operations have brought more embarrassment to the embassy in the last few years than during the entire Cold War period," he started. "At least then these types of actions could be justified ideologically and politically, but now? It is precisely the likes of agency hotheads who stall relations between our two countries. Here we are, the Bureau, trying to build a working relationship, assuring the Poles our mission is not only important for the U.S. but for the security and peace in this region and across the world, and here come the cowboys from the CIA—spying and spoiling years of work on the part of the legats' office."

"May I remind you," Loomis said, showing the first signs of emotional distress, "that there is no such thing as a friendly nation when the security of the United States is concerned? I can't rule out the possibility of an operation being conducted in cooperation with the Economic Development Agency. Not everything goes through my hands. It's this damned departmentalization. It's happened before and will happen in the future when operations are controlled directly from Langley. But apart from that, have any of you thought that perhaps Sito's death had nothing to do with Bray and his organization? As Stan just explained, officer Sito was up to his ears in organized crime. Maybe someone out there, in the echelons of the underground, thought Sito was stepping too much on their toes? Another dead cop—it's commonplace these days." Loomis ran his eyes over the legal attachés' faces and fixed his gaze on Stan's. "I wouldn't want to be in your shoes."

"That's good . . . that's good." The DCM did not seem to notice the last remark, his mind spinning. "A terrorist, gang-related attack. The embassy will have to issue a statement, of course: 'An officer of the Federal Bureau of Investigation barely escaped a terrorist attack while working on a joint case with the Polish authorities. . . .' "

"Sir," Powell objected. "The Polish authorities had not asked for any cooperation, and, what's worse, the UOP suspects the CIA's involvement in EDECA. God knows what proof they may have. They're not going to play along, not if they suspect espionage."

"Leave it to the politicians, Mr. Powell. Diplomacy is a powerful tool in skilled hands. Things look different according to the way they are portrayed. I will discuss this with the ambassador. For now, the important thing is to reject any connection with the diplomatic mission other than the legats' officially sanctioned duties. As for the extracurricular activities of our embassy's staff"—he turned to Loomis—"I will relay the information to the secretary of state, who will discuss it directly with the DCI and the director of the FBI. What I expect of you, gentlemen, is to act as befits diplomats of the American diplomatic mission. Is that understood?"

Chapter Four

"That son of a bitch Loomis is lying up his ass," Ed Powell exploded the moment the three legats entered their quarters. He proceeded to his desk and collapsed on his executive leather chair.

"Something's up, all right," O'Brien agreed. "And it stinks if you ask me. First we look up Bray and EDECA; the next thing you know, we're called off, Bray turns up stiff in the woods, and the Christians in Action are on the scene."

The two looked at Penskie. Stan stood by his desk, drying his wet hair with a small flannelette hand towel. He seemed distant and lost in his thoughts, his eyes wandering to the window, unfocused.

"Stan?"

"Yeah?"

"There's more to it than what you'd already told us, isn't

there?" Powell pushed himself away from the desk and leaned back in his chair.

Penskie weighed the answer in his mind. Sito warned about possible embassy involvement, but from what little he had time to explain, and from Penskie's observation of Loomis, this lead pointed toward Central Intelligence. In its impossibility it made sense: the abrupt cancellation of the inquiries into EDECA, called only a day before Bray's body was found, and, what further increased Penskie's suspicion—Bray's child support signed after his death. The CEO did not have preauthorized payments; the last payment was made by check, contrary to Bray's previous payments, all made via online banking. It could mean only one of two things: Bray had predated his check, or someone who had no access to Bray's online accounts wrote it for him. In the latter case someone either did not know Bray was already dead, or knew it but wanted to stop the FBI from looking into his affairs. To think that the Bureau was involved was insane. Or was it? After all, what did he know? Three years away from Washington, in isolation from the perpetual gossip that circulated the corridors of the FBI headquarters whenever a borderline activity was undertaken, had kept him ignorant of the latest of the Bureau's endeavors. As for Ed and Dave, his colleagues and friends, they had had more than one beer together, and more than one brush with the Polish underground, which led to one unwritten rule: Stick together and cover each other's butts. To think one of them—and due chiefly to the chain of command that someone could only mean Ed Powell—could be hiding something or working behind the others' back was absurd. Yet the suspicions were tearing him apart. He felt deep inside that the Bureau could not be responsible for Robert's death, but his friend's words kept ringing in his head: *I think the embassy . . . the FBI . . . the UOP . . . they're all involved in it*. No! He had to make the decision now. He could not continue on with the burden of uncertainty on his mind.

"Yeah," he started cautiously, "Dave's right, the whole thing's fishy. But Loomis has a point: Sito, just as any one of us, has enemies, the Piastów mob being the latest addition to the fan list."

The notorious mob from the suburban city of Piastów had started with the usual car thefts, extortions, and kidnappings of local businesspeople, and grown into one of the largest and best organized crime groups in the country. It was the reason the legal attachés were forced to carry their weapons with them at all times. The Piastów mob practically monopolized the European auto theft and smuggling ring. Cars, after being stolen in Western Europe, were brought to mob-controlled or owned garages, and then scattered all over the country, where they were "fixed": VIN numbers changed, repainted, and so on, and sold at dealerships or the ever popular open-air car markets, to be legally transported across the eastern border to Russia and post-Soviet republics. Piastów's turnover from the car business alone was estimated at tens of millions of dollars. Of course, like any other rapidly growing enterprise, the Piastów mob ventured into other sectors of underground economy: alcohol, tobacco, narcotics, electronics, and arms. The latter in particular, now that the Polish factory that specialized in AK-47 production had closed down because of political pressures, was the most profitable avenue to enter into. But the arms trade proved to be the proverbial last nail in the mob's coffin. A controlled purchase of AK-47s, staged by the combined forces of the legats from Moscow and Warsaw offices, along with the *Urząd Ochrony Państwa* and *the Centralne Biuro Śledcze,* affectionately referred to as the Polish FBI, brought an end to the mob's activities. Or so it was thought until the evidence showed high compartmentalization of the gang. Though hundreds of criminals and bribed officials from Polish and other governments were arrested and put behind bars, many of the gang's operations remained unhurt. It was now obvious that only one sector—that of the illicit arms trade—had been shut down. The organization continued to operate and threats were directed at those officers who participated in the crackdown. The list of casualties was growing, and the confrontation often was as explicit as an open war.

"What do you make of this CIA connection?" Ed asked.

"Chrissakes, Hank is right going straight to the DOS. Loomis won't talk. This can only be resolved at the highest level. The question is: Do we wait idly by or do we pursue the lead while it's still hot?"

"Pursue what? What do we have that we can get a hook on?"

Penskie slipped on a dry shirt and sat down in his chair. "Sito stole the investigation report from his office." He noticed the exchange of quizzical looks. "He believed his suspension came directly in response to his uncovering the EDECA connection, perhaps even that agency's involvement in the murder of Andrzej Borysewicz, the late prime minister."

Powell sat up in his chair.

O'Brien blew out a loud whistle.

"I would not be surprised if it turned out that the report was the reason for his assassination."

"The report? Do you have it?"

"No," Penskie answered angrily. "I was too busy saving my butt, but I did have a chance to look at it. I tell you, the stuff was explosive. Borysewicz wasn't very prudent about the sort of business contacts he kept, and the detailed database he maintained proves it. According to the report, among his partners were some of the biggest gangs in this country, but what is really frightening is the involvement of the CIA. . . ."

"If there was any CIA involvement at all! Loomis is the coldest SOB this side of the big water. I'd be the first to admit it, but not even he would be covering a lost cause, not when the embarrassment of the American mission is at stake. The DCM won't permit—"

"Oh, c'mon! Loomis knows it is the DCM's statutory authority to oversee all activities of the mission. If it ever came out that the spooks' meddling caused this crisis, the INR would have to step in and the operation would be pegged out. He'd never acknowledge it."

O'Brien shifted uncomfortably in his chair. With the least field experience among the three legal attachés, and being the youngest, he possessed what the others did not: a keen, open mind, ready to accept the least plausible scenario, even if it involved his own government. He was often the one to ponder questions the others would not consider viable.

"Do you think, then," O'Brien asked incredulously, "that it was the CIA? I mean . . . who killed Borysewicz and Bray . . . ?"

Penskie looked at his friend. Despite often being made fun of and pushed aside when it came to making decisions, Dave was in fact a very skilled analyst, very reminiscent of Sito. It often surprised Stan, and he always scolded himself for thinking that way. After all, Stan was only two years older than David. True, his and Sito's success made them the talk of the season within the Bureau as well as bringing a more lasting impact on the way organized crime was battled, but Dave was not exactly a greenhorn either. His marks at the academy were in the top third percentile; his field experience could benefit from longer exposure to the scum of the earth, but still, how many agents fresh out of Quantico were posted as legal attachés, or even assistant legal attachés? David O'Brien's ardent curiosity was a quality to be reckoned with. What if it was the CIA that killed Bray, Borysewicz, and Sito, and tried to kill Penskie? The thought made his skin crawl.

"That is a question I prefer not to answer affirmatively, but I think we have to take it under serious consideration." Stan broke his silence and related his conversation with Sito.

Stephen Pearson's hands trembled as he poured freshly brewed coffee into his extra-large mug. The secure communications traffic with Washington would be at its highest priority since . . . he could not remember the last time, for nothing as major as THREATCON had happened during his two year post to the Warsaw embassy since September eleventh and the following days. It looked like this was going to be a long day and he had to remain sharp and focused—too much was at stake. His concern, however, was not the embassy or its employees, but his own life and freedom, the latter perhaps more terrifying, for he feared prison more than anything else.

He slid the headphones off his ears and picked up the telephone.

"You should not have called me at this number! Your call could be intercepted, and of all people *you* should know this, you fool!" an angry voice responded after Pearson identified himself.

"You wanted to be informed immediately if anything of importance happened, and I believe we may have a situation." The statement was enough to calm the rage of the person on the other end. "Penskie knows more than he should. If they follow the trail my exposure will be imminent!"

"Calm down! Nobody's going to know anything about you when all the bridges are burned and our own people are on the scene!"

"If Alpha finds out—"

"Don't worry about it! Do your job, don't draw any attention to yourself, and cease all communication with us. *We* will contact *you*." The connection was terminated.

The categorical answer was somewhat reassuring, and Pearson inhaled deeply. He looked wearily around his small communications center and took a long sip of coffee. His hands did not stop trembling.

Utter bewilderment was the initial reaction. It was too outrageous to be true. They were prepared to believe the Central Intelligence Agency's involvement in the EDECA. After all, the agency had had its privileges expanded after the World Trade Center had been reduced to rubble, and its agents' presence in any governmental entity abroad was to be expected. But to say that the CIA could have anything to do with the underworld, other than to penetrate it and use it for intelligence gathering, was unthinkable. To say that the Central Intelligence Agency was playing an active role in the underworld's activities by providing it with logistical and operational support was insane. It was like saying that the same Piastów mob that the FBI had helped bring down was kept afloat by the CIA. Yet, that was precisely what Robert Sito had told Penskie, and paid the ultimate price for.

"Okay, let's go back for a second. What do we know about this Borysewicz?" Powell asked.

"Probably not a hell of a lot. We may need to dip into Langley's resources, but given what I've just told you, I doubt they'll release it. Borysewicz would have had to have been at the center of their attention since the eighties, perhaps even earlier. In a nutshell, he was quite a figure: chief of the *Służba Bezpieczeństwa,* state security, in the eighties, appointed and served as prime minister until the first elections of 1989. Throughout the nineties he and others were accused of fraud related to the destruction of the documents and databases of the SB, the party, and the ministry of the interior. Apparently the glow from the fires that were set to burn the files could be seen for weeks in the woods northwest of Warsaw. After the political changes Borysewicz set out to start what became one of the most popular weeklies in the country."

"The *STOP,*" O'Brien suggested.

They all read the scandalous paper for one reason or another, mostly for the spicy details of the political elite's private lives.

"It was the paper," Penskie continued, "that brought Borysewicz under the microscope of the current state security services. The weekly's thrasher revelations weren't taken seriously immediately after takeoff, the sort of *National Enquirer* news everyone enjoyed reading but hardly anyone believed. Slowly, though, a pattern emerged: A right-wing politician accused of being on the SB's payroll in the eighties resigns his post without a fight; a minister in the new government accused of having the hots for underage boys goes down, and so on. The public started to wonder: Is it all a hoax, or is there some truth to any of it? If it's only unsubstantiated slander, then how come no one fights back? After all, the country aspires to be the second America, copying its values from overseas, massive lawsuits not excluding. The latest prime minister's proposed resignation over the allegations of his being a KGB informant was a turning point, and Borysewicz's affairs were being quietly looked into. The *Urząd Ochrony Państwa* entered the scene, somehow convincing the PM to stand up and defend himself. Borysewicz could not, or would not, provide any proof to his revelations, and was forced to withdraw the slanderous charges."

"Didn't the prime minister resign over this issue?"

"Damn right he did. The bastard was probably a KGB informer, but the point was to provoke Borysewicz into disclosing his sources, which he did not. It wasn't necessary, since the goal was achieved: The PM was finished."

"So you're saying Sito thinks . . . thought Borysewicz had access to those *Służba Bezpieczeństwa* files, the same ones that were supposedly destroyed, and was using them to orchestrate the politics?"

"It's an open secret: Everyone thinks some if not most of the files were saved, perhaps microfilmed; only hard, paper copies were destroyed. Sito was convinced it was the MO of the murder. The prime suspect being foreign intelligence . . . the Central Intelligence Agency. The spooks want these files."

"How does this tie in with the Economic Development Agency?" Powell asked after a moment of grim silence.

"It may only be a coincidence. See, Borysewicz branched out into other avenues over the years. I can't be very precise—I can't remember everything Sito said—but the guy had stakes in some of the largest and wealthiest holdings in this part of the world: from the communications industry, natural gas and oil from Russia, to transportation, and from manufacturing to distribution of high-tech military products. He was immensely rich and even more powerful. His one word could cripple the country, halting the oil and gas inflow. As in so many other cases of former communist regimes' high officials, the source of his money was thought to be a mere drop in the ocean of the multibillion-dollar scams that took place prior to and succeeding the fall of the party's reign. Hundreds of phony corporations operated by the SB, the counterintelligence, the intelligence, and you name it were laundering billions upon billions in party funds as well as foreign investment and aid funds, of which the FOZZ was only the puniest of scandals. Through covert channels, the money went into numbered accounts in Swiss banks and laid foundations for future legitimate businesses and private fortunes. Nothing could be traced or proven, of course."

"Nothing could be or nothing was meant to be found out?" O'Brien broke in. "Most of the UOP's cadre is made up of the former SB professionals."

"Well, it's open to interpretation."

"I still can't see the connection." Powell shrugged his shoulders. "Borysewicz had plenty to offer, and the EDECA could have been just seeking genuine business opportunities."

"But somehow things are more complicated than that," O'Brien said.

Penskie recalled Sito's description of the capturing of the three suspects in the vicinity of Borysewicz's villa.

"All three of them died at the police station, before anyone had a chance to interrogate them."

"How the hell did that happen?"

"Apparently they tried to break for it, managed to get a hold of some cops' weapons at the station, put up a fight, and were gunned down. The two cops who shot them turned out to be killers in disguise. They disappeared right afterward, before anyone had the presence of mind to figure out what happened. So Sito did a little digging on the three dead men and found out they worked for the *Służba Bezpieczeństwa* in the eighties as *Kopacze*. . . ."

"What?"

"Kickers. The SB came up with this outrageous plan to intimidate and frighten the state's enemies and dissidents. The kickers were usually fit young men, often judo practitioners or even soccer players who were dispatched to locations where dissidents were present. They would approach the person and kick him or her in the ankle or knee, fracturing bones and crippling that person for life. Anyway, these three later hooked up with one Małpa, or Monkey, a dealer who likes to hang out at the stadium bazaar. This Małpa, according to Sito, had previous contacts with Loomis and Terrence Jacobek, one of the two EDECA execs who paid a visit to Borysewicz, and who, once again according to Sito, were the CIA's assets. There was a snapshot in the files Robert brought: Małpa, Loomis, and Jacobek at a restaurant. Positive ID."

"Photographs can be manipulated; that's no proof."

"I agree, and that's what I told Sito, even though I could not, and still can't, see a reason for him to be making this up."

"I think you've been spending too much time with him; you're forgetting he's a UOP officer. Even if it weren't Sito, there might be someone in there interested in implicating the American intelligence, for one of a million unknown reasons."

"That is a bit far-fetched, don't you think?"

"Oh, and the CIA killing Borysewicz and then an UOP officer, and making an attempt on a federal agent, is not? I hate Loomis and his agency's guts as much as you do, but do you realize the implications of what we're discussing here?"

"Goddamnit, I do! I don't know what, if *any* of it, is true, but that's why we're here: to get to the bottom of it! If the CIA is running an operation gone out of hand where the U.S. government and its diplomatic mission are involved—and they certainly are by association with EDECA—then with what we know we have an opportunity and an obligation to warn Washington. Don't you see there's no other alternative? If we want to protect the government's reputation we have to engage, even if it means bringing the agency's cover into the daylight."

"There is no proof of the CIA's involvement. One picture does not make a story. You said it yourself: Sito only suspected the connection. It's a mystifying and quite an appealing story to any investigator, but we are not going to touch it until none other than the director himself orders us to. But if it's true that the CIA is involved I doubt we'll ever get the clearance. They like to clean their own messes."

"Ed." Penskie decided to appeal to Powell's less bureaucratic side. "We have got to strike while the iron is hot. At least let us take a closer look at the EDECA while you talk to the director. Surely there's nothing wrong with pursuing a hot lead? You know as well as I do that this whole deal stinks. If it weren't for the CIA, we'd be going after EDECA in no time. Just the fact that one of its executives was possibly the last person to see Borysewicz alive makes them suspicious, to say the least. Now that Bray is dead we should talk to Jacobek before the cops get to him."

Powell weighed the thought. He agreed with Penskie. He knew he would be sending his agents after EDECA, but he needed to convey his anger. At fifty-four, he was a good agent, but over the years at the embassy he had been burned once too often on technicalities. He had learned the hard way the importance of office diplomacy. One did not rush into things without thinking them over and over, and then discussing them with the deputy chief of mission. *We are all family here,* the DCM liked to say, *and we are all responsible for each other's actions.* But Powell was once young and eager, and he understood Stan's fervor. He understood that Penskie's desire to find out what happened came from his close relationship with Sito too, though he had no idea how deeply rooted that relationship had been. Their job was crucial to United States security—there was no doubt in anyone's mind about it—but the limitations imposed by the bureaucrats were reducing the effectiveness of their work. Although—and he was not deluding himself—it was increasingly more important for him to worry about his pension rather than work effectiveness, he would be damned if he would let anyone take a shot at one of his men and get away with it.

"I want you to understand this very clearly: We are not

investigating Borysewicz or EDECA." He paused for acknowledgment. "You are there to trace the last days of Norman Bray. Nothing more. THREATCON stands until this and the Piastów mob business are done with. I don't want either of you to leave the embassy alone, under any circumstances, and I want you to report to me every hour. I want to know your whereabouts, who you're with, and what your plans are. Understood?"

Silent for the most part, O'Brien could not contain a grin of satisfaction. After the Piastów mob crackdown the legal attachés were practically confined to the office. Their cooperation with Polish law enforcement agencies was limited to tactical data exchange and support. This was fine as far as Powell was concerned, but both Penskie and O'Brien longed for fieldwork. Young, full of life, and feeling impervious to danger, they wanted to be where the action was. Norman Bray's death provided a chance to get out of the confinement and stuffiness of the embassy.

O'Brien winked and smiled at Penskie, then rushed toward the door.

Chapter Five

Rush-hour driving in Warsaw was not nearly as challenging as that in Paris or other major Western capitals. Nonetheless, it was not for the faint of heart, and Penskie tried to avoid it as much as he could. While the major arteries, built during the Stalinist era, were prepared to handle the grandest of communist parades, including a wide range of military arsenals, one quickly realized the perils of driving in a city that was entirely rebuilt when private automobile ownership was reserved for only the privileged. The error in planning became obvious only some fifty years later, when the streets became increasingly jam-packed with new car owners sprouting like mushrooms after the rain and causing major headaches for other drivers and pedestrians alike. The smaller, narrow streets that crisscrossed the city—and those were the majority—were cramped with parked, double-parked, and triple-parked cars, their owners mocking or oblivious to the existence of any parking regulations. Most drivers whose livelihood depended on their four wheels knew that shortcuts in this city simply did not exist. However crowded the main thoroughfares appeared, one survival rule was to be observed: Keep to the main road. The smaller streets, however tempting, led only into death traps. Adding to the frustration of nose-to-tail traffic, the city's drivers knew no fear when it came to squeezing in or overtaking, never slowing down while making their move. How they did it—constantly switching gears with one hand, the other handling a mobile phone, and engaged in passionate conversation—was anybody's guess.

Penskie parked the car at the lot on Plac Bankowy, in front of City Hall. He looked up at the blue steel-and-glass skyscraper directly across from him, where the Economic Development and Cooperation Agency occupied one of the top floors. It was one of those ultramodern business towers built during the Polish boom of the nineties, where glitz and luxury were the signs of the most elegant, richest, and most exclusive. They were well beyond an average person's conception of an office place. The foundations and the frame of the building were first erected in the mid-seventies, but never completed, due to perpetual shortage in the state's purse. It stood there empty, wind blowing through the steel skeleton, inspiring stories of haunting until a private consortium took over and finished it within what seemed the blink of an eye. It had been a prime office space ever since, largely due to its central location in proximity to the mayor's office, where most new business ventures sought the city's approval.

It was a late afternoon made darker by the cloudy sky, and the numerous bus and tram stops were quickly filling with lethargic commuters. The elevators in the skyscraper spewed out masses from the ground-floor lobby and returned empty to collect more. The doors slid open onto an impeccably clean marbled hallway, which led to a double glass doorway. Beyond it the legal attachés saw a crescent desk with a young woman in her mid-twenties. She sat in a swivel chair, slightly twisting it from side to side as she spoke into a small headset attached to her ear, her hands playing with a stapler on the desk. Whether because of the casual atmosphere of the office or the late hour—many offices in Poland were open eight to four—she allowed herself to continue the conversation well into the visitors' arrival. The Americans smiled. Poor customer service in a country where rapid economic growth left other fields far behind was a day-to-day occurrence. When the market, it seemed, could expand indefinitely, one did not care much about such subtleties as customer service, and the best way to deal with the fact was to keep one's temper about it.

"Dzień dobry, w czym mogę panom pomóc?" The young woman took notice of the visitors, neither of whom saw her terminate the call, private in nature, it would seem, as the headset was hooked up to a cellular phone rather than the bulky office unit.

"Dzień dobry, we'd like to see Terry . . . Terrence Jacobek." Penskie switched to English, hoping the use of the current CEO's first name would assure certain familiarity.

"Do you have an appointment?" She did not budge, a barely audible accent in her voice as she reached for the computer mouse to check the schedule.

"No, I'm afraid we don't. See, we're here simply to pay a courtesy visit."

"Well, I am afraid he's not in the office today, but if you like I can schedule you in for . . ."

Something in her attitude struck Penskie as odd. It was not common lack of courtesy, but rather aversion, as if every customer who walked through the door were cutting into her precious private time.

"What is it, Ania?"

A woman appeared by the side of the desk. She wore a peach suit of a silky material that spelled out designer make; slim trousers accentuated the length of her legs, while the top buttons of her jacket were open, revealing the swell of her bust. Her sandy hair was short, casually waved over her forehead; her blue eyes were intelligent and invitingly smiling. The woman's beauty was striking. Penskie always had trouble assessing the age of women dressed in business attire, but he guessed she must have been in her early thirties. Despite her age and appearance there was a certain aura about her that called for respect. From the first glance she emanated strength, a person used to being in charge. Her voice, though gentle, was firm.

"These gentlemen are here to see Mr. Jacobek, but they have no appointment, and, as you know, he is not—"

"Yes, I am afraid everyone's gone for the day but myself." She pointed to a sheaf of papers under her arm. "Just running last errands before Christmas shopping. Perhaps I could be of help? Mollie Banks, chief operations officer." She extended her hand and almost dropped her package.

"We're with the embassy. We've met Terry before and were hoping to ask a few questions about a matter we've been working on, perhaps over a drink . . . ?"

"I had no idea Terry was a barhopper, the hapless fella."

"You must be new here. We haven't met before." Penskie smiled as he introduced himself and O'Brien.

"Only arrived not two weeks ago. Listen, if it's all business, why don't you come into my office, and perhaps I can answer your questions? Just have to drop these off at the photocopier." She gave them directions and went off.

Mollie Banks's office, like all others at the agency, was composed of a thick and soundproof glass wall separating it from the hallway and adjoining offices. The company believed in teamwork, but with enough privacy to assure unrestricted use of one's creativity. Penskie walked over to the large window overlooking the red rooftops of the Old Town. In the descending dusk he could make out myriad sparkling lights on the river and a steady flow of traffic lights on the Dąbrowski Bridge. The view was soothing, an ideal view for someone with a stressful job. *Does Mollie Banks look out the window often?* he wondered.

Banks was either a very organized person, Penskie thought, or she was not spending much time in her office. The desk was clear of the usual clutter that haunted office desks the world over. A designer pencil holder, a small stapler, a file segregator, a Rolodex, and a monitor were the only objects on a desk twice the size of Penskie's. He realized there were no personal knickknacks, not even photographs.

"The woman obviously has a thing against computers." O'Brien was fingering the personal organizer in a soft leather binding.

"What?"

"The addresses. She doesn't trust the computers."

"What are you doing?"

"What do you mean? Just seizing the opportunity."

"Put it down. We can just ask for Jacobek's address."

"Low profile, remember?" O'Brien walked off to one of two chairs standing in front of Banks's desk. "Do you think I should ask her out?"

"Who?"

"Ania. She seems—"

"Hope I wasn't too long."

Penskie blushed, almost caught red-handed, and shot a quizzical look to his friend. "Quite a view you've got from here," he said loudly to cover his trepidation.

"The agency occupies the entire floor and each office has a nice view, but the eastern side *is* the prettiest. There is something about the river that adds a little . . ."

"Peace of mind?"

"Yes." She smiled. "Just a little perk for the senior staff."

"Does your staff rotate a lot?"

"Not at all, at least not since I've joined." She smiled again. "Tony Blake and I are the only newcomers in the last year. Good work environment, I guess."

"What happened to your predecessor? Quit along with the CEO?"

Something like a shadow covered her face. The momentary twitch around the corners of her lips drew Penskie's attention. He had to force himself to keep from staring at them.

"Terry . . . Terrence Jacobek took over the duties of the chief executive officer. I was sent in his place. You didn't know that?" She noticed the uneasy looks the legal attachés exchanged between themselves. "What exactly is the embassy interested in?" The casual smile receded from her face, giving way to a businesslike tone.

"We would like to ask some questions regarding Norman Bray."

"What did you say you do at the embassy?"

Too fast, Penskie thought.

"Legal attaché office . . ."

"I hope you don't mind showing me some ID?"

Legats stood up to pass their credentials across the large desk. Banks studied them closely.

"Federal Bureau of Investigation," she said finally, while tapping the edges of the desktop. "Tell me then, Agents . . . O'Brien and Penskie." She had to double check Stan's name, and continued defiantly, "What sort of investigative jurisdiction does the FBI have in here?"

"What makes you think we're investigating?" Penskie responded with a question. *Too quick, too prickly,* he scolded himself. He looked into the woman's eyes.

She blushed and returned his gaze but did not respond.

"Like I said, we just want to ask a few questions, but perhaps we're talking to the wrong person, since you've obviously never met the man." Not the most fortunate ending, he thought. He wanted to prolong this moment, to feast his eyes on the sight of this striking woman, but there was something about her that was beginning to make him angry. It was, perhaps, the imperious manner with which she spoke and looked from behind the desk. Perhaps it was the fact that in a few short minutes—very short, if he did not change his stance—he would leave this office without a chance of seeing her again. Mollie Banks, a woman he had met for the first time only moments ago, was beginning to dominate his thoughts.

"Perhaps we can talk to Ania, the receptionist, then?" O'Brien asked, oblivious to Penskie's mind-set.

Mollie Banks's reaction to the question drew the legal attachés' attention. She realized it belatedly, and blushed even more.

"I am certain that won't be necessary. Ania, you see, is new here. . . ." She covered awkwardness by speaking quickly.

"I thought—"

"Yes, well, she's a temp. They come and go, you know, hardly an event worth mentioning. The moment you memorize their names, there comes a new one." She tried to be more cooperative and as inviting as she was at the beginning; only her eyes lacked a smile. "Perhaps if you filled me in on the nature of your interest in the former CEO . . . ?"

"Mrs. Banks—"

"Mollie, please. *Miss* Mollie Banks."

"Ah." Penskie returned her smile; he liked the direction the conversation was taking. "I won't beat around the bush with you, then. There is no investigation . . . yet. But your agency will no doubt be overrun with the police, asking questions, rummaging through your files, the usual. Quite frankly, I am surprised you have not heard from them yet."

"What are you talking about?" she asked bewilderedly, and looked at O'Brien as if searching for confirmation of this outrageous statement.

"You *will* need the assistance of the embassy. I'm afraid we have some bad news. Norman Bray never made it back to the States. He was murdered right here in Poland."

"Oh, my God!"

She appeared genuinely shocked, Penskie noticed, not without some satisfaction. He let the news sink in, watching her reaction closely.

"How did this happen? And why?" she asked dejectedly.

"We don't have the details yet. The police found the body on the weekend and identified it only last night," O'Brien explained.

"Mollie," Penskie started gently, "the police may raise some questions that may be . . . er . . . difficult for the agency."

"What do you have in mind?"

"This may be just a coincidence, but no doubt it will be explored. Bray's death may be connected to your agency's affiliation with Andrzej Borysewicz."

Penskie knew he had hit the spot. Banks hesitated only a split second, but it was enough to give her away. She was caught off guard but masqueraded perfectly. Not a trace of acknowledgment crossed her face or her eyes, and there was only a split-second delay. Strange thing, Penskie thought: Despite its being obvious that the woman was involved in something, it made her seem even more alluring. There was now an aura of mystery surrounding her, and stimulating his mind.

"Who?" Mollie Banks asked, too late to cover the fact that she knew very well.

There was a knock on the door. Ania, the receptionist, was standing behind the glass. She awaited an inviting gesture from Banks, a coat hanging over her left arm. O'Brien, sitting closest to the door, stood up courteously to open it. He pulled the knob and took a step back, stunned by the incredible sight: An automatic pistol until now hidden under the woman's coat, was aimed at his abdomen. He made a mechanical move that probably saved his life: He pushed and slammed the door at the woman. She lost her balance, the bullet only ripping through the sleeve of O'Brien's jacket. Standing awkwardly, in a half turn, his legs splayed and barely able to keep his balance by holding on to the door handle, he was struck by a kick to his groin. As he was falling in pain he registered the glass shattering into sparkling little pieces, and Ania's legs hastening away. The commotion and shouts reached him some moments later. Out of breath, he saw Mollie Banks standing by her desk with a pistol in her hand.

Penskie got up to his knees, pushing away the chair he had sat in only seconds before.

"Are you okay?" he shouted to O'Brien, whose eyes were filled with tears.

Still out of breath, David tried to answer but was able only to nod.

"You'll be fine; she only kneed your balls!" Penskie patted him on the shoulder and followed Banks, who stormed after the receptionist.

He caught up with her in the hallway, looking at the light indicator above the elevator doors.

"She could've taken the stairs! To your right, at the end of the hallway!" Banks cried out.

There was no time to ask questions. Who was Ania? And who was Mollie Banks? Two women who did not hesitate to fire their weapons. *Their* weapons! Businesswomen did not carry guns; things had not come to that even in Poland, not yet, anyway. Very few women would have had the presence of mind to use a gun in similar circumstances. All he, a trained FBI officer, was able to do was lurch down to the floor, pulling the chair in a desperate attempt to protect himself from the gunfire. By the time he withdrew his Glock, Banks had already fired back at the receptionist, shattering the glass wall. He felt a sudden burst of embarrassment. He did what anyone would have done, but it did not make him feel any better. He was not *anyone;* he had been in far worse circumstances before. The thought made him angry, but also injected an increased dose of adrenaline through his veins. He kicked open the heavy steel door that led to the dim and cold concrete stairwell.

He stood in the dark for several seconds until he heard a very faint noise somewhere below. Footsteps. He raced down, skipping three, four steps at a time. Some dozen flights later he could hear the thumping of the woman's soles more clearly. How many floors had it been? He lost track, but was almost certain she could not escape him. He was catching up. He was good at running stairwells; he and friends had organized races back in their adolescent years. They would fly down the twelve-story stairwells, barely touching the steps. Of course, that was a long time ago, but he kept in good shape, and his speed increased as he got closer to the woman. He started noticing numbers on the doors as he passed them at blistering speed, holding tight on to the handrail, centrifugal force almost ripping his arm out at every turn. Five floors to go; he could see the woman now, only one flight of stairs between them.

Penskie caught up with Ania on the ground level, only moments before she would have been able to reach for the doors to the lobby. He grabbed her arm, but his hand slipped and pulled on the strap of her purse, ripping it off. He lost balance and fell to the ground. Crawling onto his knees, he met the barrel of a gun pointed at his torso. The woman hesitated.

"I don't want to shoot you! I will if you make me!" she warned.

Penskie reached for his weapon, and at that moment he felt a heavy blow that threw him back to the floor.

He stood up when the door closed behind the woman, a grimace of disbelief on his face. He realized he was holding on to the purse, the bullet somehow having gotten stuck in it and saving his life. He could hear screams coming from the lobby and cautiously opened the door. The woman was struggling with two men in blue blazers. Security guards. The gun in her hands must have alerted them. For once the omnipresent security guards in Polish establishments had come in handy.

Penskie started toward them when someone's hand slid under his arm.

"Slowly walk out with me!" Mollie Banks said quietly into his ear.

Chapter Six

The *Urząd Rady Ministrów* on Aleje Ujazdowskie was a complex of three-story, neoclassical buildings dating back to the turn of the twentieth century. It housed the council of ministers and the state council offices. The windows of a large conference room on the third floor looked out southward onto a large wooded park. The yellowish walls of the room were decorated with old tapestries and oversize paintings in fanciful frames. Lights were dimmed, and heavy lush brown curtains were drawn. Despite the nonsmoking policy, cigarette smoke hung in the air, forming layers of thin blue clouds. Five men seated at the long table were browsing through documents and eight-by-ten-inch color photographs. The meeting was assembled quickly, in response to the recent daring murders of a number of prominent figures. The *Urząd Ochrony Państwa's* investigating officer's death was topping the list.

"I think we should at least acknowledge the possibility that Officer Sito was murdered *because* of his investigation," a man dressed in the uniform of a police general, who held the office of chief of state police, said with anger. "Mister Minister, deliberately discarding the likelihood of such a scenario may pose a security risk for any of our leaders, as well as to the country. Sito was on the right track; that much is obvious to me."

"The *Urząd Ochrony Państwa* does not discard *any* possibilities, no matter how outlandish," objected the director of the UOP. "But, that said, it is our belief that such suppositions are premature. True, a number of significant figures from our country's social pages have died sudden and violent deaths in rapid succession, but there's no evidence to support allegations of a political conspiracy. None of these people hold . . . held any offices of importance to the security of this country. On the contrary, they're all private citizens now whose successful businesses are in one way or another tied into the underworld economy."

"Wasn't your officer investigating the murder of Andrzej Borysewicz as well as some of the earlier murders?" The deputy prime minister looked across the table at the director.

"Yes. It is most regrettable that Officer Sito had to die, but gentlemen, you mustn't draw hasty conclusions from this incident. In fact, we believe his death had nothing to do with Borysewicz's murder. Sito helped bring down one of the most notorious gangs in the country, whose members would like nothing better than to see him dead. I'm afraid that is a dreadful reality for most of our officers these days."

"Mr. Czapla, what do you make of this?" asked the minister of the interior.

Stefan Czapla headed the *Biuro Ochrony Rządu*, the government security agency, whose task it was to protect the government officials and politicians as well as visiting foreign dignitaries. The BOR's range of authorities was strictly classified; the general public knew only that it was a formation under the command of the minister of the interior. It was this agency that once provided round-the-clock protection for Andrzej Borysewicz, among other dignitaries of the times.

"I agree with General Smolarczyk," Czapla said. "Political motive cannot be ruled out. But in the case of Borysewicz, who as the head of *Służba Bezpieczeństwa* in the eighties was personally responsible for hundreds of human sufferings, even deaths, one must also take into consideration old-fashioned revenge."

"Revenge after so many years? Why wait so long?"

"With all due respect, sir, there's no expiration date on the years of misery some of these innocent people were subjected to. There could've been no opportunity before, or perhaps someone waited for the perfect moment? Who knows? But, imagination aside, from what I understand, the case was quite simple: a burglary. The murderers were apprehended, weren't they?" He turned to the general, who was about to answer when the deputy prime minister interjected.

"Why don't you brief us all on the affair, General? We heard only bits and pieces, some of which are most puzzling and contradictory. Perhaps it would be best if we could all hear the same story. The prime minister is deeply concerned with the situation, and both I and the interior minister need a clear assessment of the situation for tomorrow morning's briefing."

"Very well," the police officer began. "Last Saturday at around three-thirty in the morning, the police received an anonymous call about a break-in in progress. The cruiser arrived just in time to find three men fleeing the estate. Whether they had accomplices on the outside, who saw the police arrive, or simply could not find anything of value and were leaving empty-handed was uncertain at that moment. The officers filed a statement"—the general pulled out a sheet of paper from his briefcase—"in which they describe the suspects as frightened, shocked, bewildered, and professing their innocence. The officers then entered the premises, and the scene they discovered startled them beyond anything they could've expected."

The general encouraged the panel to reexamine the pictures spread on the table. They showed the late Andrzej Borysewicz's body as well as various close-ups. The pictures were quite self-explanatory, but the officer proceeded with the description nonetheless.

"The deceased was seated straight up with his ankles, wrists, and neck tied to a high chair with plastic wraps—I believe they're called zip-ties—generally used for coupling together wires and cables in offices all around the world. There was a needle in his left arm, with a thin tube attached and leading down to a bucket."

"A *bucket?*" the deputy prime minister asked in perplexity.

"An ordinary galvanized garden bucket. Filled with some two liters of blood."

"They bled him to death?" the interior minister asked incredulously. "Why?"

"Presumably, it was a form of interrogation. A painless torture of sorts, where the interrogated has a choice: Speak or watch your own blood drain out of your body."

"Jesus Christ!" The minister sighed.

"Do we know what they were after?" the chief of the *Biuro Ochrony Rządu* asked. "I mean, it wasn't just a haphazard break-in, was it? They were after something, weren't they?"

"Borysewicz was a wealthy man; his collection of stamps was estimated to be worth millions of zlotys, and the coin collection ten times as much, but I'm afraid I can't answer this question." The general looked ill at ease.

"Haven't you questioned the killers? Surely you have at least a partial idea what happened?"

The general sighed. "They're all dead. Shortly after being taken into the *komisariat*, they managed to get hold of a gun, or so it was thought, and were shot down. The reports are quite unclear about the incident. There was a commotion, shouts; weapons were drawn and fired, and three bodies lay on the ground. All we've been able to establish was that someone"—the general lowered his voice—"impersonating a police officer started the panic, shot the three men, and fled the station before anyone could make sense of what happened."

Silence accompanied the officer's statement, the listeners too awed to interrupt.

"Impersonating a police officer!" The UOP director broke the silence. "Shooting three killers in police custody! *Inside* the police station! Gentlemen, this illustrates the point I have been trying to make for months and months. The police force is not prepared to handle complex cases involving organized crime. The law enforcement is the laughingstock of all criminal elements in this country. . . ."

"Yes, yes, we know, Mr. Director. Had the *Urząd Ochrony*

Państwa's budget been raised we'd be in a land of eternal happiness and free of crime," the deputy prime minister said impatiently.

"The budget alone is inadequate, sir. What good is it if we can't be on top of current events? Jurisdiction, access to police records and investigations, and better cooperation. This agency needs money as well as the authority—"

"The director has a one-sided integration in mind, no doubt," the police officer broke in.

"Gentlemen, this is an issue for the *Komisja Senacka do Spraw Służb Bezpieczeństwa i Porządku Publicznego,*" the deputy prime minister said. "We're here to establish the implications of the tragic incidents that involve once-prominent figures in Poland's history, some of whom hold . . . held positions vital to this country's economy and security. Let's be honest: The pattern is quite clear and very troublesome. Someone is liquidating our defense, communications, fuel, and a dozen other strategic departments' contractors. What I . . . what we, the prime minister and the cabinet, want to know is, who's behind it and what are their objectives?"

"I think, Mr. Minister, the reason we're not getting anywhere with the investigation is because of the assumption that all the killings have anything to do with the victims' business activities," the general explained. "Yes, there's a pattern here, but so far neither of us has been able to provide any hint as to the motive. What I find even more troubling is that it may lie in the victims' past. I believe Mr. Czapla is right: There's another pattern, one that Director Szczepański has foolishly discarded."

"This is preposterous!" the director of the UOP objected.

"I'd like to hear what the general has to say, Director!" the minister of the interior said. He never favored the UOP, primarily because, unlike the *Biuro Ochrony Rządu* and the police, the *Urząd Ochrony Państwa* was independent from the ministry of the interior. His office had no direct control over this agency, and, like so many other left-wing cabinet ministers, he simply feared the UOP's growing powers in addition to its involvement in politics. The UOP's tapping of social democratic party members' phone lines and checking of their mail was a very hot issue these days.

"Let's take the Borysewicz case as an example." The general took the initiative. "Has anyone here been to his estate? Let me tell you then: It is a fortress! A two-meter concrete wall rigged with sound and vibration sensors, which are also scattered throughout the property; infrared cameras on most trees; state-of-the-art alarm system wired directly to a private security company, a subsidiary of one of Borysewicz's companies, with a two-minute response time; round-the-clock sentry on the premises . . . to name only the basic, most obvious facts. A few simpletons, who make their living selling stolen properties on the stadium bazaar market, bypassed all this, killed the man, looked around his home, and left without any of the goods they make their living selling each day. If it seems too far-fetched, then there is a good reason for it." The general leaned back in his chair to have a wide view of the others. "Gentlemen, whoever killed Borysewicz made a big mistake!" He paused. "These three men were police informants!"

A commotion just short of pandemonium broke out. Usually staid men were outshouting one another. All but one. He was sitting still, his eyes focused on the general's.

"The three men who were apprehended were framed. They were acting with the knowledge and operational support of the police and in cooperation with the *Centralne*

Biuro Śledcze. They were wiretapped, and the police entry was carefully planned. There's no doubt in my mind the break-in was orchestrated to conceal the true events. Someone hired these men as scapegoats. That someone knew Borysewicz would be killed that night. It is my personal regret that the operation misfired, but I assure you, it is only a matter of time before we find out who's behind it. I want you to understand, however, that the truth may be very surprising indeed."

"What are you driving at, General?" the deputy prime minister asked.

"I can't say anything other than that all the murders in question had one thing in common: All of the deceased were once very close to the security and intelligence apparatus of communist Poland. In fact, they all held the highest jobs in these departments: chief of the *Służba Bezpieczeństwa*, the intelligence, the counterintelligence, and the army intelligence, but then again, you all know that too."

"Indeed we do, but correct me if I'm wrong, General: Haven't all these departments rivaled one another?" the chief of *Biuro Ochrony Rządu* asked doubtfully.

"Quite. But they all had one thing in common: They all were in the possession of some of the most sensitive secrets and information in this country. And they all have destroyed their databases. Or at least made it look that way."

"You're not seriously suggesting those files *weren't* destroyed? This story comes back like a boomerang!"

"Oh, I am quite certain they were securely put away! Perhaps not all, but certainly the most important files, the ones that provided the influence and power necessary to stay immune and safe in times of witch hunts, when the former oppressors are now the ones being hunted."

"Christ!" The deputy prime minister sighed. His mind ventured back to the eighties. Martial law was called, and the members of the solidarity movement were arrested and placed in the detention camps, the minister being only an activist then. Solidarity was declared illegal and consequently shut down. Some of the most active members, considered most dangerous to the system, were found dead, among them a young priest who was drowned and his body severely mutilated. Years later the guilty were prosecuted, but it was terribly obvious to everyone, including the judges, that they were only the immediate killers who followed orders from the top. Those who gave the orders to shoot the striking workers of the shipyards of the north and the coal mines of the south were never held accountable for the atrocities. The names of Borysewicz, Jagoda, Jaruzelski, Kiszczak, and others frequented the press and the prosecutors' statements, but they remained untouchable. *The dossiers. What other explanation could there be?* the minister thought. Hundreds, if not thousands, of solidarity and opposition members, who were detained at that time, signed documents prepared by the *Służba Bezpieczeństwa.* These signatures opened the prison doors, set them free, and let them return to their families, lovers, and spouses. Those documents seemed like such a small price back in the days when communism seemed unbreakable and everlasting. Back then, those documents merely stated the allegiance to the government, but the same documents interpreted in the nineties and today meant collaboration with the hated *Służba Bezpieczeństwa*. If those documents were not destroyed, as everyone thought and assumed, then somewhere out there was a file, which bore his—the deputy prime minister's—signature.

Jezu Chryste! The minister covered his face.

Gen. Stanisław Smolarczyk started his Polonez; a Polish-made car he parked in the lot in front of the *Urząd Rady Ministrów*. He was outraged, yet satisfied. His suspicions were proven. He had bluffed about those three thugs being police informants, but the deception paid off. At first he did not want to accept the possibility, but this Officer Sito of the UOP who brought the news to him was so persistent in his desperation. His death only lent credibility to his story. Oh, if he only had listened! With Sito also perished the findings he had unearthed while working on the murders. But no matter; he had seen it in the man's eyes only minutes ago. He was guilty as charged! But why? Why kill? To support his own political agenda? Or was he working on orders from someone else? Some other figures who were placed even higher in the echelons of power? The others in the meeting? The dossiers Borysewicz and others were suspected of having preserved could crush one's opponents, so to find out who stood behind it appeared to be an easy task: Find out who benefited most. But, the answer was: everyone! There was not a single cabinet minister whose political roots did not date back to the dreadful days of the eighties. Days of turmoil and betrayal. *Madness!*

The general shivered at the thought. He would need an ally to bring the truth to light. But at this stage he could trust no one, other than the president himself. He would seek a private consultation first thing in the morning. But first he had to prepare what little he had. He glanced at the briefcase resting on the passenger seat, as if to make sure it was secure. The evidence had to be compelling enough to convince the president that the director of the *Urząd Ochrony Państwa,* the agency that was to stand on guard for the country's security, was in the business of murdering and conspiring against the state's interests! That poor bastard, the deputy prime minister, would not last long in the office. True, he gave the case to him, the chief of police, but there was no doubt in the general's mind that the minister was afraid the director of the UOP might undermine his position with the knowledge of his signature on the *Służba Bezpieczeństwa*'s documents. Oh, well, sooner or later it had to come to that. Giving the case to the chief was a last gesture of decency. Not that the *Urząd Ochrony Państwa* would not engage anyway, but at least the minister would be able to save what little would be left of his honor.

Fifteen minutes later the general pulled over in front of a ten-story concrete building in the Ursynów district. He saw the light in the kitchen, where his loving wife of almost twenty years waited for him with a warm dinner standing by. He smiled at the thought and turned the ignition off. The last thing he saw was a hooded figure standing next to the car. A series of short, muted gunshots shattered the glass, the bullets ripping into the general's throat and penetrating his chest. The killer walked slowly to the passenger side, opened the door, and reached for the briefcase.

Chapter Seven

Stan Penskie stared at Mollie Banks with awe. They were sitting inside the legal attaché's Opel SUV directly across the square from the Economic Development and Cooperation Agency's offices. Banks was sitting in the front seat and O'Brien, who was the last to leave the building, was in the back. The woman was searching the purse Penskie had kept hold of during his struggle with the receptionist.

"Who are you?" Penskie asked slowly and deliberately.

"Here's what saved your life. That and a small-caliber handgun." Banks was holding what was left of Ania's cellular telephone. The unit was badly damaged, deformed and incomplete, small shattered parts still inside the bag.

Penskie could not help but think the woman was stalling, avoiding his question. His surviving the shot seemed distant and far less important. It was done with, over. After all, he had been shot at before. What bothered and angered him more was the unknown.

"What the hell is going on in there?" he asked with determination.

"It is a long story, and a very sensitive one, Agent Penskie," she answered finally without looking at him.

"Then I suggest you make time, Miss Banks!" Penskie grabbed the woman's arm, forcing her to look at him. "What just happened there may be directly linked to one of the biggest murder cases in this country and you . . . you and your agency are somehow implicated."

"Will you arrest me, Agent Penskie? On what authority? What charges?"

"I am sure the Polish authorities would be happy to receive a lead on the case that has put the police and security services on alert. We are here to cooperate and lend operational support, you know."

Banks sat motionless. She was studying Penskie's eyes for a trace of deceit.

She found none.

"All right," she answered resignedly. "The USG, much like yourself." She paused briefly and added defiantly, "And that's all I can tell you, so let's just drop it."

"I'm afraid you'll have to do better than that. If you had worked for the United States government you would have your office at the embassy, or at least the embassy would have been notified of your presence in the country."

Banks placed the handbag on the dashboard and shifted in her seat. She did not wear a holster. The handgun weighed uncomfortably in her side pocket. She removed it.

"There are government agencies that cannot be identified

overtly, Agent Penskie. I'm afraid *you* will have to take my word for it." Banks shook off his hand, the move causing her arm to rise, and a pistol pointed at Penskie's chest.

O'Brien, who had noticed Banks remove her pistol, drew his weapon in alarm.

"Easy, miss!" he warned.

"You fools!" she exclaimed. "You have no idea what's going on!"

"Try us."

The woman turned away and looked out the window. She murmured something incomprehensible and sighed. After placing her handgun in the door pocket, she reached in and withdrew a small device from her inner jacket pocket. The device resembled an ordinary pager, though it was smaller. She activated it and pointed at Penskie, her outstretched arm drawing circles in the air. She repeated the procedure on O'Brien. Apparently satisfied, she turned the device off and placed it back in her pocket.

"Just making sure no one else is hearing this conversation," she explained.

"Spectrum analyzer?" Penskie asked incredulously. "Let me get this straight. You are supposed to be a business-woman, an executive at a zillion dollar company. A visit to your office results in a bloodbath, you get shot at by your own employee, you run around the building with a loaded weapon, and it is *you* who is not trusting *us*, FBI agents?"

"Trust? Let me tell you something about trust, Agent Penskie. The Economic Development Agency has done more for the United States during its presence in Eastern Europe than the combined efforts of all the embassies in this region. Only a few weeks ago it was this close to establishing a relationship that would have provided the U.S. with unsurpassed economic domination in this part of Europe and perhaps around the world, until someone from the embassy, someone in the position to have this kind of information, alerted the Poles about the true nature of EDECA's founders and its sources of information."

"Which is?"

Mollie Banks realized she had gone beyond the point of retreat. She shrugged and added slowly, "The Economic Development and Cooperation Agency is a . . . is the most important intelligence operation since the Cold War."

In a private ranch in the Arizona desert, the property of the brother of the president of the United States, an unscheduled and unpublicized meeting was taking place. The president was speaking with the secretary of state. John Allcombs arrived at the ranch under a great deal of secrecy. Not even the president's family, nor his secretary or his security detail, was aware of the identity of the visitor. The president insisted on the secrecy, and to his own security men's distress, the wish had to be granted. The unprecedented move was the result of very unusual circumstances. The president knew about the forces within his administration who were ready to rebel against his plan. In these times of unparalleled national unity there were people who did not agree with his visions of global security and his war on terrorism. They agreed in principle but there the agreement ended. They had their own plans. Those people—and their ranks were growing—could be monitoring his every move, influencing his foes and confusing his allies. These people had to be stopped, but how did one stop those who held offices responsible for the very service one required? The answer lay in a very distant place, where an assembly was to take place in less than forty-eight hours. Forty-eight hours to change the faith in his presidency, and the faith of the world. All this in the hands of only one man, a man to whom he would remain indebted as no other president ever had to an individual. Of course, at that point—a point of victory—it would no longer matter, for he would not be judged.

"Whom can we count on?" the president asked.

"The Brits, for sure. Others . . . who knows? Alpha does, however, have many other supporters, and it would not surprise me if he did manage to turn the scale to our advantage. He's proven his negotiating skills in the office."

"I am not so sure a negotiation is such a good idea at this stage. Why not send our boys to assure the right result? We still have control of the army."

"We cannot enter into an open confrontation with the organization. The element of surprise will be gone—no doubt their intelligence is on high alert these days—and how do we send our troops to a different country, anyway?"

"Don't we have some of our boys . . . somewhere . . . in the area?"

"In Germany. But, Mr. President, I strongly discourage the use of force. I do believe in Alpha's ability to seize control. We must wait. Alpha *will* deliver."

"John, I really want it. I want the organization and its resources."

"I know, Mr. President. I want it too."

"I am really fed up with having to beg for the green light to go after the Osamas and Saddams of the world. We are America, for crying out loud, and I am the goddamn president!"

"Soon none of it will be necessary."

The president sighed. He trusted in Alpha's strength and capability, but he knew Alpha's American background hindered his chances of winning the support of the council. The war on terrorism was a reminder that even their closest allies did not agree with the American vision of war.

"What am I supposed to do with those . . . traitors, when this is over?"

"The NSA director will be removed. The arrangements have been made."

"What are you talking about, John?"

"I didn't mean it like that. He will be removed from office. The others I wouldn't worry about. They are just pawns. Keeping them will assure their loyalty, magnified by your forgiving generosity."

"I don't like the idea. I'd much rather not see them in the administration ever again."

"It's all politics, Mr. President." John Allcombs spread his arms helplessly. "It's all politics."

Penskie was enraged. The Central bloody Intelligence! So that was it: Norman Bray died as a result of some operation gone wrong; by paying the overlooked alimony the agency was trying to cover things up. Sito had uncovered the truth and got killed. *Jesus!* The agency's mistakes killed his sister's fiancé! He swallowed and clenched his fingers on the steering wheel.

"Was it . . . was it worth whatever the hell it is you're after?"

"What do you mean?"

"What do *I* mean?"

In times of extreme anxiety Penskie confused languages,

the tongue of his childhood, and his Polish accent, came back with a strength that made his pronunciation close to incomprehensible.

O'Brien realized his friend was about to lose his cool. He did not understand the reason behind the outbreak, but he knew the symptoms—blood rushing to Stan's face, and mumbled speech. It did not happen often, and certainly the recent events did not seem that traumatic—they had been in much worse circumstances together. Stan needed a break, or . . . or there was more to this case than he had shared. They needed to talk, O'Brien noted.

Perplexed, he rushed in to help.

"Three people died—three that we know of, that is. Stan barely made it out alive this morning, and only half an hour ago, three more corpses would've been added to the list, had it not been for a bit of luck, and all this because of your operation. What else is it going to take for you to get whatever you've set up to accomplish?"

"EDECA does legitimate business—"

"Since when does the United States government seal business deals with blood?"

"Look, this isn't getting us anywhere. The only reason I'm still here talking to you is because I believe you have nothing to do with them; and the fact Ania tried to kill me, presumably because I could tell you things, only adds to my conviction."

"Them? I'm afraid you're talking riddles."

Banks sighed and sat back. She looked at Penskie, whose face was still turned away, looking out the fogged window.

"You really have no idea what's going on, do you? How did you . . . how did the FBI get involved in it then?"

"The chief executive officer of your agency was murdered. Question for a question: Who's *them?*"

"There is no easy answer."

"Give us a little credit, will ya? We're not as dumb as we look."

She appreciated the attempt to break the ice. She realized these guys were shooting bullets in the dark. Poor fellas, they had no idea their world was about to turn upside down. She shrugged.

"In a nutshell? They are a powerful international conglomerate, identities or objectives as yet uncertain, but chaos and destabilization of world power structures, perhaps financial markets, cannot be ruled out as their goals."

The legal attachés sat in silence.

Penskie turned away from the window. This woman startled him; everything about her was electrifying, from the way she talked, the way she looked and walked, to the information she offered.

"And they—the powers able to destabilize the world—are right here in Poland?" he asked sarcastically.

"The brains appear to be here. The executors are on Wall Street, in Tokyo, London, Paris, Moscow, Beijing, and in the governments of each of the world's most powerful nations and economies."

"A variation on Carroll Quigley's network of secret political societies or a continuation thereof?"

"Your sarcasm notwithstanding, we believe it's a fact."

"Who is *we,* Miss Banks?"

"My turn to ask a question. Can we be on first-name basis again?"

The tension on Penskie's face relaxed.

"The EDECA, much like the U.S. Agency for International Development, was established to provide loans, grants, and technical assistance, but localized only to the Eastern European region. Unlike USAID, it is in no way affiliated or otherwise connected to the embassy or any other American government mission."

"But—"

"It's only a front. It was meant to look like a government organization, to lend it the necessary credibility, to achieve their goals. Norman Bray must have learned about the true nature of the agency and was killed."

"You're saying the EDECA is a hoax? But how is it possible? We've been in touch with Washington. We've had specific memos and instructions from the state and the Bureau detailing the procedures and conduct of the investigation while dealing with EDECA. It *is* a government agency!"

"Nothing but an ingenious masquerade, I'm afraid."

"Who's behind it? How did they manage to pull it off?"

"We are dealing with masters of deception, Stan. The Central Intelligence Agency—"

"You have got to be kidding! Not even the CIA could organize and run it. EDECA is too big. I just don't buy it." Penskie stamped his foot on the floor mat.

"Is that why Bray was killed? He found out who signed his paychecks, or was he with the CIA himself?" O'Brien continued the thought. Where conspiracy was involved he did not discard even the most outrageous possibilities. This case was more appealing to him than chasing hoodlums. Cases such as this one were the reason why—and he strongly felt it now—he had joined the FBI in the first place.

"I doubt it. The Company does not normally place its officers in the top positions. Too much exposure, for one thing. And no, the EDECA is not even a government-sanctioned operation, even though it was likely formed by people from Washington, people so influential they could provide the illusion of legitimacy and offer political support should the secret surface; you witnessed it firsthand. The CIA's experts are among these people. Despite their intentions they are not who they seem. They are traitors, but not in the sense we know from popular fiction or cases such as that of Aldrich Ames. They are a different breed. They may call themselves, or even be perceived as, patriots, for what they do is seemingly in the interest of the United States."

"Who are they?"

"They are extremely hard to find, though you may think there is nothing easier than to find who's covering the EDECA. However, if you look at the vastness of our administration you'll realize it is not impossible to lose it in the red tape, with the help of strategically placed assets, of course."

"How do you know this?"

Banks hesitated.

"I am with the inspector general. We investigate allegations of wrongdoing within the Central Intelligence Agency."

"Spooks within spooks."

"The inspector general is independent. There's a necessary and pragmatic reason, really. The agency, especially in the days of cutbacks and failures, such as Nine-eleven, cannot afford to entangle itself in affiliations that make the public wonder whom it actually serves."

"You said, though, that Central Intelligence established the EDECA to break this international . . . what you might call conglomerate."

"No, you misinterpreted my words. The EDECA was

formed with the assistance of some CIA officers and resources, and whatever their reasons, these people no longer work for the United States, Stan. Furthermore, those are the people who killed Bray."

"And Robert."

"Who?"

"Someone who came too close to the truth." Penskie shook the thought off and caught a quizzical look on his friend's face. David might be suspecting something. Perhaps he should have told him? It would be awkward at this stage, but he knew he could not leave any room for the slightest doubt in his friend's mind. In this job there was no room for doubts. Your partner was often all that separated you from a bullet. If there was no trust, you might as well pose as a target. He would have to tell O'Brien—soon.

"Those . . . renegades work with the conglomerate?" O'Brien asked.

"Well, that's the confusing part. Some of the recent events seem to indicate quite the opposite. There is evidence of internal struggle, the case of the prime minister Borysewicz—"

O'Brien whistled lengthily.

"Borysewicz was in it?" he asked disbelievingly.

"Wait a minute," Penskie said. "If they're no longer working for or as the CIA, and not with the conglomerate, then . . ."

"Maybe they work for themselves . . . I don't know. Another possibility is that some faction of this organization does not like what's happening. It could be that they want to stop the process."

"What is happening? What process, Mollie?"

"Like I said, the organization controls a vast part of the

world's trade and has access to markets America cannot dream of entering, and to governments we have no diplomatic relations with. The list is long, but there are people, organizations, and governments who do not want it to happen, who will go a long way to stop it."

"Was Ania one of the people who want to stop it, or was that just an outburst of a frustrated employee?"

Banks ignored the sarcasm.

"Two possibilities: Either it's Polish counterintelligence or . . . er . . . or . . ." She picked up the wreck of the cellular phone and proceeded to disassemble what was left of it. She managed to lift off the deformed battery and sighed with satisfaction.

"We may be lucky after all."

"What are you doing?"

"When you came into the agency, and after you had gone to my office, I noticed Ania whispering into her cell phone headset. When I passed her desk she paused and gave me this strange look, not her usual look when she does something other than her duties, but a . . . conspiratorial one."

Banks removed a miniature plastic card from underneath the battery of the telephone.

"Here we are," she said triumphantly. "One of you has a cell phone?"

"I'll be damned!" O'Brien handed over his.

Banks swiftly removed the battery and replaced O'Brien's SIM card with Ania's. She activated the phone and checked for recently dialed numbers. She muttered the last one and sighed.

"My God, it's Jacobek!"

Penskie shifted in his seat. "Sito was right on the money! Bray and Jacobek visited Borysewicz together. Bray disappeared after the first visit, and Borysewicz was killed after the second. The question is why? Why did they have to die? You said the EDECA was on the brink of striking the biggest deal—what was it?"

"Borysewicz, as you know, held the keys to some of the major industries in Poland, and Bray negotiated a close cooperation with him. But it is becoming obvious now that the game had a different objective. I assume you know what Borysewicz did before he became the prime minister? Well, the Company has long believed that someone had to be in possession of the names of the former Eastern Bloc intelligence services' sleepers who operated in the States and elsewhere under nonofficial cover. Parts of these databases were recovered after the German unification—the Czechs simply offered theirs to us—but others have remained beyond our reach. Some within the Company still think that those sleepers are run by the current intelligence services and collectively control billions in liquid assets. I admit it is an old story, but there must be some truth in it. No agency would simply give up on their assets only because the country changed its political line. If you think about who is the most obvious person to know, or perhaps to be in possession of this information, the name of the commanding officer comes to mind."

"Borysewicz!"

"Jacobek must have been after the list."

"So are we to assume that Jacobek got a hold of the names and is not going to pass them along to the U.S. government? Who is he working for, then?" O'Brien asked.

"Sito had a snapshot of Jacobek and Loomis together. Perhaps Jacobek acquired the list for Loomis and the government?"

"The list is a gold mine. Whoever has it can name *any* price."

"Hold on a second. Let me see if I've got this straight," O'Brien said. "Afraid their identities may be exposed, not the CIA, but this *organization* created the EDECA, supposedly a government agency, to act on its behalf. The reason they want these names kept from the government is simple: imminent exposure."

"That, in turn, means that the EDECA was formed by . . . the sleepers?" Penskie added with doubt; he was not sure he followed his friend's thinking.

"Those would have to be the highest-placed sleepers ever!" David exclaimed enthusiastically.

"Since the day I arrived in Warsaw I've run into nothing but obstacles," Banks started. "Those who were supposed to be on our side, aiding me in the investigation, were in fact driving me away from it. Jacobek is with the Company . . . and so are dozens of others who were to help me find out who's gone astray. I was beginning to believe it was the station chief, Dan Loomis, but I suppose I have to exonerate him now." She pondered for a moment in silence.

The legal attachés were much too overwhelmed by all the information to speak out. They remained quiet for a while, immersed in their own thoughts. This was no ordinary chase after crooks, thieves, or thugs. The picture Banks painted in front of their eyes showed a far-reaching conspiracy. To create and run an organization such as the Economic Development and Cooperation Agency one had to have access to very high places. The confusing and conflicting orders from the Bureau's headquarters might very well point to a traitor within their agency, perhaps even to somebody they knew and respected. That was not an easy thought, and if it came to that, nothing would be able to expiate the fact that the FBI harbored a traitor. In their minds, being in the position to uncover the identity of that person or persons was a debatable accomplishment.

Banks had to recall their attention.

"Well, I guess we can thank the circumstances. Whether it was Loomis or this Officer Sito who stepped on their heels, the fact is that they have been exposed; they panicked and made mistakes. No doubt they will take further steps to cover the trail; the murders are a sign they are working on it. We should follow the scent while it is fresh and before more people have to die."

Terrence Jacobek lived in nearby Nowe Miasto, or New Town, a deceiving name, considering the area dated back to the fifteenth century, when the community separated from Old Warsaw and received its own municipal administration. After the almost complete destruction of the city center during the Second World War, the New Town was meticulously restored to its former glory. Today it was hardly distinguishable from the Old Town complex, and was every bit as charming and interesting. Unlike the neighboring Old Town though, it was largely a residential area, and many visitors and locals preferred it to the Old Town for its stately and quiet cobblestoned streets, free of tacky souvenir shops and countless school groups.

The apartment house Terrence Jacobek lived in was less than ten minutes on foot from the Economic Development and Cooperation Agency's offices, but it took just as long to drive to it due to a complicated network of one-way streets. It was a newly renovated four-story building with a wide marble stairwell. There was no elevator—most of the older buildings lacked this luxurious innovation—and the light in the stairwell was not working. The city lights reflecting from low clouds shone through a large skylighted ceiling, providing enough of a faint glimmer to notice the contours of the steps.

"You'd think in a place this ritzy they could afford to replace the lightbulbs once a while." O'Brien pressed the light switch.

"Apartment fourteen," Banks whispered. "It should be on the top floor."

"Yeah, it figures. Doesn't it strike you as somewhat suspicious that it is always the top floor when there is no elevator? Must be a masonic conspiracy." O'Brien chuckled.

"Look at it this way: For every floor you clear one cigarette from your lungs."

"What's the point? Gonna need one as soon as we climb to the top."

The amount of light coming from the glass rooftop was stronger at the top of the stairwell. Here Penskie could see a large plant standing in the corner, and despite the still-poor visibility, he recognized a ficus benjamina. He had one just like it in his place, but it was not doing very well. He could not believe how big and luscious this one had grown. He approached the plant to touch its leaves, suspecting it to be artificial. At the same time O'Brien lit his cigarette lighter to find which of the three doors led to Jacobek's apartment. The tiny flame gave enough illumination for Penskie to recognize that there was something peculiar about the plant. It seemed to have an abnormally thick trunk. He reached in to touch it when a sudden rustle of leaves startled him. The trunk was moving! It split into three, and Penskie realized someone had been hiding in the shadow. He instinctively lurched to the side, reaching for his handgun. The move probably saved his life, as a quiet click and a small burst of light indicated a fired weapon. A scream followed from behind him where his companions stood. It occurred to him one of them may have been shot, and in enraged passion he emptied the magazine of his Glock into the silhouetted figure. Moments later he saw the shape slowly, as if in a slow motion movie, bend backward, right over the waist-height handrail, and a muted thump followed.

"That son of a bitch was waiting for us!" he shouted, and cautiously approached the handrail. He could not see the bottom floor.

"He's been hit!" The woman's shout caught Stan's attention. It took him a split second to realize she did not mean the killer. David O'Brien lay on the floor in the fetal position, holding his abdomen, subdued moans indicating he was alive.

"Go down and check on Jacobek! I'll get an ambulance!" She was dialing O'Brien's phone with one hand, while attending to his wound with the other.

Penskie ran downstairs holding on to the handrail, so as not to lose his balance in the darkness. He should have expected this. Jacobek had to be on alert after having received the call from Ania, but between the three of them they had been almost certain he would not be home. What was he doing in his apartment, or in the city, or even in the country, for that matter? If Jacobek had killed the former prime minister and got hold of the names he would not be waiting for the cops to show up at his door. Perhaps, then, he did not acquire whatever he was after—or, the thought suddenly occurred to Stan, it was not Jacobek at all. It was possible the killer had murdered Jacobek and was about to flee the building when they showed up. In either case their chances of finding the answers had largely diminished. As the thoughts ran through his mind, Penskie could not withhold a loud curse.

Street lamps allowed enough light to pass through the glass doors, and cast a glow on the floor. Penskie could make out a figure lying on the floor, its limbs twisted unnaturally. He approached it carefully with his gun directed at the body. He checked the carotid artery for signs of life, and sighed. The man was dead. He holstered his handgun and stepped over the body to see the face of the person.

Had Mollie Banks not been talking to the emergency dispatch she would have heard a muffled cry of astonishment. The body was that of the economic attaché of the American Embassy and the Central Intelligence Agency's station chief, Dan Loomis.

Chapter Eight

It was early afternoon in Washington, D.C., when four men gathered at a nondescript house in a quiet residential area. They had never used this house before; they never met in the same house, and they seldom met face-to-face under one roof. It was one of the rules stipulated by the organization. This time their meeting was of such magnitude that it required the presence of all four of them. Still, secrecy was paramount. Each man arrived on foot, his car parked a block or two away; the counterintelligence would not be a reason for concern; through the organization's resources they made sure the premises were not under surveillance. Nosy neighbors, on the other hand, were always something to be reckoned with. The house was one of many similar homes scattered around the country; it was occupied at night by a person who worked long day shifts, and never returned home before eight or nine in the evening. There were also other homes whose occupants worked night shifts, so as to provide maximum versatility for the organization's meetings. The occupants were an unwanted but a necessary part of the scheme. The houses had to have the appearance of being occupied, first because of the neighbors; second in case of possible surveillance. The counterintelligence, or even ordinary cops, might be interested in receiving tips from sleepless or curious neighbors who never got invited inside and never received RSVPs to their own invitations. For that reason the occupants had to undergo routine security checks. They were low-key members of the organization; their duty was to keep the house bug-free, maintaining the state-of-the-art equipment that counteracted any possible eavesdropping. Nothing that went on inside could escape outside of such a home's walls. To assure even greater security the organization often owned the houses next door as well. In such cases a subterranean tunnel linked the homes; the members entered one home and used the passage to another one, where the actual meeting took place. If anyone were curious about strangers arriving into the neighborhood, possible surveillance would then be directed at the house they had entered.

Despite the countersurveillance equipment in place, the first man to arrive used a portable scanner to ensure that the equipment was functioning properly. As if not fully trusting the arrangement, he withdrew a small device from his briefcase—a white-noise emitter, courtesy of the Central Intelligence Agency—and placed it on the windowsill, careful not to disturb the blinds. The blinds, much as many other items in the house, were especially designed to accommodate the needs of those who would use the premises—not only did they allow no light to be visible from the outside, not even the slightest trace of it, but they also stopped possible electronic attempts at eavesdropping by emitting pink and white noise.

Shortly three more men arrived, one by one.

The emergency meeting commenced. The mutual concern was the upcoming general assembly of the leaders of the organization, driven by the very serious prospect of the American takeover. The organization, as explained earlier in Arlington by the National Security Agency's director, needed a new approach, a new direction, which was to go hand in hand with the United States' interests, thus crippling the organization's sovereignty. Naturally this did not go over well with the organization's council, used to making international decisions without being tied to any political factions or governments, other than making use of them for its own benefit. It had taken over a decade for the organization to achieve the status and power it currently enjoyed, and America's pushing for its sole control, after having little part in building the organization, was likely to cause major upheaval. For the first time in its history the organization faced a crisis. Other than the occasional internal restructuring, an affectionate term for the discarding of its undesirable members, it had never coped with internal strife of this magnitude. It stood on the verge of an open conflict. It was time for its members to choose sides. Before the terrorist attacks on the World Trade Center, the choice of its American members was personal, usually the profit and power the organization was able to offer, but after the terrorist attacks, even the most selfish found a patriotic streak in themselves. It was time to use the organization's resources to benefit the United States of America. It was time to stand side by side with Alpha and the president.

Tonight these four men would have to decide. Alone, none of them could stand up to the National Security Agency's director, the leader's deputy for the East Coast, but if they joined forces they stood a chance. History would not forget them, and these were historic times. The director of Central Intelligence knew where their sympathies lay, and he banked on them. Tonight was the night he would demand the removal of the National Security Agency's director from the organization's highest position after Alpha's. At times such as these, a man who did not stand up for his country was a traitor, and this afternoon's meeting proved the NSA director would follow the organization in its current state. A traitor.

The four men mutually agreed: The time had come.

The hospital on Ulica Wołoska belonged to the ministry of the interior and was considered one of the best and technologically most advanced hospitals in the country. Doctors of all specialties longed to practice in this facility, and citizens who needed medical attention hoped to receive it there. The notion of the hospital's superiority was certainly true during the communist era, when it catered to the elite government officials, its equipment being the latest the West had to offer and in many cases not available in any other medical facility in the country, but nowadays Poland's elite preferred to seek medical treatment at better-equipped private clinics. As dubious as the reason for jealousy was, state employees who were treated here considered themselves privileged and were subjects of envy among the general population, who could not be admitted to Wołoska Hospital.

Stan Penskie was waiting in an empty doctor's office offered by an obliging surgeon who thought a foreign diplomat deserved more than the waiting room. This did not matter to Penskie, who hardly paid any attention to the surroundings, his mind engrossed in endlessly pondering the day's events. He turned over every word, every scene, every facial expression of Sito's, then Loomis's; even what the legats said and did from the minute Robert had shown up at the café. It was not easy for anyone to witness two violent deaths, especially of acquaintances and friends. Even a highly trained professional was only a human being. Stan prayed to God that David would survive the operation; somewhere deep down he could not help but feel it was his fault. He should have exercised more caution, and after the conversation with Robert he should have taken the necessary steps to confirm his information. If he had, David would have been fine. The trouble was, he cursed himself, that after being shot by the receptionist—and even as they were climbing the stairs to Jacobek's apartment—he still believed deep down that Sito's account was too outrageous to be true; it belonged in a fictional story rather than real life, especially his life. He had seen girls, children of thirteen, with their faces slashed for refusing to work as prostitutes, with their fingernails torn out, even their eyelids cut off; he could believe any atrocity possible, but he could not admit the possibility of a conspiracy and treason in his own government, in his own workplace, among people he himself lunched with. Yet Loomis's shooting at them could not be explained otherwise. Regardless of how important a case one worked on, one did not go about shooting at one's own colleagues. And Loomis had to know—he must have recognized Dave and Stan's voices in the darkness. *Jesus!* He realized he had not spoken to Margaret yet. He panicked.

He did not want her to learn of her fiancé's death from the news. He had to call her now.

Penskie stood up, ready to return to the car for his cellular phone, when the door swung open and the surgeon walked in, in the company of Ed Powell and Hank Russell.

"How is he?" Penskie asked the doctor.

"He's lost a lot of blood."

"Is he going to make it?" Penskie pressed.

"Rest assured, Mr. Penskie, your colleague is in the best of hands. The bullet went in deep and his condition is serious, but we believe his life is no longer in danger."

Penskie sighed and caught a quizzical look on Powell's face. He saw how badly Powell wanted to ask questions but was holding them back; some things were better discussed without the meddling DCM.

"What happened?" the deputy chief of mission asked when the doctor left the office.

"What happened was," Penskie replied slowly and icily, "that Loomis shot Dave."

Powell was quiet. Russell, too enraged to speak out, was pacing in the confines of the small office. Penskie's phone call had been understandably sparse—the line was insecure—but a coded message left little doubt that a serious accident had happened. Two American diplomats were shot. Given the earlier incident at the café, the embassy stepped up its THREATCON, and all events scheduled for the evening and the coming days were immediately canceled or postponed. The staff at the American Embassy was at risk. Standard procedures were followed, but how did one react to news that one American diplomat had shot another? There was no procedure for one's emotional response. Disbelief. Anger. Words and questions were coming to mind, none of which could be spoken out loud. The place was not right; the conversation had to wait.

The helplessness of the situation filled the air with tension. The three Americans stood without a word.

The door opened and an impeccably dressed man with a few gray streaks in otherwise raven-black hair had walked in. The deputy chief of mission recognized him instantly and his face changed expression.

"Ah, Mr. Kubas is from the diplomatic protocol of the ministry of the exterior and will assist us with the burden of dealing with the police and the authorities."

"I just received a word from the doctors that Mr. O'Brien will be all right." The man shook hands with the Americans. "Please accept my deepest sympathy at Mr. Loomis's death. What a terrible tragedy."

The diplomats exchanged glances. Penskie knew situations such as this one—though never in his career had he heard of one American diplomat being shot by another one—tended to drag beyond the limitations of his patience. He seized the opportunity to excuse himself. The moment was calculated precisely; Penskie knew Russell would not bicker in front of the man from the ministry. Instead he caught an expressive look on the DCM's face, indicating a clash to come.

"Hold on, Stan!" Powell caught up with his deputy in the long hallway leading to the exit. He waited till they passed the reception desk and went out of the building.

"What the hell is going on?"

Outside, in the dark visitors' parking lot, Penskie turned around and waited for an elderly couple to pass.

"I don't know. But it goes beyond the EDECA; at least that much is clear."

"What do you mean? Langley?"

Penskie did not reply.

"*You* shot him, did you?"

Silence gave away the answer.

"Jesus, Stan!"

"That son of a bitch shot Dave! He waited for us; he was there for the kill, Ed!"

After his deputy's distressed phone call, Powell assumed it was Jacobek who had shot both diplomats. He chewed on Penskie's revelation, the fact that Loomis could be the assassin still not being processed by his mind. He pulled Penskie toward a darker area of the parking lot, where large spruces blocked the lights cast by the building.

Penskie did not want to talk; his anger gave way to a quiet numbness. He wanted to escape, to regain his balance and strength before he set out to find those responsible—and find them he would, so help him, God! He knew, however, that he could not walk away, not now, not when he was the only witness, and the killer of a fellow diplomat. The embassy would deal with the Poles, taking that burden off his shoulders, but no doubt it would put his life through the mill. He would need all the help he can get. The legal attaché, Ed Powell, was not only his immediate superior but a friend too. Penskie would need friends. Powell should know what had happened, not only as his boss but also as a friend.

Penskie told Powell the events of the evening in quick words drained of emotion.

After discovering the identity of the man he had just shot, Penskie had run back upstairs. He could hear locks being turned in people's doors as he passed them, but no one looked out. O'Brien still crouched on the floor, while Banks was trying to stop the bleeding. With his handgun drawn Penskie had tried the door to Jacobek's apartment. It was not locked and he proceeded cautiously. The lights were out, and a cigarette smell lingered in the air, an indication of someone's recent presence, but no one was inside. Penskie realized that in a heavy smoker's home the smell just might be embedded in the furniture, the walls, becoming a part of the surroundings. The apartment had been searched: Books, clothes, papers, little tidbits, all were piled on the floor in the middle of each of the three rooms. He checked the kitchen and found the kettle was still warm. Jacobek had been home today.

Penskie could hear the sirens nearing and he withdrew. Banks was still attending to David and seemed to have the blood flow under control. She insisted on coming along to the hospital, but would remain in the car.

Penskie hoped she was still there.

"Do you trust her?" Powell was intrigued by the woman's assignment. "I mean, it's pretty explosive stuff we're talking about. What do you know about her? Can you be certain Loomis wasn't shooting in self-defense? You said it was dark. . . ."

"Look, I don't know how the CIA station works—it's not something they brief us on—but I am sure Loomis knew who we were; he must've heard our voices, for crying out loud!"

Powell's shoulders droped; his hopes to find a flaw in the story, anything to explain the event as a tragic mistake, had vanished.

"Christ! The Poles will want to talk to you. What am I supposed to tell them? What about Hank?"

"Stall them."

Stall them! Tomorrow's arrival of the state department's Bureau of Intelligence and Research officers, at the express wish of the secretary concerned with the American government activities, specifically the mysterious Economic Development and Cooperation Agency, was headache enough. God knew Powell did not need it. The holidays alone were taking their toll on his nervous system, with the wife pushing the celebrations and preparations to the extreme. Constant overtime, overdue vacation time, it was all accumulating too quickly. He knew he could kiss the Christmas and New Year's break good-bye. His only consolation was—and he found it perversely satisfying—that the entire mission was in for a major shake-up, with repercussions that would send shock waves to Washington. The United States government would have been lucky if the disappearance of Norman Bray had turned out to be a plain murder case; however, today's events assured Powell that the case had a gloomy and staggering overtone.

A spurious American government agency was suspected of meddling with what looked like state security issues of the host country! And if that was not enough, a diplomat who also happened to be a Central Intelligence Agency's station chief was shot by an FBI officer while staking out an apartment of the EDECA's chief executive officer and a possible CIA operative. Loomis, Loomis! What was his part in these events? Was he following orders from headquarters? If so, the case would be buried deep, and, short of a handful of pencil pushers, no one would ever know what had really happened. Even without a proper investigation Ed Powell knew what happened: The Central Intelligence had screwed up once again. It was not hard to come to this conclusion. The agency had been going through tough times since September eleventh. Government pressures stretched its operational abilities beyond limits already believed to be unattainable. It was very likely that someone out there lost control of the situation—a situation that eventually outgrew the agency's capabilities. Powell, however, was not going to accept such an answer, not when his friends and deputies were being shot in the process. He must see to it that someone answered for the blunder. *Damn spooks!*

"We have to talk," he said grimly.

"Unit One to Center. We've located the subject and are in position," the man with a slight Russian accent said into his headset microphone. His orders were confusing. The man they were not to shoot at the café was now to be protected. Of course, they knew nothing of the reasons behind such an order, but the way things had changed unexpectedly cast suspicions beyond the ordinary. They had been with the organization long enough to realize something was up. As a general rule, the more confusing and conflicting the orders, the more serious the trouble was. There were times when little was demanded of them—protection of a VIP, or a convoy, slow and routine jobs usually, or occasionally a cleanup was ordered. The importance of the man within the organization determined the complexity of the job. Some of the biggest fish had their own armies of trained bodyguards, but unless one had field experience, say Chechnya, no training could provide enough skill and the necessary mind-set to protect one's master. The man with an accent was one of the best in his field, with practice obtained in the Caucasus Mountains, Afghanistan, and as far off as the Balkans, not to mention his service whenever an assassination was required. His experience as a hired killer also made him the best protector; there was no trick of the trade he could not understand and take countermeasures to prevent. Alpha knew whom to give the job to, but hiring him also meant the FBI officer was of extraordinary importance, for his services were required only for extraordinary cases.

The one thing the man sometimes regretted was not knowing why. He was asking himself this question more and more often. The constant routine was just no longer satisfying.

"He must not interfere. Should the circumstances call for it you can use force to stop him, but remember, from now on you are personally responsible for his safety," the voice from the headphone speaker responded. "Do not let me down."

Chapter Nine

The inspector general's safe house was a simple yet ingenious choice, and one of the favorite among intelligence agencies worldwide. What better place to keep one's anonymity than a busy hotel? The Europejski Hotel on Krakowskie Przedmieście was only a stone's throw from the university campus. It was a two-story neo-Renaissance building rebuilt and expanded many times since it was erected in the early eighteen hundreds. A suite was kept reserved in the hotel for a large American East Coast university whose lecturers and scientists stayed there during visits to the affiliated University of Warsaw. To provide a sense of legitimacy, visiting professors would indeed occupy the suite and occasionally entertain their Polish hosts. The arrangements for the safe house were made in haste, in response to growing concern over the CIA's involvement in unsanctioned activities, and inevitably there were loopholes. A stay at the hotel during university breaks risked raising the attention of the management or the cleaning staff; nonetheless, it provided a relatively secure place in a pinch, to organize help or a rescue mission.

Seated on a sofa in front of a long oak coffee table, Ed Powell listened to his deputy with growing impatience and incredulity. "I say, it is just too far-fetched! What was Jacobek still doing in his apartment, or even in the country, if he's got the files Borysewicz supposedly offered for sale?" He gazed at Penskie and Banks and understood. "The obvious answer is, he hasn't got them!"

"We should consider another option," Mollie Banks responded. "We've assumed it's the files, but perhaps Jacobek's interest had a different objective altogether?"

The statement had a staggering effect on the legal attachés. It showed, despite the internal investigation, that the inspector general had no idea what his office was after. The answers Ed Powell was expecting to find were not forthcoming.

"Are we way over our heads? What are we, the FBI, doing here? What are we supposed to do?" He asked the questions into the air.

"This isn't just an internal problem of the CIA anymore, Agent Powell," Banks said. "We're not dealing here with rogue officers stealing office supplies. We're talking a broad conspiracy, for lack of a better description. We're talking about a hostile operation with the appearance of a legitimate government program. With Loomis's attack we know the station chief was not only involved but possibly ran the operation at this end. We can't rule out the possibility that someone else at the embassy has been working with Loomis. Finding a possible accomplice should be your first priority. We also need to find out which parties in Washington are behind the creation of the EDECA, and who else should do the job but the FBI? See, I do believe our agencies should have worked on it from the start. But what's done is done. You're in it now, whether you like it or not. The question is, How do we get to the bottom of it without getting ourselves killed?"

"Why wasn't the Bureau informed of the investigation, particularly the part of it taking place on U.S. soil?"

"The inspector general believes it was an internal CIA matter. Of course, I can see now that it reaches far beyond the Company, but I have no evidence to question my orders. Quite frankly the entire investigation is just guesswork."

"But you must have some idea who's pulling the strings?"

"There is a preliminary list of suspects, those who may directly or indirectly provide—or be standing behind those who unknowingly provide—cover for the EDECA. You must understand, some, if not all those people who are directly involved may be in the dark as much as we were about the true nature of the Economic Development Agency. For all we know, the brains behind the creation of the agency may not even be associated with the EDECA anymore. After all, it's been three years since it was created."

"*Po nitce do kłębka,* follow the thread, as the Polish like to say. Can you get those names for us? The inspector general's resources may not be adequate, but combined with the Bureau's they might just do."

Banks thought about it for a moment. She did not have the order to involve a third party, but she did have the authority to use all means necessary to succeed in her investigation.

"I would not risk direct communication with headquarters—we can't be sure who's listening—but I might be able to log in to our databases, as well as the CIA's. I'll need access to some hardware, though."

"That can be arranged," Powell replied. "The embassy keeps notebooks for our staff. They are used primarily for downloading e-mail while on the road and are wiped clean upon each return. I'm not sure what kind of software you'll need. . . ."

"All I need can be downloaded from the Internet."

"Fine." Powell checked his wristwatch and spoke to Penskie. "Meanwhile we should concentrate on finding this Mr. Jacobek. It's about eighteen hundred hours in Washington and probably too late to talk to anyone."

"I wouldn't talk to anyone, Agent Powell. At least not until you get a chance to verify the party is beyond any suspicion. Even then, you could never be too sure."

The legal attaché wanted to object. This woman was over her head. Living in the world of lies, half-truths, and illusions had taken its toll on her. She saw conspiracy everywhere, including the Federal Bureau of Investigation, but so far it was only Central Intelligence that stood behind the affair. In all honesty, he learned that the CIA always had an agenda within an agenda, presumably to confuse possible observers. He had read a lot about the work of the intelligence world; he had friends in the agency. He knew the Soviets did it all the time, which meant that so did the CIA. It was not just a legacy of the Cold War. It was a day-to-day business. Banks might believe somebody out there had crossed the agency, but was living a double life not the very essence of the work of the Central Intelligence Agency's officers? Were they able to distinguish reality from the assumed lives they took upon themselves? Who was to say what was or was not true? Who could guarantee the people on the preliminary list were not perfectly innocent government servants, and others only led to believe they were the conspirators? In fact, who was Mollie Banks? His first order of business upon his return to the embassy would be to verify Banks's identity. To rely solely on information coming from the sources of the Central Intelligence Agency would be too abstract; he would have to read between the lines. He needed concrete information based on evidence. He needed the resources of the Federal Bureau of Investigation. Powell sighed. He was getting too old for this job. Had it not been for his wife, who loved the lifestyle his work bestowed—the chance to travel and to experience the cultures of the world—he would have been back in his Maine log cabin, having taken early retirement, walking his dog, stretching in his recliner, and watching hockey on television.

Powell sighed again and shook the feeling aside.

"Well, that can be avoided altogether. What I was proposing was that I'd try to get on LEO. See what we can dig up."

"Leo?"

"Law Enforcement Online, a computerized communications and information service for the community. I doubt it will contain anything of interest to this investigation, but it's a start, as Stan pointed out." Powell put his decaffeinated coffee on the table and stood up.

"I don't think it is wise for you to return to your homes." Banks stood up too. "We should assume they might be monitored. If you need a place, there is plenty of room here."

"I don't think I'll be able to leave the office in the next few days." Powell grinned.

Penskie smiled appreciatively. The thought of falling under surveillance was only secondary to a stronger desire: He did not want to part with this woman. Banks's vibrant personality and independence had dazzled him from the moment he saw an automatic in her hand, back at the offices of the Economic Development and Cooperation Agency. Her presence of mind, the ability to take offensive action while the two of them, trained field agents, were stunned by the violent and unexpected event—and the gentle care with which she had held David's head in that dark stairwell—engraved in his mind a picture of a tender soul underneath a strong exterior. Mollie Banks—a woman he was beginning to fall for.

"You realize this will be taken out of our hands," Powell said during the short drive to the embassy.

Penskie did not reply, his mind engrossed in the abrupt and surprising twist of emotions, from the grief of losing a friend, to the shock of killing a human being, to feelings for a woman he had met only hours before.

"I know what you're thinking about, but unless we can get something to go on by the morning, Hank's gonna have us flown back to the States," Powell continued.

"Yeah?" Penskie roused from the depths of his thoughts.

"You all right? Seem absentminded today."

"I killed a man, Ed."

"You did your job, and if the woman is right, you did your country a great favor, too."

"Somehow it doesn't make me feel any better."

"It never will, Stan. Which is why I'll understand if you decide to call it quits."

"No. I want . . . I need to know why."

Sun Valley in Allegheny Mountains, in West Virginia, was a small town of some four hundred inhabitants, half of them seasonal, a village really. It had a sizable population of newcomers, wealthy retirees, and well-to-doers who got out of the wireless and high-tech markets early enough to afford land and mansions in this isolated and pristinely clean area. The original Sun Valley had expanded greatly to accommodate the new citizens; new mansions were built on secluded wooded lots several acres large, attracting the rich and famous. Here one could be assured of privacy and a peaceful existence, never bothered by one's neighbors or passersby, seeing other people only in the town market hall, and, of course, only if one chose to do the shopping oneself, for most everyone in this town had live-in house help.

One of the older mansions, a six year old, twelve-bedroom stone cottage outfitted with a small private air-strip, was exceptionally busy; exceptionally, because it normally stood uninhabited throughout the year. Scattered around the property were twenty-four security guards, a private battalion of former Special Forces soldiers, armed to the teeth and ready to stand up to anyone who would threaten their employers. Mobile ground-to-air missiles were positioned and manned at all times; a special communications detachment monitored the latest in jamming technology. No electronic equipment, including satellite eavesdropping, could penetrate the property. Such were the measures necessary to protect one of the most powerful men in the world, a man whose one word could overthrow governments.

Two men had arrived in Sun Valley to meet face-to-face with the man to whom they swore allegiance. One of them was the director of the National Security Agency; the other was the governor of California. Both were the leader's deputies for North America. The visit to the Sun Valley mansion was a last step on their leader's tour around the world to build a coalition against Alpha and the American takeover. Gone were the days when the leader could simply eliminate opponents; it was his very objective to transform the organization, to break free of its militant past, a decision that helped to create an empire, but that ultimately might cost him the leadership. About the organization's future he did not worry; it would survive, for no one could ever refuse its resources. He knew he had a long way to go before the ultimate goal was reached: creating a political and economic balance across the world. He had made many mistakes along the way, and a lot more would be made, but of one thing he was positively certain: The American leadership would break the fragile balance the organization maintained. If Alpha succeeded there would once again be only one power dictating to the world its own will. He cursed himself for not noticing sooner the direction Alpha was heading. It was the British members' conniving efforts that had clouded what was truly happening. Did they not realize that selling the organization to the Americans would undermine and damage Europe's fragile political influence, crush its economic strength, and bring it to its knees? Another two, maybe three years and the organization would completely blend in, becoming the binding element between the world's political, economic, and military alliances that had alienated the world's nations. Instead the world might be heading for a disaster. With the resources the organization held, America could build a universe unto itself. It would be the renaissance of the feudal times, where the rich and powerful would bathe in luxury and indolence as the rest of the world would exist only to provide their riches and would bend over backward to every demand. He was not an idealist; he would be the first to admit the organization was based on autocratic rule, and sooner or later someone would have reached for leadership. But he also had a keen vision of the organization's future and its role as the only power able to halt America and her race for political and economic dominance. Europe was losing ground, and with the U.K. becoming an American enclave, Europe would have no choice but to rise. It spelled disaster. America in the eyes of her president was the only superpower left, a yokel notion that could trigger another Cold War. Should he put an end to it now, before the rift became deeper? Some of the council members who stood by his side demanded complete eradication of the problem. They did not share his vision of a peaceful resolution, but that did not shock him; many of them came from totalitarian backgrounds. The Russians were advocating a bloody resolution, and half the Islamic members, as well as those who had had any issues with the Americans, were supporting them. He could go along with their wishes, but it would be a step backward. The organization was no longer operating along those lines. It could achieve its goals by means that went hand in hand with the times. Strangely, though, while it had the means to exert pressure on groups, organizations, countries, and the masses, it could not control one individual, the president of the United States. Maybe his council was right. Perhaps some heads would have to roll?

He knew he had the majority support of the council, and

if Alpha decided to go ahead, both he and his puppet, the president of the United States, would be thrown into oblivion. He had the means to do it. He did not like the idea of playing by force, but he would not hesitate to use it. The future of the world was at stake. He was a citizen of the world, a man who could make a difference, and therefore it was his duty to act. Noblesse oblige. This was the reason he had traveled to Sun Valley, to relate his orders to his deputies. In two days the council would vote overwhelmingly against the American option, and if they were met with any defiance the plan would be put in place. The president would be replaced and, more important, Alpha would be eliminated.

Chapter Ten

The suite smelled of lavender and moisture when Penskie returned with two embassy computer notebooks and a pair of scrambler-equipped mobile phones. He placed the large duffel bag on the sofa, next to Mollie Banks's clothes, and began unpacking its contents. He was placing everything onto the nearby coffee table, slowly and meticulously, wanting to prolong the moment, though he knew he could not wait any longer. He had to talk to Margaret.

He dialed the long-distance number to Kraków. She was not home. He tried the mobile phone. Her cellular telephone provider answered with an automatic error message. The recipient was unreachable. *Strange.* Worried, he checked his Palm Pilot and dialed a number of a friend of his sister's. He woke her up, and sighed with relief when Jana Haug informed him the class was on a short camping trip—four days in Silesia, due back tomorrow afternoon. It was very likely there was no signal in the Karkonosze Mountains, especially during snowstorms. Nothing to worry about.

He sat down aimlessly on the sofa. That would explain why Margaret did not telephone. An agent's death was mentioned on the evening news; he had heard it in his car on the way to the hotel. Margaret had no access to the news. He realized belatedly that Sito's name had not been mentioned. Neither was his. It was a deal reached between the embassy and the police.

Mollie emerged from the bathroom wearing a hotel robe, a towel over her head.

"Just ordered some fresh coffee and canapés. Hope you're hungry. I don't think I could eat anything."

He did not understand. He just sat there and stared at her, a blurred figure in a veil of hot steam. She looked diametrically different now, he realized, but still there it was: Behind that strong façade was a gentle and sensitive woman whose feminine aura emanated in the steam that followed her from the bathroom. Penskie was taken by her transformation. The robe added a homey, relaxed touch to her bearing; her face had a soft texture that a hot bath and steam created, and she looked even more appealing than in her designer business attire.

She pulled the flaps of the robe's collar together and said, "I'll need new clothes, something more comfortable than this." She pointed at the clothes scattered over the sofa. "Think they may have a store downstairs?"

Penskie realized he was gaping. He stood up and walked over to the minibar in an effort to cover his embarrassment. "I'm sure they'll be happy to oblige." He pulled a miniature bottle of Wyborowa vodka and a Hortex lemon juice. "Care for a little relaxant?"

"Oh, God knows I could use it, but I have to stay awake." She approached the sofa and examined the notebooks Stan had brought. "Not exactly top-of-the-line, are they?"

"It's the difference between ritzy corporate execs and humble government servants." He realized his answer might have unintentionally been too snappy. He was still under the influence of the woman, her close presence making him uneasy.

"Well, I am sure they will suffice." Banks appeared not to have taken notice. She looked around for a telephone outlet. She located it by the desk and carried one of the notebooks there. "Tell me, are you related to Ze . . . Zee-beeg . . ."

"Zbigniew Penskie. My father."

"Seriously?" She paused momentarily to face Stan. "So you're Polish then, are you?"

"I was born here, but my parents left the country when I was thirteen."

"I don't mean to sound too clichéd, but your English is excellent. I've heard somewhere that nine is the deciding age for losing one's accent."

"I've always had a knack for languages."

"I really admire people who can master other languages," she continued while powering on the notebook. "Where do you live in the States? New York?"

"How can you tell? My father's a prof at NYU."

"Oh? I didn't know your father taught. I studied at Columbia, but lived in the Village. Your accent . . . I have an ear for accents, though I am terrible at pronunciation."

"How did you end up with the inspector general?"

"Through Central Intelligence."

"You were recruited in college." It was more of a statement than a question.

"I was a bit of a nerd, I suppose, but contrary to popular belief the Company is not composed solely of thugs. What's your story?"

Penskie could not help but think this exchange of questions was a test. Avoiding answering direct inquiries, both were assessing each other's validity. It occurred to him that Banks might want to verify his biography through the CIA's sources. He was glad Powell was doing the same at the embassy, but what could be found in a file stashed in the depths of supercomputers could not replace a person-to-person interaction, the nuances in one's voice, eyes, and facial expressions.

"Foreign languages, Slavic in particular."

"But of course! With centuries of multicultural society, who can speak better Russian, Ukrainian, or Byelorussian than a Pole?"

"Russians, Ukrainians, or Byelorussians."

"Right." She laughed. "But no foreigner can imitate those accents better than a Pole. Take me. My grandmother was Polish, but I can hardly pronounce Zee-bee-g-niew or Dwo . . . Dworzec Główny."

"I see what you mean." He laughed genuinely.

"Would you believe I took a year at Przegor . . . Prze-go-r-zały Institute?"

"The one near Kraków?"

"Could there be another place with a name like that? And yes, after Columbia it was either that or back to Toledo."

"Is that where home is?"

"Just outside." She shifted her attention toward the computer. "Okay, what have we here? Government servants not using the world's most popular Web browser?"

"Personal choice of our computer people. Something to do with security and privacy."

"No kidding," she replied absentmindedly. "Still, you should consider other players out there." She punched in a sequence on the keyboard, which activated the modem. Moments later she entered the URL of a popular underground search engine. "Wonder if the AltaVista people ever filed a copyright infringement lawsuit?"

The name was so cleverly similar he did not realize at first what she meant. When he saw it on the screen, he could not withhold a burst of laughter.

"Oops, I suppose I shouldn't be downloading illegal software onto the embassy computer . . . and in the presence of an FBI agent," she continued.

"Well, we can always call it a sting operation," Penskie answered as he leaned over her shoulder.

Some of the Central Intelligence Agency's resources for field operatives were located in offshore servers with no connection to headquarters. A password and specific decoding software were necessary to allow entry. While even the most basic of the CIA's resources required positive identification to access them, some general information was available without complicated security measures. Some resources were stationary, kept on servers indefinitely, and were considered low-security data, often available through other government agencies' portals; there were also servers operational only for the duration of the investigation, and entry was restricted only to investigating officers and their support team, who updated and maintained the information as it became available.

The latter was also true of Mollie Banks's assignment. In conjunction with the inspector general's resources, she had access to certain of the CIA's databanks, a move made possible through a high-level agreement reached between her office and the parties within the CIA who were concerned with that agency's integrity. The inspector general thought the problem was so serious only absolutely essential staff had been assigned to the investigation. The result was, it quickly became obvious to Stan, that information pertaining to the case Banks was working on was very scarce and lacking any systematic data collection method. Still, there were numerous personnel files of suspected probable or possible creators of the Economic Development and Cooperation Agency. Some of the files contained details ranging from health records to food preferences, while others contained only one word: *classified.*

It took the better part of the night to recognize that the connection between the late Prime Minister Borysewicz and the founders of the EDECA had either been expertly removed, was nonexistent, or was not accessible through the available sources. Cross-reference checks presented no results. Not finding the answers they were looking for, discouraged and tired, Mollie and Stan looked at each other hopelessly. As a last attempt to find any link or even a starting point Mollie pulled out the Economic Development and Cooperation Agency's personnel files. While the files produced nothing of significance, Penskie recalled a photograph in Robert Sito's documents: Norman Bray, Terrence Jacobek, and Małpa. Małpa—the only link to a case that had produced four corpses to date, at least to his knowledge, and had put the embassy on THREATCON.

What Banks and Penskie did not know was that it was also about to become the case that put the entire U.S. intelligence community in a state of the highest alert.

* * *

Jonathan Berr, the inspector general, was awake when the phone rang. His only daughter, Helen, was in the hospital, about to deliver her first baby three weeks prematurely. Although Berr was worried about Helen—she was thirty-six and single—he also was acutely excited. He was going to be a grandfather! There were a few things he still expected from life, though none more anticipated than his first grandchild. He woke up Marion, who had just gone to bed, and within minutes both were in their Lincoln, heading toward Washington. Berr was normally a cautious driver, seldom exceeding speed limits. A serious collision some fifteen years earlier taught him the meaning of the word *accident*. An accident was an accident—you couldn't expect it. Tonight he was speeding from the moment he left his driveway. They had barely crossed the city limits when a red pickup cut him off at an intersection. Had it not been raining that evening the Lincoln's brakes would have been enough to avoid a crash altogether. Still, it was nothing serious, a fender-bender really, but he had to pull over to get the insurance settled. The driver of the pickup got out of his car and approached the Lincoln. Jonathan Berr rolled his window down to apologize; it was his fault—he should have stopped at the intersection. Before he could utter a word his gaze fixed on the muzzle of a pistol equipped with a silencer. Neither he nor his wife heard the shots, and in all probability neither of them felt the bullets that penetrated their foreheads.

Some 180 miles away by air, in Sun Valley, the director of the National Security Agency had switched off his digitally scrambled satellite telephone and turned to the governor of California. The leader had left an hour ago, and was on his way to Europe; he would have been pleased with the smooth way the inspector general had been neutralized. It was his, the NSA director's, trademark.

"It's done," he said matter-of-factly. "What should we do about the woman?"

"The leader did not mention anything, which we should assume means to leave her be. I don't believe he'd be too happy to hear about another corpse. The inspector general should have been approached and won over to our cause a long time ago. Unfortunately for him, there is no time right now; we cannot take any chances. As for the woman . . ." The leader's deputy for the West Coast paused and approached the large fireplace. The fire was slowly dying, and he pondered throwing another log in but changed his mind; the meeting was over and they would soon part. "She's nothing without the inspector, but I think we should contact the leader nevertheless; it's his territory and he should decide. For now, let's shut down the servers and leave her be. The leader may want to use her to get through to Penskie. I know I would. . . ."

"Which . . ." the leader's deputy for the East Coast started, then stopped abruptly. "Right." He suddenly understood.

Chapter Eleven

Boasting eighty thousand seats, the *Stadion Dziesięciolecia* was the biggest open-air stadium in Poland. Raised for the tenth anniversary of the People's Republic in the mid-fifties, it was rarely filled to capacity or even served the purpose it was created for. Through the decades it had been used for grandiose communist ceremonies as well as occasional sporting events, annual harvest festivals, rock concerts, or religious gatherings, such as the pope's 1983 visit to Poland. But years of neglect had caused the stadium to deteriorate and eventually it was deemed unsafe for the public.

In the early nineties, the abandoned venue attracted street vendors and small time traders, quickly becoming a popular marketplace where hard-to-find goods could be obtained. The idea caught on, and in a short time it was transformed into one of the largest daily-open air markets in Europe, drawing vendors from beyond its eastern frontiers: Latvia, Lithuania, the Ukraine, Russia, and as far as Mongolia, China, and Vietnam. The *Stadion*'s daily turnaround was estimated in millions upon millions of dollars, and it could be as high as tens of millions—no one was counting. The only thing certain was that buyers and sellers alike flocked to the market from all corners of Eastern Europe to buy or sell everything from homemade cheese, used clothing, hardware, electronics, and pirated music and software, to the most advanced and top-of-the-line merchandise in all imaginable categories. The vast majority of items for sale fell into two categories: stolen goods and fakes (cheap Chinese imitations). Both categories offered, for example, cellular telephones, cameras, expensive watches, objets d'art, and designer fashions. The *Stadion* was also the place to acquire genuine high school or university diplomas, fake or stolen credit cards, a fine choice of handguns, luxury cars for a fraction of the price, and villas on the Mediterranean or Black seas. Here even the proverbial sky was not the limit: rumors had it that ballistic missiles and, adapted for the civilian market, military planes and helicopters from the former Soviet Republics could be arranged.

Stan Penskie enjoyed the *Stadion.* It had a buzz about it he had never experienced in America. It was alive. The rush of shoppers squeezing in between stalls was like blood flowing through veins of a living organism. It had been a place where all races, religions, and languages intermingled as in Babel. It had been a long time since he had visited the market, not since the legats' participation in police stakeouts in the spring. He knew about the intricate network of vendor security personnel who roamed through the market scanning for undercover police officers. Initially, those merchants who needed protection for their products and bodies employed a group of strong young men, but quickly it became evident that a more serious arrangement was necessary, particularly among those who offered counterfeit merchandise. Into this niche came a well-organized group of racketeers, imposing their own services and rules associated with them. Their ranks often derived from unemployed or deserted military and Special Forces personnel of the former Soviet Bloc countries. They were well paid, well armed, vigilant, and ready to stand their ground in a clash with the Polish law enforcement agencies. Regardless of the legality of their services, their presence at the *Stadion* provided peace and order among rivaling merchants. Brawls were rare and quickly suppressed. To the amazement of the local precinct even the pickpocketing rate dropped dramatically. In fact, it was that very anomaly that triggered an increased police interest in the daily life of the market. The police suspected the organized racketeers of terrorizing the victims enough to keep them from filing complaints; it was the only logical assumption. No one on the force considered that the racketeers had lowered the crime rate with their swift and on-site dealing with petty thieves in the name of the protection of customers. They accomplished what the police could not: They provided a safe environment for the merchants and kept the cash, keeping folk coming and the show rolling.

The *Stadion* operated daily from break of dawn to about eleven, when business slowed down and vendors dispersed to other parts of the city. The best finds and business deals were struck at the earliest hours. Penskie left the hotel at seven. It was another gloomy and wet day. Were it not for the bitter chill that morning, he realized, he would have had a hard time avoiding being recognized by security. He pulled the hood of his parka low onto his forehead and raised his coat collar above his chin as he approached the Washington Roundabout. He followed groups of anxious shoppers as they poured through the main entrance and formed an enormous, slow-flowing river of faceless hordes. The trade expanded from the entrance and inner stadium onto the surrounding areas; shopping or just browsing would slow the flow and cause immense backups, accompanied by hard cursing; stalls of clothing and shoes along the main alleyway, filled with cloned labels of the most desirable designers, did not help alleviate the traffic problem.

The last days before Christmas brought a record number of visitors, so that it was difficult to maneuver between the anxious last-minute shoppers. Penskie had to make his way to the entrance, where he expected to find the items Małpa dealt in. He elbowed his way through the mob, knowing his chances of finding the man he was looking for were very slim, if not nonexistent. Eventually he located an area where paramilitary and military equipment was sold. He approached and hovered around every stall, assessing various items until he realized all the vendors were Russian. Their products ranged from brand new and used military uniforms, medals, communication equipment, and cold steel to parachutes and blueprints of armored vehicles, planes, and missiles. Components of machine guns were sold in such a way that one could purchase and completely assemble an AK-47 without having to risk imprisonment for buying an illegal weapon. For the asking one could assess those items that were not displayed, such as live ammunition and ready-to-use weapons.

As time progressed Penskie grew more weary and disappointed. Małpa, he realized, had either fled the city or was perhaps too big to be dealing himself. Any one of those who sat in the cold, shivering and embracing thin cups of tea, would be only small pawns in a bigger game. Someone like Małpa was likely to finalize large transactions himself, or so he hypothesized. Penskie approached a stall with a large selection of military paraphernalia and picked up an item. He asked to speak to the person in charge. His posture, tone of voice, and foreign clothing spelled *money*. The seller took out a sleek cellular telephone and punched in an SMS message. A minute later a middle-aged man arrived. He was dressed in a leather bomber jacket, the type favored by most vendors and those who wanted to accentuate the fact that they had lots of money to blow. It was not Małpa. Apparently not satisfied with a deal on two dozen night-vision goggles, Penskie moved on, leaving the dealer disappointed. He repeated his trick elsewhere, but apart from being offered a truly great deal on what looked like authentic Russian orthodox icons, he still was not anywhere near finding the man he needed.

It was not until about three hours later, when the rush began to ease up, both traders and shoppers slowly retiring to parking lots and public transportation stops, when an oddly familiar face rushed by in Penskie's peripheral vision. He knew he had seen this man before, though he could not remember the circumstances. The familiar face and something about the man's behavior caught Penskie's attention, and he followed the man's gaze. Blood rushing through his veins, he realized the man he found was following Małpa! Was he a bodyguard? Unlikely, since he kept a considerable distance, which in a crowd this dense would not provide him adequate response time in case of an attack. Was he a police officer tailing a suspect? It was the obvious answer; the man must be an undercover policeman, perhaps one of those Penskie had met during one of the joint investigations. Suddenly someone ran into the man, causing his furious reaction. He turned back toward the person who had so carelessly, though unintentionally, bumped into him, an African dealer of imitation brand-name jeans, and said something in a muted voice. As he was turning back, Penskie recognized the look in the man's eyes, a look he knew all too well from his undercover work on the streets of Chicago. It was a look of a hunter in pursuit of prey.

Małpa walked with self-confidence, stopping here and there to exchange a few words with some of the vendors. Apparently not aware of being followed, he headed for the northeast exit, dense with shoppers and vendors with brightly colored and bulging bags the size of wine barrels. Penskie, being only five feet behind the killer, had noticed the man's right hand slide into his washed-out army jacket. He was closing in on Małpa, ready to strike at any moment, Stan observed with helpless dismay. There was no time—he had to act now.

Penskie lurched ahead, pushing aside an elderly woman with a large wool blanket from the Ukraine who was blocking his way. Her angry cries and the commotion caught the attention of the would-be assassin. He briefly turned his head around, and his eyes locked with Stan's. Instantly recognizing danger, the killer raised his arm and aimed ahead, toward Małpa. In rage Penskie grabbed on to the man's jacket, pulling him closer and then immediately pushing him away into a display of small objects on the ground. The man slipped on some small Matryoshka dolls and lost his balance. The gun, equipped with a silencer, flew high into the air; the man grabbed onto a passerby and they both fell down. Before the two hit the ground, Penskie was already some five feet away, fighting his way toward Małpa, who watched the event with growing consternation.

Realizing he was being pursued, Małpa jump-started toward the exit. Struggling through the masses Penskie managed to push through the narrow gate, Małpa only ten or twelve feet ahead. Outside the gate both men were able to trot, maneuvering inside the thinning crowd.

"Małpa, wait!" Penskie cried out in Polish.

They approached a large parking lot with hundreds of cars, vans, and buses filled with merchandise. Małpa could easily disappear in this maze, Penskie realized. The arms dealer headed for the area occupied by shabby tourist buses from the former eastern republics of the Soviet Union. They carried loads of day-trippers who came to this "Western" capital to make a złoty or two, selling anything and everything from gold jewelry and vodka to Matryoshka dolls, all carried in tremendously large bags. They traveled all night, often after being stuck for hours or even days in lineups at congested border crossings, and headed straight for the market as it opened in the morning, and if they did not sell out their items, they slept at the nearby train or bus stations—money to pay for a hotel was not allotted in their slim margins—until they made enough of a profit to return home for another load of merchandise.

Penskie followed Małpa behind one such bus. The man tried to negotiate a tall chain-link fence, the toes of his large boots sliding out of its small links. He realized he was not going to make it, jumped down, and reached into the small of his back.

"Don't even think about it!" Out of breath, Penskie yelled

out in Polish, "Keep your hands out so I can see them. . . . Slowly . . . That's it. Turn around and face the bus."

"You a cop?" Małpa asked, arrogance in his voice. "We can talk, but we have to get out of here . . . they'll come after us."

"Who's *they*, Małpa?" Penskie asked while frisking the man. He pulled out a Scorpion automatic and slipped it into his parka's side pocket. "Turn around." He stepped back. "Who's *they?*"

Małpa heaved a sigh and shrugged. "Are you new or not from around here, *glino?*"

"I'm not a cop." Penskie hesitated a moment. "I'm an American."

Małpa focused on Penskie's face. "You're that FBI cop who got shot yesterday!"

Suddenly his eyes wandered over Stan's shoulder.

"Drop the gun!" a voice commanded in English. "Do it!"

Penskie sensed that it was not the killer he had left behind. If it were, he would have been shot in the back already. He considered his options, dropped his Glock to the ground, and slowly turned around. The man was dressed in plain clothes, but something in his posture and the way he held the weapon gave him away. *A cop,* Penskie thought. "I'm an American diplomat," he started, and realized the man must have known that, since he spoke English.

"Back away from the gun and face the bus," he answered in Polish. "Both of you!"

Partly because of the command and partly due to moaning coming from behind, Penskie turned just in time to see Małpa slide onto the pavement, arms at his chest. The man looked shocked and frightened. Blood showed through his fingers. *What the hell . . . ?* Penskie watched with astonishment.

Someone grabbed him by the shoulders and pulled him to the ground.

"Get down!" the stranger shouted as they both fell. He rolled under the bus, pointed the gun, and scouted the immediate area.

Still in shock, Penskie looked back and forth between the man with a gun and Małpa, who lay on his side, in a fetal position, groaning. Only now did it come to him that Małpa had been shot. It could not have been the stranger, though. It had to be the killer who managed to find them and carry on his deadly assignment! Penskie stood up cautiously and looked above the roofs of the cars. He saw the barrel of a gun pointed in his direction. He froze, focused on the man who held the weapon. His eyes were fixed on Penskie; he could see them clearly from the distance of about twenty meters. It was only a split second, but in the assassin's hesitation Penskie could see the man shaking his head, as if in disapproval. *It must be an illusion. Why isn't he firing?* In that instant he heard a shot from behind, and the assassin disappeared. Penskie realized it was the man he thought was a policeman who had fired. Moments later he saw him run stooped over after the killer.

The moaning at his feet broke the spell. Penskie leaned toward Małpa, trying to assess the wound. The man was dying; barely audible sounds came out of his throat. Stan leaned closer to grasp the meaning of the words.

"Piąta . . . mię . . . mię . . . między . . . na . . . ro . . . dówka . . ."

Stan was crouching over the ailing body, administering what first aid he could, when the man he labeled a police officer came back, pistol still in his hand. He touched the carotid artery and pronounced, "It's no use; come on!" He pulled Penskie's shoulder and handed him his Glock.

"Who are you?' Stan hissed.

"We have to get out! You can't be seen here!" The policeman gestured toward the onlookers whose heads stuck out from behind and above parked cars.

"Bullshit!" Penskie exploded. "Who the fuck are you?"

"Robert Sito was my friend. . . ."

Chapter Twelve

Xian-Tao Chu was signing last-minute directions for managers and directors of various departments within the corporation he chaired. In less than a few hours his jet would be taking off for Europe, and he wanted to catch at least a short nap beforehand. He could never sleep on board, not since that fateful flight when he was almost shot down en route to the organization's council meeting two years ago. And over Chinese land! Of course, since then the rebel members were caught and killed, slowly and in excruciating pain, but ever since he believed that someone, somewhere, was waiting to take his seat, whether it be within the organization or the corporation he headed. Ch'in Corporation was an empire unto itself; it supplied the world with close to 60 percent of its electronic components for everything from VCRs and DVD players to the automotive industry and the latest in electronic warfare. The world depended on his products as much as the Western markets depended on cheap Chinese labor to make substitutes for almost everything, now that unions had made "Made in the USA" or "Made in the United Kingdom" products hyper expensive. Xian-Tao was big. He was above the law in his homeland. There was no law enforcement agency or politician that would dare stand in his way. The only thing he feared was the organization. But, after the last incident in the air, two fighter jets would accompany him over China, and then all along the way to Europe various countries would provide similar protection. The leader made sure of this. He was not about to lose one of his strongest supporters in a conflict with the Americans.

Haleb Aram Ashur was a poet—not one of those employed by the state to write pamphlets about Saddam, but a true poet in his heart, torn right out of European Romanticism. He had never published anything; his poems were written in vain and destined for his desk drawer only. No one would ever know about them, not Saddam and not even the leader. His job as Saddam Hussein's aide for Iraq's economic upsurge in the Middle East was secondary to his hidden passion. Had it not been for the leader, who needed his presence in the Iraqi government, he would have long retired to some romantic village near Heidelberg, where he had gone to university. He had to sacrifice his own desires for the bigger cause, for he was but a particle in the aggregate so misunderstood by the world at large. *Ein Teil von jener Kraft, die stets das Gute will und stets das Böse schafft:* A particle in the force that tries to make good, but only bad it does, as he liked to paraphrase the great Goethe, his only and true idol.

Haleb had left the presidential palace and ordered his driver to take him home. It was still early afternoon in Baghdad, but Haleb had to prepare for tomorrow's meeting. He would not have had to leave this early, except he had a private consultation with the Syrian and other Islamic representatives in Damascus on their way to Europe. The leader had asked him to emphasize the need for the support of the Muslim members.

Haleb did not mind his clandestine job on behalf of the leader; in fact, he thought he could do much good for Iraq through the organization's resources. He did not resent Saddam Hussein's efforts to build an arsenal of weapons of mass destruction, but he despised his internal policies; one did not treat one's citizens as enemies. That was where the organization would step in and bring a new and better future for Iraq, he reasoned. Alpha promised a swift removal of Saddam from power and quick withdrawal of the American troops from the Middle East in exchange for the Muslim support. Haleb agreed, even though he often had doubts about Alpha's politics. What bothered Haleb the most was Alpha's support for the regime, and the presidency in the United States was a regime veiled in democracy that was striving to tear Haleb's homeland apart. He knew, despite his patriotic pride, that his country could not stand head-to-head with the power of the United States; he was not blind. It pained him even more to see what was happening within the organization; any rift was bound to weaken its position, not only in Iraq but on a global scale too. It had taken the better part of his life to help build an organization that would finally bring an end to such ancient colloquialisms as religious, cultural or political hostilities. The organization was capable of turning the world around.

He believed in it and supported it wholeheartedly. The secret lay in complete denunciation of all political or religious agendas. Those may have still functioned in the world of physical boundaries, governments, and nations, but on that sublevel where the organization existed they were relics of times gone by. That is, only until the president of the United States crawled out of his cave and he and Alpha decided to put an end to the organization's global revolution because it was not good for America. Of course it was not good for America, for where the organization existed there was no America, no China, Russia, or Iraq. There was only one world with a mutual goal: to thrive without subdivisions of the so-called First or Third World. It was not just an idealistic jingle. It was possible. It was already happening. Slowly—one could not change in a decade what took over hundreds of years to build—but it was happening. And in his small way Haleb was a part of this process, a misunderstood man who had found his place in time and history, a poet with a dream.

Yevgeny Ostipovich Snegov drew a deep breath. He had just gotten off the phone with the minister of telecommunication. His consortium has been granted a license renewal for its nationwide chain of television and radio stations, Russia's largest independently owned media network. The leader had been promising resolution for close to a year now, a year of bitter legislative battles against the president and his personal quest to destroy Snegov and his empire. Perfect timing. He knew the leader would wheedle the license sooner or later, and he knew it would come in the form of a theatrical gesture, the fancy of a man who always got what he wanted. Except that in this case it was hardly necessary; Snegov would never support the idea of American leadership. There had been far too much animosity between the Russian and American members in the first formative years of the organization. Both parties agreed then that the organization was too precious to be subjected to such enmities. The decision was a godsend; it elevated the organization to levels unimaginable in the wildest of dreams. He and the Russians, as well as all other partners, had benefited from the organization's existence beyond anything possible in a single lifetime already, and there was more to come. Someday the telecommunications ministry would be his. The leader had said so—but even without the organization's help it was going to happen. He was immensely popular among the people and a good portion of the administration. It was the conflict with Snegov that was responsible for the president's declining popularity. Who knew? Someday maybe even . . . Nothing was unreachable for a man in his position. He was not a sentimental man, but he knew he owed a great deal to the organization, and he was not going to let it down. Tomorrow Alpha would leave emptyhanded.

Chapter Thirteen

Penskie followed the stranger's Daewoo to a secluded riverbank near the Siekierki power plant. The plant was surrounded by acres of fruit and vegetable orchards, as well as small allotment gardens where retirees grew carrots, chives, tomatoes, and other plants cultivated for home consumption. Distant sounds from the highway construction site were thumping in the wet air. The sun was breaking through thinning clouds, and mist from the river and wet earth had covered the area. One could not see beyond ten or fifteen meters. It was a good place for a clandestine meeting—or a murder . . . Penskie realized it was foolish of him to follow the stranger to such a place, but deep down he felt the man was not out to kill him; he would have done it in the stadium, or let the killer do it.

The scrambled cellular telephone rang. Ed Powell spoke about a new development that required Penskie's presence at the embassy. The legal attaché's words were spare, but excitement in his voice suggested a breakthrough or a leap forward in the investigation. He also had good news from the hospital: David's state had been upgraded to "recovering," and the doctors expected the youngest of the legats to be released from the hospital as early as New Year's Eve.

The Daewoo continued down a six-meter-high embankment and parked on a meadow dotted with black cinders—signs of picnickers and fishermen. Penskie got out of his Opel and followed the stranger to the sandy beach. Muddy water flew by, swiftly and with a steady hum.

"I used to come here as a child with my parents," the man started. "The river would dry out and sandy islands would form. We'd hop from one to another . . . you could almost cross the river that way. A number of people drown each year trying to do this."

"Who are you?" Penskie asked icily.

The stranger took out a flip wallet from his Gore-Tex coat and handed it to Penskie, who read out loud: " 'Paweł Urbaniak . . . *Urząd Ochrony Państwa . . .*' "

"What is not printed is my position . . . deputy director of counterintelligence." He offered to shake hands.

Penskie stood idle. Was it a pitch? The rescue at the *Stadion* parking lot . . . the reference to a friendship with Robert . . . The man knew about his relationship with Sito! He knew the reference would have dispersed Penskie's doubts. It did. It convinced him of the man's honesty. Robert would not have told anyone but a friend.

"Well, Deputy, who killed Robert . . . and why?"

"If you meant to ask who fired the gun, then it was the same man who killed Małpa—Sasha the Trigger." Urbaniak took out a crumpled pack of cigarettes, strong Polish Klubowe, and offered one to Penskie, who shook his head in rejection. The deputy director lit his, took a deep puff, and continued, "Gun for hire. Credited with at least four gang-related hits this year alone. Not associated with any particular group—an independent contractor, so to speak. Ukrainian, deserted from Spetsnaz during the Soviet withdrawal from East Germany back in the early nineties. Eluded the police, the *Centralne Biuro Śledcze*, and the UOP ever since. Quite possibly with the aid of the extensive network of the KGB's and GRU's leftover sleepers."

So that was it! Penskie's mind wandered off to the Wilanowska Café. The man in a washed-out army jacket was Sasha the Trigger. The same man who killed Robert Sito. To think he was so close! Blood rushed to his head. If he had only connected the two events, he could have taken him down. Or been taken down himself. Then Penskie recalled the look in the man's eyes in the parking lot. The assassin did not shoot, but he had hesitated, almost as if killing Penskie would have been against his orders, something his heart did not agree with.

Stan shivered and said angrily, "I could have had him today!"

"Oh, Mr. Penskie . . . or do you prefer Agent? I feel just as bad about Robert's death, but I am glad you did not shoot Sasha. It's the closest we ever got to him."

"We?"

"My men are following him as we speak."

"You mean . . . you let him go?" Penskie cried in astonishment. It was incomprehensible. It made no sense. "You saw him kill a man, you knew he killed Robert, and you let him go?"

"Małpa was a scoundrel destined to end up in a ditch

sooner or later. As for Robert . . . rest assured Sasha will pay for his death. For now, one must not forget Sasha knows a hell of a lot about things vital to the security of this country—your country, Stanisław . . ."

"Oh, spare me your melodramatic crap! He's a killer first and foremost. He murdered Robert, supposedly your friend, and you let him go! Do you really think a Spetsnaz killer who eluded you for years is going to let some gumshoes follow him around?"

"I have confidence in my officers. Sito was my friend too, not a brother-in-law-to-be, mind you, but a good friend nevertheless."

Urbaniak knew! Penskie was in shock, even though the thought had earlier crossed his mind. It was unnerving. It put Urbaniak in control, and as any investigating officer knew, relinquishing one's control was the number one mistake. Still, Penskie was too weary to bother with elementary rules of interrogation. He wanted to know right now, and this man had the answers.

"Why? Why Sito? Why . . . all this?" Lacking proper words, he made inexpressible gestures with his arms.

"I trust some patriotism and loyalty to the country of your birth is left in you, Stan, because what I have to say is beyond just a cop-to-cop relation. . . ."

"Save it. You're making this into a stage play. I was thirteen when we landed in America. I've spent twenty years of my life outside of Poland. Do you seriously think this is going to work on me?" Penskie laughed a nervous laugh. He was in the dark about the meaning of the events, Urbaniak's allusions only adding to his confusion. *My God!* It hasn't even been twenty-four hours since Robert had been killed, and he had learned of things that required a think tank to make sense of. "As far as this is concerned, I am an FBI officer and I want the bastards who did this!"

"I'm afraid you're going to have to choose whether you are a cop or a brother and a son."

"What?"

"That's not all, Stanisław. You will have to decide whose side you're really on."

"What the hell did you mean about my father?"

"I'll get to that in a moment. First I want you to listen, and very carefully, because I may not last long enough to repeat this. I am going directly against my boss's orders, and against the state interests."

Penskie wanted to object. Instead he bit his lips to prevent himself from shouting. He was tired and lost and, at this point, ready to accept any arrogant son of a bitch who had the answers. He sat on a large cold log and listened.

Urbaniak repeated most of what Penskie had already heard from Sito at the Wilanowska Café. True, Robert Sito had died while relating it, a tragedy of personal proportions to Stan, but somehow the same information told now by the chief of the counterintelligence department of Poland's premier intelligence agency, the state security agency, added an even more catastrophic angle to the story. Sito's flight with the investigation files was undertaken with Urbaniak's help in order to protect the information gathered thus far. It was in danger of being buried by the bureaucrats in the *Urząd Ochrony Państwa.* Even though Penskie already faced the deadly consequences of having just brushed with the truth behind the murders, it was not until now that he fully appreciated the magnitude of the revelations.

"So all this over the files?" Penskie asked incredulously. "Dossiers of informants, snitches, and the scum of the earth? Are they even real? Haven't they all been destroyed?"

"Destroyed? Sure . . . after being microfilmed and digitized. No falling dictatorship will leave itself defenseless. What was destroyed forever were operational documents that could lead to exposure of those who gave the orders to shoot the miners, the shipyard workers, plans for the annihilation of the opposition, and so on. But the existence of the informants' dossiers provided immunity from prosecution. No one in their right mind would destroy such valuable information. There's always the possibility some fresh-out-of-school, idealistic new prosecutor may want to bring charges. That's when a quiet reminder to his or her superiors, often on the ministerial level, of his or her past steers them off to more important tasks, like prosecuting the real criminals, those who threaten the growth and the stability of our emergent economy. . . . What we're talking about is much bigger than a bunch of names. Big enough to have the CIA eliminate FBI officers who threaten to expose the operation . . ."

Urbaniak paused, as if letting Penskie object or contradict.

Penskie did neither. As incredible as it all sounded, it could certainly explain why the legats had met such opposition when looking into the EDECA affairs. But that was too easy a conclusion, and too outrageous even to take into consideration. No one out there, whether in the Central Intelligence Agency, the government, or especially the Federal Bureau of Investigation, was killing American diplomats in the name of some elusive operation. Loomis could not have been following orders from the CIA. That was preposterous!

Urbaniak studied Penskie's face for emotions, and, satisfied that his comment had brought out the desired effect, continued, "The ministry of the exterior and your state department agreed to wrap it up quietly, and you've guessed whose job it is to make sure it stays that way. They expect *us* to cover things up, to make sure that no one digs out the truth."

"What is the truth?"

"Loomis wasn't turned over. He wasn't working for us; nor did he shoot your friend because of some old quarrel. He was following orders from Langley."

"Why?"

"Because these files are a key to information your government wants more than anything else in the world." Urbaniak paused.

"There's no need to be so theatrical. You brought me out here, you saved my life, you can spell it out for me!"

"I want to make sure you understand the significance of the things we're talking about. The list . . . the names . . . it's not just some old operatives of defunct services and times long forgotten. These people are active to this day."

Penskie did not reply immediately. Urbaniak's intonation suggested another pause. The man was positively annoying.

"Why are you telling me this? Why aren't you working through proper channels?"

"I'll level with you, Stanisław. I don't know whether the Bureau is in on it or not, but the fact that you've been misled and shot at makes me want to believe at least some of you are in the clear. Bet you've been thinking the same thing . . ."

"In on what?" Penskie was on the verge of losing patience.

"Don't you see it? The existence of a powerful network of spies, operatives, or whatever you want to call it is what the American intelligence community needs to survive and thrive. And don't fool yourself—they're not after it to expose it or destroy it. Once they have the names, the data, contacts, the whole organization, they'll be able to seize control, to run it. You know why? Funding . . . employment . . . survival. The existence of a powerful threat to the security of the United States will open the pockets of Congress."

Penskie stood up. He looked into Urbaniak's eyes and took a step back.

"To convince Congress to shell out funding would require a threat of enormous proportions, not some bunch of geriatric patients from a bygone era. You're a lunatic! There are problems the United States and the world have to face that are more important. The war on terrorism . . . Iraq . . . Security services across the western hemisphere have received an influx of manpower and funds because of the terrorist attacks. There *is* plenty of money available for them. You can even say it's a renaissance time for intelligence and security agencies. . . . you're way behind the times."

Urbaniak did not take offense. He pulled out another cigarette and lit it. "Ever heard of the SOUD, the system for recognizing enemies?"

Penskie thought a moment. "Sure, the old communist database. A thing of the past, isn't it?"

"Not entirely true. See, when the system was created back in the late seventies, it was to provide and store information on potential and actual hostile forces that might want to undermine the Soviet participation in and organization of the 1980 Olympics. Eventually it grew into a fully operational database with inputs provided by intelligence agencies from the bloc: Bulgaria, Czechoslovakia, Cuba, Poland, East Germany, of course, as well as some Far Eastern states . . . and the Soviet Union. SOUD contained everything on everyone. There was no such thing as insignificant information, as far as the Soviet system was concerned.

"The databases were filled with hundreds of thousands of files on organizations and individuals, diplomats, journalists, politicians, terrorists, spies, and pretty much anybody who might be of interest. Both the diplomatic missions and intelligence networks of the participating countries supplied all they could gather, including DNA samples from such sources as hair, discarded nails, or even crap.

"Some of the mainframe computers that carried the traffic from intelligence and diplomatic posts were located in East Germany, and after the unification fell into the hands of the *Bundesnachrichten;* thus its existence became known in the West, as you said. But what the Western agencies didn't know at the time was that a similar database was created much earlier, and contained information about the friends of the Soviet system. And by that I mean sympathizers as well as active supporters, spies, politicians, organizations, et cetera."

"And you think that's what the CIA is after? The political system these people supported is no more. The world has changed."

"Stanisław, Stanisław . . . the only thing that changed is the objective. You're not trying to tell me that because communism is gone, the CIA or even your own FBI doesn't recruit spies from among the new American allies?" Urbaniak did not wait for an answer. The sense of his statement was clear. "You know it as well as I do: In this business there is no way out. These former *friends* of the old system are still active assets of the current intelligence services. It's true that many of them were discovered and turned and are now on the CIA's, the FBI's, the DOD's, and other agencies' payrolls."

"I don't buy it. A hunt for moles doesn't necessitate the killing of an FBI officer. The opposite is more probable: If what you're saying is true, Loomis is a prime candidate for one such *friend* who's gone to the extreme to protect his double game."

"We're on the same side here, Stanisław. I'm telling you this as a friend, an ally: Loomis was not our asset."

"You'd have to do better than that to convince me."

"You mean hard evidence? It always amazes me, the straightforward thinking of a cop: No evidence—no case. You'd never make an intelligence officer, dear Stan. The world of espionage is built on illusions. Things such as the so-called evidence and chance are meant to fool the enemy. They are carefully planned to facilitate a desired reaction. To learn the true intentions one must learn to read between the lines."

"What does your between-the-lines reading tell you?"

Urbaniak pulled another Klubowe cigarette from a rumpled package. He lit it, inhaled deeply, and said slowly, "All the facts tell us the CIA and a number of other agencies are actively trying to acquire the database."

The conclusion was obvious.

"So according to your thinking it's to conceal the fact that they already have it!"

"Precisely. Whether in full or in part, they've had it at

least since the mid-nineties, most likely earlier, but like any self-respecting intelligence agency, they didn't make immediate use of this information. No arrests or blown covers ever surfaced. When the first indications were substantiated, we assumed the agents were turned. However, that was not the case. They were allowed to continue their traitorous work, and do it to this day."

"Okay, slow down a little. Let me see if I've got this right," Penskie said in an exaggeratedly sarcastic voice. "The Central Intelligence Agency acquires an explosive list with evidence of a massive spy network working on American soil, and not only don't they hand it over to the FBI but they allow these assets to pass on the secrets to . . . to you?"

"To us, the Russians, Ukrainians, French, Chinese, or Bulgarians, you name it. They allow the network to exist and operate uninterrupted. Why? You should know the answer—to be in control of the information that changes hands. Except that these assets are not being fed phony secrets. Some of them bring top-quality material, and the CIA knows it and allows it. Why? Two reasons. The stakes are extremely high—survival. You realize what will happen to the agency if the truth about their knowing about the terrorist networks, Bin Laden, and others should ever be exposed? That's why they are prepared to go to extremes to keep the Bureau out of it." Urbaniak paused, his eyes far and fishy. "Of course, there is the other possibility—"

"Why choose me?" Penskie interrupted. "Why not go straight to Washington? The counterintelligence would be thrilled to expose the traitors. That is what you want, isn't it?"

"Normally I . . . the UOP would come to the FBI with it; after all, we are allies, and both our and other countries' national interests and security are at stake. Despite the authenticity and value of the information provided by our assets, they must be terminated. No"—Urbaniak shook his head—"I don't mean killed! Just withdrawn from our services. It's a done deal, since they are already jeopardized.... Hell! Burned is a more appropriate word. Besides, who would we turn to? The same people who ordered you to stay away from the EDECA and Norman Bray? The way I see it, they're a part of it."

"I'll take most anything said about the CIA, but if you're trying to tell me the Bureau is a part of this... this conspiracy, then you have one more screw loose than I thought!"

"Think about it, Stan. What do I have to gain? I just divulged some of the most closely guarded secrets of the *Urząd Ochrony Państwa*. I'm even prepared to give you names of some of our assets in America."

"Assets already known to the CIA! Where's the secret when we already have the answers?"

"*We*? That is precisely what I'm trying to explain to you. It isn't American interests the CIA represents anymore! If it were, the appropriate actions would have been taken and the FBI would have been handling it now. No, Stan, I did not come to you as an officer to an officer. I came to you as one patriot to another. Even if your feelings steer only toward your adopted country."

"What do you expect me to do about it?" Penskie asked, irritation in his voice.

"Talk to your father."

"What?"

"He was the national security adviser!"

"That was two administrations ago!"

"He's still got big influence with the president senior.

They are close friends after all. Granted, the son may not know what to do, but he'll listen to his father's old advisers. He rehired some of them, for crying out loud!"

Urbaniak was right. The new president had followed not only his father's footsteps into presidency but also his political doctrine. He simply carried on where his father left off. It was no secret that to influence the White House, one had to find access to the senior.

"I can't go empty-handed. All you've given me so far are speculations, nothing to hang on to. What am I supposed to tell him—that the CIA lets secrets leak out to foreign intelligence services who don't want them? He'll laugh me out! I need more than that."

Urbaniak threw away the cigarette butt, his eyes following its flight. "I meant to tell you this. We've taken the secretary into our—UOP's—custody last night."

"What?" Penskie was perplexed.

"Ania, the EDECA's secretary. That's how we found out about Małpa. Apparently he and Terrence Jacobek of the EDECA were close associates. Jacobek worked under the control of Daniel Loomis, but what Loomis and the CIA didn't know was that Jacobek had turned."

"You . . ."

"No, not us, nor the Russians, Bulgarians, or any other nation. Jacobek works for . . . a multinational organization."

"What the hell does that mean?"

"What the CIA took upon itself turned out to be more than it could handle. When they seized the files, with all the names and all, what they didn't realize was that it wasn't just an alphabetical list of names of individuals and groups working for the former communist regimes. They returned to service, and by the mid-nineties, when the truth surfaced, they were already a well-organized, powerful, and independent organization.

"The CIA finally caught up and saw what it was up against. Unfortunately there was nothing they could do about it, because exposing the truth would mean admitting to harboring not just foreign spies but terrorists too, and you know what your president said about countries and organizations who support terrorism? 'You're either with us or against us. . . .' Remember that?"

Penskie stood speechless. This was not happening! Fables! The counterintelligence director was telling old fables, fables so outrageous they were long discarded by intelligence agencies worldwide. He wanted to rub his eyes and wake up from a crazy dream—a dream he had already dreamed before, and he knew what was coming next.

"That's right, Stan; the CIA has all your government wants, what the rest of the antiterrorist alliance wants—the names, the organizational charts, the whereabouts . . . everything it needs to put an end to global terrorism. And it won't give it away, because it would mean the end of Central Intelligence." Urbaniak considered taking another Klubowe cigarette out, but the package was empty. He crumpled it and threw it into the river's current.

"Talk to your father, Stan. *Piąta Międzynarodówka* is a fact. The Fifth Internationale is real." With these words Urbaniak turned and walked off toward his Daewoo.

Penskie watched the officer slowly disappear into the mist. He was startled beyond words. His mind raced. Could this have been a coincidence? Małpa's last words were *Piąta Międzynarodówka*—Fifth Internationale—but surely these two men had different things in mind.

Or had they?

Chapter Fourteen

"Tell me about the Fifth Internationale."

"What?" Mollie Banks stiffened at her desk.

"You're not really here because of some agency irregularities, are you?"

She turned away from the notebook. She looked tired. They'd stayed up till the wee hours last night, perusing resources that proved to be fruitless. Penskie did not wake her when he left for the *Stadion.* Now he stood in the middle of the room in his coat and hat, his eyes fixed on hers. He had to know; he had to see it in her eyes. *This is it,* he thought. He did not care about the ultimate objective; he just wanted to know the reason, the truth.

"Not everybody in the Company is supporting it," she answered glumly. "This is not to say that we know who is, but—"

"I can't believe I'm hearing this! You actually telling me this thing is true?"

Banks looked perplexed, her eyes wide. "For a moment there I thought—I *hoped*—you'd gotten hold of some evidence!" She stood up. "Look, I'm sorry I didn't mention it yesterday by name, but I figured you wouldn't take me seriously. This story has been circulating ever since the Wall came down; it has been discarded by the biggest authorities in the field, yet it seems the Fifth Internationale is real, after all."

Banks was not trying to deny anything, and Penskie relaxed.

"Well, why didn't you say something in the first place?"

"I don't know what happened this morning, where you got the information from. You look shaken, and . . ." She pointed to his soiled coat. "But would you have believed me if I told you this yesterday?"

He took off his coat and sat down on the sofa. Would he have believed that Loomis would shoot David to protect a secret so outrageous? There could be only one explanation: The legats must have been close enough to evidence of the existence of the organization that was supposedly a hoax, a rumor spread by a practical joker, a rumor that had all intelligence agencies on the edge of their seats when it first surfaced. Could he believe this now?

"How bad is it?"

"No way of saying for sure; we receive only a hint now and then, nothing that could lead to serious conclusions, but I won't lie to you. It looks quite bad."

"*Quite* bad?"

"Since the dismantling of the communist intelligence agencies, many of their officers and operatives found employment in the Company and other Western or Middle Eastern agencies."

"Why does it not surprise me? If they can hire Gestapo officers then why not commies and terrorists?"

"Political affiliations aside, they were highly trained professionals who had an internal knowledge of intelligence beyond anything attainable before; many of them controlled networks of assets throughout the globe. Some of them came to good use during the Gulf War, in Bosnia, or lately in Afghanistan. They were cheaper and better informed than our own people, and not surprisingly there came a time when they replaced our own operatives. Before we knew it they were everywhere, recruiting assets in the name of the Central Intelligence Agency, the MI6, MI5, DSE, BND, and appealing to people's patriotism. It wasn't hard. Who wouldn't do a small favor for their own country, especially when the seemingly simple task was often accompanied by a hefty reward?"

Penskie leaned back into the deep sofa, his head resting on the back, eyes fixed on an unspecified point on the ceiling.

"They are well organized, resourceful, and omnipresent," Banks continued. "Did you know that the KGB alone was well over five hundred thousand strong? What did you think happened to the hundreds of thousands of them from throughout the bloc? The Czechs, for example, replaced almost everyone to guarantee a clean start. But what happened to the others? Did you think they just retired to the Oppenheim Memorial Park, chasing an imaginary enemy?"

Banks was agitated. She was pacing around the room in front of Stan. She awaited a response, a comment. None came, and she considered his silence degrading. She felt compelled to defend the Central Intelligence Agency.

"Well, the idea was tactically sound at the time. Rather than have them sell their skills to Iraq and other terrorist states, we offered the best or the most useful of them employment on our side. Who was to know, to imagine in their wildest dreams that by that time they were already organized into a powerful entity with its own goals, finances, and strong leadership?

"When the first signs of trouble emerged, we captured and questioned a handful of the most likely suspects, small fish in a sea of sharks, but I tell you, even if half of what we've learned is true, it is frightening. They control banks, multinational corporations, key fields in national infrastructures, and have their own people in the highest government entities. We've estimated their opening budget—money funneled from secret and official accounts of individual members of the party, intelligence agencies, and state-owned corporate giants, such as the national television networks and petrol industries, monopolies on the grandest of scales—to be upward of one hundred billion dollars, perhaps as much as twice that. And that was over a decade ago. Do you realize how much money that is? A billion, two billion, or a hundred billion, it all sounds the same to you and me: It's unimaginable. But look at it from a different standpoint: The entire U.S. intelligence community receives about thirty billion a year, not counting the post–September eleventh influx. The Brits finance their intelligence with some five billion. The Swiss defense budget is in the region of five billion francs. . . . They were big, Stan. They were big from the start. And they've grown since."

She paused. Penskie's silence was unnerving, but she decided to ignore it. She was on a rant. Weeks of undercover investigation, being thrown on her own resources, not to mention the assassination attempt, all this took its toll on her emotional state. Not sure how to continue, what to add to what already seemed incredible, she subsided into complete silence.

The change was absolute and shocking, but Stan did not notice. He was engrossed in his own thoughts.

The Fifth Internationale, the subject of countless debates and even more rumors and tales. A shadowy organization of former intelligence and secret service officers and operatives who came together after the winds of change swept through the world, leaving thousands of them unemployed, their futures uncertain, their skills no longer required. The subject so loved and cultivated by the press, but never quite crossing the stage of a rumor. But a rumor feared to have originated out of a legitimate concern. To this day the Federal Bureau of Investigation's vast corridors of intelligence data contained a sizable section devoted to the nameless organization. Much of the intelligence concluded a not-so-secret fact: Many former operatives found employment in the private sector. The Gulf War, and then the Balkans, distracted the intelligence community from pointless debates, and no one took arguments into consideration: Could the market, even one as fast-growing as that of Eastern Europe, absorb hundreds of thousands of specialists in a field as rare as spying, while at the same time national job statistics were recording unemployment levels unthinkable during communist rule, when everybody was supposed to have employment? Could people who knew things that no state in the world would like to reach media or foreign intelligence simply walk away, survive on unemployment benefits, when the value of their knowledge was sky-high? Was that knowledge of any value today? Was it valuable enough for Loomis to shoot David? It could be if one were to take seriously what Banks and Urbaniak had said: The Central Intelligence Agency was trying to prevent the information from being discovered. The CIA's actions were not bound by ethical standards of such law enforcement agencies as the FBI, particularly after they'd gotten their green light to commit assassinations in the name of United States security. But was this all the CIA wanted kept out of the limelight: the existence of a secret and elusive organization of unthinkable resources and proportions? Or was it the fact that it held the keys to this organization and let it slip away? What did Urbaniak say . . . ? *The CIA . . . won't give it away, because it would mean the end of Central Intelligence. . . .* Having prior information about terrorist networks such as Al Qaeda would do much harm to the CIA, but it did not justify killing FBI agents.

His mind hovered around the conversation with the officer of the *Urząd Ochrony Państwa.* He recalled the strange comment: *Talk to your father. . . . The Fifth Internationale is real. . . .* Why should Zbigniew Penskie, former national security adviser to the former president of the United States, know anything about it? He had been out of the office for over a decade now, two presidential terms, an eon in the fast-changing world of the nineties and the beginning of the new century. As far as Stan knew—and he had a fairly open relationship with his father—Zbigniew Penskie had nothing to do with politics anymore.

He wanted to tell Mollie about his morning and the meeting with Urbaniak. He wanted to ask, to share his thoughts and doubts, and to hear her opinion. He could not. No matter what he felt, he was too experienced a field agent to give in to temptation. He had to see what Powell had uncovered about her, this woman who appeared out of nowhere with stories that could shake the world's most powerful intelligence agency—perhaps even throw it into oblivion.

He excused himself and walked out of the suite under an ad hoc pretext, leaving Banks perplexed.

Outside, in a small parking lot, he took out his cellular telephone and dialed a number in Kraków. He paced in anxiety. Zbigniew Penskie did not answer. He ended the connection and dialed 00-1-212, then seven more digits.

Ruth Sagowitz, the corpulent assistant to Professor Penskie at New York University, was surprised. The holiday break had started last Friday, and by now Zbigniew was supposed to be with his family in Poland, she thought. She had been sitting the professor's cat, Shakespeare, since Saturday. Hadn't Stan heard from his father yet? The old man suffered from hypertension, and she expressed her worry. Stan did not even have to ask—she would take a cab over to the professor's place and make sure he was all right. Stan left his cellular phone number with Ruth and asked for a call as soon as she had any news. He got into his car and drove away.

Stan was worried. Hypertension did not prevent Zbigniew from indulging in the two or three daily coffees he refused to give up. And they were not the cappuccinos, frappuccinos, or any other coffee drinks so popular nowadays. Zbigniew Penskie grew up on *zalewajka,* strong, black coffee steeped Turkish style, a habit picked up during countless and sleepless nights while he was with the Polish Solidarity movement.

When the martial law was declared in Poland in 1981, the

family was caught unaware while skiing in the Austrian Alps. Returning to Poland meant certain imprisonment and possible death under mysterious circumstances for Zbigniew, a high-ranking member of *Solidarność*, and a life in misery and persecution for his wife and children. The family chose freedom and uncertainty. After months in a transitory camp for refugees, the Penskies received visas to the United States of America. Holding a doctoral degree in political sciences, Zbigniew received tenure at one of the East Coast colleges, where he specialized in communist affairs. His hard line position toward the communist system eventually landed him a post as national security adviser to the president of the United States. Being a close associate of the then–vice president, he remained in the office after new presidential elections. Zbigniew Penskie was generally credited with increased American support for the opposition in Poland and the final demise of the regime, which eventually led to the collapse of the entire system.

Stan did not know much about his father's professional life after the Cold War had ended. When the Democrats took office, he retreated into writing memoirs and giving lectures. When Poland gained full independence and the new government lifted his death sentence, given in absentia by the communist court in the early eighties, Zbigniew Penskie became a sort of a celebrity in the old country. The press and radio and television stations were lining up for interviews with the legendary Solidarity fighter who was forced to seek refuge in the West.

Stan knew that his father remained a close friend of the former president, and that during his work he had met many influential people, who were reinstated after the president's son won election to the White House. Zbigniew's influence in the new administration was something that Stan had never given a thought to, though, he now realized, it must have existed, if only by acquaintance.

It was Zbigniew Penskie who had persuaded Stan to take the offer from the Federal Bureau of Investigation's recruiters after his graduation from NYU. Penskie was always a lively child, seeking every occasion to spend his energy and to find fulfillment in areas of interest. Poland's martial law, a national tragedy, and the refugee life it bestowed on the family proved nothing more than a big adventure for the young man. To him it was an extended holiday and travel. Years later, after graduating from the university and facing a prospect of following in his father's footsteps by obtaining a doctoral degree, Stan eagerly listened to Zbigniew's advice and did not reject the Federal Bureau of Investigation's recruiters. A life that offered more than lectures and lunching at university cafeterias was more in line with his nature. He appreciated the opportunity for the kind of life the FBI had presented, and he plunged into it, never regretting his decision.

Until the last presidential elections, which had caught Stan on-duty in Poland, apart from the usual long-distance relationship the family would meet several times a year at Zbigniew's estate in Kraków, south-central Poland, with politics seldom discussed. After the elections, however, Stan realized now, his father had spent much of his time in the United States, hardly ever visiting the country of his birth. This could mean the old man was once again entangled in politics, perhaps even working with the new administration. Stan was hoping to see his father in three days' time for Christmas, but the events of the last day—and Urbaniak's statement—demanded immediate contact.

He started keying in the number on the telephone again, then paused. *Oh, God!* His hands were trembling! He shivered at the thought of the terrible news he had to deliver to his sister, but almost immediately found relief in the fact that the conversation with Zbigniew might provide the answers Margaret would expect. Just how his father could have the answers, he did not know, but he hoped to God he could say earnestly to her that Sito's killer would pay for his death; a typical male rationale that was not going to bring Robert back, he realized, while pulling up to the embassy gate on Ulica Piękna.

Chapter Fifteen

There was a sense of rushed animation in the embassy as Penskie entered the main building. The marine who was sitting behind an elongated desk in the front lobby greeted him with a stoic expression, but all other staff hurried through purposefully. One of them was Ed Powell, who was passing with a thick sheaf of papers and a cup of coffee. The legal attaché could not contain his excitement.

"Where've you been? Hell broke loose around here, everyone's on the edge, and Hank thinks somehow it's all your doing."

"Tell you in the den." Penskie nodded at the marine.

Powell glanced over his shoulder and lowered his voice. "Yeah, c'mon. Got some tangy juice from F-eighty-one."

F81 was the designation for a field station operated by the National Security Agency in Bad Aibling, outside of Munich, Germany. It was a part of a larger network of similar facilities encompassing the entire globe and known under its code name, "Echelon." Formed during the Cold War by the United States, Canada, the United Kingdom, Australia, and New Zealand, Echelon served as a communication surveillance system. Through its array of sophisticated equipment it intercepted a vast amount of military, diplomatic, commercial, and civilian communications. Satellites, microwave stations, radio listening posts, and ordinary wiretaps connected directly into phone lines, and fiber-optic cables collected voice, fax, video, radio, Internet, and any other form of electronic communiqué that occurred at any given time in any place around the world. As communications were intercepted, they passed through supercomputers equipped with custom multilingual dictionaries that filtered the messages according to the criteria supplied by intelligence agencies of the countries operating the network. The keywords included anything from names of people and institutions, nicknames, phone numbers, and Internet and e-mail addresses to license plate numbers, bank accounts, or any other terms of interest. When intercepts satisfied the criteria, they were appropriately categorized, analyzed, and forwarded to interested government agencies, such as the Federal Bureau of Investigation.

Powell put the paper cup of coffee on his desk. He shoved the papers to one side, on top of an already large pile of other files, and punched in a sequence on the intercom.

"Marv, would you like us to come down now? . . . Oh, okay, thanks." He hung up, turned to Penskie, and asked with a trace of angst, "What happened? You look like hell."

"This'll help," Penskie picked up the coffee cup from Powell's desk. He drank a mouthful and placed it back on the desk. "Bit of a rough morning," he started, then changed the subject. "What's this stuff from NSA about?"

"Ah, for once the No Such Agency sent some interesting material, and in record time, too." He shuffled some papers until he found the right one and handed it to Stan. "Read up."

Penskie grinned as his eyes scanned the text.

He finished reading and was about to start over when Marvin Cleft, the chief of embassy security, walked into the office, a notebook under his arm.

The man sat down, set up his computer on Powell's desk, and powered it on.

"Listen to this." Cleft clicked on the screen of his notebook.

A voice from internal speakers poured out in English: "You should not have called me at this number! Your call could be intercepted . . . you fool. . . . Penskie knows more than he should. If they follow the trail my exposure will be imminent. . . ." The voices were distorted but audible.

"This phone call was intercepted yesterday at seventeen hundred hours. It originated right here, in this building," Cleft explained when the playback ended.

Powell sat grimly, evidently having heard the message already.

Penskie was too absorbed by the mention of his name in the message to react. He was standing, still holding the transcript, his eyes moving from one man to the other, as if he did not understand. When the impact of the intercept finally dawned on him, his head tilted backward and a loud gasp followed.

"Give us the full spiel, will you, Marv?" Powell broke the silence and shifted in his leather chair.

"I won't say this very often, but I'm glad the NSA has got the chip to decipher the scrambled communications of our diplomatic missions. This phone call was made using a secure line at seventeen hundred. Most staff were still in the building, but since not everyone has access to the scramblers it narrows the list substantially. We've used the voice imprint to find the bastard. It wasn't easy, since he used voice-distortion software in addition to the scrambler. The NSA's equipment must have been set on priority monitoring, 'cause the quality is damn good, if you ask me. On the other hand, our own SCE came up with *nada*. Darn pansies . . ."

"I'm not sure I'd like the Special Collection Element's scope of responsibilities to include spying on the embassy's employees," Powell cut in.

"Well, at times it might be a justifiable—"

"Who was the caller?" Penskie cut in impatiently.

"Stephen Pearson," Cleft answered matter-of-factly and shot a quizzical gaze at the legal attaché.

"Stan doesn't know yet," Powell explained to the chief of security.

"Know what?" Penskie asked.

"Pearson was killed by a car last night on his way to the Sheraton. The car came in from around the curve from the Plac Trzech Krzyży, ignoring the red light. Cops said it happens all the time in that spot. They have been ticketing regularly there," Powell explained.

Too awed to comment, Penskie collapsed onto an available chair. He looked wearily around the room.

"Serves him right," Cleft said coldly. "If anything, I regret he can't be questioned about it. Would make our job easier."

"Tell us about the recipient," Powell reminded him.

"Ah, there is good news and there is bad news. Our friends at F-eighty-one managed to pinpoint the location of the cell phone that received the phone call. Incidentally, that's only possible if the phone is under surveillance. Random monitoring would not have shown this data—"

"Cell phone location?" Penskie interjected.

"Yeah, basically all cell phone systems can be used to track down the location of a caller. Still, even when a phone is not in use, as long as the battery is charged and it is turned on, its location and number can be determined, thanks to signals each unit emits. The signals are picked up by base stations, which in turn enable monitoring parties to identify the geographical area, at the very least. And, if such a phone is equipped with the PHL chip, as many of the newer and all embassy phones are, one can pinpoint the location to within meters."

"What's a PHL? You have to level with us."

"Stands for Personal Handiphone Locator. The Japs came up with it a few years back. Have the right equipment and you can see where your wife is shopping for your Christmas pressies." Cleft made the last remark to Powell. It was a bit of an office joke. Powell and his wife constantly telephoned or sent SMS messages to one another. Whether at an important meeting or a pub crawl, chances were the legal attaché would be spending part of it on the phone with the missus.

"He's probably got her on hold right now," Cleft continued. "C'mon, man, let the lady know what you want before you end up with another bag of socks!"

Even Penskie could not refrain from laughing.

A smile still on his lips, he asked, "So who's the subject?"

"That's the bad news. I'm afraid the phone's been cloned or otherwise rigged. The scan registered tens of different accounts. Unlikely that any of 'em are linked to our man. It's a custom trick used around the world. Back in the olden days they used one stolen phone per call and trashed it before the call could be traced. With the digital age you can input hundreds of SIM accounts into one of those toys and use it permanently, constantly generating new accounts as needed and switching between them automatically and at random. There's software on the black market—seen it myself at the *Stadion*—that will generate these numbers virtually endlessly. Purchase an additional loader and you can program whatever you need without ever having to pay bills, thus avoiding disclosing your address to the billing department. Mind you, that still does not prevent your location from being identified."

"Where was that cell phone traced to, then?"

Powell looked up something on one of the sheets of paper that occupied his desktop.

"That's just southeast of Kraków, a small village called Nowa Wieś. We've looked it up. Not much there but some two dozen houses and an enormous castle, a museum you probably heard of. Most guidebooks claim it to be one of, if not *the* biggest in the whole of Europe."

"Did you look it up in your guidebook?"

"Hell, no! Just remember reading about it. Almost went there with Melanie last summer . . ."

"Our people from the consulate say the village is a bit off the beaten path. It's one of those places you can't get to very easily; there's no public transport nearby, very few tourists. . . ."

"So the call's recipient could've just been visiting the museum. A villain with a knack for medieval arts."

"On a Monday, and at five in the afternoon?" Penskie cut in.

"What?"

"Most museums are closed Mondays."

The simple observation startled his colleagues. They looked at each other and sat back in their chairs.

"Shit!" Powell cursed.

"Better send a recon team from the consulate to take a discreet sweep of the area," Penskie suggested.

"I'll get on it right away," Cleft stood up, picked up his notebook, and stormed out of the office.

Penskie pushed back his armchair. The constant tension of the last twenty-four hours was showing on his face. The initial upset caused by Urbaniak's reference to his father subsided. He was sitting numbly, his mind active but continuously veering off to the revelation brought upon by the intercept. Zbigniew and Margaret. Two conversations he feared and loathed at the same time, both for quite different reasons. The possibility that his father might still be working for the government was troubling. It was not just that the old man was back in politics, but the fact that he would even consider returning to it after it caused so much grief to his family. His mother, for instance, never quite got over the stress of the Solidarity years, when arrest was expected any day, and sooner or later was inevitable. Living in exile in America, a second home for Zbigniew and the kids, felt like only a transitory station in life for her. She never quite blended in. Though they never spoke about it, living the life of a wanderer was blamed for her illness. It was an unspoken bone of contention between Stan and Zbigniew. Stan was proud of his father, for the values he represented and fought for, but he never forgave him for his mother's suffering. Their relationship was neutral, perhaps even cool, but both men held quiet respect for each other. Stan because he knew he would choose the same path his father had, if put in his shoes. And Zbigniew because he understood Stan's feelings, and was grateful for whatever emotions Stan had left for him. This sensation grew stronger with each passing month and year. Zbigniew needed his family. Stan knew it, though he learned to appreciate it mostly through Margaret's persistence, and he was ready to reconcile his feelings. This family Christmas was to be it: a bridge to reunification and absolute forgiveness. Zbigniew's return to politics could shatter it.

"That was mighty fast of the NSA to forward the intercept," Powell broke the silence. He was holding the transcript of the phone call in his hands. "Come to think of it, I don't recall receiving anything this fast from them. Ever."

Penskie looked up. Something in Powell's statement stirred his mind.

"Normally it takes two to three days to process these things before they're sent out, unless . . ."

"Unless it's an executive order, such as wartime activity or a pending operation!" Powell put down the paper and looked anxiously into Penskie's eyes. "Are you thinking what I'm thinking?"

"They know! The NSA knows who . . ." He bit his tongue. The NSA knew who was behind the Fifth Internationale! There was no other explanation. The random intercept was one thing, but monitoring the location of the person who received the phone call required prior knowledge. The message from Bad Aibling was not part of standard procedure. *My God!* Was the National Security Agency leading them on? Why was there no official word from the Bureau? Why was the NSA bypassing headquarters? Something was wrong! He knew it sounded absurd, but he had learned to trust his hunches, regardless of the level of absurdity. He recalled Sito's warning—*the FBI . . . both governments . . . they're all involved. . . .* Preposterous! Yet he saw no alternative. He refused to accept the possibility that the FBI was implicated. That left only the National Security Agency and the Central Intelligence Agency. Did they work together? It was one thing to suspect foul play on the part of the CIA, but expanding the sentiment to the NSA implied an operation of extreme proportions. Neither he nor Powell nor even the headquarters would be cleared for such information. There was, however, one way to find out. The fastest, the safest and the only way he knew was through his father. He had to talk to Zbigniew Penskie.

"What're you thinking?"

"Not enough sleep is all." He made light of the question. He should tell Ed—he knew he should, but the feeling was there. For the first time he withheld something from his partner. He did not want to lie, but he did not want to talk either. He felt blood rushing through his face.

If Powell noticed anything, he kept it to himself expertly.

"Hank is going out of his mind." The legal attaché changed the subject. "As you can expect, the Poles have a million questions, and then some. You know how the DCM feels when his staff is not accounted for."

"Where is he, anyway? It's awfully quiet here. . . ."

"The hospital. The INR teams arrived this morning. They're trying to talk to Dave. They want to talk to you, too. Should I call Hank and tell him you're back?"

"Stall him!" Penskie bridled. "Don't think I can deal with him right now."

"He's gonna have my ass fried if I let you go. You're to stay put and report to the man."

Stan's telephone rang. It was Zbigniew Penskie. Ruth Sagowitz had found him. The kindly old woman was out of her wits worrying about him. It was cruel of Stan to scare her so, his father said. Zbigniew was in Poland, having landed this morning. A slight delay, a stopover in London extended to two days. Nothing to worry about. He wouldn't mind seeing Stan. Of course, he would understand if the assistant legal attaché of the American Embassy was too busy . . . No? That was wonderful! It was too long since they had seen each other.

Stan agreed to meet Zbigniew in the evening. He was dumbstruck. The call was so unexpected he barely spoke a word. He was anxious and relieved at the same time. And he knew what he had to do.

"Anything wrong?"

"Banks has some news," he lied, and instantly scolded himself. It was wrong. Nothing in his friend's behavior or in anything he said had called for such deceit.

"Yeah." Powell sighed. "A terrible tragedy. The CIA's on alert, making half the embassy staff jumpy, too."

"What are you talking about?"

"The inspector general," Powell answered, and shot Penskie a quizzical look. "Murdered last night. His wife too . . ."

"Jesus!"

"Yep, cops are considering road rage, but I think we can rule it out. Oh, and that reminds me . . ." Powell sifted through papers on his desk. "Ah, here it is."

Penskie glanced at the single page. It was a printout of Mollie Banks's personnel file from the Central Intelligence Agency.

"Miss Banks worked for the ops department before she was assigned to the inspector general's. Had to pull some strings to get this," Powell added. "She doesn't know yet?"

Stan shook his head.

He waited.

"Okay," Powell said finally. "But have your cell phone and stay in touch. Lemme know what she's got."

His concerned eyes followed Stan to the door.

Chapter Sixteen

If rush-hour city driving in Warsaw was considered nerve-racking, out-of-town travel in Poland was for only the most determined and daring. With a poor network of motorways and only a handful of double-lane highways, Polish motorists were confined to single-lane roads—one narrow lane in each direction for travels between most major cities. These roads posted maximum speeds of up to ninety kilometers per hour, with drastic speed reductions in urban zones. The virtual nonexistence of bypasses meant a winding, tedious, and tiring drive through plentiful villages and small towns. Most drivers, however, wired from the excitement of near-misses during overtakes (where one was expected to give way to more aggressive drivers, whether coming from behind or ahead, by means of driving on the shoulder, while the car overtaking went up the middle), seldom slowed down in the urban areas. These areas were favorite stakeout spots for speed-checking police cruisers. Neither the police nor dangerous road conditions nor annoying if often unwritten road rules were able to deter more and more drivers from taking to the roads. The excellent, fast, and timely railroad service could not provide the freedom that owning and driving one's own automobile offered. The result was that Polish roads were becoming more congested and increasingly more accident-prone. Placed along some of the most dangerous stretches were sad reminders of how careless driving ended—like a wrecked car, crumpled up like a pack of cigarettes and placed on a platform by the side of the road, beneath it a billboard with a current count of dead and injured at this particular juncture.

Penskie had accelerated to keep pace with the traffic flow—the safest option when the slower-moving cars had the additional danger of constantly being pushed to the often nonexistent shoulder by more aggressive drivers. The E77 was one of the better roads; the route from Warszawa to Kraków to Zakopane was among the most frequented in the country. Still, the drive that would have taken two and a half or three hours in Western countries would be equaled only by breaking speed limits, and most drivers did.

Mollie Banks insisted on coming along after hearing about the NSA's communications intercept. The death of the inspector general was devastating. There was no trace of doubt in her mind that it was a direct result of the investigation, and as dreadful as it was, it proved the investigation had hit the spot. Somewhere, somehow, they had stepped on the Fifth Internationale's toes. The trouble was, she did not know where or how. The logical conclusion would have been the shooting at the Economic Development and Cooperation Agency's offices, and the subsequent death of Daniel Loomis, the CIA's station chief. Terrence Jacobek had found out about her and notified his accomplices in Washington. It was a reasonable assumption, until Penskie mentioned her personnel file. She appeared baffled as she held the single page in her hand.

"How did you get this?"

"Ed got it. You checked out."

"But *how* did he get it?"

"What do you mean?" Penskie sensed her anxiety.

"You can't just *get* it. This is so classified not even the director of operations has access to it."

"He said he had to pull some strings," Stan answered bewilderedly.

"There are only two ways of getting hold of this file—the inspector general or the DCI. Both need to consent to any such request. I doubt it would have been granted to the FBI, and most certainly not to some legal attaché way overseas. No offense, Stan, but I am working on the most covert operation ever undertaken by the Company." She paused and looked into his face. "How did Powell get this?"

"I don't think I like where you're going with this," he answered angrily.

The implication was unsettling. It was true he had had a hunch, an unspecified feeling that something was wrong when he talked to Ed Powell, but he reconciled it in his mind as having something to do with his personal life. If asked how, he would not have known. A hunch, a gut feeling, was an indispensable tool in the mind of investigators the world over.

He did not answer. He needed to think. In a few short hours he would see his father. He feared what he might find out. He did not want to drag his family into something that might be entirely unrelated. Margaret's fiancé and his friend were killed, but Zbigniew Penskie could not have been associated. Stan wanted to believe it, and the conversation with his father occupied his entire mind.

His cellular telephone rang. He pressed the green key and listened.

There was no answer.

Annoyed, he shoved the phone back into his breast pocket.

Highway E77 cut through the monotonous landscape of Mazovia. Mollie Banks sat quietly, her eyes wandering over the passing scenery. It was a moist and dark day, early evening quickly approaching. The lights of the oncoming traffic were inducing sleep. She was tired, but sleep was not coming. Her mind was active. The inspector general was dead. The investigation was abruptly halted as it started to gain momentum. It left her without guidance or backup. Whatever she did from now on would be up to her. She was the sole interpreter of the evidence and leads, and as the inspector's successor was responsible for a handful of other investigators working under deep cover, no doubt feeling just as scared and abandoned as she did. She would have to assume command. The investigation must continue. It was more imperative then ever. She would have to contact the others.

Banks powered on the notebook. Her resources were limited, but they included dial-in numbers to servers that housed what was left of the resources pertaining to the investigation. One of the emergency procedures consisted of a series of messages posted to certain newsgroups. They were innocent in nature and unrelated to the inspector general's office, the Central Intelligence Agency, or any other government department. As a precaution the messages were coded with simple yet effective ciphers. Chances that such a message would be intercepted were next to nil. It would have to have been specifically targeted. That would have meant betrayal. Each member of the team was supposed to check the newsgroups on a regular basis. Where the facilities existed it was possible to receive the forwarded message via cellular phone. Most of the members opted for this alternative, as it provided almost instant communication. No direct member-to-member contact was permitted.

She had used the embassy cellular telephone to dial in to the server. Normally the call would have been relayed through a series of other servers before reaching the desired one, but that did not happen this time. The connection could not be established. The server was not responding. She checked the signal strength. It was high. The communication had been severed. The unthinkable had happened.

"You must retrace every step you made in the last twenty-four hours. It can't be a coincidence. Your investigation has been exposed. Find out what the broken link is." Penskie's eyes showed worry, but his voice was calm.

"I have to contact my team. Warn them somehow." She was not panicking, but a strong concern was evident in her voice.

"Can you contact the office?"

"Out of the question. Every log-in is monitored."

"You can use my father's computer as soon as we get to Kraków. You must have other means of contacting them."

"This was not supposed to happen. It was supposed to be foolproof." Her voice trembled. She had to regain her calm. She fell quiet.

"Yes, there are other means," she spoke again after a while. "Come to think of it . . . this is all so parallel it's scary," she added shortly.

"What?"

"Our communications. The way it works. It's the same for every intelligence agency out there, I suppose, as it is the same for the Fifth Internationale."

"How do you mean?"

"For example, the bottom never contacts the top directly. There are emergency procedures, of course, but the fact is, the lower ranks have no idea where the orders come from."

"But they do receive their orders and the means to carry them out." It was a statement.

"Simple but effective ways, some of them good old tested relics from the Cold War. One man we caught was using a submersible device that he would toss in the water. The device would surface after a while and send burst messages through a satellite, then drown when finished. Untraceable accounts, dead drops that change each time, the location given only after the delivery takes place, inconspicuous messages in newspaper classifieds, Web sites with password-protected entries, e-mail messages imitating spam, text embedded in digital images, Internet guestbooks, newsgroups . . . the possibilities are endless."

"There is a task force that monitors the Internet communications. Why not use them to find the Fifth?"

"Stan, we only started taking it seriously a few weeks ago. The possibility of the Fifth Internationale's existence was not even considered as an option. It was determined years ago, when rumors first started to spread through the community, that no such thing could exist. Of course, the Company played a key role in denouncing these rumors.

We know it now, but to this day we still have no concrete evidence that such an organization exists. Some stalled and misdirected investigations, a few arrests and murders—nothing that hasn't happened in the past, or didn't happen on a regular basis."

"You have your proof. The inspector general's death. Your servers . . ."

"It's not proof, Stan. It's a . . ." She paused abruptly.

"What is it?" Penskie sensed rather than saw that she picked up the notebook and inspected it. It was almost dark now; a slim line of light above the horizon where the sun had set was the only reminder of the daylight.

Banks turned on the ceiling light and continued checking the computer. "Who takes care of your notebooks?"

"Why?"

"Have you checked it for spyware? Does the embassy monitor your usage of these machines?"

He did not know.

"God! I should have checked it." She gasped.

"Are you saying someone was monitoring your online activity through the notebook?" Stan asked incredulously.

"Through software," she corrected, "and I think you know it's not just anyone."

"Now look." He lost control for a split second, and the car veered off to the side. "Ed and I are friends! We have worked together for years."

They had just passed the last cluster of houses of the small town of Węgrzce. Stan drove behind an unusually slow-moving Skoda van with Slovak plates, and he had just overtaken it when he noticed the red flashing-light of a traffic police officer on the side of the road. He cursed but slowed down and pulled over.

The policeman approached the door; another one came to the passenger side, a flashlight in his hand.

"Dobry wieczór," said the first policeman as he saluted.

"Dobry wieczór, Officer. We're diplomats with the American Embassy. How can we help you?" Penskie pulled out his flip wallet and held his diplomatic accreditation so the officer could verify it. Oddly, the policeman was more interested in the passenger than the documents. His gaze cut through the poorly lit car interior like a knife.

The other policeman approached the rear of the SUV and scanned the inside of the vehicle, a powerful flashlight penetrating every dark nook and cranny.

"You are still in the urban zone." The policeman pointed at a white road sign with the name of the town, located some twenty meters ahead and glowing in the car's headlights. "You've broken the maximum allowable speed limit and overtaken another car where it's prohibited. That continuous line is there for a reason." He gestured toward the direction Penskie came from. "I'm sure the rules are similar in America and in many other parts of the world; would you agree with me?"

It was not the rude treatment most policemen exercised. It was not the first time Penskie was pulled over, so it came as a surprise; Polish traffic police, short of the Russian police force, the GUI, were among the rudest he had ever encountered. What also drew his attention was the peculiar way in which the policeman moved the flashlight to his left hand, his right resting on the holster while he scanned the road in front and behind. At the same time a movement on the right side of the car registered in Penskie's peripheral vision.

"Oh, my God!" Banks cried out with astonishment, and

watched as her empty McDonald's paper coffee cup flew off the dashboard and landed on her lap. Her cry was lost in the strenuous revving of the engine. Penskie had a habit of stopping the manual-transmission car in first gear. At the first sign of irregularity in the policeman's behavior he released the brake and floored the accelerator. The car jump-started but quickly fell into a spin on the wet pavement and skidded into the oncoming-traffic lane. The driver of the oncoming car flashed his high beams as Penskie tried to regain control of the vehicle. He pulled back into the right lane just in time to avoid collision.

The first bullet hit the back window as soon as he evened out his vehicle. He lowered his head, fingers clasping the steering wheel. Banks tried to reach for her small knapsack and pull out her Walther .38, but the continuous acceleration kept pressing her into the seat. She had managed to reach the knapsack when Penskie switched to second gear. The second bullet hit the tire, and Penskie struggled to keep the SUV from veering off into the oncoming lane. He compensated by pulling the steering wheel to his right, causing the car to skid.

The roadside ditch was shallow enough for Penskie to drive out of it, especially in four-wheel drive, but standing water and a ruptured tire made it an insurmountable obstacle. Penskie realized he would not be able to drive out of it, and he turned off the ignition. He got out of the vehicle and peered down the road from behind the trunk. Cars were whizzing by, but none slowed down to offer help. In the headlights he could make out two silhouettes running along the side of the road in his direction, not more than fifty meters away.

He heard Mollie's feet tap in the water behind him. He rushed back around to the front of the car.

"Hurry back this way!" he yelled out. In the dim light of the car's interior lights he saw Banks point her Walther and fire three shots at the front passenger seat. He understood that she had destroyed the notebook. He slammed the door shut and pulled her out of the ditch and into an open field. They ran, stooped, in the direction of the police cruiser. Wet grass, fallen leaves, and traffic muffled their steps as they ran in the dark, and dense thornbushes and short trees concealed them from the road.

Through the branches they could make out two silhouettes advancing stealthily toward the SUV. The only thing separating Banks and Penskie from the killers was bushes about six feet high. The men had stopped and exchanged a few words. One of them started for the bushes in an obvious attempt to encircle the Americans. Banks had stooped, her weapon pointed at the approaching man. A sudden screech of tires was followed by two shots. A muffled cry indicated that one of the policemen had been wounded; the one who tried to cross the bushes had returned fire.

Startled, Penskie pulled Banks to him firmly and said into her ear, "The cruiser."

He did not think about the arrival of another automobile and the shots. Was it an ally? He did not care. The primary objective was to get away. With the policeman shouting words he could not make out and engaged in an exchange of fire, he hoped to reach the cruiser and drive off to safety. It could not be more than another fifteen meters, he thought. It was a risk, but Penskie was almost certain there were only those two officers. They always traveled in pairs. But then again, those were not ordinary cops. . . .

The soil was firm under their feet now. He could not hear Banks's steps or hear her breath, but he felt her presence behind him. The police *Polonez* stood on the side of a narrow dirt road facing the highway. Penskie approached the car cautiously. There was no one inside. He opened the door. The keys were in the ignition, as he had hoped. He started the car as Mollie buckled up in the passenger seat.

The wheels spun and the *Polonez* lurched forward. Penskie joined the traffic heading north, back in the direction he came from.

He sighed with relief. They were safe. For now . . .

Chapter Seventeen

"I don't understand how you could have failed."

"The man must be on the edge. He sees conspiracy and treason in every step he takes. I don't see any other reason for him to suspect that my men were not real cops and to anticipate their intentions. They were professionals."

"Perhaps it was the woman. Could she have recognized them?"

"Impossible."

"But she got away. She's alive."

"Alpha is watching the FBI man. Sasha, his protection, arrived and interfered in time to stop my men from completing the assignment."

"Of course Alpha is watching the American! He's leading him in. How could you not have anticipated that?"

The man had no answers. His orders were to kill the woman. He had failed. What more could he say? He sat in his car, staring through the windshield into the headlights of the passing cars. The silence on the other side of the call was paralyzing.

"Her investigation—" he started.

"It's not her I worry about, nor the CIA, FBI, or the Martians. We had a plan. It hasn't been followed through. As insignificant as they are, when little things start to fail, you lose the ability to control the situation on all fronts. This woman was supposed to die. Penskie was to meet with Alpha—alone—to thwart Alpha's plans. Having the woman at his side will make him weaker and cloud his perception. He may not be able to stand up to—"

"If I may, sir," the man in the car interjected softly, but firmly. "Perhaps it's not a bad idea . . . Sparing the woman may prove advantageous when he fails to stop Alpha."

A moment's pause on the line made him regret the interruption.

"How do you mean?"

"His psychological profile, as well as ample observation, suggests that he might feel a certain attachment toward the woman. When he finds out how utterly and completely he has been betrayed and abandoned, he will turn toward her. They will grow closer. He won't want to lose her. It will make him vulnerable. Reaching him will be that much easier."

"What about his father? The sister?"

"Threatening the life of his father may not be as effective. There is too much resentment. He has lived on the edge of society; his mind and heart have roughened; he's been lied to. The sister personifies innocence. Killing her will either shut him down into a cocoon or turn him into a bloodthirsty avenger; in either case he will become useless. I suggest we wait. He *will* turn to the woman. It's only natural."

Silence. The leader was considering the thought. His American deputy had mentioned something to that effect, but he had discarded it—or did he misinterpret his deputy's intentions? He really needed to rest. He had not slept in three days. The weeks of preparations and enormous tension were taking their toll on his aging body. His mind was clouded. It made him angry. He had to remain in control. Tomorrow. He had been counting down days and hours, the most important hours in his life, hours that might prove catastrophic for him, his organization, and the world.

The leader agreed.

It wasn't a bad idea, thought the man in the car. He had come up with it ad hoc, in a desperate attempt to save his own life, but he had come up with a gem. It was true; he had studied Stan Penskie to the smallest detail. It was only natural that the legal attaché would turn to the woman when he found out. If the woman had come into the picture sooner it would have made it easier; they would have grown more attached. Still, he was almost convinced it would work. Almost, because the next move belonged to Alpha, and if Alpha played his cards right, he, Marcin Twardoch, would be a dead man. Nothing would stop his leader from ripping his heart out and feeding it to his alligators. He shivered. Rumors circulated about the leader being insane. Perhaps they were planted on purpose, like the information that it was his unbalanced leadership that had caused the rift in the organization. The leader had lost touch with reality, living a dream in dreamlike surroundings. His private zoo was the latest on the list, the fancy of a man gone mad. The leader should step down, the rumors had said, but no one dared take any action.

Not until Alpha decided to take over.

The man sighed. Alpha, the leader, it did not make any difference to him. He would be just as devoted to Alpha as he was to the leader. He served the organization. His job was to follow the leader's orders, sane or not.

"They were waiting for us!" Penskie said angrily. In Węgrzce he had left Highway E77 and drove into the night along the narrow, single-lane roads heading west and south. There was no saying when, if at all, a search for the police cruiser would commence. The longer he drove the more dangerous it became. Kraków was not more than fifteen kilometers away. The small road he decided to take wound its way through tiny hamlets and would add another five, perhaps ten kilometers. The chances of running into patrol cars were slim on such roads. What worried him were roadblocks around Kraków. Naturally none of it mattered if *those* cops were not cops at all, which meant a deadly strike could come from any direction, without his ever seeing it come.

"Who knew about your trip?" Mollie Banks asked.

"I haven't told anyone."

"Powell?"

"No! I made the decision on a whim." It was partially true. It was a last minute decision, but not telling Powell was his choice. He remembered the hunch and it made him angry.

"Could the hotel have been bugged?" he asked quickly to shake off the unpleasant thought.

"Or the car? The notebook? And who were those people who showed up at the last minute?"

He did not answer. In the absurd web of events that led

to his pursuit of an imaginary organization that was the Fifth Internationale, with quite real corpses and shootings, CIA officers killing FBI agents, and coverups that reached Washington, a small tracking device planted in the notebook was practically a given. Every officially registered car from the diplomatic pool was equipped with a tracking device; he recalled those who advocated the removal of these devices arguing their potential harm—anyone with the right equipment could tap into the frequency and monitor the embassy staff's whereabouts. If someone wanted to find him, they had it made easy. He shook his head. The woman had done it: The seed of mistrust had taken root. Ed Powell kept coming to mind.

He decided to abandon the car a fair distance from his father's home. He fooled himself into thinking that his destination was unknown to those who followed him. Even if it were, he was not going to make it any easier. He drove through small villages to Mydlniki, making circles to make sure he was not followed, and continued on to Krowodrza, a suburban district of Kraków. There he abandoned the car in front of a high-rise student dormitory and continued on foot.

He was very anxious and worried. Zbigniew was not answering his telephone. After the incident on the highway he kept trying to warn his father. Chances were that whoever wanted to get through to him might want to harm his father too. He should not have allowed it to go this far. He should have known better than to drive to Kraków; it was a giveaway! He had put his father in grave danger!

Mollie Banks was keeping pace.

The legal attaché was racing.

Not a word was spoken.

Zbigniew Penskie's house stood in the hilly Wola Justowska, less than three kilometers away from the student dormitory. Wola was a residential quarter, with spacious villas built after World War I. It was located on the edge of a large wooded park where residents of the city flocked on weekends in search of greenery, fresh air, and peace. From Ulica Piastowska, Penskie could make out the lights of the hotel by the Kopiec Kościuszki, a thirty-four-meter mound raised by the residents of Kraków in memory of their great hero, Tadeusz Kościuszko, who had also distinguished himself in the American War of Independence.

Penskie picked up his pace, his anxiety rising with every step that brought him closer—closer to the truth. He did not want to admit to himself that it was not only his concern for his father, but also the answers the old man held that lured Stan to his ancestral home. Answers that led to perhaps the biggest threat to the United States since thousands of nukes had awaited the push of the red button within arm's reach of the succession of deranged old rulers of the Kremlin. He scrutinized every car as they climbed the steep and narrow street Zbigniew's house stood on. He recalled times when three, maybe four cars were all there would be. Now there was a long line of them parked along the curb all the way to the entrance to the park.

Mollie and Stan walked casually up the street, a couple on a romantic walk to the hotel or in search of privacy in the quiet park. At the top of the street, satisfied as to the lack of surveillance, Penskie led Mollie to a three-story house surrounded by a wrought-iron fence.

The gate opened smoothly and quietly. The door to the house was unlocked. Penskie took out his Glock and unlatched the safety. A dimly lit hallway led directly to a spacious living room. He did not know why he did not call out to his father or otherwise announce his arrival. He did not know why he tiptoed either.

Something was wrong.

His anxiety spread to Mollie Banks. There was something about the house that made her feel uneasy to a point that it sent shivers down her spine. The wooden floor creaked with every step, and there was a strange smell in the air. Barely audible sounds of sacred music were pouring in from an indistinguishable direction. Sort of like an old church somewhere in the countryside, she realized. Candles, wood polish, scents, and . . . lack of fresh air! That was it. She guessed the house stood empty for most part of the year, and that discovery put her at ease. She unzipped her coat.

The only source of light in the living room was a tall floor lamp with a dark shade. Penskie could make out a figure in the shade of a deep comforter in front of the fireplace. The fire was dying, shooting faint, blistering flashes of light. In one such flash Penskie recognized his father. Zbigniew Penskie's head was thrown back, his mouth open, and his eyes . . . Those eyes! Open, unfocused, and faraway eyes that terrified Stan. The eyes of a dead man.

Chapter Eighteen

Penskie rushed to his father.

"*Tato!* Dad!" he cried out, trying for the carotid artery.

"What? What is it?" The old man woke up, his voice startled, eyes alert.

With the lamp directly behind him, Stan's face was lost in the shadows. "Who is it?" Zbigniew asked, sudden fear in his voice.

Penskie knelt by the comforter.

"It's me, Stanisław," he gasped out.

"Staś?" Father raised his eyebrows. "What's wrong, son?"

Stan stood up, breathing heavily, the anger in his eyes giving way to relief. He realized Zbigniew's eyes were fixed on his Glock. Penskie holstered it.

"Never knew you slept that way, with your eyes wide open," he said with reproach.

"Learned it during my years in office. The things you

pick up in politics—those dragging debates, senseless quarrels that put you to sleep . . ." The comment did not bring a smile to his son's face, as Zbigniew had hoped. He stood up, his voice composed and succinct. "What's happening, son? Why the weapon?"

"Dad," Penskie started hesitantly, "you have to leave the house."

"What? What's this all about?" Zbigniew sensed someone's presence at the entrance to the living room. He turned around. "Who's there?"

"My name is Mollie Banks, Mr. Penskie." The woman made a step forward.

"An American?" Zbigniew shot an inquiring look to Stan. He walked to the woman and courteously kissed the top of her hand.

"Dad, Mollie's with American intelligence. There's something we're working on together. In fact, it's the reason we're here. I believe you may be in danger."

"I thought you told me this Piastów gang business was over?"

"It's not that; the Piastów affair is over, more or less. This thing goes back to the States, possibly as far back as your term in office."

Zbigniew's face changed. He turned slowly and walked across the room to his liquor cabinet, then took out a bottle of Starka but did not open it. Holding the bottle in his hands, he spoke barely audibly and without turning to face his son. "They finally reached you, did they?"

"What?"

"They said they would if . . ." Zbigniew turned abruptly and looked into his son's eyes. "But it's not what it looks like, Stan! Whatever they said, it's not true!"

Stan stared at him numbly. This was not right. It was not what he had expected, what he had hoped for. . . .

"What in God's name are you talking about?"

Zbigniew appeared surprised. He glanced from Stan to Mollie.

"Which arm of the intelligence are you with, Miss . . . Jones, was it?"

"Banks. I'm not exactly with the intelligence, sir."

"Ah, who with then, if you don't mind my asking?"

"Inspector general's office."

"Ah, Jonathan 'the Grizzly' Berr," Zbigniew said, audible relief in his voice.

Neither Mollie nor Stan acknowledged the familiarity the former national security adviser had shown. Something was wrong. The tension was evident in their postures. They stood awaiting something inevitable, not knowing what it would be.

Zbigniew looked at Mollie.

"How did you find out?"

The question startled Penskie. He glanced at Banks. The woman stood expressionless, at ease, and did not return his look.

Seconds that felt like an eternity later, Mollie approached the small letter desk in between two cathedral windows and sat on a wooden chair.

"We've broken through the ring. People talked."

Zbigniew listened intensely, weighing the answer in his mind. "Yes, I suppose I wouldn't divulge the secrets of the investigation either." He shrugged and turned to his liquor cabinet, where he poured three small glasses of Starka. He offered one to Mollie. "You're soaking wet, Miss—"

"Dad!" Stan cut in impatiently.

"I want you to understand it wasn't a matter of choice." Zbigniew raised his arm in a gesture that meant, *Let me finish.* He handed the remaining glass to Stan, who accepted it mechanically, without planning to drink it. "When your mother fell ill shortly after our arrival in America, we didn't know what to do. We had no money, no insurance, didn't know anyone, and had nowhere to get help from. Things were looking so grim we even contemplated going back to Poland. When help was offered, we didn't care where it came from. We would have worshiped the devil himself, if need be. All that mattered was the operation that saved your mother's life. Our benefactors even offered to pay for the convalescence, years of prescription drugs, hormonal patches, the chemotherapy. . . ." Zbigniew took a deep breath and nodded his head as if to reassure himself of his decision. "It didn't matter where the money came from."

"What are you saying, Dad?"

"You and your sister were too young to understand at the time."

"I remember! The Polish-American Congress offered money through collections and from its Freedom Fighters Fund."

Zbigniew nodded.

"When your mother recuperated I went to thank our benefactors. The Congress had no record of any financial or other support extended toward our family. I kept insisting, but it didn't accomplish anything. I figured it was just a big mess within the organization, so I thought I'd repay by joining in and working for the cause. They helped me get tenure, which later led to the White House. That's when they called in my favors."

"They?"

"A man came in with the receipts I signed and demanded cooperation. They said I was an investment. . . ." Zbigniew looked up into Stan's eyes. "What was I supposed to do? What could I do?" he cried out.

Stan pivoted around. It could not be true! His father a traitor? Insane! Impossible! An adviser to the president of the United States receiving paychecks from . . . from whom? The communists? He envisioned Zbigniew in the early eighties, in their cramped apartment in the Village, the hardships the man had had to go through, not being able to contact, let alone see his own mother, who lived alone in Kraków, for fear of reprisals. The years in exile, away from his homeland, family, things familiar, his loss of cultural identity, having to abandon values he fought for with such devotion and sacrifice . . . No, Zbigniew Penskie could not have been a traitor!

"Who was it?" Stan asked icily. Something had triggered his memory.

"What?"

"The man who came to you."

"The man . . . I didn't know then; what did it matter?"

"Names! Who was your case officer? Who handled you?"

"Handled? Oh, it was always the same person."

"Oh, my God! I can't believe I'm hearing this!" Stan was pacing around the room. *Jesus! Anything but this! Not now!*

"Stan, hear me out. It's not what it looks like—"

"What the hell is it supposed to look like? My father, the hero of two continents, a traitor!"

"Do you really see me as a traitor?" Zbigniew was taken aback. "Sometimes sacrifices must be made for the bigger cause, and Stanisław, what's more important than yours and your forefathers' homeland, the country your ancestors gave their lives for, so that you, your sister, and your children could live with dignity and pride?"

"You must be turning senile; this melodramatic bullshit has no effect on me. Working for *Służba Bezpieczeństwa* to demonstrate your love of the country? Give me a break!"

"For *Służba Bezpieczeństwa?*" Zbigniew's jaw dropped in astonishment.

"That's no way of talking to your father, Stanisław!"

The voice had startled all three of them. Zbigniew remained motionless, his eyes unexpressive and fixed on the lone figure standing in the shadows.

Stan's initial shock turned into anger; his face reddened.

"You!" he roared.

Banks, noticing the reaction of the legal attaché, withdrew her Walther .38 in one swift move, unnoticed by anyone in the room.

Standing in the doorway was the deputy director of the *Urząd Ochrony Państwa.*

Chapter Nineteen

Pawel Urbaniak was at ease, leaning nonchalantly against the door frame. He looked as if he had been inside for a while; like someone who was no stranger to the place. He wore a casual wool jacket and a light blue shirt unbuttoned at the collar. He had no coat. His clothes were dry and he appeared warm, unlike someone just coming in straight from the cold winter evening.

Penskie stood speechless. The appearance was so sudden and came at such a tense moment that he had not moved. Strangely, though, his anxiety began to subside. Urbaniak's presence shifted his attention away from Zbigniew, and his sinking anger centered on the UOP officer.

"Stanisław, Stanisław . . . I tried to appeal to your patriotism, but apparently it had no effect on you. The way you treat your father . . . I suppose it's not entirely your fault. It's the lack of family values and cultural ties that America bestowed on you." Urbaniak pounded his chest with a fist. "You've become hollow inside. . . . It's a terrible shame, because, as I told you, your country needs you."

"My country? Is it the same country that revoked my parents' citizenship and put them through years of hardship? You are a damned fool, Urbaniak!"

"Tsk, tsk . . . You don't seem to fully appreciate the magnitude of the matter you are dealing with. You're probably thinking, A bunch of old apparatchiks and their hound dogs, the SB, who had a hold over the nation are now racking up the profits and living it up. But, think bigger; think country and homeland, freedom and independence. . . ."

"You're mumbling. The country you served has changed; the freedom you advocated was only for the chosen. You are living in a dream, a dangerous dream."

"Is that what you told him?" Urbaniak looked at Zbigniew. "Zibi, Zibi . . . after all we've been through together! That was uncalled-for, old friend." Urbaniak pushed himself off the door frame and walked over toward the fireplace. He stopped and turned around. "Well, I suppose it would've been hard to explain to a young boy what his father *really* did."

Zbigniew closed his eyes. He shrugged and waved his arm in a gesture that meant, *Go on with it; finish it off.*

"Very well," Urbaniak carried on. "Correct me if I drift off the topic . . . all those years can cloud one's memory." He turned to the woman. "Do you mind, Miss Banks?"

She glanced at Stan, who did not return her look, too absorbed with the shocking events. After a few moments of hesitation she lowered her weapon and holstered it.

"Thank you." Urbaniak bowed his head slightly. He looked back at Stan and started pacing back and forth in front of the fireplace. "Your father wasn't exactly an innocent victim of muddled turns of history, Agent Penskie. To the contrary, he was . . . how do you say it in America . . . a major player. In fact, were it not for your father and others like him, Poland might have wrestled with adversities similar to those of some of our neighbors to the east and south." Urbaniak stopped abruptly and stared at Zbigniew. "Isn't it so?" Something in the shape of a smile showed in the old man's eyes. Urbaniak looked back at Stan. "Yes, despite a certain aura of celebrity you can call your father a nameless hero, whose true accomplishments will never see the light of day, like those of so many others in our line of business."

"Your line of business? Are you involved in treachery as well, the fastest-developing profession of all time?"

"Don't be too modest with yourself. Think bigger. Try state, and indeed global security, my hot-tempered friend," Urbaniak said angrily. "As far as national security is concerned, there are no proscribed activities. Whether under the communist or any other rule, the national interests must be guarded and fought for."

"You're kidding me, right? Whose national interests did you fight for in the eighties? Moscow's?"

Urbaniak ignored the insinuation. "What Zbigniew, your father, did, he did in the name of the country, whether you believe it or not."

"Spare me the crap!"

"Great catastrophes, like martial law in Poland, had proven to be among the best opportunities for intelligence penetration. People migrate, flee, and seek asylum by the thousands. Placing one's own operatives among them is like sowing grain. Whoosh . . . whoosh . . ." Urbaniak made a wide gesture.

Penskie's eyes shifted back and forth between Urbaniak and Zbigniew. His father a plant from the start! Preposterous! Yet here he was sitting in a chair amidst all these allegations, his eyes focused on an unspecified area of the wall, a quiet, resigned old man, with a former officer of *Służba Bezpieczeństwa* in his living room. All these years his father and mentor, the one who encouraged Stan to join the Bureau, and later to accept the post in Warsaw "to clean up the country of all the scum, to help build a better place, one that could proudly be called a part of Europe," his father was an asset for the hated *Służba Bezpieczeństwa*—and, with the later shift of power, also the UOPs?

"Dad?"

Zbigniew looked up, the expression on his face obscured by the dim light of the lamp. "Let him finish, Stan."

"I'll spare you the details, as you so politely requested," Urbaniak continued. "Suffice it to say that Glasnost and Perestroika marked an end to values such as patriotism and devotion to idealism and gave room to pursuance of one's own interests and downright treason. Yes, that was one of the greatest letdowns in the history of ideology. The number of people who betrayed, dropped out, or were forced out of the ranks was unprecedented. Those who had the presence of mind were able to foresee the future. They took actions that later led to the creation of what is sometimes referred to as the *Piąta Międzynarodówka,* the Fifth Internationale.

"When the Soviets were crumbling into pieces, the arms race slowing and the nuclear confrontation risk diminishing, the world took a deep breath and sighed in relief. Soon, however, it became evident that there was an entity capable of posing an enormous threat not only to our country but also to the world at large. Despite the reorganization of the Eastern intelligence and security agencies, the famous *lustracja,* the old networks continued their existence and they flourished better than ever, in part thanks to the lack of accountability and boundaries drawn by governmental entities. They were self-governed and self-financed, very well financed. . . . And they were driven by a more powerful goal, one stronger than an ideological allegiance to their political leaders: self-preservation. A dangerous fiber in creature and man alike, but catastrophic in an entity with the power of the *Międzynarodówka,* and with its influence on various militant and terrorist organizations."

"Where is this leading to?" Stan asked impatiently.

"You have to realize there were people on both sides who longed for a stop to this insanity. It wasn't just America and its allies who were afraid of the captivity and restrictions, both national and individual, that communism represented. In its early stages the Fifth looked like a new transnational body created by our friends in Moscow in order to strengthen the ties within the bloc, a countermeasure to Mikhail's reforms. The thought that it could be a new and independent formation was never considered. And because of that misconception, first contact was initiated. Forward thinkers on this side of the Iron Curtain sat down with the Americans, the British, and the rest. The threat was so real, and the resources needed to fight this new force were so great, that there was literally no one left in the intelligence services to foresee the total collapse of the system."

During the speech Urbaniak moved behind the lounge chair Zbigniew was sitting in. He stopped there and leaned against the back.

"Your father was never our asset, Stan. To the contrary,

Zbigniew Penskie drew freely on the CIA's resources, from the American financial aid against communism, while freedom-fighting in the ranks of the Solidarity. . . ."

"What about these *helpers* from the Polish-American Congress?" Penskie shot out after a sigh of relief.

"No one hated commies and the whole system more than I did, and no one bestowed more effort to fighting it than I, Stanisław." Zbigniew shifted in his chair. "I was prepared to make significant sacrifices for the cause, even if it meant collaboration with foreign intelligence."

"So it was the Central Intelligence that paid the hospital bills?"

Zbigniew did not confirm. He reached into his pocket for a pipe and a bag of tobacco.

"I thought the agency didn't operate in the States at that time?"

"Let's not go into this right now so as not to embarrass your friend." Zbigniew looked at Banks. She stood by the large window in the farthest corner of the room, her face lost in the shadows. "It wasn't just the CIA, though. It was a combination of forces, a joint operation run by various intelligence agencies. When they revealed themselves as the true benefactors, they didn't have to blackmail me in order to get my cooperation, not as an asset, of course—although it could be read either way—but as an adviser on Eastern European affairs. Pawel, Director Urbaniak, is wrong in one respect. I did not work for foreign intelligence while still in Poland. The CIA may have sponsored the Solidarity, but my loyalty was undivided; it belonged to the country." Zbigniew lit a match and brought it to his pipe. He inhaled deeply until the tobacco took the flame. Satisfied, he continued. "Anyway, at that time Gorbachev's reforms released a herd of hungry dogs whose appetites for the riches of the modern world were strong after decades of isolation and poverty in the homeland. They were professionals from all areas and levels of government institutions, including intelligence and counterintelligence, but also universities, science laboratories, various sectors of the cultivated and controlled underground, as well as the limbs of the law—"

"Mafia?"

"Ha, ha . . . Mafia is a kindergarten fraternity in comparison with what became of these scattered and disorganized but skilled minds and muscles—"

"The Fifth Internationale."

Zbigniew took a puff. He savored the taste.

"Why has it been allowed to exist, and grow to its present state?"

"Its true nature had not been discovered till it was too late. For the longest time we thought we were dealing with the old intelligence organizations. The Fifth even retained the old bloc's areas of responsibility, and that fact fooled us the most. The East German members of the Internationale continued to provide a technological base, the Czechs supplied SEMTEX and other weapons, the Poles did the reconnaissance and intelligence gathering, the Bulgarians supplied the killers, and the Russians coordinated the whole thing. No one thought there could be a new Hydra growing on the old carcass. In fact, we still can't be sure it *really* exists."

"What?"

"Well, until people like Urbaniak came forward, we thought the newly created agencies simply took over the old networks, the legacies of their predecessors, and in many instances they did, and nobody on either side was surprised. Friendly nation or not, one doesn't just stop spying. The only countries America doesn't spy on—that is not to say that we don't actively keep ourselves informed on what's happening there—are Canada and Britain. What happens when, say, an American is caught spying in Warsaw or vice versa? It is usually quietly wrapped up. A normal business day resumes. At least it did for a long time after Poland gained independence, even after it joined NATO, and until Urbaniak on this side and our DCI got together and said, 'Why not slow down, your people are becoming too bold.' Wasn't it so?"

"Something to that effect," Urbaniak replied.

"Right. It was then that both sides realized they had no record on any operations that were conducted by their respective agencies. Which meant that somebody out there was using resources and assets that were either frozen, inactive, or simply long discarded by the CIA, the Poles, the Czechs, and so on. Somebody not only had access to this highly classified information but was capable of reactivating and running long-forgotten networks, and quite efficiently too. That's when old fables in the community came back as possibly having a particle of truth in them. The Fifth Internationale, a secret society of former and current covert operatives, could actually exist.

"When we took this approach we realized that if the leads were interpreted as if it did exist, then it grew far beyond a network of intelligence officers and their operatives. It simply could not exist without political endorsement, some form of corporate sponsorship, as well as cooperation from those existing agencies that derived from the communist ones, but it also crossed the ranks of its former enemies."

"Are you telling me the CIA could really be a *part* of the Fifth Internationale?"

"There is no other agency that would want to shake off the oversight of its activities more than Central Intelligence. The Fifth is bound by no rules other than its own survival. Sustainability and growth as well as independence present tempting prospects for any organization or business."

"But there is no concrete evidence that the Company or its officers are working with or for the Fifth." Mollie Banks spoke for the first time.

"The only evidence of the Fifth's existence, if one can classify it as such, is the death of Premier Borysewicz," Urbaniak answered.

"How's that?"

"Borysewicz contacted the Americans after September eleventh with what he called evidence that the Fifth not only exists but is well and thriving all across the world."

"Evidence?"

"Certain names, contacts, internal structures, and the whole terrorist arm of the organization were supposed to be delivered to us as part of the Fifth's database."

"And Borysewicz had this information? The identities and whereabouts of Al Qaeda members?"

"Did he have it? He claimed to have been one of the founding leaders of the Fifth, which, according to him—though earlier also supposed by us—had a working relationship with all of the formerly intelligence-sponsored terrorist networks."

Stan and Mollie's eyes met. This part agreed with what Banks was sent to investigate. The top-secret information release Borysewicz negotiated with the United States through the person of Terrence Jacobek, a CIA officer working under unofficial cover. Negotiation that resulted in bloodshed was indicative of the volatility of the information. The deaths and shootings did not directly point to the Fifth Internationale, but they certainly proved that whatever it was that Borysewicz had to offer created or proved the existence of a split in American intelligence—Loomis's shooting David and staking out Jacobek's apartment, presumably under some false pretenses. Of course, it could be much simpler than that. Daniel Loomis, economic attaché of the embassy, could simply have been a traitor selling his services to the highest bidder. Shooting an FBI officer was not necessarily a sign of belonging to some fabled organization.

"I suppose you wonder why Borysewicz offered this information in the first place?" Urbaniak broke the silence.

Penskie nodded.

"As a result of a power struggle and an imminent takeover within the Fifth," the director answered.

"A power struggle? You make it sound like it's some kind of cabinet shuffle or corporate restructuring."

Urbaniak shrugged his shoulders.

"And you bought it?" Penskie turned to Zbigniew.

"People become traitors for millions of reasons, in some cases for the sheer thrill treachery brings. *Power struggle*—to us these are only words, but to Borysewicz it could've meant the world. He was worth billions. Who knows, maybe it was the money? Perhaps with the loss of his position within the Fifth, and without its resources, he could've lost it all."

"Could have, shmould have. It's all suppositions! Why did he choose the Americans and not the UOP? After all, Borysewicz operated in Poland, was a Polish citizen. . . ."

Penskie exploded. He felt he was continually balancing on the edge of unknown.

Urbaniak blushed and glanced at Zbigniew.

The old man remained unmoved. He continued matter-of-factly, "According to Borysewicz, the UOP is controlled by the Fifth."

"I've also heard that the CIA has control over the Fifth."

"And in a sense it does, but its control is a blackmail of sorts. You see, knowing about the existence of the Fifth Internationale and having its partial database is a powerful tool in skilled hands. The CIA may not have the control, but it is able to exert pressure on the Fifth's decisions and its operations. That's why Borysewicz's offer came directly to the National Security Council."

"How do you know all this?"

"I am on the National Security Council's advisory board. Central Intelligence . . ." Zbigniew halted briefly and looked at Mollie. "Central Intelligence is the reason Borysewicz decided to come forward. The CIA wants complete control over the Fifth, and is closer than ever to achieving this goal."

Penskie sat down on the old couch that stood perpendicular to the lounge chair his father occupied. The statement was staggering, and suddenly, for the first time since this madness began, things actually started to make sense. The Fifth had penetrated the CIA, which in turn had created the EDECA, supposedly a government agency that secretly spun a web around one of the most powerful men in the country, to acquire information that opened the doors to the leadership of the Fifth Internationale. The moment these thoughts crossed his mind Penskie became confused. Did Jacobek acquire that information? Where did he disappear?

The States? Or did he stay in Warsaw? If Borysewicz had been killed Saturday night, after a visit from Jacobek, the alleged killer, then what was the EDECA's exec doing in his apartment on Monday when Ania, the secretary, had called him? The thought had already occurred to Penskie that she might have been calling Loomis, who was scouting Jacobek's apartment, to alert him that someone was on the way. But the CIA station chief had his cellular telephone on him! Penskie shook his head. That was another possibility. The call may have been for either. According to this scenario Jacobek could still be on *their* side. The right side. Whatever the hell that meant. It was all speculation. And it confused Penskie even further. He went back to the original picture: Ania called Jacobek to warn him off, and the fact Jacobek was still in the country would have to mean Borysewicz's database did not switch hands. Could it also have meant that the CIA was battling the rift from within? How else to explain Loomis's role? Furthermore, if Loomis was not with the Fifth, if he did in fact represent the part of the agency that did not give in to the Fifth's lure, then why shoot the legats? And what part did Banks play in all this? Countless thoughts flew through his mind, giving birth to numerous theories, none holding ground as the right one. Penskie realized he was at as much of a loss as ever. He looked at the woman. She did not appear surprised by Zbigniew's revelation, but then again, she was investigating an immense conspiracy within the agency. She must've already come to terms with the vastness of the cancer that was eating it. She was prepared for any scenario.

"We must assume the database is still in Poland." Banks was reading his mind. "Jacobek would not be in the country otherwise."

"Actually, Terrence Jacobek—" Urbaniak started but was interrupted by Stan.

"Did you come up with some sort of strategy? I mean, you weren't going to sit and wait, were you?"

"Understandably, I couldn't have used the intelligence community's resources, which leaves us at a bit of a disadvantage, but it doesn't mean we just sit with our arms crossed."

"How is it understandable? What makes you so certain your agency has been penetrated or is under control of the Fifth? Which, by the way, you said you weren't sure exists at all. And if you know it, then why not stop it?"

"I know what you're thinking: Arrest the traitors and voilà! I assure you if it were only that simple it would not have been an issue. In fact, we were prepared to arrest one of the suspects, perhaps the most significant of them all, but alas, we were too late. He was killed along with the secretary of the Economic Development and Cooperation Agency." Urbaniak bowed his head toward Banks.

"Ania?" she asked in amazement.

"Who was it?" Penskie asked.

Urbaniak took time before he replied. "The director of *Urząd Ochrony Państwa.* We've been watching him for a while. Yesterday Ania was delivered to a safe house, where she was to be interrogated by the director himself. Both were murdered by the director's own security detail." Urbaniak paused and moved closer to the fireplace, facing the room. He sighed and continued. "They are everywhere. We cannot win by rogue confrontation, but we may just succeed with the help of an intelligent, if not cunning, match."

Stan did not respond, but his eyes gave away his attention.

"If we can't reach the Fifth, we should make them come to us," Urbaniak continued.

"How do you propose we do that?"

"What is it the Fifth doesn't want the CIA to get hold of?"

"Their database."

"Precisely. So we make them come to us; we make them believe we've got it. They'll come out."

"But we don't have it, and if they know we don't have it—"

"That may change."

"What are you talking about?"

"We'll come to that in a minute. There is just one more thing we must straighten out before we go on. It's Jacobek."

"Did he sell out to the Fifth Internationale? When? Why?" Banks asked.

"As I was trying to explain to you a little earlier," Urbaniak said, "Jacobek is neither on the Fifth's nor the CIA's side in this conflict. Jacobek is working with us."

"What?"

"Loomis was wholeheartedly devoted to the Fifth. It was one of the leads Borysewicz allowed us to follow in order to convince the National Security Council that the Fifth was real. The reason you didn't know about it"—Zbigniew turned to Banks—"was because Jacobek responds directly to the NSC."

A muted sound could be heard from inside the house, a squeaky sound Penskie recognized instantly as the old stairs to the second floor. This time he was quick to pull out his Glock and approach the door. His back to the wall, handgun at his shoulder, Stan noticed three pairs of eyes staring at him uncomprehendingly. Obviously no one else in the room noticed or heard anything. Zbigniew and Urbaniak appeared at ease. Banks shifted her gaze to the shadows in the hallway outside the living room. Stan could swear her face went pale. He stepped out into the door frame, his Glock in his outstretched arm.

"Stay where you are!" he yelled out.

"No, Stan!" someone cried from behind.

A figure approached the room from the shadows of the hallway. A man in his forties with short hair graying at the temples and an expensive-looking, impeccably fresh suit was all Stan could notice before the man spoke.

"Hello, Mollie."

Chapter Twenty

"Terrence!" Banks came forward, out of the shadows, perplexed. "This *is* a surprise."

"Same here, I assure you." Jacobek appeared relaxed as he casually crossed the room and shook hands with Mollie.

"Come, now, you must've known I was connected with the Company. With the distance you kept all this time . . ." she said more composedly now, her voice lowered.

"Quite, but the inspector general's investigators are not exactly best friends of the ops department. Besides, only now can we speak of our allegiance to the same Company." The words were exchanged quietly, and in an almost conspiratorial whisper.

"There is no allegiance, Terry. I work for the IG now, *not* the Company."

In another part of the room, though only steps away, Penskie watched Jacobek and Banks as they stood face-to-face, speaking quickly as if they were long-lost friends who had to catch up on their life stories.

"All this time you knew about him? And you didn't warn me about Loomis!" Penskie spoke to his father with reproof.

"Never expected you or the legats would get involved."

"I almost got killed, Dad! A friend from the embassy is in a hospital! How's that for involvement?"

"I'm sorry, Stanisław. I really am. I don't know if I could live with myself if anything happened to you because of it. Please forgive me." Zbigniew stood up as he spoke. He approached Stan and stopped two feet away with his arms slightly spread out, a gesture that could have been read as an anticipation of an embrace.

The moment was tense. Everyone in the room froze, watching father and son.

The attention did not escape Penskie. The whole situation was utterly theatrical. It was a combination of the dramatic appearances of the two men and the way the father had approached the son. He could not quite make out his mind as to whether Zbigniew sincerely meant to apologize, or did it solely for the effect. In any case, he could not simply forget what happened. He felt he should have been informed. Sito could still be alive!

"How long have you been involved in it?" Stan asked softly, pretending not to notice his father's eagerness for truce.

"Since after September eleventh, but we didn't get a break till Borysewicz's death. Please do believe that had I known this would endanger you in any way, I would have either asked the director to recall you to Washington or brought you in on it sooner."

"Brought me in sooner? What on Earth does that mean?"

"You knew Stan would be coming to you?" Banks added.

"More to the point, I knew that once Stan got the lead he'd find the connection sooner or later. To make sure it happened sooner rather than later, Director Urbaniak was kind enough to hint at my involvement and to start you off with the idea that the Fifth Internationale exists. Of course, I realize now that this should've been done much earlier."

"Apparently I'm not the only one to have found out about you and the investigation."

"How do you mean?"

"I . . . we have been given a chance at life, Dad. I can't even tell you how many times I've been shot at since yesterday. The last time was not even an hour ago, just outside the city, on the way to you. Had it not been for someone who arrived in time to distract the killers; the exchange of gunfire . . ." The statement hung in the air, throwing Zbigniew and Urbaniak into discomfort. Penskie noticed their reaction. "Was it one of your people?" The question was for the deputy director of the *Urząd Ochrony Państwa.*

Zbigniew Penskie and Urbaniak exchanged quick glances. The director shook his head.

"Dad, I don't think you're safe in here," Stan reminded his father of his earlier concern.

"Nine of my men are outside, watching the house and the surrounding area. Three more are inside. You're in because we let you in. We expected you," Urbaniak said.

"What about Margaret?"

"There's been a violent storm in the mountains. It will be a while before the roads are plowed, but she should be home by tomorrow. There's someone close by to watch over her," Zbigniew replied. "Come, I'd like to show you something," he added.

They all left the room and followed the old man to the basement. A small area was enclosed to contain the furnace; the remaining space had walls finished with cedar paneling; books piled up loose as well as in cardboard boxes and stacked up to the ceiling worked as dividers creating narrow lanes, as in a maze. Old vinyl records filled one whole wall, floor to ceiling. Elsewhere were different family mementos: a baby crib, a rocking horse, boxes labeled as Stanisław's or Margaret's and containing schoolbooks. It was an ordinary basement, similar to any other in the neighborhood. In the laundry room the washing machine stood on a wooden pedestal. Zbigniew reached behind it and unlatched a lock, pushing the machine aside. The pedestal was on a swivel tray bolted to the floor. Beneath it was an opening cut in the concrete floor, perhaps two feet square. Narrow wooden steps led to a small room seven feet high, where walls were lined with metal shelves stacked with electronic equipment, computers, monitors with live pictures, a paper shredder, scanner, printers, and various other machines whose purpose Penskie could not tell. Once everyone had descended to the room there was very little space left to move around, not without having to run into electrical cords or filing cabinets.

"When did you have this done?" Stan asked with astonishment, his eyes wandering from one item to another.

"I had a little cubicle, perhaps a third as big, dug in 1980, when the *Milicja* started knocking on our doors more and more often. It was a small hideout, excavated over a period of some months, when you were at school. Only your mother and I knew about it. We used to keep some *Solidarność* material in here. It was expanded recently to accommodate the needs of the operation—a communication center from which we monitored the EDECA's progress with Borysewicz and kept in touch with our friends."

"Apropos of Borysewicz," Banks said to Jacobek, "what was the connection between him and Norman Bray?"

"The prime minister was a bit of a pessimist, or perhaps a realist, who foresaw that the rift within the Fifth would escalate and in all likelihood would turn into an open battle. He would rather have seen the dissolution of his creation than have it fall under the Company's control. When Norman approached him, as a representative of the government, Borysewicz was ready to hand over the information, the proof of the CIA's involvement and its prior knowledge of the terrorist networks that brought down the World Trade Center and hit the Pentagon. Bray, the poor fella, had absolutely no idea what he was getting himself into."

"He wasn't even briefed?"

"No. He was genuine. He was told only—through government channels, of course—to initiate contact with the president and chairman of some of the largest holdings in Poland. If Borysewicz would've handed the database over to him, I doubt Bray would've known what it really was. Loomis must've sensed something fishy going on and killed the CEO."

"What happened last Saturday?"

"It was the night I was supposed to receive the database, but for some reason Borysewicz wavered, was uncooperative. . . ."

"So you killed him." It was a statement.

"No!" Jacobek cried out. "The man needed more time; he had doubts!"

"Then who did?"

"Loomis, of course."

Penskie told them about the photograph of Dan Loomis with Jacobek and Małpa, and finished coldly, "How can you explain this?"

Zbigniew searched the small desk cluttered with office supplies, filing folders, notepads, computer disks, pens, and myriad other things.

"Was this it?" He produced the photograph Robert Sito had had in Wilanowska Café.

"How did you get it?" Penskie studied the image, Urbaniak and Jacobek peering over his shoulder.

"It's a printout. The image was digitally manipulated. Came to us by e-mail. We presume it was meant to confuse us and possibly set us at odds." Zbigniew shrugged.

Penskie looked at him doubtfully. It was too easy, not convincing enough.

"Looks pretty real, but you can't take it seriously," Jacobek said.

"Who's the man next to Loomis?" Banks asked.

"Małpa, the man who supposedly masterminded the murder of Borysewicz. His men were framed, arrested, and then killed at the precinct," Urbaniak replied.

"What happened to the database? Did Loomis get hold of it?" Banks continued.

"Loomis's role within the Fifth was to make sure the exchange would not take place. We can presume he thought it did happen, hence his presence in my apartment. Assuming that he secured Borysewicz's database—and he must've, since the cops found nothing in the villa—he probably wanted to find out whether I got a copy or not. When there's digital technology involved there are always multiple copies. One can never be sure."

"So where is it? The database Loomis seized."

"Erased? Returned back to the Fifth's headquarters in Nowa Wieś? Who knows?"

"So that's it! Nowa Wieś is the HQ," Penskie said. No one seemed to have thought it strange that he should know about Nowa Wieś. He continued, "Then why bother with this guesswork? Why not raid the estate and seize whatever resources of the organization you want? Surely there are forces in the Polish justice and law enforcement systems that are not corrupted?"

Urbaniak approached the small desk. He found a manila folder and withdrew two typewritten sheets of paper.

"Your father and I have considered forcible action before, but frankly we didn't think the two of us were capable of penetrating the property." He shot a quick glance at the former national security adviser and projected a wide smile. Everyone stared at him in anticipation. "That was a joke. . . . Anyway, the use of external force would not necessarily guarantee success. Before we proceed into that I'd like you to hear something." He glanced at the papers in his hand as he spoke. "The Nowa Wieś castle complex belongs to *Polski Związek Biznesu*, Polish Business Alliance, which contains some of the wealthiest and most influential corporations in the country. The castle is one of the largest in Poland, boasting three hundred and sixty-five rooms, one for each day of the year, apparently. It was badly damaged during a series of wars beginning with the Swedish surge of the seventeenth century and continuing with clashes with the partitioning armies over the next two centuries. During World War Two the castle underwent significant alterations and renovations when Hitler planned to use it as one of his shelters. The walls were reinforced and the already extensive subterranean complex was expanded. Later the retreating Germans caved in and flooded parts of the underground, apparently to destroy and conceal those secrets that could not be evacuated safely in sight of advancing Soviet troops. The castle stood abandoned after the war until it was purchased by *Polski Związek Biznesu* and turned into a museum and a luxurious conference-slash-hotel center for the PZB's important clients and members. The PZB even aspires to host the World Trade Summit in the castle's grounds once Poland joins the European Union."

Urbaniak's monotonous voice glazed through the narration without any intonation or emotion, the cold voice of someone who had been acquainted with the information and presented it only for the benefit of others.

"The PZB is chaired by Tadeusz Balcer, president and chair of numerous holdings ranging from Russian gas and oil distribution, transportation, and communications to art galleries, banking, hotels, and casinos. His fortune was built on one of the first and largest chains of currency-exchange offices that sprang up in the late eighties. Incidentally, he owned these *kantors* jointly with Andrzej Borysewicz. . . ."

The significance of the information did not escape Penskie and Banks, who exchanged glances of understanding.

"To illustrate the wealth of the duo in the early nineties, let me point out that it was the Artico company, owned by the two, that withdrew all the hard currency from their exchange offices to finance the covert purchase of Poland's debt from international creditors, an operation that ended up in a scandal so vast its repercussions languish in the courts of the country to this day. That's not all. Both men and their companies were involved in many of the biggest scandals of the past and present decades: smuggling Jews from the Soviet republics to Israel, arms dealings with Iraq,

Iran, and North Korea through Nicaragua and other banana republics, drug trafficking, money laundering, and so on. Needless to say, none of the charges ever resulted in the two men being convicted. That was mainly because their dealings often balanced on the verge of illegality, taking advantage of the loopholes in the newly resurrected Polish democratic legal system, in accordance with common-law principle, which states, 'What is not forbidden, is allowed.'

"The results of the HUMINT reconnaissance to Nowa Wieś, conducted by a counterterrorist unit of the *Urząd Ochrony Państwa,* revealed a highly sophisticated security system." Urbaniak took a sip of tonic water and turned to the second page of the document. "The castle grounds consist of seven hundred and twenty hectares of densely wooded hills. The entire area is enclosed with a high iron fence topped with closed-circuit video cameras. Penetration revealed additional cameras scattered throughout the terrain, along with infrared, acoustic, and laser trip sensors. Also, around-the-clock sentry patrols crisscross the grounds at varied intervals. Incidentally, these guards are former Special Forces soldiers trained regularly in SpecWar tactics by the officers of various army and ministry of the interior CT units. In the opinion of the four-person recon unit, the only way to raid the castle and to achieve an element of surprise is to send in airborne troops." Urbaniak threw the sheet on the tabletop and leaned back against a metal shelf organizer.

An uncomfortable exchange of looks followed his lecture.

"Well, not your ordinary business club, is it?" Banks broke the long silence.

"Shit, the place is what it was intended to be in the Middle Ages: a fortress!" Jacobek cried out.

"Without special training and equipment, none of us can successfully penetrate the compound, and as much as I'd like to see it I don't think we'll be parachuting ourselves," Urbaniak started, but then realized the joke was already passé, and the grin vanished from his lips. "About the only option with any chance of success is the use of a professional counterterrorist unit; however, it would be a very risky undertaking, given the level of penetration of the UOP by the Fifth."

"The recon team that prepared the report? Can't it be trusted?"

"They were contracted by the PZB to evaluate the level of security in the castle and its grounds. The same unit participates regularly in the training of Balcer's guards. The part of the report that covers the inside of the castle is missing from the *Urząd*'s files. It's as though this part"—Urbaniak shook the two sheets of paper—"was left to deter possible action against the property."

"Perhaps the missing part revealed weaknesses in security."

"True."

"Which would suggest that an infiltration *is* possible."

"Okay, what you're saying is, we're on our own. There is no force in the whole country that can do the job? I don't believe it!" Banks said.

"Without knowing the level of penetration of the country's law enforcement—" Urbaniak started.

"There is GROM," Penskie cut him off.

"We thought about it," said Zbigniew.

"And?"

"First of all," Urbaniak answered, "Balcer's guards are trained by the UOP and occasionally by GROM's officers, too. Second, GROM falls under the ministry of defense's jurisdiction. Quite frankly, I don't think they'd cooperate, based on what little information we have. I mean, what can I tell the minister? 'Sir, please lend me your elite unit, because I think my own agency is penetrated by the biggest hoax in the intelligence world'? Even if they took the Fifth Internationale seriously, they'd need a really good reason to dispatch their troops—which, may I remind you, we don't have. It's more than likely, though, that they'd call for suspension of the *Urząd Ochrony Państwa*, a budgetary rival. No, I'm afraid that's not the way."

"You worry about your damned budget?" Penskie asked incredulously. When no reply followed he shook his head in disbelief. "What the hell does it take to get the crooks in this country?"

"With a recent history of autocracy, our government must be very careful not to make hasty decisions based on unsupported intelligence, suppositions, really. We need strong evidence."

Penskie told the group about the intercepted telephone call and the location of the recipient.

"That's better," Urbaniak responded. "Still, not enough to convince the minister, not without calling a cabinet meeting, and there is no saying whose interests the cabinet members represent. My office is investigating a few individuals."

"Right, gentlemen, if the Poles are of no use, then it leaves only the United States. We must rely on American resources," said Mollie Banks.

"Impossible." Urbaniak pushed away from the shelving unit. "The number of troops necessary for the action is too great to allow them into the country without raising suspicion."

"What about the embassy and the consulate?"

"The embassy has no such resources," Penskie replied. "We can count on the legats' office for tactical support, but as far as manpower goes—"

"I would question Powell's agenda, Stan."

Penskie gazed into Banks's eyes but did not respond.

"What's this about, son?"

Banks replied instead. She told him about her suspicions. It was true that nothing concrete could be laid on the legal attaché, but until proven otherwise she suggested avoiding all contact, not only with Ed Powell, but with the embassy altogether.

Penskie recalled his superior's request to stay in constant communication, and the order to report to the deputy chief of mission.

"I'll have a chat with the secretary of state. The DCM will be off your back," Zbigniew assured his son. "About your office, though. Who knows about your trip to Kraków and this house?"

"Nobody. And I think Powell *can* be trusted. We've worked together for three years. I know the man. He's straight and by the book, but he will stand for the unit's integrity, and the legats are one such unit, isolated in a sea of bureaucrats and pencil pushers. Fieldwork does that to people; it binds them closely together. Besides, keeping him in the dark is not a good idea. You know what happened to me and David, my colleague, who ended up in the hospital."

Zbigniew thought about it. He exchanged glances with Urbaniak and Jacobek, who nodded their heads in agreement. Both of them worked in the field and knew all too well this angle of human bonding. Zbigniew himself had his share of covert fieldwork while with the Solidarity, whether distributing "illegal" materials or organizing rallies and sabotage. Of course, his experience was quite different; Solidarity was always crawling with informants and traitors. The sort of work Stan, Urbaniak, and Jacobek did was closer to combat situations, where things were simpler, and good and evil were clearly defined. In confrontation one had only two choices: Shoot or be shot. The moral fiber of one's colleagues was easier to read and understand, something Zbigniew never experienced personally and had to rely on his partners for. As far as he knew anyone could have been an informant of the *Służba Bezpieczeństwa* back in the eighties, or of the Fifth Internationale today.

"Fine, other options explored, we'll consider Powell," he agreed reluctantly.

"Other options?"

"Yes, there is one thing—a person, rather. It's someone from Balcer's inner circle; someone who does not agree with his vision of the organization's future. He's made contact with us. . . ." Zbigniew raised his arm to quiet his son. "We don't know who it is, except that he appears to be very high-ranking, with full access to Balcer and the command of the Fifth. He's offered to deliver the database to us in exchange for certain prerogatives. I won't go into details right now. Suffice it to say he does not want to be identified; he's afraid of exposure. Apparently, and these are his own words, the Fifth is everywhere. Therefore he won't bring the database to us. We have to come to him."

"How?"

"To the castle."

"But it's impenetrable."

"Maybe, maybe not. The assessment Director Urbaniak

was kind enough to read pertained to penetration from the outside. Is it as hard to succeed from within? The corporate area must be somehow connected to the museum."

Mollie Banks understood.

"When I lived in Poland, one thing that always worked when trying for off-limits areas in museums, art galleries, et cetera, was to play a dumb tourist. You just walked over the ropes to see the item up close or to enter rooms that were closed to visitors. Boldness was the key. When confronted you simply babbled incomprehensibly in your foreign language and at worst were told to withdraw. Most museums have *Wstęp Wzbroniony* or *Nie Dotykać* signs, but what foreigner knows what they mean? I've only rarely seen explanations in other languages."

Zbigniew, Urbaniak, and Jacobek gazed at her uncomprehendingly.

Penskie projected a wide smile. *Brilliant,* he thought. *One may not be able to enter the Fifth's territory forcibly, but with enough luck and cunning, one may just stand a chance. Brilliant and simple.*

Zbigniew cleared his throat.

"That won't be necessary, not to mention how unlikely it is that you should find just such a door that leads to the corporate area. All we have to do is get inside the museum. Our man will find a way to make contact."

Banks and Penskie exchanged glances.

"What's the trouble then?" they asked in unison.

"The trouble is that neither of us can enter the castle without alerting the security, both the state-of-the-art electronic and human."

"Send somebody else."

"This man won't trust anyone, unless . . ." Zbigniew paused and looked at Stan.

"Dad, spell it out."

"Unless it's family, or someone else whose allegiance to us—to me—cannot be doubted."

"Family? Do you mean . . . me?"

"He's asked for you specifically. That is why we had to bring you in."

Chapter Twenty-one

Kraków was not one of those tourist destinations that overwhelmed a traveler, yet it provided a satisfying stroll that left a lasting impression. Its picturesque historic center was one of a handful in the country that did not suffer either complete or extensive damage during World War Two. As a result of this favorable fate the old town's authentic medieval charm, complete with cobblestone streets and topped with a prestigious place on UNESCO's world cultural heritage list, drew countless visitors year-round.

The surrounding countryside was scenic, filled with charming villages, picturesque castle ruins, and captivating scenery. It had long been admired by Poles, who hiked, biked, or jogged in large groups or solo every day of the week, rain or shine, along numerous tourist trails that crisscrossed the region.

The presence of a large university in Kraków with a sizable foreign student population as well as Nowa Wieś's situation near a busy tourist route to the Auschwitz concentration camp, were the reasons why two foreigners who decided to break their journey to see the isolated castle did not raise the staff's attention. The Nowa Wieś museum was one of the finest in the region. Surrounded by limestone upland, the castle stood atop a wooded hill, accessible only by a single-lane paved road that wound its way through dense woodland. Tourists usually hiked an hour and a half from Kraków across the highlands, or mountain-biked, instead of taking the infrequent public transportation. Thanks to the mild climate of the region, the castle and a picnic under its massive structure was a popular destination and pastime even during winter. This year, however, the winter was out of the ordinary; meteorologists noted record low temperatures and snowfalls. Much of Europe experienced weather that was drastically different and unseen in decades. Nowa Wieś was no exception. The hills that surrounded the castle were covered in fresh white snow, and the trees were pressed down under its weight. The municipal roads were barely plowed.

The young couple who had just arrived on foot at the visitors' parking lot, outside the large gate that led to the castle grounds, appeared in awe at the sight of the imposing structure. They gaped at the medieval walls encrusted with coats of arms of former owners, and snapped photographs with their cheap disposable point-and-shoot camera, ill chosen by the unprepared tourists, who did not anticipate the wealth of subjects worth photographing on their European vacation.

A plowed path led from the parking lot to the castle's main gateway. On either side were single-story brick buildings that housed souvenir shops, a cafeteria, and washrooms for the visitors. It was the only way to the castle, providing access for delivery trucks as well as visiting dignitaries. Visitors were not allowed to drive past the cast-iron, electronically operated gate. The path branched off just before the castle and led to a wooded parking lot marked as private, where more than twenty luxury vehicles were parked that day. Some of the cars had foreign license plates, but the distance did not allow for more accurate distinction.

The main entrance to the castle was closed for another thirty-five minutes; visitors were allowed in only by guided tours commencing every hour. A handful of tourists lingered here and there, waiting for the next tour. Nearby were gardens maintained in various styles, each occupying its own terrace carved in a steep slope of the hill, and offering magnificent views of the forested valleys.

The young couple wandered into the lower levels of the gardens, passing burlap-wrapped trees and shrubs. The walking paths were plowed, the park benches cleared of the fresh white fluff. They reached the bottom terrace and followed a narrow gravel path along a high spiked iron fence.

"During the communist rule locals picked mushrooms in these woods," the man said. "Now it's all fenced up. Private."

"Reminds me of some of the French châteaux where owners are obliged to open certain parts to the public, but the rest remains off-limits," replied the woman.

"Feudal days are no more. The owners of the property are just guardians of national treasures belonging to the people. Or so they like to call themselves," the man commented absentmindedly. His eyes wandered to the trees, the statues, and a small pagoda in the far corner of the garden. He raised the camera to eye level, while the woman posed next to a carved statue representing a bearded man with horns, hooves and a tail. "Smile . . ."

They continued along. Suddenly the man stopped and knelt to tie his shoelaces. He remained in this position long enough to draw the woman's attention.

"What is it?"

"This place is wired better than a military base. See that green stick with a few bare branches?"

"Yes," the woman answered hesitantly.

"Doesn't it strike you how green and unnatural it looks? A luscious, springlike green at the end of December?"

"It's an exotic garden." She was facing rows of bushes tied with a string.

"No, I meant in the woods." He stood up and nodded toward the dense forest with only small amounts of snow on the ground. "It's a disguised vibration sensor. There must be more of them scattered about the park. I have an idea that when triggered they activate those cameras." He pointed his head toward something in the branches of an old oak. It looked like a birdhouse. "They are independently powered, meaning that to disable them you can't just cut off the main power line."

"The report was right. There is only one way of entry."

"With this level of security on the outside I doubt it will be any easier on the inside."

"No, I suppose it won't be." The woman smiled as she posed in front of the romantic pagoda. She glanced at her wristwatch. "It's time."

They climbed the limestone steps and followed the pathway to the castle's entrance. Six other visitors queued to enter through the narrow door that opened through the five-meter-tall black iron gate. Inside was a large vestibule that could accommodate a truck. The doors had closed behind the visitors. Initial darkness was penetrated only by a small amount of daylight that poured in through a narrow slit above the gate. The darkness prompted the visitors to remove their sunglasses. Slowly light began to fill the vestibule. Flabbergasted, the guests felt trapped and began to pace around from wall to wall. The vestibule had white walls with a strip of black glass that ran along both walls. It was about sixteen inches wide and placed some five feet above ground level. Soon another door creaked in the front, and seconds later its two wings slowly opened to allow a view of the courtyard. Visitors scattered, marveling over richly sculptured walls and the magnificent well that stood in the middle of the courtyard. One person did not join the common excitement. He lowered his head and followed his companion in distress.

"I hope we're not in their database, because, if I'm not mistaken, we've just been scanned."

"What? Where?" The woman smiled, but her eyes showed concern.

"In the vestibule. That black glass. I think they used a biometric scanner. I saw this system at an exhibition in Budapest a few months ago. It's used for iris recognition. The latest the industry has to offer."

"Aren't you exaggerating? I don't recall having my eyes scanned."

"I think you're confusing it with the retina scan used for identification purposes. Iris recognition in the post-Nine-eleven era can be done without you ever knowing it. It's just a picture taken with a very high-definition camera. You can disguise yourself with a wig, a beard, contact lenses, or even plastic surgery but you cannot change your immutable retinas. It is a better discriminator than face recognition software used in airports, better even than DNA testing. I just hope this scan goes directly to the desk of our man. . . ." He paused as they approached a door with a sign that read *Wejście,* entrance.

Just as the last visitor disappeared inside, the woman rushed in behind. Inside she stopped so abruptly the man bumped into her.

"Damn," he muttered.

Four large men in blue crested jackets blocked the door.

"Good morning, Miss Banks," said one of them. "We've been expecting you, Mr. Penskie."

"Has the contact been made?" asked the director of Central Intelligence, a trace of anxiety in his voice.

"It turned out better than we could have hoped," replied the director of the National Security Agency. "The younger Penskie not only followed the lead, but spoke with his father and was retained at headquarters this morning, local time."

An animated exchange of voices followed the statement. The men were congratulating one another. It was only early morning in Washington. The NSA director's call for an emergency meeting in the wee hours of the night sent shivers through each one's spine. Today was the day that would end the waiting and release the tension that had kept them awake for days.

The Central Intelligence director remained unmoved. Over the last few days he had had time to think—to really think and rethink his involvement. Their involvement. September eleventh unified the nation like no other event in recent American history. Yet these men, including himself, were drifting away from the president, when their place was to stand firmly behind him no matter what his intentions, for even in his extreme the president's actions had only one goal: to make America strong. So thought the NSA director, and so did he. Their ideas may have differed, but in the end they all endeavored to make America better and stronger. He may not have agreed with the American option, but it was his sworn duty to serve his country and his president. It was not, however, the moral dilemma that prompted his pondering. He began to lean toward Alpha and the president's line. After the September eleventh attacks it became painfully obvious that America would sooner or later become isolated in her desire to strike preemptively whenever and wherever the state and world security issues called for such action. The trouble was that American and world security did not necessarily go together in the eyes of the world. Regardless of the influence the organization held, nothing could change it. Worse yet, the organization more often than not followed a course that was contrary to American interests. It was a paninternational body set on benefiting itself and itself only. The director was once a military man; he worked for years in G2, and such values as motherland and nation were important to him, particularly as he grew older. It was time to give his services back to the country. Yes, it was time for change. He must not waver anymore. He would play his cards carefully. The NSA director had power over the others, but forced power it was—power built on fear and blackmail. It was natural that they would want their freedom, the power to make their own decisions. Turning them should not be hard, especially if Alpha showed his capability today. Today was all they had. Before the meeting in Europe ended they should all be on Alpha's side—the American side.

"Does his father know about it?" someone asked when the excitement subsided.

"Oh, he will find out within an hour or so."

"Will this stop Alpha from intervening during the council meeting?" asked another voice.

"The young FBI agent is our collateral. Zbigniew Penskie will not allow any interference that could endanger his son's life. Alpha will fail."

"How can we be sure that everything goes as planned?"

"I think we're beyond planning. At this stage the success of the operation lies in the arms of providence." The NSA director chuckled. "Of course, we have greatly helped our cause by securing precise timing and retaining organizational integrity." He glanced at his watch. "The council meeting will commence in about seven hours. I do not foresee any trouble."

"What about the embassy? The deputy chief of mission there is a man of influence, his father could stir up trouble here in Washington."

"The DCM is a presumptuous man who can be controlled if we play to his vanity. I would not worry about him. The ambassador is keeping an eye on things."

"What about the intelligence and research team?"

"The only forcible action open for Alpha is to take the headquarters by storm. The Polish government would not allow our forces to cross the borders without prior agreement. The last NATO training activities took place months earlier in northern Poland. Our men have been withdrawn. It was a great tactical move on our part to reschedule it in light of the coming summit. As for the four INR men Alpha's brought, they are hardly a reason for concern."

"But is the leader aware of their presence? Sending the

INR to the embassy might pass unnoticed. Given what's happened to the embassy's staff it's to be expected that the team will be dispatched. It's expected and therefore not taken into account as a threat. It may appear to be a routine investigation. There may only be four of them, but we don't know about other resources available to Alpha. We must not underestimate him."

"I assure you the leader is well aware of the INR team's arrival. We remain in constant communication. Everything that takes place on American soil is instantly relayed to our headquarters. And as you all know, the headquarters is a fortress, more so due to the extraordinary meeting taking place today."

"Then we have nothing to worry about?"

"It would not be prudent to celebrate victory before the battle. We can be reasonably certain of our plan ending successfully. We should, however, exercise caution and must be prepared for the unexpected factor. We will wait and we will watch. I hope, gentlemen, that you will be comfortable here. Relax and let history take its course." He stood up and added, "Fresh muffins, tea, and coffee urns are in the hallway. Make yourself feel at home, for this will be your home for the next seven to nine hours."

The DCI listened with amazement. This self-centered buffoon was confining them, locking up some of the most powerful men in the nation! The fact that such extraordinary measures were called for by the director of perhaps the most secretive of all agencies could come only as a result of immense fear. The confinement meant also that he knew or suspected the DCI's sentiments. Moreover, and despite his confident poise, he did take into consideration the very real possibility of Alpha's victory.

* * *

The embassy was in a state of animated turmoil. There was not a section or a single employee that was not subjected to the deputy chief of mission's outburst of frustration. Hank Russell's ego boiled in acid over the unthinkable affront. His kingdom had been threatened. Hard-earned dominance over his subjects, meek servants of the United States government, was being taken away from him. While it may have been the state department's God-given privilege to assign people to their posts, it was his, the deputy chief of mission's, duty to make sure they met their obligations. Therefore it was his right to know what these obligations were. Stan Penskie's unexpected reassignment to a classified intelligence mission was a kick in the groin—the DCM could not ensure that the embassy's good name would not be jeopardized. After all, his employees' conduct reflected not only on the United States but also on him personally. The latter concerned him even more.

In his office Hank Russell spoke to Cr. Ray Stockwell, the chief of the four-person team of the intelligence and research branch of the state department.

"It is your responsibility to see to it that his conduct in no way reflects harmfully on this embassy."

"Sir, we are forbidden from interfering with the legat's ops," Stockwell replied composedly, his eyes laughing. The old fool had no idea he was playing to the team's true mission.

"It is within the INR's statutory authority to handle issues that arise in the course of intelligence and security operations abroad, is it not?"

"Yes, but—"

"Commander, I'm not suggesting that you interfere with

the operation. I simply demand that you ensure that this activity is conducted in harmony with the embassy's diplomatic functions."

A knocking at the door cut into Stockwell's reply.

"Come in," Russell said irately. "Ah, you've met our chief of security. Marvin will assist you with your task. The ambassador is at our consulate in Kraków; therefore everything comes directly to me. I expect a detailed report and analysis on my desk at close of business every day. You can start with Penskie's whereabouts and objectives."

"Sir," Marvin Cleft started, "we can't do that without violating the state's—"

"This is my turf, gentlemen. The embassy is my responsibility, and you follow my orders. Am I clear enough?"

"Yes, sir."

"I have a meeting with the minister this evening. I will not be sitting there like a damned fool. I need answers. Give them to me."

When Stockwell and Cleft left the room, Hank Russell sat in his executive leather chair. Oh, the humiliation of the last two incidents involving the legats! It was bad enough that Central Intelligence had to operate under diplomatic cover; now the Federal Bureau of Investigation was adding to his stress. He took a sip of hot green tea. Ah, it was so refreshing and relaxing. He finished the cup in a few large gulps, taking pleasure in the hot liquid scalding his lips. It took away the anger. He felt better. *Ah, well, that's all part of life's rich pageantry*. He liked to use his favorite expression from cinematic history. *Pull up your socks, Hank; twenty-five years in the government's foreign service taught you to clench your teeth and do your job. Administrations come and go, but you are still here. Why? Because you damn well know your job!*

Chapter Twenty-two

"What do you mean we must assume the worst?" Zbigniew Penskie was startled. His right hand froze in midair, the flame of a lit match flickering under his heavy breath.

"Only that it's been over two hours, and tours last forty-five minutes. They should've been back by now," Jacobek answered. He was sitting in the backseat of a navy blue BMW SUV.

"They should have worn a transmitter," Urbaniak said from the driver's seat. He pointed to a small unit on the dashboard. It was a miniature receiver the size of a Palm Pilot. It picked up a wireless signal from a transmitter the size of a dime, showing the geographical location of the subject on its color LCD screen.

"We all decided it was too risky, a sound precaution, given what's taking place in the castle today. In any case, a jammer would probably be activated, preventing any signal penetration," Jacobek said.

"You should have told Stan the truth!" Urbaniak rebuked him.

"You don't know my son! He believes in the letter of the law, the Constitution, and the clearly defined values that made America the country that it is. He wouldn't understand!"

"How do you know? You didn't even try to convince him otherwise."

"There was no need for that. That man was supposed to pass the database to Stan during the tour, an inconspicuous brush; that was to be my son's whole involvement."

"Clearly you've underestimated Balcer."

"We don't know they were apprehended. They might be hiding," Jacobek said. He pointed to the secure telephone placed on the armrest between the front-row seats. "I don't think we have a choice."

"If they're in hiding and are unable to communicate, a phone call might break their cover, not to mention it is unlikely that any communication will go through." Zbigniew Penskie spoke composedly, but his voice showed a trace of anxiety. He was beginning to worry. It was supposed to be a safe and quick operation; the man had assured him of it. He could not afford to raise any suspicion among other members of the organization, despite his high position. Zbigniew believed he knew who the man was. He knew more about the organization than he admitted to his son. He suspected the identity of the man who offered to pass on the database, but was afraid the news would have a negative effect. Stan was very devoted to his job, his adopted country, and to the ways the Bureau conducted its business. He would not understand. Telling Stan that the ambassador of the United States was the contact, the high-ranking member of the Fifth Internationale, would have discouraged him. No, it was better this way. He would be shocked upon finding out who was going to meet him, but the extraordinary circumstances would not have left time to ponder. He would need to get out of the castle. The database had priority. The explanations would follow later.

"Let's hope it's set to vibrate," Zbigniew said, and picked up the telephone in his shaky hand. They'd better have turned off the ringer. He dialed the number. He misdialed and tried again. Ten seconds later his face changed. He listened intensely for about a half a minute, and then his arm dropped.

Urbaniak picked up the telephone and brought it to his ear. There was only silence.

"What was it?" he asked.

"It was Balcer. They have Stan and the woman. They know about us. I am to stay away from the castle, and if any suspicious activity is detected in or near Nowa Wieś, they'll . . . they'll kill him."

Urbaniak and Jacobek exchanged glances. Allowing Stan to enter the castle was a mistake. The elder Penskie was a strong man belonging to a generation prepared to lay down their own freedom and life for their country—common sacrifices among Solidarity members in their fight for freedom, but to sacrifice one's own child was different from sacrificing one's own life. Both Urbaniak and Jacobek were married and had children, and both understood the severity of the plight Zbigniew was facing.

It was Jacobek who observed that Stan's capture provided a new opportunity. Balcer had made a mistake. Kidnapping was a serious matter, and kidnapping an American diplomat called for a stern response. It took him almost a quarter of an hour to convince Zbigniew of the necessity for quick action. In Jacobek's opinion, Stan's life was in danger whether Zbigniew withdrew or not.

As the CIA operative was presenting his case, the director of the *Urząd Ochrony Państwa* grew more and more fond of it. Jacobek was right: Kidnapping Stan presented their cause with new opportunities. They now had a viable reason to call the minister of defense and request the backup of the army.

Zbigniew objected. He demanded nothing be done, believing himself impervious to threats or harm. The false notion likely derived from his cushy years in Washington, Jacobek noted. The CIA man believed it was precisely this sort of politicizing from behind the curtain of oblivion that made the United States vulnerable to threats such as terrorism, and was responsible for the country's inability to face crisis situations that arose around the globe. It was people such as Zbigniew Penskie who decided where and how to respond to threats from the warmth of their offices or over brunches with other eggheads, accidental warriors whose decisions rendered the United States unable to strike quickly and accurately.

Jacobek clenched his teeth but did not voice his disapproval when Zbigniew demanded they wait. The old man actually believed he could leave his son's life out of it! Ludicrous! But the former national security adviser was in charge and he, Jacobek had only one thing to do—obey. He did so, and nothing would have changed Zbigniew Penskie's mind had it not been for the ringing of the secure telephone Stan had left behind.

It was Ed Powell.

* * *

It took the legal attaché only two minutes to convince the deputy chief of mission to formally request the Poles' assistance in freeing the American diplomat. As he learned about the situation this cocky FBI agent had gotten himself into, Hank Russell grew more than keen to act on it; he was happy. Stan Penskie's kidnapping was his chance to get back at those who dared meddle in the internal workings of the embassy. If the intelligence operation failed—and it was evident that it already had—he would have a case against those parties in Washington who were using diplomatic missions to do their dirty work. He realized, with apprehension, that he should discuss his move with the ambassador, but when his effort to contact him failed on the first attempt, he did not retry. The ambassador was unreachable. It was an unthinkable breach of security, but it put a smile on the DCM's face: It was now up to him to make the decision. He picked up his telephone and dialed the number to the minster of foreign affairs, who in turn mobilized the defense minister.

Not two hours after his conversation with Zbigniew Penskie and Robert Urbaniak, whom Powell had met before on official duty and was able to confirm his identity by answering a series of short questions, the legal attaché was on the way to a small airfield, where a PZL W-3 Sokół helicopter awaited takeoff. The consulate's reconnaissance team's findings prompted Powell to telephone Stan. He suspected his deputy of having gone to Nowa Wieś without his approval, and the Nowa Wieś castle was a suspicious place, to say the least. The advanced security systems, combined with the presence of armed patrols and small units monitoring antiaircraft missiles, told Powell what he suspected: The castle was a probable location of the Fifth Internationale. He did not stop at this discovery. He had contacted one of his best sources in Washington, a man he had known and trusted for years. His father-in-law was a member of the National Intelligence Council, with access to data so classified only a handful of people in the nation had access to it. Something told Powell that the lack of intelligence information on Tadeusz Balcer in the FBI's and CIA's databanks could not be coincidental. Men of smaller significance had pages and boxes in these agencies' computers and filing cabinets. There had to be a reason why Balcer's file was nowhere to be found. What his father-in-law passed on to him, on a line so secure it was beyond even National Security Agency' reach, had a staggering effect on the legal attaché.

Balcer had to be stopped.

The information was sensitive to the point that he had to lie to Hank or, as he convinced himself, to tell a half-truth. Stan Penskie, a United States diplomat, had been kidnapped by a terrorist organization. Powell related it to the deputy chief of mission, who in turn said the same to the minister of foreign affairs. The wheels were set in motion.

The car pulled up in front of the gate to the airfield in Okęcie, where two commandos in full combat gear greeted Powell and escorted him to one of the two Sokół helicopters. Sokółs were Polish-made twin-engine combat helicopters widely used by Polish military forces. Although not the ideal equipment for the formation that was GROM, whose wish list centered on a UH-60 Blackhawk, they had to suffice until appropriate funds allowed for purchase of the American aircraft. Inside were eight GROM soldiers armed with HK MP-5 submachine guns, Tantal 5.45mm and Beryl

.223 assault rifles, and CZ-85 and SIG-Sauer P228 pistols. In addition, the legal attaché recognized two HK PSG-1 sniper rifles.

The unit's commander, who identified himself only as Reszka, showed Powell to his seat, and the two Sokółs lifted off immediately.

The legal attaché knew only the basic facts about GROM, as briefed by Marvin Cleft. Although one of the youngest, the unit was already considered one of the best counterterrorist formations in the world. Formed and trained with the aid of the American Special Forces and British SAS, GROM, or Thunderbolt, proved its special warfare skills in a number of hostile situations that took its members around the world: Haiti, the Balkans, the Arabian Peninsula, Afghanistan, and lately Kuwait, near the Iraqi border, as part of Poland's support for military action against that country. On the home front GROM participated in a number of high priority missions, including the breakup of the notorious Piastów mob, whose operations spanned the world. Most members of the GROM were pulled from various formations of the army and had undergone a rigorous elimination process, which left only the most physically and psychologically fit for spec war. They were the best of the best. The elite.

Reszka was aware of the mission's objective, which was to free the assistant legal attaché of the American Embassy. He was surprised to find out about the existence of a second hostage, a woman, also an American citizen. He did not like surprises. Good thing this civilian had the good sense to share the information before they landed. He sighed and passed on the photographs of Stan Penskie and Mollie Banks to his soldiers and remained uncommunicative for the duration of the flight.

Chapter Twenty-three

The room in which Penskie was locked was not what one would expect from a posh conference center in a medieval castle. It had twelve-foot high ceilings, painted and peeling walls, and was cold. Sparse furniture consisted of a small solid wood table beneath a small window carved in a three-foot-thick wall some eight feet above the floor and a single scratched up chair next to a narrow metal cot. Judging by the distance to the room it was probably located at the far end of the castle from the entrance, Penskie thought. But it could have been anywhere, since they made numerous turns and took three flights of stairs to reach it. He climbed on top of the wobbly table and pulled himself inside the window well. It was narrow and he had to slide in with his arms stretched alongside his body. There was no glass. Thick bars on the outside discouraged any attempt to escape nearly as much as did the view. He pushed himself close enough to see a steep rocky hill that sloped at the bottom into a deep wooded valley. The only way out of the room was through the solid wood doors. The door was thick enough to muffle the sound of the bolt after the two thugs pushed him in. He could not hear where they took Mollie. He knelt down, his head to the floor, to peer through a slit at the bottom of the door. It was no use. All he could see was a pale wall across the corridor. He wondered whether she was taken to the adjoining room. He knocked on the wall. It could not have been as thick as the outside wall, but it was thick enough to deter any attempt to communicate through tapping. He scanned the room for an air vent or water pipes. There were none. Then he realized it would have been useless even if he had found a radiator. He did not remember Morse code, even though he was once really good at it as a scout in junior high. He sighed, sat on the crude chair, and waited.

It was almost five hours later that Penskie's bladder reached the limits of sustaining the pressure. For the next ten minutes he hammered on the door and called out for the guards. Two arrived armed with pistols and escorted Stan to the washroom down the hallway. It was a long corridor of perhaps twenty doors similar to the ones to the cell Penskie was locked in. The smells at the end of the hallway suggested a kitchen, and he realized the cells were once servants' lodgings.

Instead of returning him to his room, the guards ushered him farther. He asked where they were taking him but was ignored. Countless doors and two flights of wide staircases later they walked into a large hall richly decorated with heavily gilded portraits, genre pieces, and huge mirrors. Here and there was a small table or a display cabinet with objets d' art, decorative vases, and intricately designed tabletop clocks. This was more of a museum than a place of business or leisure. The lack of any signs or ropes suggested that this was not the section of the castle that served as a museum. This had to be the corporate area. Some thirty meters into the elongated hallway was a double door. It opened the moment Penskie neared. Two guards stood on either side of the door frame. They nodded to the ones who ushered in the legal attaché, and the duo turned around and headed back.

A large electric chandelier and a series of wall sconces lit the large chamber with tapestries on the walls and murals on the high ceiling. Life-size portraits of knights in armor hung on the walls, and a set of armor guarded each corner of the room. One wall had two cathedral windows that offered spectacular views of the sunset and the surrounding hills.

A slim man with gray hair, dressed impeccably in a tailored suit, stood by one of the opened windows, a cigar in one hand and an octagonal glass in the other. His eyes, though bloodshot and tired, were smiling, his posture was relaxed. A great sense of relief showed on his face.

"Mr. Penskie, how nice of you to drop by! Please, can I offer you anything, a drink or a smoke, perhaps?" he opened jovially, his arms spread out as if in an invitation to an embrace, though from a safe distance.

"I don't drink before proper introduction," Penskie replied icily.

"But of course, please forgive my inexcusable manners." The man approached the large desk that separated him from Penskie. "Tadeusz Balcer, castellan of this estate." He smiled widely.

Penskie remained silent. A lingering hope that his captor was the mysterious man who was supposed to pass on the database had vanished. Tadeusz Balcer, the leader of the Fifth Internationale. The power this man represented and the wealth he possessed were secondary to the strength that was evident in the way he carried himself. Not physical strength, but one associated with his position. This was the man who could crush markets, buy whole countries, and overthrow governments. Of course, only if rumors about the Fifth Internationale's potential were true.

"*Gość w dom, Bóg w dom,* as we Poles like to say. You're welcome to stay as long as you like in my humble estate, Mr. Penskie."

"Wouldn't want to impose on your hospitality."

"Ah, do fill me in on the reason for your most unexpected visit then. What brings you in?"

"How about your goons' assertive persuasion?"

"It's true they can be very firm when it comes to fulfilling their duties, but one can hardly blame them in this world of ambiguity and fallacy. They convey a certain assurance and stability where there is none."

Penskie jerked his head impatiently. "Where's Banks?" he asked, then realized belatedly that his anxiousness might have exposed a weakness. "What do you want from us?" he added aggressively to cover his abashment.

"The question is, what do *you* want, Mr. Penskie? After all it is *you* who contravened on *my* privacy."

"All right, why don't we cut to the chase? We know who you are and we know what you represent, so you may as well face it: The game's over!"

"Hmm, such arrogance illustrates lack of training in diplomacy. Frankly, I was hoping we'd have a more interesting chat, you know—allusions, insinuations, smoke screens. . . . It's so much more refined and challenging to reach an agreement without being so crudely plain." Balcer paused and walked back to the window. He looked out and continued, "You are so different. You're not at all like your father."

If it was Balcer's objective to get Penskie to lose his composure, then it misfired. Stan was more surprised than upset. The fact that Balcer may have heard about his father was not at all strange. Zbigniew Penskie had his fifteen minutes of fame extended to hours, weeks, months, and even years after the media first went into a frenzy over his career in Washington. He was still quoted on various topics ranging from security to economy, and gave interviews during hot debates on the Polish position as the only European NATO member that shared borders with Russia, however antiquated the issue was. What struck Penskie as odd was not the mention of his father, but the use of his father in reference to some agreement. What did that mean? And what possible agreement could he reach with Balcer? Was it possible that Balcer was the mystery man, after all?

Penskie stood motionless, uncertain how to respond.

Balcer, who was peering over his shoulder, motioned for Penskie to approach the window. One of the guards followed but was stopped by his boss's gesture. Balcer turned around and once again motioned Penskie to move closer, his face brightening.

"I'd like you to see something. A most interesting lesson, I assure you," he said rapidly.

Penskie walked over to one of the windows. The sky gave way to gray dusk with the last traces of lilac over the horizon, darkness quickly swallowing the snowcapped woods beneath. He could make out several figures lurking on the verge of light cast by powerful lamps that illuminated the castle. They looked small from the height of Balcer's office, but their objective was obvious: to enter the castle covertly. Balcer gave an inconspicuous signal to the guards who remained by the doors. One of them muttered something into a headset microphone, and Penskie witnessed a scene that made his flesh crawl. A sudden movement behind each one of the intruders was so unexpected that he could not even gasp out a protest before their throats had been slit and their bodies slowly slumped onto the ground. Despite the poor lighting and the distance the picture was clear: Those four men were killed. The logic of the action escaped Stan. Why would Balcer resort to killing? He could just as well have incarcerated them. Who were these men? And what was the lesson he was supposed to learn from it?

"What the hell was that?" Stan's eyes were wide in bewilderment and rage.

"That was just an example of what the lack of consensus leads to. These four poor souls were only a representation of their employers, but the message will reach even farther. Hopefully in the future it may be averted; perhaps a hostile action may not even be considered at all. . . ."

"Okay, nice show, but staging it won't accomplish whatever it is you want from me."

"Oh, I assure you, for all intents and purposes it was as real as you and I standing face-to-face. An unthinkable occasion only a day or two ago, and quite an accomplishment on your part too, Mr. Penskie."

"I don't buy it."

"You should know enough to believe it. The fact that you're here would suggest that."

"Who were they?"

"Those were agents of the notorious intelligence and research office of the department of state, whose secretary's fickle conduct irrevocably crossed the boundaries of my patience. Personally, I'm against such radical measures, but some of my associates believe in a more rigid treatment of various parties who are set upon bringing damage to my and my colleagues' interests."

Penskie burst out laughing. He laughed a long, loud, and nervous laugh he was afraid to end. He could imagine how the INR agents had ended up in Nowa Wieś and on whose authority, but the sheer fact that Balcer could simply eliminate them with a flick of a finger was unnerving. Whether this was a staged play, and Penskie believed it was, or a true event, one thing was obvious: It was a show of strength intended to intimidate him. The question was: Why? Why would a man of Balcer's position *need* to intimidate the assistant legal attaché of the American Embassy?

Balcer watched the American, his arm delivering the cigar to his slim lips in a smooth, nonchalant gesture. Despite the event he remained relaxed and self-assured. The room was quiet. The guards standing by the large doors watched Penskie with intensity. At the slightest danger they were ready to spring into action to save their leader. The leader knew it would not be necessary. Penskie was not the sort of man to hurt a worthy opponent in a brutal attack. He was too smart for that. In this respect he was a lot like his father; with his enduring stamina he would challenge intelligently. His psychological report was clear about that.

"Well, now that you've decided to drop by we may as well make the best of it," Balcer broke the silence, and motioned Penskie to one of the two comfortable seats that stood across the desk.

Balcer too sat in his large wooden seat. Penskie was not an expert in antiques but the seat looked like a throne—massive, dark, and sumptuously encrusted. It was somewhat higher than the deep, soft leather seat Penskie sank onto. The entire surroundings were surreal. He felt like a suppliant at a feudal court. He refused to feel intimidated by it.

"But first," Balcer continued, "why don't you satisfy the curiosity of an old man and tell me, What may this most surprising visit of yours be attributed to?"

"Your guards suggested that we were expected."

"I would very much like to hear from you your reasons for coming here."

"Curiosity killed the cat," Penskie replied in an attempt to defy the intimidation.

"Yes, but vigilance saved the mouse."

Was it a threat? A reminder of the standing of power? Neither was necessary, for it was clear Balcer had the upper hand. He knew more than he was willing to share, and he had already demonstrated that he could take life without a wince.

"You have forcefully confined me and my friend. You owe us an explanation," Penskie replied boldly. He was losing patience with the old man's babble.

"All right, let me put it this way. I know why you think you are here, but can you be sure that what you think you know is true, Mr. Penskie? In other words, are you here because of your own perceptiveness or have you followed clues left for you to find?"

"For someone who claims to know the answer you seem to have an awful lot of questions," Penskie started. He wanted to take charge of the conversation. He realized he had to provoke this buffoon, to force him to lose ground. "The problem with you is that you're overconfident in your position, but the power, money, control, and influence you rely on in high places didn't prevent you from overestimating your strength. Sorry for being so crudely plain, but I want to be very clear on this: Your and your organization's days are numbered, Mr. Balcer."

"And what are your conclusions based on?"

"The jig is up!" Penskie shrugged. "*Międzynarodówka* is no longer a secret, and sooner or later your operatives will be weeded out and disabled."

"*Międzynarodówka*? . . . You're right, our organization is no secret, and if truth be told, it never was. Well, not for long, anyway. Even so, the American scenario proved to be the better one, one that assured the unprecedented growth we've experienced. Growth that benefited all interested parties, not excluding your Federal Bureau. So, you see, by meddling with what you don't understand you're on a course to destroy the very foundations your country's intelligence and security community are based on. To put it more directly for you—our organization's existence cannot be threatened, will not be threatened. Not because of our strength. We're too much of a threat to be destroyed. That is not to say that there weren't such attempts, but those who tried and undoubtedly will try in the future have been and will be dealt with swiftly and crudely. Oh, please sit down, Mr. Penskie; had I wished to kill you, you would have been dead before you knew why. In fact, I may have saved your life instead."

There was a quick spark in Balcer's eyes. His iris opened and closed in a split second. It did not escape Penskie. Balcer was lying. Which part was he lying about?

"Those INR shooters followed you here not to rescue you, as you may have hoped, but to eliminate you. Are you surprised? You needn't be, if you understand what you've stepped into."

"Why don't you enlighten me then," Penskie replied with such sarcasm it could not have been read as a question.

"I don't blame you for such an attitude. After all, being blindfolded by your own, lied to, and deliberately deceived would make anyone suspicious and wary."

Balcer was not the first one to imply penetration of the Federal Bureau of Investigation, various other government entities, and even the embassy. Some events, like the circumstances of the shooting at Jacobek's apartment building, played into such suggestions. Therefore Penskie's reaction, or the lack of it, was not what Balcer had hoped to see. Penskie realized it and it made him feel sure of himself. He had a small victory. True, it was shocking, even terrifying to think that something to that effect was possible, but the anguish of the past two days had finally changed to numbness. Nothing, he thought, could move him, no matter how absurd and shocking the revelations this man could present. Not even if he were told there was no one left to turn to for help. Except for Zbigniew, that is. Family ties could not be diminished by any outside events.

"Is there anyone left you can trust, Mr. Penskie?" Balcer seemed to have read his mind. "You think you have stumbled upon a conspiracy, and you think you know who's behind it, perhaps you can even identify persons who are high in the ranks of this . . . what did you call it? *Międzynarodówka?* Clever. It has been called so many names. . . . So you pursue the leads that are conveniently laid out for you, leads to an organization so powerful yet so secret that no one ever was able to prove its existence. You just happen to find proof in, what, two days? Well, never mind that. Say, just for the sake of argument, that you *did* get a break, that you *did* find a weak link, or a way that might lead investigators to this organization and to break it. I ask you, with what you've learned about us, to whom do you turn now, Agent Penskie? Who can you trust as not being an operative of *Międzynarodówka*?" A barely visible grin hung in the corners of Balcer's lips.

"The president."

"Yours or mine?"

Penskie did not reply.

"Okay," Balcer continued. "So you reach the president, who in turn designates a special committee to eradicate the problem, assuming he won't simply wish to take possession of the organization, of course. Anyway, what makes you think that someone on that committee won't be a member of *Międzynarodówka?*"

"As I already pointed out, you overestimate your reach."

"Do I?" Balcer pulled out a drawer from his desk and took out a recordable optical disk. He inserted it into a notebook computer that stood on the side of the desk and performed several quick operations with a cordless mouse. Finally he swiveled the notebook so it faced Penskie and pushed it slightly in the legal attaché's direction. "Please." He invited Stan to view the screen.

Penskie stood up and walked over to the desk. There were no seats next to it and he decided to sit nonchalantly on the edge of the furniture. He pulled the computer closer and glanced at the screen. He felt his stomach come to his throat. He could see a directory structure of a folder named USG. Subdirectories were named after various organizations within the United States government, such as the FBI, CIA, NSA, and some dozen other intelligence-gathering organizations, as well as Congress, and the White House topped the list. He opened the directory labeled "FBI" and saw that it was further divided into subdirectories named after various departments of the Federal Bureau of Investigation. He worked his way through divisions within departments until there were only documents that bore names of people. He clicked on one of them, and a personal file opened up on the screen. It contained a photograph and data on an individual named Jonathan S. Herlihy, code-named Spear. Links on the main page pointed to such documents as his career with the FBI, medical history, family connections, financial records, and more. Included on the front page was a brief note that read, *Since July 27, 1994,* followed by a list of names and events that linked to other documents.

Penskie browsed frantically through the database built in the form of an Internet Web site. He realized the names were those of the people who were operatives of the Fifth Internationale, complete with every detail of their personal and professional lives. He stood in front of the desk, no longer able to control his anxiety, searching and opening documents at random. He worked his way back to the top of the directory and through further links, which pointed toward various institutions of public life in the United States: universities, media, state and municipal judiciary systems, along with police and military forces.

Balcer halted his perusal.

"I think you get the idea." He stood up and reached for the notebook. He pulled it toward him and closed the lid.

Penskie was now standing in front of the desk, visibly shaken.

Balcer sat down and continued, "It is only disk one. Similar information pertaining to other countries is kept on other disks. That's tens of thousands of individuals in all areas of government and public life. Trust me, Agent Penskie, there's no operation anywhere in the world that can be launched without our knowledge, no matter on what level and with what security measures in place when the decisions are made."

"What do you want from me?" Penskie hissed out, his teeth clenched.

Balcer stood up and walked to the window. He remained silent for a minute and turned slowly to Penskie.

"You could put an end to it."

"Unit Five to Alpha." The voice in the two-way radio was loud and clear. The transmission must have come from close range. "The assembly is over. We are reading movement throughout the property. The guests will be departing shortly."

"Understood. Keep your positions and wait for my signal."

The man replaced the receiver and spoke to his companion.

"Balcer will make a final appearance; then they will begin to disperse. My guess is we have about an hour."

"Everything seems to be as planned," replied the second man. He held a satellite phone in his hand. The phone was connected to a Palm Pilot. The color screen showed a moving object, a small red dot on a map similar to ones showing flight progress on jumbo passenger jets. "GROM should be arriving in about twenty, perhaps twenty-five minutes."

"All right, send your men to neutralize the jammer and

stand by to activate the landing strip beacons. I don't want them to be looking for just *any* landing space. I don't want GROM to run into our people by accident."

"Our people are in position to storm Balcer's C-three-I. The radar will be shut down before the helicopters enter their range. As for our people, the danger of their running into GROM is minimal."

"Nevertheless, we must be prepared."

"If we are unsuccessful in gaining control of their C-three-I, we'll still have a chance of acquiring the database. Balcer will flee the castle. We should assume he would have some part of it, if only in his Palm Pilot."

"I doubt he would carry it around, but even so, it would be only a partial database."

"Yes, but through it we can re-create the rest."

"It will take years. I'd rather it had not come to that."

Alpha's aide remained silent. He knew better than to argue. Having only a partial database meant a serious decrease in the organization's effectiveness. It was not what Alpha and the president needed to fulfill their plans. But it was Alpha's fault. He was stubborn not to acknowledge the possibility that the council might choose to stand by Balcer's side. It did. Now there was nothing left for them but to race against the approaching GROM troops. They did not doubt that GROM would succeed in taking over the castle. If Alpha's men did not get there in time they might be forced to destroy the command, control, and communication system in order to protect the organization's database from falling into GROM's hands.

Chapter Twenty-four

Penskie listened to the statement not without a great sense of relief. Somewhere in the grand scheme of operations that lay beyond his comprehension, his life was considered necessary. The alleged leader of a supposedly almighty organization needed a low-key attaché of the American embassy. What was planned for him did not matter. The immediate conclusion was more important: As long as his existence was beneficial to Balcer, for whatever reason, his life was not in danger.

The finding put Stan at ease.

"Is it hope or worry I detect in your voice?" he replied boldly.

"Drop your chivalric façade for a moment and hear me out, please," Balcer answered coldly, and waited for an indication that Penskie was willing to listen.

It suddenly occurred to Stan that Balcer, as was true of

so many men of high standing, was surrounded by an aura of eccentricity, even madness. And Penskie could not decide which was most prevalent. To head the Fifth Internationale, with everything that was attributed to it over the years, if by reputation only, one had to be of a particular mind-set. With the very thin line between eccentricity and madness, Penskie decided it better not to defy a man for whom killing, whether a man or a fly, meant merely the motion of a finger. Who knew, perhaps the life of a pesky fly was held in higher regard than that of a human being? The assistant legal attaché did not reply, but his eyes glistened with rage.

"Thank you. Before I come to the point it is important that you are aware of basic facts about our . . . about the Fifth Internationale." The leader continued, "When it was first formed it was largely a militant organization. You have to understand that most of the founders whose background was army or security services believed in the old ways of ruling with an 'iron fist,' something the changing climate was less and less fond of. But there were many others, more forward thinking, who understood that survival depended on quite different skills: the subtlety and shrewdness of diplomacy and the audaciousness of corporate ferocity. The latter, being outnumbered, had to give way, and watched their creation become just another spinoff similar to, but much broader than, the KGB, *Służba Bezpieczeństwa*, or Stasi. The Fifth Internationale had the contacts and resources of all these organizations, backed by hard-liners from the Komitet Centralny, along with their funds and contacts in the leftist organizations around the globe. Now, don't get me wrong, Agent Penskie: Strong leadership was what helped the Fifth establish itself and survive the havoc of the late eighties and early nineties, but the narrow-mindedness of its bullying leaders never allowed it to cross the thin line between underground and legitimacy. Sort of like the Piastów mob that gave you such a run. To make things worse, somewhere along the way the Fifth had to struggle to keep what little independence it had. Call it a hostile corporate takeover, if you wish, the new player imposing his own rules and deciding the future of our organization. The Fifth became a pawn in the hands of a ruthless player, one who was not interested in its stable growth and its breakoff from the less-than-commendable past. He wanted a villain, someone to do the dirty work when required, and a reason to gain Congress's acquiescence to keep the budget flowing its way when post–Cold War business began to dwindle."

Penskie listened with growing angst. He did not like the direction Balcer was heading. As much as he hated to admit the most outrageous theory possible when hypothesized by Sito, Urbaniak, or Zbigniew, the same told by the leader of the Fifth Internationale, an organization whose existence still seemed absurd in the back of his mind, made it definite. He found with a degree of surprise that he no longer doubted the existence of such an organization now; he only hoped the Fifth Internationale was not anywhere near as broad and potent as it was being presented. Penskie had been around long enough to tell when someone was withholding information; he had learned through his work to recognize clues the average person did not: Every twitch, every muscle spasm, every gesture and eye movement told a story that words did not. For the first time, the person speaking of *Międzynarodówka* seemed genuinely sincere—Penskie could not help feeling that all the others, including his father, were withholding something crucial from him.

While he had no reason to doubt either of them, perhaps with the exception of the deputy director of the *Urząd Ochrony Państwa*—and only because he inexplicably disliked the man—Penskie assumed they improvised where conclusive data was missing. It occurred to him now, and not without a great deal of discomfort, that it was very likely that they purposefully withheld some aspects of the evidence known to them. Balcer, in Stan's mind, was either better at this game or he was telling the truth. In either case, playing naïve seemed the right approach to make Balcer speak. In all honesty he did not have to pretend. He was confused, and in particular as to the role Balcer planned for him.

"The Central Intelligence Agency *already* controls the Fifth Internationale?"

"With the collapse of the Soviet Union, the ultimate villain of the twentieth century, America remained the only superpower in the world. However, while this presented a great opportunity to instill in and carry on that image of a hegemonic state with her numerous, still-existing enemies, the United States did not want to appear as the gendarme of the free world—a contradiction in terms, you see. Yet someone had to do the job. When the freedom or the needs of the free world needed to be defended or aided with the use of the U.S. Special Forces, the move wasn't exactly welcomed with open arms. Take Somalia, for example. So instead you contracted better-suited and nondescript members of the Fifth Internationale, who derived from all corners of the world, including the troubled nations, speaking their language and understanding every nuance of life in those regions. There was no need for expensive military or peacekeeping operations, no need for intricate infiltration—

their operatives were already in place. They were native to those places, yet their loyalties lay with the organization. When you hear from time to time that democratic powers within seized control and led the nation in the right direction, or something similar, the way the media likes to phrase it, you can't help but wonder who stands behind it.

"Of course, it wasn't just the Central Intelligence Agency who had a sweet tooth for *Międzynarodówka*. It was the entire United States intelligence community, aided by your government, a move quietly approved by numerous governments around the world. You see, it's in most everyone's interest that an organization such as the Fifth Internationale exists and remains under control. Whether it should be the American control is often debatable, and less and less appealing to all sides, including certain parties within the United States. So, to answer your question: Not the entire organization succumbed to the Americans. What I have in mind is what you may consider our militant arm, the darkest of dark legacies of the Cold War. While we, the organization, struggle, trying to distance ourselves from that part of our past, at the same time creating a countermeasure to the American bullying tactics and bringing a ballast to the international scene, they are just as persevering in their attempts to swallow all other aspects of our operations. The day will come when the American people will demand answers. Your government will need a scapegoat. Or worse yet: Having complete control of the Fifth Internationale will place it above judgment and accountability. Personally, I believe the latter to be their ultimate goal."

Balcer paused. The news was devastating, if not absurd,

to the uninitiated. He had to force himself to deliver it in small doses so as not overwhelm Penskie. Too much information offered might have the reverse effect and render it more doubtful. He wanted this down-to-earth agent to believe him. Some things needed to be downplayed while others were emphasized. In the end, Penskie would have to come to his own conclusions, and it required a certain finesse to steer him in just the right direction. Balcer was not disappointed.

"So all the fighting, the deaths of Bray, Borysewicz, and even Loomis, they're the result of internal strife?"

"They're the most regretful consequence. I can't begin to explain how dreadful I feel about it."

Penskie watched the leader from across the desk. The light was poorly placed to permit ample observation, or perhaps it was carefully planned that way; a sconce on the wall directly behind the leader blinded the person sitting opposite. Penskie could not see into Balcer's eyes—the Pole's face was sunken in shadow—but for a brief moment he thought he detected a slight twitch or a grin on the slim lips.

"You bastard! You just killed four men out there! Your entire story is a bunch of lies!" he exploded.

Balcer shifted uncomfortably, his face turning toward the light from the chandelier hanging off the ceiling and revealing his expressionless eyes.

"All right, Agent Penskie, you've called my bluff. It's true that those men weren't killed. The event was staged, done for a very good reason: I had to show my associates that I agree to their terms. I couldn't be with them to witness their reaction; I was afraid something in my behavior could betray the truth, as you just found out. I just hope *they* believed it. I mentioned to you their attitude toward the Americans, and their ideas about running this organization."

"The 'iron fist,' yes." Penskie answered angrily. Balcer was good. It really made Penskie uncomfortable. He was no longer sure of himself. He could not read this man.

"It's true, Mr. Penskie, our organization is divided. A few years ago the leader would not need to look back, or seek a majority to make decisions. But alas, the times have changed. Perhaps it's for the best. The organization's reach is so vast it's only natural that various parties should have a vote when it comes to making decisions about their regions of influence. Sadly, it can't be achieved without a complete break from the American intelligence. We're working on it, though. Two years ago the French, German, and other governments of the NATO and G-seven countries received tips about the existence of an American-run top-secret organization with operatives in their countries' government institutions and vital infrastructures. Although political allies, these countries' national interests are often poles apart, so as you can imagine the reaction was quite severe. The relationships between these countries and the USA stiffened, which reflected in the lack of support for war with Iraq, or opposition to your antiballistic missile system, among other things. The allies insisted that the organization be either disbanded or its operatives withdrawn. The USA not so much refused, but maintained its innocence. That's when Andrzej Borysewicz came to the scene offering certain concessions in exchange for these countries' support in breaking off from under American control."

"I thought Borysewicz contacted the Americans," Penskie replied, anger still in his voice.

"There are powers in your country that want to put an end to it too. They are vital to our offer."

"Which is?"

"The Fifth Internationale will terminate its terrorist links and expose its operatives working in countries such as the United States, France, Germany, Britain."

"Why are you suddenly so concerned about your image? The terrorists, the militant streak in you, it's kind of . . . becoming."

"Just the legacy of dark times in human history. We are ready to cross over. We do not need arms to achieve our goals. Neither does America. I am quite confident your government could easily resolve many issues with diplomacy rather than troops. In fact, let me use this as an analogy. The United States is a lot like the Fifth Internationale. Disband your armed forces and you might be a welcome and respected partner in such places where no American citizen would dare venture without an armored vehicle."

"Fantasy aside, I still find it hard to believe you'd do that, give away your operatives. It would mean annihilation for you, and as someone told me, it's self-preservation that prompted the creation of the Fifth, that kept it growing. . . ."

"It's no longer a matter of survival, Agent Penskie. The Fifth Internationale cannot be simply erased. It's so entwined in every aspect of life that it's no longer possible to separate it without serious consequences to the global economy, not to mention security. The attacks on the World Trade Center and the Pentagon are only examples of what an intervention of outsiders can lead to."

"*You* were behind September eleventh?"

"No, you have to learn to listen," Balcer answered angrily. For the first time during the conversation he lost patience. "That tragedy would not have occurred had the CIA stayed away from the Fifth Internationale. The world's terrorist networks cannot be controlled using Cold War tactics, which the agency employs. To penetrate the gutters one doesn't recruit operatives at diplomatic receptions. Central Intelligence failed because it tried to clutch at matters beyond its comprehension and ability to control. Not to mention what America represents. Will it come as a surprise to you if I tell you that the United States of America's foreign policies are not received fondly in many parts of the world? Your president doesn't seem to see it that way. When the world learned who stood behind what it considered patriotic movements, it erupted. The World Trade Center was a warning."

"Bin Laden and Nine-eleven triggered the race to war, not the American involvement in combustible regions of the globe."

"Wars are not fought by individuals, Agent Penskie. Your president would not dare storm Iraq had it not been for the support of the American people. It goes for Bin Laden, too. Osama is just a pawn, an ejaculation of the right moment in history. And like your president he's an expression of countless minds. Unfortunately we are living in such times when terror and wars are still the most common ways of settling our differences. Links to militant and terrorist organizations are something I'm not proud of, but at least when in our hands these forces were under relative control. It's a common misconception that the Fifth Internationale was built on terror. Forgive me if I won't divulge names, but you can trust me when I say that some of the wealthiest, most powerful corporations and true global giants comprise a network of thousands of companies and institutions that are the foundation of our existence. In a way, the Fifth Internationale is just a pawn like your president, or Bin Laden. We were able to form and exist because we were needed, and we are needed now more than ever. There is no government on the face of the Earth that would want us destroyed, because destroying us would mean serious economic and social downturns in their regions. See, we are a product of history, Agent Penskie. What the world gains through our existence is the return of the balance of power. By withdrawing Americans from militant and terrorist networks we allow the rest of the world to participate in the progress of events rather than be silent witnesses to the unilateral tactics of a bully."

"What does such generosity entail? What's in it for you?" Penskie asked with sarcasm. He was positively certain that this respectable-looking gentleman was a madman.

"To paraphrase the famous words: It's not what we expect the world to give us; it's what we can give to the world. What the United States is trying to achieve, a worldwide unity with common objectives, is predestined for failure for the simple fact that the world will not accept the Americans dominating. The United Nations more often than not represents totally different and unacceptable views to those of the U.S., and U.S. opposition makes the U.N. inoperable. *We* can be the body that ties the world together, that leads it to a peaceful growth existence."

"You." Penskie snorted.

"Yes, because we are not constrained by such antiquities as nationalism and local patriotism. But I understand your skepticism. Individual profit. It's been with us throughout history. Always will be. Sure, some—hell, many—will profit. The drive to prosperity is after all what the world was built on, and as an American you should understand it better than any. But what the world can get in exchange is far more precious. You have to understand that whether or not the Fifth's links to militant organizations are terminated, the process of our economic and political growth cannot be stopped for the simple fact that we are not some identifiable entity that can be isolated and removed. We're an integral part of every aspect of the global economy and political structures. We exist but we cannot be pinpointed and eradicated. We've grown beyond that point. It's not even that we're so powerful—"

"Yes, yes, you've already said that. But if you are as mighty as you imply then why not put an end to it yourself?"

"The chaos that would erupt as a result of such confrontation would have dire effects on a global scale. You saw what happened when the Towers fell. What will happen if members of Congress start to die, what if your politicians, intelligence officers, and civilians are killed—and killing is the only way to achieve this kind of success. A war, Agent Penskie. A war worse than any other: a civil war. Americans killing Americans. As I've tried to explain to you, we're not a particular entity that can be identified by a set of principles, policies, political affiliations, or geographical boundaries. Rather, we are what the circumstances, both local and global, call for. Those individuals you just saw on the computer can be eliminated as easily as they were recruited. There are organizations, even governments in the world that would be more than happy to send assassins after these Americans, whether in the name of a holy war or a million other reasons. What's worse, there would be just as many Americans ready to do the job. And what's ironic in all this: The Fifth Internationale would profit still, whether the world was flooded in blood or sunbathed in rays of eternal happiness and peace. If you were led to believe otherwise then you were quite misled. We don't want a war. We are civilized people, Agent Penskie. Some of our members and supporters are Nobel prize winners. Violence and hatred are not virtues we care to cultivate."

"Ah, money and ethics! You want to clear your conscience by offering the world prosperity! What a pile of crap!"

"Tsk, tsk . . . Working with the scum has roughened your soul and narrowed your mind. The cynicism is blindfolding your thoughts."

"Why don't you skip the sermon? I care as little for your ethical outlook as you did when you murdered Sito!"

"Sito?"

"Robert Sito, the UOP officer who brought out the evidence of a cover-up in Borysewicz's murder. You didn't even know his name, you son of a bitch! What do you know about ethics?"

"Case in point. It's reached the stage when it's no longer possible to tell who's who. What this man uncovered could not damage the Fifth Internationale. The only thing that could be hurt by such evidence is the UOP, and whoever else is directly interested in the puny information Borysewicz had to offer. If the truth was to surface that the UOP was covering up, the only party this would harm is the UOP. The *Urząd Ochrony Państwa* killed this man to protect itself. There's no going further. Please! Sit down and let me illustrate it for you. Thank you. See, you know now that the Fifth Internationale exists, but did you believe that man then?" Balcer paused, his eyes locked on Penskie's. "You see, then. Did this man even know what he'd stumbled upon? It goes for the world at large, too. As far as the world is concerned there is no such thing as an international alliance of—pardon the expression—*spooks* and corporate moguls. It makes a fun read while waiting at the supermarket and fingering through the *National Enquirer*, but no serious media producer would ever take on the subject, other than to stir their readers' emotions and sell a few extra copies. Hell, we've published such stories to boost sales of our papers, too. Would it ever . . . has it ever interested the officials? No! Because it's too outrageous."

"Either that or because you control legislature, as you control the UOP."

Balcer ignored the hint. He glanced at his watch. The conversation had lasted longer than he had anticipated, but at last this young man was sufficiently primed for Balcer to lay the case in front of him.

"As Borysewicz before me, I am prepared to release the names of those individuals who are responsible for the militant arm of our organization. Furthermore, your government will have the complete information on Korea's weapons-of-mass-destruction program. We'll give them to you, along with the details on how to neutralize them without going into war. You could be the savior of hundreds or perhaps thousands of lives, Mr. Penskie."

Penskie did not reply immediately. It was clear to him that Balcer was trying to appeal to his conscience. That devious bastard!

"How come I get the feeling it's a sign of weakness, not conscience?" he asked sarcastically.

"You are quite wrong. The backbone cannot be destroyed. Besides, the world is better off with us rather than without. Ousted communists may have formed it, but the Fifth Internationale does not rule with a whip. If we've learned anything, it's that one cannot enslave others indefinitely. Eventually the resources needed for that purpose would outgrow one's ability to supply them. Examples can be found throughout human history: Those enslaved will seek independence regardless of how long it takes, eventually eroding their captors from within. Tell me, could the Solidarity have ousted the communists by letting its militant arm, the *Solidarność Walcząca*, bomb party assemblies or assassinate party delegates? Of course not! So is it a sign of weakness? I'd call it common sense with a degree of shrewdness. Face it, Mr. Penskie, America did not end up as the only superpower because it had more nukes. No. There comes a point when it no longer matters how many weapons you have in your arsenal when only a fraction can send the entire planet out of orbit. It was the Marshall Plan that provided the best learning experience. The answer is very simplistic but accurate. It was the multiplicity of George Washington's likeness in virtually every corner of the world." Balcer withdrew a single one-dollar bill from his slim leather wallet. It was crisp. He raised it and showed it to Penskie. "Money! Of course, tanks helped a great deal in many places and in many circumstances, but it was your green buck that proved to be a far more effective weapon. Military action may end in fiasco. What an embarrassment! Money will go much farther."

"Economic sanctions did not oust Castro."

"I'm not talking about sanctions. Cash, dear Stan. While the United States bans dealings with Cuba, her allies—Canada is a good example—enjoy good relations with the dictator. In effect Castro can laugh at Washington. I'll let you in on a secret: The Fifth Internationale can make such an embargo truly effective. How? Because we are not bound or slowed down by diplomatic babble or public relations. We can afford not to look back once the wheel is set in motion. Why? Because as far as the world is concerned we don't really exist."

It was clear to Penskie why Balcer's speech was so effective: The man was mad. He had to be to believe his own words. He wanted to be the savior of the world. It made him extremely dangerous. Whether or not the Fifth Internationale was real, or perhaps was only coming into existence, Penskie had to play his part very carefully. He realized he had to outwit someone worse than a master of deception. He had to convince a crazy man with a finger on a trigger that he agreed with his vision.

Below ground level, in cellars excavated some five hundred years earlier and expanded in the 1940s for the chancellor of the Third Reich, a group of men gathered around a long wooden table. They were deciding the fate of a traitor, a long-standing member of their organization who almost gave them over as prey to those savages from Central Intelligence. The council meeting was over and the voting turned out as expected: With the exception of a few who took the liberty to withhold their vote, no doubt in light of the sentiments held by the majority, all members decided against the American leadership. It took a decisive veto and a lot of convincing on the current leader's part to forestall their demands for complete removal of all Americans from the ranks of the organization. The council members were angry. The American position on Iraq showed beyond any doubt that the Americans would seize power to rule unilaterally, an impossible-to-accept slap in the face. Within the organization there were no superpowers, no richer or stronger allies. Together they formed one successful entity where all members were equal. The uncovering of a conspiracy to sell out the organization to the American intelligence called for a strong response. They all agreed it would have to be a spectacular act, one that would put off even the slightest hint of such intentions in the future. It would have to be harsh and generous at the same time. The latter was already in effect: The American members who refrained from voting or voted against Alpha would be allowed to return home. To demonstrate that loyalty was not without reward, those men would be elevated to higher positions in their home country—the organization would need new deputies, and the governments there would need new leaders. On the other hand, treason would have to be treated with the reaction that it called for: severe punishment.

"Don't take it personally, Mr. Ambassador. Certainly you must understand the position our organization found itself in, and hopefully it will help you appreciate what we are about to do," said Moshe Klein, the Israeli delegate.

The ambassador from the United States of America lay on the elongated table, his limbs spread out and chained to the tabletop. His mouth was gagged but he was no longer making attempts to plead for humane treatment. Physically exhausted from his earlier struggle, he lay in complete numbness, only his eyes, moistened with tears, showing signs of life.

"Let's get it over with already! The traitor does not deserve the courtesy of being spoken to," said Rijn van Boerg, the South African delegate.

"Let's hear suggestions then," said Yevgeny Ostipovich Snegov, the leader's Russian deputy. He turned to Alosha, a young public prosecutor from Moscow and his personal aide. "Have them set up the cameras and switch on the lights. Perhaps the sight of the equipment will help us come up with the most appropriate tool?"

Alosha spoke on a two-way radio, and a moment later lights illuminated the hall where the conversation was taking place. It was a large oval cavelike dwelling cut in the rock directly underneath the castle. The walls were left unfinished, the sharp edges of rock glistened in the lights. Along the walls stood equipment whose function was not immediately clear. Museum plaques explained the gruesome purpose it was used for. The hall was the part of the museum that housed a large collection of medieval torture paraphernalia. A collection of simple cat's-paws and head and bone crushers and more elaborate items, such as the Judas cradle and intricate hanging cages with pointed spikes, comprised the most anticipated exhibit in the museum. The centerpieces of the exhibit were an inquisitional chair equipped with mechanisms to force its hundreds of sharp spikes into the body, and a variation of the Maiden of Nuremberg, a sarcophagus with elongated spikes that were driven into the flesh of the person locked inside.

"Couldn't we just drive pins under his fingernails and send him home as a *living* example?" asked someone with a low resistance to instruments that inflicted pain.

Nobody answered. Everyone was looking around like excited schoolchildren.

"Everything here is so positively poetic in its ancient and guttural primitivism, it's hard to choose a single item." Haleb Aram Ashur stood in front of the large bone-breaking wheel, his eyes wide-open in fearful admiration.

"It would be a true feast for the eyes, but alas, we cannot spend eternity here. Today is actually Christmas Eve, the holiest of holidays. Our families await us," said one of the Poles, and glanced at his wristwatch.

"Right. Before we disperse we should like to hear what is going to happen afterward. The body," someone said.

"Indeed," someone else added. "One can't even bury bodies in the woods anymore, as exemplified by the . . . what was his name, the American from the Economic Development Agency? Anyway, the body was found, and it brought unnecessary attention—"

"This was an ad hoc operation; our man had not thought it over. This time there will be no trace; no one will ever have a chance to conduct a postmortem. Follow me," said Snegov. In the far end of the chamber he stopped before an enormously large cast-iron vat with an open top. Underneath it was a stack of wood, as for a bonfire. "Some of you who had your share of interrogative experience in the sixties and seventies should remember this simple solution for disposing of undesirable evidence after an interrogation ended with a dead body . . . those frail enemies of the state. Gentlemen, may I present you with the venerable flax bleaching pot? Any organic matter boiled in it long enough will dissolve without a trace." He looked upon the surrounding faces with a smile. He was genuinely pleased to be able to surprise his peers with something simple yet practical.

While the group assembled around the cast-iron vat, two men arrived carrying a tall tripod, a digital video camera, and a large light reflector. They proceeded to set up the equipment amidst the animated conversation being conducted around them. Unnoticed by the stately men torn between impalement and skinning, personal favorites of the Far Eastern delegates, the two activated the camera to record the events taking place, its lens directed at the council members instead of the condemned. One of them opened the oversize camera bag he carried on his shoulder, but instead of taking out photographic or video equipment he firmly pressed a small detonator into the C4 plastic explosive that filled the bag.

Chapter Twenty-five

"What will happen to those American operatives you are willing to expose? What will happen to the Central Intelligence Agency?" Stan asked with a degree of genuine concern. Somewhere in the outrageous plot had to be a reason for Balcer's taking the time to talk to him, to seek his cooperation.

"It will help them make the right decision. Something that should've been done with the collapse of the Soviet Union and the end of Cold War: reorganization. Your country needs an intelligence agency capable of surviving in the new times. A whole different mode of thinking and operating."

"But that would render USINTEL inoperative for years!"

"There is no need to exaggerate, Agent Penskie. The Czechs did it, and their intelligence functions well. It's not my place to suggest this, of course, and ultimately it's up to you, the Americans, to sit down and seriously think it over. Just remember: September eleventh was fully preventable." Balcer glanced at his wristwatch. "This is, however, beside the point right now; we have other concerns to consider. My part in helping your decision makers to find the right answers is setting you off in the right direction."

"How do you see it done?"

"Take it directly to the director of the FBI."

"Why can't you do it yourself? From what I've seen you must have people close to him." Penskie pointed at the notebook computer.

"Two reasons. One, it'll work only if the truth is told by someone on the inside, someone genuine. Would you have trusted the enemy when they came to deal with you? Your arrival here presented us with the second good reason: your relationship to Zbigniew Penskie, a man of the highest moral virtues, a man whose word means something to the president himself."

"Why not go directly to the president, then?"

Balcer shook his head. He paused, and Penskie thought for a moment he was not going to reply. He did. He spoke slowly and deliberately, as if the question were anticipated.

"The current president is the sort of man who would be more than happy to keep the status quo, perhaps even reach for more. Having someone else do the dirty work would be a blessing for any leader. The World Trade Center and the Pentagon are a small price to pay for what he'd get in exchange. No. The news has to be delivered to a clean party, led by a powerful voice that can successfully oppose the president's advisers. Why? Because there is no doubt that they will press him to keep control of the Fifth Internationale. I am sure of it."

Balcer's last words left no doubt as to the sources of his information.

Penskie understood.

"You have people close to him and won't give them away?" he asked in a voice that suggested a readiness to barter.

Balcer smiled, but did not respond.

"How many other operatives will you not expose? How many federal agents will you keep?"

No response.

"Give me a reason why I should do this. How do you expect me to react, knowing any one of my colleagues might be working for you?" Penskie raised his voice.

"A day will come, Agent Penskie, when the FBI will grow to appreciate our . . . cooperation. There is no reason why it shouldn't benefit both sides. We could be your link to all intelligence and police forces around the world. Think about it. No boundaries for the exchange of information. An Echelon-like web of global law enforcement community."

"With you pulling the strings."

"We could have had it by now had it not been for the CIA's possessiveness."

"Right," Penskie said doubtfully. "Let's just concentrate on today."

Balcer reached to a wooden box on the side of the desk. He opened the lid and offered Penskie a cigar.

The assistant legal attaché declined.

"You will deliver the names of those of our operatives who are necessarily expendable to make your director appreciate the gesture." The Pole spoke while snipping off the end of the cigar. "I would like him to see that I'm willing to cooperate. Whether he likes it or not, I think he'll have to agree that certain mutual concessions are worth the ultimate goal, though the goals may be quite different for both parties. Your country gets the truth. We can enter a new stage in our existence, one without the dark legacy of our past."

Penskie did not reply. He remained quiet, pondering the conversation. Balcer's information proved even more staggering than the earlier speculations of Mollie, Urbaniak, and his father. His quick browse through the database revealed that virtually every department of the Federal Bureau of Investigation had been infiltrated by the Fifth Internationale's operatives. Links he had no time to follow pointed to all departments of the government, including the Pentagon. Balcer was right: The Fifth Internationale was powerful, but his desire to break free of the CIA's elusive control over the Fifth's militant arm lowered Penskie's opinion of its strong position. Balcer's story was flawed. The question was, How? Could the Central Intelligence Agency control only one, bloody side of the Fifth Internationale without having decisive influence on the rest of the organization? It would make more sense that the agency was able to control the entire organization. It would explain why Balcer sought help from the outside instead of taking care of the problem from within. But such interpretation was even more frightening. It meant the CIA controlled not only the entire American intelligence, and possibly the army and government, but also those departments in other countries in which the Fifth had highly placed operatives. Which was worse: influencing the world by applying economic pressure, as favored by Balcer, or by deploying armed and deadly mercenaries and terrorists, the option—according to Balcer—supported by the CIA? Neither should be allowed to happen. As a naturalized American and an intellectual, Penskie could not stand the view of America's forcibly dictating its terms to other nations. He had never supported violent confrontations, believing in diplomacy and international cooperation on issues that demanded outside intervention, especially in trouble-stricken areas of the world. The Fifth Internationale's being able to reach this level of international unanimity, as described by its leader, had an appeal to him, and he understood how it could appeal to many around the world, but the Fifth represented the views of a clique, who stood on guard for their own interests. Penskie was not naïve. The Fifth did not care about the welfare of people; it cared about its assets in various regions of the world. Being muddled in questionable associations threatened the Fifth's economic growth. By helping Balcer get rid of the CIA, he was not supporting a better alternative. He understood that a structure as powerful as the Fifth Internationale, without proper oversight, should not exist, and the chance to put an end to it was in his hands. Whether Balcer was taking advantage of him for his own gain, or whether he was genuinely concerned about issues other than his own pocket, Penskie decided to play along. The FBI agent in him took charge.

"I'll do it," he said without looking into Balcer's eyes.

Balcer eased visibly. His tight lips rounded as his jaw relaxed.

"The director of the FBI is visiting Eastern Europe and will be lecturing at the International Law Enforcement Academy in Budapest the day after tomorrow," Balcer said straightforwardly as he reached into one of the drawers and took out a compact disk. His cold eyes were fixed on Stan's.

The disk was sealed in a plastic wrapper and bore the label of a popular Polish rock group. It looked like a brand-new musical disk, complete with a small shopping bag from a department store in Kraków. "This copy was prepared some time ago." He pushed the disk across the desk. "It contains the database, or rather excerpts of what you browsed a few moments ago. The information is secured with a sophisticated code that would take years to decipher should this fall into undesirable hands. Once this disk reaches the director, we will contact him with the appropriate codes."

"How am I supposed to deliver it?"

"No doubt your every step will be monitored the moment you leave these grounds. Were it not for the *Centralne Biuro Śledcze* and the stepped-up army air reconnaissance along the borders I'd lend you an aircraft, but as things are, I'm afraid you'll have to put some legwork into it. Four of my people will help you cross the border and complete the mission. Have you any specific questions before I proceed with the plan?"

His telephone rang, and Balcer excused himself.

Penskie was ready to enter battle stage two: What happened to the woman he was with? During their conversation Balcer did not mention Mollie Banks. Now it was Penskie's turn to demand answers and concessions. He was not going to leave without Mollie.

Stan watched Balcer's face grow tense during the short telephone message. He could not help but hear sporadic words: *GROM? . . . What happened to the radars? . . . How could they? . . . Who gave the orders? . . .*

Soon Balcer replaced the receiver and motioned to his guards, who at the same time were communicating with someone else through their headset radios. One of them approached the desk and helped Balcer gather things off the tabletop and shove them inside the spacious drawers.

"I'm afraid our time is up. You'll have to leave immediately," Balcer said to Stan. He placed the notebook and a Palm Pilot in a silver briefcase he picked up from the floor. He continued gathering more items when sudden gunfire erupted in the depths of the castle's hallways. Balcer locked the briefcase and chained it to his wrist.

"Follow me," he said to Penskie.

"What's happening?" Stan asked anxiously.

"Somewhat unexpected and very unwelcome visitors," Balcer said composedly.

The guard finished clearing the desk and joined his boss and Penskie at the large door. He turned around and pressed a key on his small wireless converter. There was a muted thump inside the desk, and gray fumes started to pour through invisible cracks. Satisfied, the guards opened the doors and ushered the leader into the enormous hall. They started across, their weapons drawn. Short bursts of machine gun fire were now more audible. Still, they were distant, and Penskie could not determine the direction they came from. It could have been inside as easily as outside.

The party approached the large fireplace made of white marble, its mantel six feet high. Inside was a single pine log two feet in diameter and four feet long, obviously serving decorative purposes only. The fireplace must have been used from time to time, though, as its walls were covered with black soot. One of the guards bowed down and walked into the chimney. He pushed on one side of the wall and it swiveled open. The guard walked inside and switched on the lights. There was a narrow corridor, poorly but sufficiently lit by low-wattage lights installed in the low arched ceiling. Balcer went inside and motioned Penskie to follow.

"Where is the woman?" Penskie took a step back and walked into the remaining guard.

"She'll meet us on the other side," Balcer replied but was interrupted by a sudden noise.

The doors to the grand hall swung open and two more guards rushed in, their automatic rifles drawn. At the same instant two windows shattered and two figures dressed in combat gear landed on the floor and turned somersaults. Just as the first assailant regained his posture, kneeling on one leg, the newly arrived guards opened fire. Bullets ripped through the man, throwing him back. Before he fell to the floor the second man placed two precise shots in both guards' foreheads. Their heads sprang back under the impact as their bodies slumped to the ground. They continued squeezing the triggers, bullets leaving zigzagging lines on the ceiling. The guard who stood behind Penskie fired a frantic round at the soldier. Some of the bullets hit the chest and the bulletproof Pro-tec helmet, but the man was alive, crouched on the floor holding on to a shattered knee.

The incident took no more than twenty seconds, but to Stan time had stopped. He watched as the events unfolded in front of his eyes. The arrival of the commandos, the deaths of the two guards, and the return of gunfire happened so quickly he did not have the presence of mind to classify the situation as threatening. He did not duck to the floor or seek refuge inside the large fireplace. He stood frozen until the shattering silence that followed the guards' shots broke the spell. The silence roused him to reality. He noticed with his peripheral vision that Balcer was gone. As the guard reloaded his Beretta and approached the wounded commando, Penskie followed him and struck a powerful blow between the guard's collarbone and the neck in the area of the lower cervical vertebrae. He caught the unconscious body and lowered it to the floor.

"Thank you, Mr. Penskie." The soldier gasped in pain. "There is a helicopter waiting for you outside."

Stan was taken aback by the use of his name. He knelt down and wanted to help the man.

"No. You must go." The GROM commando raised his voice. He pushed himself toward the wall and sat against it. "You will find a small landing pod on a hill about a kilometer northwest from the castle. Here." He withdrew a cellular telephone and flipped open the keypad. The large liquid crystal display, the length and width of the telephone, illuminated and a map appeared on the screen. "It is blueprint of the castle and the grounds."

"Let me help you," Penskie started falteringly.

"No. There is no time. Go now!" the soldier said in an assertive tone.

Questions ran through Penskie's head. Questions he could not ask. There was no time. He looked at the soldier with hesitation. He could not leave a wounded man.

"I will be all right," the soldier said. "Go!"

Penskie picked up the unconscious guard's automatic pistol, and, without looking back, he darted through the door and down the cold staircase.

Chapter Twenty-six

"Alpha has struck after all," the national security adviser said. He looked at his companions with a grim expression. "We all know what that means. He's left us no alternative."

"Why wasn't Agent Penskie's presence used to stop him? Wasn't that the plan?" The attorney general pushed his glasses firmly onto his nose, his eyes fixed on the East Coast deputy leader of the organization.

"The leader firmly opposed such measures. It's not our place to question his actions; it's entirely possible the young Penskie will still serve his purpose, as the situation dictates. Unfortunately our communication with headquarters has been disrupted. We must rely on the emergency procedures. But when the call comes, I won't be surprised to receive the orders to execute plan Clean Sweep. We must ready ourselves, gentlemen. This is a historical moment."

"Removing the president from office is not something

many are given the opportunity to do," the secretary of defense started cautiously. "Not to mention when at last the nation and Congress stand firmly behind him."

"Neither the nation nor Congress has ever been charged with the extraordinary task of keeping our great country strong both on the national and international scene. The president's actions threaten our country's historical opportunity. His takeover of the organization will place us in complete isolation."

"There are some who might argue otherwise. They might say that having such control will assure our unfettered complete supremacy for decades to come."

That was new. They had asked questions before, but none had ever dared speak something so bordering on defiance as this. Has he become oversensitive? It had been a long and stressful day, one far from over, and his senses may have become sharper. He glanced over the faces gathered around the large living room. None were looking at him. Their eyes wandered from wall to wall, from one hanging picture to another, from bookcase to bookcase. None dared look into his eyes but the director of Central Intelligence.

Suddenly the national security adviser understood. They had rebelled. Alpha had reached them.

"Will it protect us from the likes of Al Qaeda or the Saddam Husseins of today and tomorrow? Many of our counterparts from other parts of the world will undoubtedly withdraw from the organization. We'll lose the edge that keeps our people and our land safe." He spoke calmly. He knew he had to play to their weakness, that one subtle sentiment all of them shared: their patriotism. The sentiment that flapped aimlessly like a forgotten pair of old long johns on a clothesline until cold weather forced the owner to make use of them again. "Superpower or not, we cannot afford to stand alone. Do you realize what we're headed for when the war on terrorism, or some new fancy of our government, is fulfilled and over with? A day will come when we'll be rid of our enemies. We'll have to create new ones. Who is the most likely candidate? Who stands in the way of our expansion? Whose aggressive industries are gaining the edge over ours? It's a natural process, gentlemen. Take control of the organization and you risk a breakup. The world once again divided. Without the independent organization, the body that binds us all together, we are looking at a whole new war, one just as bad as the Cold War. Europe will never sink to the position of our servant. We'll be forced to fight against our allies, very powerful ones. No country, however great, can sustain such pressure. Recession, poverty, civil unrest . . . perhaps dictatorship . . ."

"Keeping the status quo only deepens our dependence. America is losing her identity. Mere membership within the organization lowers *us* to the position of a servant. The American people have worked long and hard enough to see their country lead the world. It is, after all, their money that paid for it," said the defense secretary.

"The American people know very little about the rest of the world, and care even less about it. Membership in the organization helps open their eyes to the world, and what's more, it helps the world see us in a different light. Shutting ourselves up deepens the rift that began forming even amongst our allies. Look at Europe, France. . . . Hell, look even closer: Look at Canada, gentlemen. Our border-screening of their citizens alienated our closest neighbor. It's only the beginning. Separatism is a mistake!"

The Central Intelligence director rose from his seat and looked around the room. It did not take long to convince the others to join the president. While the initial reluctance could be attributed to the sheer fear of challenging the organization, their benefactor for many years, the events in Europe played a key role in their final decision. They began to believe that the organization was not so powerful after all. That it was possible to stand up to it, something no one ever dared to do before. Each one of them had joined for different reasons, none of them known to the DCI, but he knew one thing: All had succumbed to the one virtue that now bound them together—America. Whether driven by patriotism or fear, the latter skillfully exploited by the director, they all switched in anticipation of a confrontation. If America were to ambush the organization as if it were a country, as a military power, there would have been only one outcome: Their heads would have rolled together with other members'. Whatever their personal beliefs, one desire accompanied them throughout their lives: being on the winning side. The president seemed determined to annex the organization by all means available to him. That spelled war. War meant victory for the president. For, whatever resources the organization had in her possession, she could not stand up to the United States. It did not matter that the organization could not fall under attack as a military target. Short of its headquarters it had no borders, no assets whose destruction could cripple its existence. To control the organization one had to acquire its databases. The information was the key. If the leader was foolish enough to hold it all under one roof, in Nowa Wieś, then it had become a target. The trouble was, the headquarters was on foreign soil. How could the president achieve his goal? The answer was simple: the Polish army. They knew the organization never aspired to controlling the armies of the countries in which it operated. Which meant Alpha took advantage of this oversight on the part of the leader and his council. With the army at his disposal Alpha would succeed. There was no point defending a lost cause. All there was left to them was to save their lives and join Alpha and the president.

"We've decided unanimously to join the president," the director of Central Intelligence spoke on behalf of the others. "Our decision is final. All cells under our command will follow our orders."

At that instant the others stood up in support of the director's statement.

The national security adviser remained motionless in a circle of determined men. No longer shy and avoiding his eyes, they stared at him boldly and provocatively, like schoolboys caught in mischief who denied allegations despite positive evidence against them. A barely visible grin disfigured the corners of the national security adviser's lips. He understood that the basis for their disobedience lay in fear. And when faced with fear they would turn once again.

Chapter Twenty-seven

The rooms and chambers were distinctly regal in their calm and spacious atmosphere. The low ambient light accentuated selected objets d'art, skillfully displayed on mantels and pedestals. Ornamental sculptures, rich paintings and tapestries hanging on the walls, exceptional workmanship in every detail of every item, combined with the complete lack of people would have delighted any art historian and aficionado. It was as if one were miraculously transported to the Louvre, or the Hermitage after-hours. Great masterpieces representing centuries of human expression in art were crushingly overwhelming.

Penskie had not noticed, let alone appreciated, the amazing collections amassed in the rooms he passed. His mind concentrated on re-creating the route he had been brought along by the guards earlier that day. What seemed fairly straightforward—follow a series of chambers and hallways that should take him to a large staircase—turned out to be complicated and unnerving. The blueprints provided by the GROM commando were illegible to him. He did not recognize any familiar objects en route. According to his calculations he should have found the staircase long ago; instead he kept entering more rooms that looked the same. Just on the verge of losing his patience he decided to pass one more doorway, then turn around; somewhere along the way he must have missed the staircase. He jerked the handle of the large door and sighed with relief. A long cold hallway led to the staircase. He had found it! He could now hear agitated but distant voices coming from the depths of the castle, occasional gunfire breaking their monotonous whine.

Two flights of stairs later Penskie recognized a narrow concrete hallway with a row of cells. He ran past numerous doors, some of which were closed, until he reached the room he had been locked in during the day. He assumed Banks was kept in one of the adjoining rooms. The closest ones stood empty.

"Mollie!" he called out.

Nothing.

"Mollie!"

He could hear a distant thumping at the end of the hallway. Someone was knocking and kicking on the doors. As he approached the end of the corridor he recognized male voices. They were shouting in English.

"Who are you?" he asked.

In the momentary pause that followed he could hear a muted and incomprehensible consultation.

"We are Americans," a voice finally replied.

"With the embassy," another one added.

"Who are you?" Penskie repeated.

"Intelligence and research."

Penskie was taken aback. Balcer had not lied. He did not kill those INR agents.

"Agent Penskie?" the first voice asked hesitantly.

Stan did not reply.

"Agent Penskie, you are in grave danger! We've come to help you get out of here. You must leave immediately. Go back to the embassy."

"How did you find me?"

"Your father," the voice replied after a short pause.

"What about my father?"

"Your father requested the embassy's assistance after you were kidnapped. Open the doors, Agent Penskie. We must get out of here. This place . . . it will be blown up."

Penskie pondered the answers. Balcer did not lie when he said he only staged their deaths. He also said they came to assassinate Penskie. How did he put it? *They came to eliminate you.* But was the leader telling the truth? He knew one side was manipulating him but could not begin to guess which.

"What's this about blowing up the castle?"

"Explosives have been planted. We've come to take you out."

"How do you know this?"

No reply.

"Who are you?"

"Let us out, Agent Penskie. There's no time for it."

Suddenly he heard his name called out from the far end of the corridor. In the dim light he could not make out the identity of the person. It was not Banks; he was sure of that. The voice was male and called him by his first name. Penskie withdrew behind the doors of the closest cell. He could not see the man, but from the growing strength of his voice he knew the stranger was nearing. At the next call something in the man's voice struck him as oddly familiar.

"Ed?" he asked from the safety of the cell.

The legal attaché approached cautiously along the cold wall, a Glock in his outstretched arm.

"Thank God, we've made it in time!" he exclaimed.

The presence of another person alerted the confined intelligence and research team commander. In a loud voice he demanded immediate help and release.

Powell rushed in to the door but his deputy cut him off.

"The scoundrels might be working for the Fifth!" Stan explained.

"What? Why are they locked in then?"

"I don't know; there are too many unanswered questions." Penskie pulled his friend's arm and headed up the far end of the corridor. Powell followed hesitantly. The angry voices of the Americans soon subsided.

In quick, erratic words Powell explained the events that led to his presence in Nowa Wieś.

"Apparently the Defense knew about Balcer, but their hands were tied because of tremendous corruption within the government and law enforcement. Whenever they caught a lead and were ready to move in they were stalled, and eventually the case got thrown out. Can you imagine the level Balcer's organization is able to reach?" Powell concluded.

"I can." Penskie patted on his pocket. "I've got it, Ed! I've got the names . . . not all . . . some, but it's a start!"

"What do you mean?" Powell kept pace alongside Stan.

"Balcer, he wants me to . . . Well, never mind. He gave

me excerpts of the Fifth's database. They want to clean it—clean themselves in order to break free from—get this—American control!"

"What does Balcer want you to do?"

"Take it to the director. Have him clean the USINTEL and—"

"You bought it?" Powell stopped in bewilderment.

"Yes . . . no . . . I mean, yes to the fact he wants to shake off the CIA. No to his reasoning. Anyway, we've got to stop him; he has the complete database on him!"

Penskie resumed his pace. Suddenly he turned to Powell. "Any idea what happened to Banks?"

"How can you be certain he's not misleading you?" The legal attaché appeared to have not heard the question.

"What?"

"Those names Balcer gave you. How can you be sure it isn't calculated misinformation intended to sow mistrust and have it blow us up from within?"

"I can't, but there is a way to find out: Compare it with the original. Balcer's got the disks on him."

They had reached the end of the corridor and stood at the beginning of another one. To the left was a plain wall with a suit of armor of a medieval knight. To the right the corridor led to the staircase, a small nook on the side. Powell turned toward it.

"There's a helipad on the neighboring hill, some few hundred meters to the north of here. If Balcer wanted to escape it would've been the surest way."

"I know. He's probably gone by now."

"Maybe not. GROM are watching it. Come on," Powell stepped up pace.

"But Banks—"

"She lived in Poland for two years, Stan," the legal attaché said over his shoulder.

"Studied. I know. In Kraków. So?"

"In her second year at the institute she got a job at *Art and Artists* magazine, an English-language monthly owned by Borysewicz until it was allowed to go bankrupt. At that time Borysewicz cochaired Artico, a company that at some point operated billions in government funds, secretly buying the country's foreign debt at preferential rates from Western financial institutions. Artico's cochair was Balcer."

"I know this," Penskie replied, a trace of anger in his voice.

Powell looked back, not certain what his friend knew about—that Banks worked for the magazine or about Artico's dealings. The latter was a matter of public knowledge. The Artico affair resulted in one of the biggest scandals in the country's history, mainly due to billions lost in unexplained and untraceable financial operations.

"Banks worked for Balcer before she was recruited by the CIA, Stan."

Penskie gasped and stopped abruptly, pulling on the sleeve of Powell's parka.

"Sorry about that, but it'd only come through after you'd left." Powell paused, apparently alarmed by the focused expression on his deputy's face.

Penskie stared at the end of the corridor, into the small nook. It was a dark concrete area with an arched ceiling not more than six feet high.

"There's someone in there!" Stan whispered with anxiety.

"You imagined it."

"No. There was a man in there, looking at us. At first I thought he was going to shoot, but he changed his mind and . . . disappeared."

Powell focused his eyes on the nook.

"Maybe it was a GROM commando? They know me and have a picture of you."

"It was a civilian. Where're we going?"

"I told you, there's a passage from the castle to the landing. Come, there is no time!" Powell pulled out of Penskie's grip and in just a few long leaps he reached the nook. He pushed on one side of the wall and it opened. "No one in here." He motioned for Penskie to approach.

Stan advanced cautiously. It was a small storage room; old mops, galvanized buckets, dirty rugs, and crumpled cardboard boxes lay on the floor. Broken-down storage shelves leaned under the weight of paint cans and jars of impossible-to-determine substances. Behind a large stack of old wooden crates the wall was darker than elsewhere, a cold breeze coming from its direction. The dark area proved to be a small door leading to a narrow passage similar to the one Balcer entered upstairs, inside the hearth.

"How did you know about this passage?"

"I . . . we . . . GROM found the landing and the entrance to it. They had the castle's blueprints."

"How did you find me?"

"Your father . . ."

"No! How did you know where to look for me in the castle?"

"What are you driving at?" Powell stared coldly into Stan's eyes. A single lightbulb flickered under the low ceiling, casting long shadows on their faces.

"This place is enormous, with countless corridors and God knows how many rooms!"

"Don't let it get to you, Stan. You've been running in circles from one bizarre lead to another. There is no conspiracy! No Fifth Internationale! No penetration! Balcer's been under suspicion for industrial espionage and grand-scale corruption in the States, Germany, Japan, and half the world's countries. *He* is the villain. The only reason he's still at large is because he knows no allegiance other than to money. He'll steal secrets from someone today and to call off the chase will offer something to his victim or persecutor tomorrow. I'm talking dealings made at the very top of the government ladder. That is what makes it look like a conspiracy, Stan, and it is a conspiracy, but not the sort you were led to believe. The conspirators are those who make a mockery of the law enforcement and intelligence agencies. The bastard steals our latest technology, so we go after him, but he offers something our government can't pass up, like the Chinese or Korean nuclear development plans, or in this case Al Qaeda. That's right, you guessed what happened: We got called off. This time, however, he went too far. He's acquired our ABM plans, and the USG is not going to deal."

"He stole our antiballistic missile system plans?"

"According to the director he did."

"The director told you this?"

"We put our lives on the line here, yet we know nothing about what's going on, so I confronted him."

"You *confronted* the director of the FBI?"

"You keep repeating me. Yes, I have some influence in Washington, you know."

Penskie slouched resignedly.

"So this is why they kept us away from Borysewicz," he said quietly. He raised his head, sudden alertness in his eyes. "Who's running it then?"

"You'll get a kick out of this one—the state department, which I guess at this end means Hank."

"Shit."

"Yeah."

"Those INR agents didn't come after me then?"

"I wouldn't trust Russell to that extent . . . but I'm told their only job is to make sure you don't mess up the DCM's brilliant plans."

"Balcer knew they were coming. He expected them. He knew you and GROM were coming, too. It means he's got someone else at the embassy . . . or even worse—the state department."

"It's over. His reign, his corruption, everything is over. He must have been captured by now. These commandos are top-notch. We'll soon know everything about his operations. Come." Powell bowed his head and walked into the tunnel.

"He's gone by now," Penskie murmured doubtfully, but followed his friend.

The corridor was not more than five feet high. They walked briskly at first but soon had to slow down. It was tiresome having to walk half slouched, constantly looking for the industrial lights in metal cages that required bending even lower. Penskie soon lost count of his steps, annoyed with the soreness in his neck caused by the awkward position in which he was forced to walk. After what seemed an eternity Powell stopped in front of a small steel door. He pushed the door open and froze. The cold muzzle of an automatic rifle touched his forehead. A very bright light shone directly at the gate, bringing tears to his eyes.

Chapter Twenty-eight

"Can either of you fly this thing?" Balcer asked.

Dumbfounded by the turn of events, the Americans did not reply. Balcer was free; two commandos lay on the side of the landing area. Balcer's pilot had been shot and killed in the short battle that had erupted when they entered the landing. Four helicopters stood in a row—GROM's two Sokółs, a small Super Puma, and a Rah-66 Comanche belonging to Balcer. The latter was custom-ordered, stripped of visible weaponry and painted in indigo.

Balcer was enraged. Ignoring Stan's question about the presence of Mollie Banks, he approached one of the GROM soldiers, who lay slouched on the ground.

"I guess that leaves only you," he said, and motioned one of his guards.

A bulky man in a leather bomber jacket and chinos stepped forward. He cut the surgical tape binding the soldier's legs and lifted him effortlessly off the ground. The commando grimaced as his arm was pulled. He had both hands tied behind his back. A wet blot on his left bicep indicated a wound. His face showed pain but his eyes remained defiant. The guard dragged him over to one of the Sokółs. Soon the blinding beam of the searchlight was redirected toward the woods.

"I hope our deal stands despite this little interruption?" Balcer turned to Penskie.

"I'm afraid things have changed since," Penskie answered, thinking about Mollie.

"Ha! I suppose it is Mr. Powell's doing?" Balcer shifted his weight to face the legal attaché. "We've never had the opportunity to meet face-to-face, but I've always appreciated your integrity and considered you a loyal comrade."

"What the . . ."

"Come, now! Who got to you? I'm not buying that sudden-change-of-heart twaddle!"

"You son of a bitch!" Powell darted forward, his fists hitting the air as Balcer dodged them.

A powerful blow on his neck threw the legal attaché to the ground. He lost consciousness. The second one of Balcer's guards stood over the American's body, automatic pistol aimed at his temple. He stepped back on his leader's command.

"Goddamn you!" Anger permeated Stan's voice.

"I don't know what arguments your friend used to make you change your mind, but if I may remind you: Once a traitor always a traitor."

"What?" Stan hissed.

"You haven't looked it up?" Balcer appeared surprised. "I would have thought you would have verified your own unit in the first place."

The thought had not even crossed his mind. The legats a part of Balcer's organization? Preposterous!

"You're bluffing!" Stan replied, a barely discernible hesitation in his voice.

"You're holding the answer in your pocket, Agent Penskie. The CD . . ."

The rotor started its slow rotation, the piercing whine drowning the rest of the sentence.

Balcer instinctively bowed his head and motioned Penskie to board the helicopter.

The events that followed caught both men off guard. Balcer stood on the edge of the area lit by the helicopter's powerful searchlight, while the security man stood between his boss and Penskie. The noise and darkness immediately behind Balcer provided a suitable condition for the assault.

Balcer stood erect, his oddly stiff position alerting the guard. With his pistol raised the Pole took a few steps toward his principal. Only now did Penskie notice a gleam in the dark, just above Balcer's neck—a pair of eyes. Soon he could make out the silhouette of a person holding a gun to the leader's forehead. The two started backward toward the entrance of the tunnel, step after step. With his back safely covered by the rock where the entrance was hidden, and with a clear view of the landing, the captor shouted something into Balcer's ears. The leader hesitated a moment, but a jerk of the muzzle prompted him to motion a silent command to his guard. The guard dropped his weapon and withdrew three feet.

The overall confusion was short-lived. The second guard who escorted the GROM commando to the helicopter had finally noticed the events taking place outside. He directed the searchlight at the tunnel entrance, blinding everyone in its path and revealing the captor's identity.

The disarmed guard on the ground roared in fury that was lost in the helicopter's noise, a yawnlike expression on his face, and rushed in large leaps toward his boss. Halfway along the way Penskie tripped him up and the man tumbled down. As the guard struggled to get up on his feet, Penskie crashed a knee into the guard's back and pinned him down, twisting the man's arms.

Inside the helicopter the guard, preoccupied with the searchlight, momentarily lost sight of the GROM soldier he was supposed to monitor. This one moment of carelessness was enough for the soldier to apply a grip to the guard's neck. Seconds later the guard's body went limp and dropped to the floor.

Penskie looked past Balcer's shoulder into the tense eyes of Mollie Banks.

She watched the events unfold, and despite Penskie's gestures she continued to press the muzzle of a pistol to Balcer's neck until the helicopter's engine slowed.

"It's okay!" The legat's reassuring voice penetrated the subsiding noise.

With the guard immobilized, arms tied behind his back with a leather belt, Penskie walked up to the woman.

She finally eased her grip, pushed the leader away, and approached Penskie.

They embraced each other without a word.

Banks was wet and shivering from the cold, her wool sweater covered with small icy pellets. Her lips trembling, she explained the events that had brought her to the landing. She was ushered by one of Balcer's guards who was supposed to prepare the helicopter for takeoff but was ambushed by the soldiers and killed in the exchange of gunfire that followed. Shortly after, two more guards arrived from the woods, not from the tunnel as was anticipated, and killed one of the commandos and wounded the other. The soldier, though ambushed, put up fierce resistance. In the confusion Banks slid off the hill into the darkness, where she waited for what seemed like an eternity to her, but was likely not more than ten minutes, before Penskie and Powell arrived. During this time Balcer and his guards tried to start the helicopter. Having lost the pilot Balcer tried to contact another one. He used a two-way radio but no one responded. At this point the Americans arrived at the concealed gate.

"I saw people. Balcer had guests. Who were they? What happened to them?" Mollie asked in conclusion.

"They won't go far. Even if they do, we'll know who they were," Penskie said, and approached the leader. "The key, please."

"It's encrypted. Won't be of much use," Balcer replied coldly.

"All the same, the key."

Balcer handed over a small key and Penskie proceeded to unlock the chain that linked the leader's wrist to the silver briefcase. It was heavy. He inspected it and found a small flap under the handle. He opened it.

"The combination?" Penskie asked.

"You can't seriously expect to—"

"Now who's being melodramatic? It's only a briefcase. I'll pry it open if I have to."

"I was going to say, you can't seriously expect to solve everything, Agent Penskie. Even if you ever manage to decipher the information—"

"There are people who will take care of that."

"To whom can you entrust such a task? Will you verify them before or after you check the information? As the old riddle goes: What comes first: the chicken or the egg? *Kura czy jajko?*" The Pole laughed.

Penskie did not reply. His mind was racing. The logic of Balcer's question did not escape him. Balcer was right. Who could he trust? Who could the director trust? Could he hire an outside party to decipher the database? It was obvious the FBI could not do it, not before the allegiance of its officers could be verified. The questions mounted. The answers were vague. The more he thought about them the more confused he became. He shook his head. He had to come up with a plan. He had the database, but he was still in the heart of the enemy's territory. Trying to reach Urbaniak and father was unthinkable; he would have to postpone it. The safety of the database was his main concern. That and the woman. During his confinement in the cell, even during his emotional conversation with the leader, he did not stop thinking about Mollie Banks. Worry and longing were embedded in his heart. He could see in her eyes that she felt the same way. He could not bring himself to part with her. Not again. He shivered. He realized his feelings toward this woman were taking over his obligations. He knew he would not stop until she was safe. The moment he reconciled the thought in his mind he knew what he had to do.

Penskie approached Balcer, who began shouting obscenities.

"I could have killed you!" he concluded. "I spared your life only out of regard for your father. . . ."

Penskie pulled a handkerchief out of the leader's breast pocket and gagged his mouth, securing it with a necktie around his head. He then ordered the leader to enter the helicopter. With the help of the commando he picked up the unconscious guard and placed him on the floor next to

Balcer. They tied Balcer's and the guard's wrists to the metal beams over their heads. Before leaving the helicopter Penskie brought the briefcase and lifted it to Balcer's right hand. He opened the small flap under the handle, which revealed a tiny LCD screen and a small red light. He pulled out the leader's thumb and pressed it against the screen. One second later he heard a muted click and the light changed color from red to green.

Outside Penskie and the commando dragged the corpses out of the landing strip and farther toward the edge of the woods. At last Penskie leaned over the unconscious body of Ed Powell. He considered the short exchange of words between the legal attaché and Balcer and shook his head.

"I'm sorry, Ed. I can't afford to have doubts," he murmured, and with the help of the commando he carried Powell into the other of GROM's Sokółs.

Inside he related the supposed intended detonation of the castle and the location of the INR agents. The commando quickly relayed it to his colleagues via the radio.

Penskie then proceeded to explain his plan. The safety of the briefcase was crucial. The gunfire that could be heard in the distance suggested that GROM had not yet claimed control of the castle, and quite possibly had run into growing resistance. Flying out in these circumstances posed far too much risk. Besides, the whereabouts of the helicopter could be traced, something Penskie could not allow.

The commando understood and agreed; his job was to secure the landing. He shook hands with Banks and Penskie and hid in the woods, where he would keep watch, an automatic rifle at his side.

Stan took Mollie's hand and, without looking back, pulled her down the steep slope of the wooded hill.

Chapter Twenty-nine

Margaret Penskie, referred to as Gosia by her family, lived in a small apartment just off Plac Na Stawach, a busy weekend market square ten minutes on foot from Rynek Główny. Every weekday morning she pedaled five minutes to the American school on Ulica Warneńczyka. She was twenty-eight, single, and loving her life. Prior to coming to Poland she had spent a year in Japan and a year in Hong Kong teaching English. Such a lifestyle suited her. She had planned to go to Thailand after the summer she spent with her brother in Poland, but she met Robert Sito and fell in love. She stayed, but the only position she could find was in Kraków, a three-hour train ride away. The relationship survived the test of long distance, curiously strengthened by periods of parting.

Gosia was born in Kraków, but her memories consisted of only her immediate neighborhood, a magical world of joy and laughter. Now, after almost four months of living in the ancient city, she had rediscovered her childhood home. She was fascinated with the lively Old Town and its narrow cobblestone streets bustling with students and colorful crowds of tourists. She walked and jogged the chestnut tree-lined Planty, cycled across the Błonie or along the riverbanks, and hiked the Skałki with energy she never felt before. She loved her life. She loved this city. She wanted to stay here forever.

Margaret Penskie was positively happy. She had found a sense of identity and belonging she had never felt in the United States, though her brother often said that if any one of their family could truly call themselves American it could only be Gosia. After the family was forced to seek asylum in the West, Stan would often tease her by saying she was too young and did not have the same emotional and cultural attachment to Poland the rest of them had. She took it seriously at first, but soon realized it was only "brother talk"; older brothers were supposed to belittle their sisters—it made them feel superior. It was the threat of girls' earlier maturity that turned some brothers into patronizing boors. The truth was, she missed Poland more than any of them, if only for the girlfriends she left behind. But that was long ago, and during the years in America Stan was more than a brother—he was a good friend too. She was glad to have him close when she met Robert. She had doubts about starting a new relationship, after the last one had turned sour. Stan was there to talk to her, and to listen. It was he who lent the support necessary to remind her that not all men were like the one she broke up with. She owed Stan her relationship with Robert, the best thing that had ever happened in her life.

Margaret logged off of the Internet. Writing e-mails and chatting online with friends in the United States and Asia took the better part of the evening, and she wanted to keep the phone line free in case Robert phoned. She had not talked to him in three days. The snowstorm in the mountains prevented communication, and now Robert was not answering his telephone. He was probably busy. It happened occasionally. There were times when he worked undercover and could not afford to telephone or receive telephone calls. Personally she could not understand how someone could not find five minutes to telephone—after all, a five-minute phone call—was just a five-minute phone call—but she learned to appreciate the nature of Robert's job. Sometimes he managed to slip her a short SMS message, and it made it worth the wait. Stan insisted that men like Robert tended to be so wholeheartedly dedicated to their work that they devoted their entire conscious life to it, the unconscious being a whole other matter. Stan was right. Robert was not as much a workaholic as he was in his element. He loved his work and he gave it all his energy, but he always thought about her. He loved her and his thoughts were with her. He did not have to say it. She knew. They had an agreement whereby each day they could not talk or see each other they would touch a small silver heart each wore on a silver chain. At the specific time of day she could swear she felt a certain energy fill her body as she touched the small object. It must have come from Robert. Two days in a row now she had not felt anything. She tried to convince herself it was only a silly superstition, but it did not help. She was beginning to worry. If that was not enough, tomorrow was supposed to be the big day: She wanted her father to meet Robert, her fiancé. She glanced at the telephone when a gentle knock on the door drew her attention.

She opened the door.

Gosia did not cry. The news was so shocking that she fell into numbness. Stan could not help the comparison: Gosia was like a patient under dental anesthetic; her face was lifeless, only her eyes showing signs of deep trauma. She appeared not to hear Stan's account of Robert's death, her eyes wandering in the darkness outside the window. When Gosia did not respond after Stan had finished, he decided to leave her alone, to allow her to mourn and reflect in private. He knew she would need him later, when the news had set its roots and spread into her mind.

Mollie Banks had caught a bad chill and was steaming in the bathtub. The hike from the castle to the suburban train line was strenuous, and by the time they reached the nearest train station the weather had turned for the worse: cold rain mixed with wet snow. They arrived in Kraków within an hour and a half of leaving Nowa Wieś, but took an additional thirty minutes scouting for possible surveillance outside Margaret's building. For a city as large as Kraków, with a large university and a charming Old Town, the streets were surprisingly deserted. It was only nine, but it might have been two or three in the morning, if one were to judge by the number of people they encountered during the fifteen-minute walk from the train station.

Penskie left his sister in the kitchen and carried Balcer's briefcase into another room, Gosia's study/living room. He placed it on the desk. Inside he found the notebook he used in the castle, a removable hard drive, six recordable compact discs, a Palm Pilot, and a satellite telephone. In a slim pocket were four paper folders containing printouts of tables and figures. From the look of them Penskie assumed they were incomes and expenditures, but the numbers could have meant anything. He removed everything from the briefcase and placed every item on one side of the desk.

He started with the notebook. It required a password to boot up, and after a few unsuccessful attempts he closed it and put it aside.

The telephone was the smallest satellite unit he had ever seen: It resembled a small cellular telephone. To his surprise it was not password-protected. He checked the phone list and recently dialed numbers. Both lists were empty.

He used Gosia's desktop computer to access the recordable optical disks. Each contained a single unidentified file. The file names were incomprehensible—a gibberish of letters, symbols, and numbers. He tried opening them but to no avail.

Disappointed, he picked up the paper folders. Each contained an identical set of eleven pages of printouts from presentation and spreadsheet programs. He could not make any sense of the figures, numbers, and charts. He sifted through the pages in hopes of finding anything he could anchor his eyes on. Nothing.

He pushed away from the desk and looked around the room. The apartment was in a typical 1960s five-story concrete building, with two bedrooms that turned into living space during the day, a small kitchen, and a bathroom. The room he was in was the larger of the two, some eight or nine meters long, with a balcony that overlooked a small marketplace. He recalled that it turned busy every weekend, with vendors coming from close and far away. The first time he visited Gosia they equipped her apartment with dishes, utensils, bedspreads, and even a dining set purchased there. His eyes gazed at the copper samovar they had haggled from an older Russian lady. It stood on the coffee table, in the glory it deserved.

The memories brought a smile to his face.

He was about to stand up and brew fresh tea in the samovar when he noticed a spindle of blank recordable disks on the shelf above the desk.

Copies. He could make copies. Being able to do something, even as insignificant as copying the disks, gave him a sense of confidence and promise of better luck to come.

"How did she take it?" Mollie Banks stood in the door, her thick bathrobe tightly belted around her waist.

"It will hit her when the shock finally subsides."

"Would it help if I talked to her?"

"I don't know . . . I think I'd better see to it. Come, I'll show you to the wardrobe."

Banks followed him to the bedroom. The large wooden closet in the corner made the room look even smaller. Had it not been kept meticulously clean it would have been oppressively small. Pots of begonias in the window added color and life to an otherwise serene décor. The apartment had the feel of a temporary lodging, of belonging to a person who spent most of her time outside, using it only to catch up on her sleep.

The magnitude of her loss had struck Margaret with Stan's arrival in the kitchen. Her bother's presence brought her back from the depths of her inner thought. He reminded her of the painful truth: She would never see Robert again. She did not care about who killed her betrothed or why he had to die. She wanted to hear his name; the words Stan was speaking now helped her envision Robert's face, the shape of his lips, his body language. With every sentence of Stan's description of the fateful day, she inhaled deeply, her heart hammering, quiet spasms jerking her head up and down.

She stopped crying eventually, silent sobbing giving way to concern for Stan's safety. Penskie was not sure she fully comprehended the danger looming over his, Zbigniew's, and perhaps her own life. He was not certain he himself had fully understood. Balcer could have killed him at any point during his imprisonment in the castle; yet he let him go. Never mind his intentions; the fact remained that he did not kill Stan. Someone, however, did try to do it. Or did they? He recalled various moments from the last forty-eight hours. Sasha, who blew Robert's head off, hesitated at the *Stadion* despite a clear line of fire. Before that the secretary . . . what did she say? *I don't want to shoot you. . . .* True, she did shoot him eventually, but that was because he left her no choice. In Banks's office Ania did not fire at either of the legats—she shot at Mollie! And the cops on the highway? They were more interested in the passenger: Mollie Banks! Did Loomis aim at Banks, too? What did this mean? Were Penskie and the Bureau not enough of an obstacle for the Fifth Internationale? Was the Federal Bureau of Investigation so insignificant that they found it unnecessary to prevent its agent from probing into the existence of such explosive information as the Fifth Internationale's databases? Was Mollie Banks the key to everything that had happened? The thought was uncomfortable, but it did not come as a surprise. He realized that on some unconscious level he had suspected something. He scolded himself—*suspected* was not the right word; rather, he felt something unfinished or unsaid looming over the woman.

A telephone rang in the living room. One ring. Two rings. He realized it was not Margaret's telephone. He shot up.

Mollie Banks stood by the desk, Balcer's satellite telephone next to her ear.

"Yes? Hello?" she answered. She listened for a moment, shrugged, then pressed the off switch. "No one there," she said in response to Stan's puzzled face.

Penskie noticed she had sifted through the contents of the briefcase. One of the compact disks was still in the drive of Gosia's desktop computer. Mollie appeared not have noticed the copies Stan made.

"Even with the right software it will take time to decipher this stuff." Banks became aware of Penskie's perusing gaze.

"We don't have that much time," he replied. "I think it's best if we leave this place."

"You think the phone call—"

"Yes."

He rushed back to the bedroom and found Margaret holding a framed photograph. It was Stan who had taken the picture in the mountains: Gosia and Robert posing on Kasprowy Wierch, a deep valley with a serpent of a creek on the Slovak side in the background. He calmly asked her to put on her coat and pick up the most important sundries she might need in the next few days. She was not surprised, and complied mechanically with his request.

Mollie Banks appeared in the hallway holding a small knapsack with the notebook, Palm Pilot, the satellite phone, the compact disks, and the paper folders in one hand, the other holding the empty silver briefcase.

"You'll find a warm coat in the closet," Stan said.

When Banks disappeared into Gosia's bedroom, he

walked into the living room. The copies were stacked exactly where he had left them. He looked for jewel cases but found none. He picked up the spindle of blank disks. Originally holding a hundred, it was about three-quarters full. He placed the copies he had made in between the blank ones and placed the spindle back on the shelf.

He scanned the room. Nothing suggested his presence in the apartment. He turned off the desktop computer and leaned over the couch to pick up Mollie's soaked clothes. He stopped halfway through and decided otherwise. Whoever telephoned must know they were here. The location of the telephone must have been traced. There was no point trying to conceal it. He went to the door and turned back. The spindle. He hesitated. He walked briskly to the shelf and placed the spindle in his coat pocket. It was bulging, weighing his coat down on one side.

Stan drove Margaret's small Fiat Stilo for three-quarters of an hour before he was satisfied that no one had followed them. He stopped at one point to throw the silver briefcase into a large garbage can.

Jana Haug, Gosia's friend and the principal of the American school, lived across the river in Podgórze. The windows in her house were dark, but she opened the door promptly. She was a divorcée in her mid-fifties. She lived alone in a spacious three-bedroom home. The television set in the living room was turned on, a black-and-white movie paused. A half-empty bowl of popcorn stood on a small coffee table in front of a deep sofa. She did not ask any questions and appeared horrified at Stan's explanation of the tragic death of his sister's boyfriend. Jana took Gosia directly to the kitchen, where a large canister of Hortex ice cream materialized in front of her poor, poor Margaret. The clichéd significance of ice cream was not lost on Stan. He embraced his sister and whispered in her ear the need to keep the truth about Robert's death to herself. Keeping it a secret altogether was not possible, as it had already been on the newsstands.

Satisfied with the care Jana demonstrated toward his sister, Penskie went back to the living room, the knapsack with the items from Balcer's briefcase on his shoulder. One of the corners, a nook with a large window opening to the garden, was used as a study. He looked out the window onto the quiet street where Banks waited in the car. He watched the car for a few seconds and turned back. A computer and a printer stood on the small desk. Papers, books, compact disks, and a multitude of office supplies were piled on the desk, the monitor, the printer, and even on the floor. He smiled. Jana was a messy woman. He crawled under the desk and hid the spindle of blank optical disks on the floor, in between two boxes of computer paper and a variety of items that had fallen from the desk. Judging from the amount of dust under the desk, the disks would be safe here for weeks, or months.

Some distance away from Podgórze, Penskie used a pay phone to contact his father. Zbigniew was shaken; his voice never regained stability throughout the entire conversation. He feared Stan had perished in the detonation that destroyed much of the castle after GROM's raid. The commando responsible for securing the landing area had assured him of Stan's safe departure, but the old man envisioned his son returning to Nowa Wieś.

Stan suggested a rendezvous at a gas station on the outskirts of town. His father initially objected to such a conspiratorial approach, declaring that after the ministry of defense had successfully stepped in, the end of the organization's existence was imminent. Stan persisted.

The castle destroyed! The commander of the INR team was telling the truth. How did he know? According to Powell the team had just arrived in Nowa Wieś, and Penskie saw them from Balcer's window. They were caught before they could enter the castle, which suggested they were not the ones to plant the explosives. They knew about the plan to destroy the castle beforehand. The takeover! The INR was a part of the coalition to take over the Fifth Internationale's leadership. Once again Balcer was telling the truth: It was not just the Central Intelligence Agency.

The Aral station stood on a busy highway to Zakopane, a popular mountain resort in the heart of the High Tatras. Despite the late hour, the road was busy at this time of year, drawing tourists from all over the country. Spending Christmas and New Year's in the mountains was gaining greater popularity with each passing year, mainly due to the area's romantic surroundings and the certain presence of snow.

The gas station was one of those western facilities that filled the gap in the shortcomings of the Polish-owned chains who were ill-prepared for the boom in the car ownership of the nineties. It was modern, clean, and safe and offered more than fuel. A motel, a restaurant, or a well-equipped deli was almost invariably a part of the newly built amenities.

Penskie drove through the property, assessing the cars that were already parked outside the adjoining restaurant. Nothing suspicious drew his attention. He crossed the highway onto a dark path used only by farm vehicles. He parked the car in the wet snow on the side of the road by a wall of dense bushes. He was satisfied with the location; he could see every car as it drove in and out of the rest stop, while being himself invisible in the darkness.

The fast and dangerous living of the past days provided the necessary inflow of adrenaline to keep his mind and body functioning. Now that the one thing that had weighed the most—the conversation with Margaret—was over he suddenly felt weary. He needed a break, a nap, anything to rest and redirect his thoughts, or better yet—not to think at all. He had perfected a way to rest even while on duty. Just sit back, close his eyes, and let the emptiness descend. What most people gained from an afternoon nap Penskie achieved just by sitting quietly by the window, letting his eyes drift into the sky and allowing the innate emptiness of the universe take over his soul. Ten or fifteen minutes of gliding weightlessly in the clouds provided all the rest he needed.

He turned off the ignition and pushed back, but rest was not meant to come this time. The woman's tense presence was utterly unnerving.

Mollie Banks was sighing and turning in her seat.

"What do you think will happen next?" she finally asked, unable to remain silent.

"In any other case I would not hesitate to use diplomatic mail to send it off; in an extreme circumstance I'd courier it myself, but because of what Balcer said out there . . ." He yawned. "My father's a resourceful man, and no doubt he will help us find a way to reach the director."

"I meant . . . what will happen after that?"

"We're in for a shakeup. I can't imagine the USINTEL could be left as if nothing ever happened."

"What if it is? The status quo might be very tempting for the government."

"How do you mean?"

"Balcer's organization has big influence in, if not outright control of, major industries, banks, even politicians worldwide. To control his organization is to control those people and industries."

"If the database is incomplete or impossible to decipher it may be necessary to infiltrate the . . . Fifth, or whatever it is. There was something Ed said that makes me wonder whether any of it is true."

"That there is no Fifth Internationale? Whatever the name, you don't think Balcer could acquire such a closely guarded secret as our antiballistic missile program on his own? There had to be someone with access to this information. I can't imagine Balcer alone could have entered wherever the hell they keep this stuff. I don't suppose he just put an ad in the classifieds. So where there's more than one you can start talking network. What about Balcer's guests? Those were some very important people, judging by the security measures."

Banks was right: Whether Balcer controlled a world-spanning organization or a small network of "associates" who were able to obtain the United States government's secrets, the bottom line was that he could not have acted alone. Until all his associates were discovered, the FBI's job would not be over.

"I predict it will be an arduous investigation. In fact, I'm not sure we'll ever know the whole extent of the Fifth's reach." He paused, stricken by a sudden thought. "I guess it won't see the light of day, no oversight committees, and certainly no media, until the investigators are convinced they have fully penetrated and broken the organization."

The woman sat uncomfortably, clasping her hands without a word.

"What's the matter?" Penskie asked.

"I think you may be wrong," she started warily. "I've been with the company long enough to know a thing or two, to understand how things work, what takes priority in this business. These people, Balcer's operatives, will be turned. They'll work for us. There is no other alternative. If only a small part of what we've heard about the Fifth is true, it's too valuable a resource to destroy. To build a network such as this takes years, even decades. Balcer's enormous success could not have happened without the networks created by the KGB, the SB, all those agencies. As you're well aware, the Cold War may be over, but the old race is on: the race for dominance. Except this time it's not the capitalists versus the reds. I don't know who fights who in this round; maybe it's us against Europe, or us against the rest of the world, but maybe it's just the Company against Balcer? I don't know, but this man must be very sure of his organization if he offered you the database, even in a much-reduced form. He must realize that it's a giveaway; that in some way or other those few names he's given you will lead to the others. Granted, not all exposed traitors talk, but there are those who sell it all out. It's a matter of price. It's the nature of the game."

"You're saying those disks may contain anything *but* the database?"

She did not reply right away, as if the thought had only entered her mind and needed thinking over.

"I'm saying that it seems too easy. Just look at it from this point of view: One of the most sought-after men hands over information that offers him unimpeded protection, that *had* offered him this protection for years."

"But he only—"

"Yes, he gave you only a 'partial' database, but as I explained before, it's a gateway to the rest of it. It's the beginning of the end. What if . . . what if you were played?"

"How?" Penskie asked incredulously.

"Well . . . only Balcer can answer that question. If I were to guess? Perhaps he needed a way to transport the database outside of the country and then take it away from you. That's one thought, but quite frankly I doubt he's given it to you at all. In fact, I doubt any of these disks contain anything that can hurt him. I don't see how it could be the database, which according to everything we've heard would pretty much be the most valuable and desirable information in the world of intelligence. To carry it around in a briefcase seems unthinkable to me."

"He was fleeing Nowa Wieś. The information is encoded. The man is sure of his strength. Who would dare mug him?"

"Yes, he was fleeing Nowa Wieś, but he mentioned to you that he expected some form of an attack or an invasion. Would he have been carrying it with him? I doubt it. The database may be encoded, but even he knows there is no such encryption that can't be decrypted. Lastly, there are far more efficient ways of transporting, concealing, or sharing digital information than to carry it in a briefcase."

Penskie had to admit that her thoughts were not without merit. He had suspected trickery throughout the conversation with Balcer. His feelings, much like Mollie's speculations, were unfounded. He could not see the reasoning behind such deception. Why go through all the talking and pretending? If the disk he had received from Balcer was a decoy then the whole affair made no sense. Balcer did not strike him as a senseless man. On the contrary, he was very much to the point, a man with a reason. What was that reason? Or . . . oh, God! Could this have been? Could it have been that it was not *what* but *who?* Could it have been Penskie? Why? What did Balcer expect of him?

Stan reached to the backseat for the knapsack he had borrowed from his sister. He searched it for a moment and took out the compact disk Balcer had given him. He ripped off the plastic cover with impatience and inserted the disk into the car's stereo.

The fast, loud tones of a popular Polish rock group poured out from the speakers.

Chapter Thirty

"I'm lost," Penskie said in bewilderment. "Unless there are hidden files on this CD, readable only through a computer, then I cannot begin to fathom what he could have hoped to achieve with such deceit."

"Perhaps the fancy of a man of insurmountable might? To play an experienced field agent of the very agency that ranked him as one of the most wanted men in the world might give someone like Balcer some perverse satisfaction."

Both fell silent for some minutes. Both were at a loss. To Penskie the musical disk put everything Balcer said in the castle in doubt. The conversation might as well not have happened at all. None of what was said had helped advance his investigation. Yet Penskie knew there had to be a clue. People like Balcer did not waste time on pointless discussions with law enforcement officers. Was the disk some sort of a clue, something Balcer could not speak of directly? Impossible! The man was on his own ground, his bearing, his intonation, all the signs pointing to a man who was used to getting his way, used to speaking his mind. Perhaps the disk was some kind of a sign for the director, then? Or perhaps it had no meaning at all, and there was something else, something Penskie did not give enough attention to? Suddenly he remembered Balcer's last words: *I spared your life only out of regard for your father*. Was he trying to negotiate his safe passage out of the castle or the country? Was that all? Was Stan simply a hostage? Balcer's ticket to freedom? But Zbigniew could not have possibly been in a position to bargain with Balcer!

Penskie shifted uncomfortably in his seat. He glanced at the quartz clock on the dashboard. Zbigniew and Urbaniak would be arriving in a half an hour. He had to find something to divert his mind from the perplexity of the questions to which he had no answers.

"You never mentioned you had worked for Balcer before," he said to Mollie, reproach in his voice.

"What?"

"The magazine . . . *Art and* something . . ."

"*Art and Artists?* I had no idea who owned it! I had never even heard of Balcer then. I was a student. I was young. I liked the country. I needed something, anything, to help find a base upon which to plan a longer stay in Poland when the course ended. I did not want to go back to the States yet."

"Why didn't you tell me that before?"

"There was nothing to tell!"

"I no longer believe in coincidences, Mollie! Somebody told me recently that in the world of espionage there are no coincidences and that luck and happenstance are, in fact, carefully planned. You worked for a magazine whose owner is wanted by our government right in line with Bin Laden! You went back to the States and joined the CIA! Is it a coincidence?"

"Don't do this, Stan. There is no link between the two. *Art and Artists* was an English-language promotional periodical for foreign media. They arrived at the school looking for native English speakers. Even after the course, English was pretty much all I could hope for with my limited knowledge of Polish! The job offer was a blessing! Yes, Balcer owned it, but he also owned half the newspapers and magazines in this country."

She spoke with such zeal that Penskie could not help but retract his sudden suspicion. He remained tense, however. He wanted to believe her, and deep down he did, but his tired mind, clouded with mounting doubts, demanded deeper probing and clear answers. As quickly as he accused Banks of previous collaboration with Balcer, he refocused his mistrust on Ed Powell. Was Balcer bluffing? Could his partner and friend have had a relationship with the Fifth Internationale? He had to give credit to Balcer: The man had succeeded in planting misgivings so deep not even Stan's father could be ruled out as possible collaborator. After all, what did Penskie know about Zbigniew's objectives? Only what he was told by Zbigniew. Nothing verifiable, because the damn affair was so secretive that only a handful of people knew about it! What about those people? Zbigniew could be clean, and Stan prayed that he was, but his associates? The sheer possibility that they too could have an agenda of their own sent shivers down his spine. No! He shook his head. Balcer and the Fifth may have been powerful, but to suppose that they could have reached the top of the intelligence council was simply ludicrous. If the Soviets did not succeed during Cold War then how could a single guy like Balcer do it? He could not! Not in a million years!

About fifteen minutes before the scheduled meeting a car drove into the rest stop. It was one of numerous cars that had arrived since Penskie's arrival, and while others did not draw his attention, this one stood out immediately. All previous automobiles had one similar feature: They were overpacked with luggage, skis, and passengers; they were headed for their holidays. The latest, a black or a dark BMW, had two occupants, neither of whom was interested either in fuel or refreshments. The driver slowly circled the gas station and the restaurant, then parked in an unlit area by the air pump. The location offered a clear view of all incoming cars. Penskie assumed immediately that the newcomers' arrival was linked to his meeting. Were they Urbaniak's people securing the area? With extensive field experience during his solidarity years, Zbigniew would have mentioned something as important as the presence of a scouting party or a security unit. The conclusion was very disconcerting: His father's mobile telephone had been monitored. Perhaps he should not have used an unsecured line? Penskie reproached himself, but quickly rejected the idea. Whether secure or not, the telephone would have to have been specifically targeted for eavesdropping for the BMW team to arrive so quickly. These things took time, from the intercept and processing to analysis; it would have taken much longer than the forty-odd minutes since he had placed the call.

Minutes later another car arrived, a dark BMW SUV with two men inside. Penskie instantly recognized one of the silhouettes as that of his father. A part of him wanted to warn Zbigniew of the presence of the surveillance unit, but another part told him to wait and observe.

The BMW parked close to the highway, just outside of the illumination cast by the restaurant's windows, and perpendicular to the surveillance unit's car, almost directly in front of it.

It was almost ten minutes past the scheduled meeting, and nothing had happened. Penskie decided to act. He exchanged short sentences with Mollie, switched off the internal lights so they would not give away his location, and got out of the car. He was confident he would not be seen in the spot he had chosen. It was pitch-black. Infrequent motorists' headlights went by so quickly one would have had to stare in the right place to have noticed faint reflections on the Fiat's headlights. Penskie walked behind the bushes that grew alongside the highway until he reached a place where a cluster of decorative shrubs that were planted in the restaurant's parking lot covered his view of the SUV. He waited for a gap so as not to be seen in the cars' headlights and quickly crossed the road. He had barely made it across when the driver's door opened and Urbaniak stepped out of the car. He appeared irritated as he quickly walked toward the restaurant. Penskie watched him enter the building. Urbaniak scanned the room and walked past the counter toward the back of the building, possibly to the bathroom. Penskie scrutinized the parking lot cautiously, so as not to be seen by the surveillance unit. He approached the SUV and flung open the passenger door.

"Stan!" Zbigniew was startled.

"Dad, come with me!" Stan looked around and above the car roof.

"What . . . why?"

"Come. I'll explain later!" The sense of urgency in Penskie's voice was utterly assertive.

Zbigniew hesitated a split second. He looked quickly across the parking lot. Stan followed his gaze and cried out with astonishment. Two men were walking hurriedly toward them. Penskie immediately recognized one as Terrence Jacobek. The second man . . . *Oh, my God!* It was Sasha the Trigger, the killer of Robert Sito!

Penskie ducked and withdrew the pistol he had picked up in Nowa Wieś. He could hear Zbigniew shouting, but in his agitation could not make out the sense of the words. He stood over the hood of the car, weapon raised and pointed toward the approaching men. They were startled, but whether by the sight of the gun or the person holding it, Penskie was not sure. After a moment of indecision, Sasha reached into the small of his back and pulled out a pistol.

"Stan, it's not—" The remainder of the sentence Zbigniew cried out was lost in a blast of the discharged gun.

Sasha fell to the ground, an expression of surprise on his face.

Jacobek lurched behind the closest car, a station wagon with a set of skis on the roof.

Penskie reached in to his father.

"Quick!" he said.

Zbigniew showed striking resistance. He was refusing to follow!

"Dad!" cried Penskie. "That man killed Sito and Małpa . . . Jacobek is with him. We've got to get out!"

"No, Stan, you don't understand. . . . It's all right. They're just . . . Urbaniak . . . Oh, God, what are you doing?" Zbigniew cried out in dread.

"You bastard!" Penskie raised his pistol in the direction of the station wagon where Jacobek was standing. He paused. The scene was very odd: Jacobek was partly covered by the car, his arm raised and outstretched. He did not have a weapon, or if he did he was not going to use it. Stan did not know what to make of the strange situation. His eyes fixed on Jacobek, he pulled his father's arm.

Zbigniew struggled away.

"Stan, stop it immediately," he exclaimed. "You must listen to me—Urbaniak . . . these men . . . It's all right. Just give us the disks!"

Stan looked into his father's eyes in shock. He saw not only alarm on Zbigniew's face, but also confidence. His father knew about the surveillance car and he knew about Sasha. He knew about the disks too! But how was it possible?

Penskie took a step back, his eyes wide in astonishment. *Jesus!* It was all suddenly so clear. Balcer was right: The United States Intelligence would never give up the advantages associated with owning his databases.

"Stan, drop the gun, please." It was Urbaniak. The director stood in the entrance to the restaurant.

Penskie retreated backward into the decorative shrubs, his head shaking in disbelief. He tripped on the curb and almost lost his balance.

Car wheels squealed behind him. Mollie swung open the passenger door and shouted words he could not understand. He was overwhelmed by the terrible truth: His father had betrayed him.

Chapter Thirty-one

The Fiat headed south on the E77. After the city of Myślenice, the two-way highway wound its way through hilly countryside, quickly becoming congested due to poor visibility. On an open highway the Fiat, even though it was a semisport edition, would have been no match for the BMW; however, having a head start even of a minute on a road such as this presented an opportunity for a successful escape, though only if the driver was ready for the challenges offered by a narrow road where overtaking meant a brush with death. Penskie knew the highway very well; he had traveled it countless times, night and day. Mollie, on the other hand, had never driven on Polish highways and hesitated too long before passing other cars. It was only a matter of time before the BMW would catch up with them, but even if Urbaniak could not make up for the time loss there was no saying what resources lay at his disposal. Continuing any farther was therefore too risky, and when the car approached the exit to the city of Rabka, the driver and the passenger decided to get off. They watched the exit in the rearview mirrors. No one had followed them.

The town was asleep and, as in many small towns in Europe, the only signs of life were visible in the vicinity of the train station. A small group of people in the lit waiting room as well as the open bar suggested that a train was expected. The woman drove on three hundred meters into a residential cul-de-sac, where she parked the car, and the two hurried back to the station. It was a typical small-town railway station, with a small waiting area and some wooden benches. It was not the sort of place where the speedy InterCity trains stopped, but nevertheless two regular trains were expected within a half an hour, one headed to Zakopane and one to Kraków. The idea to return to the latter was discarded after short deliberation. Without knowing anyone to turn to for help, they thus decided they should continue on south. Despite the outrageousness of the thought Penskie rekindled the idea put forward by Balcer: to meet with the director of the FBI. Three major factors aided him in this decision. First, it was unlikely their pursuers would consider crossing the border in the winter as a plausible escape route. Second, he would not be forced to rely on anybody; it was painfully clear that they could not afford to trust anyone. And third, the two trains departing in opposite directions were bound to confuse the chasers.

Penskie knew the mountains—he had crossed the border with Sito numerous times, once in the winter—and he was certain it was within his abilities. For Mollie, on the other hand, the idea presented a frightening prospect. Not only had she never climbed rocks before; she had never been to the mountains either. The idea, however, followed by a persuasive description of a picturesque journey, won her over. She agreed to Penskie's suggestion. She did not know what she was up against, but her partner's unwavering good spirits were all she needed to believe in the feasibility of the plan.

It could work.

It had to work.

The train serviced all the minuscule towns and villages on the way, and it took close to an hour to reach Zakopane. Despite their pressing desire to cross the border immediately—as if the border were some magical boundary where all earthly troubles would be left behind—the fugitives emerged from the train in Poronin, the last stop before the Polish capital of winter sports. Poronin was a small village best known as a less costly alternative to the more stylish Zakopane, and it lingered in Penskie's memory as a place he had spent a winter break with his sixth-grade class. During the communist era it was a mandatory destination for all organized groups visiting the mountains, for it once served as summer residence to Vladimir Ilyich Lenin. A museum named after the great revolutionary was created in the house where party assemblies were held.

Numerous signs—*Pokoje do Wynajęcia, Zimmer Frei,* and *Pensjonat*—while lit, actually proved to be only a tease, for their owners, who either lacked the desire to stay awake for late-arriving guests or neglected to post messages informing of sold-out rooms, did not respond to fervently rung doorbells. The sky was clear, dotted with a myriad of sparkling stars. Dogs barking at opposite ends of the village broke the flat calm of the still mountain night; their howling was long, and their wailing sent shivers through the strangers' bodies. Visitors arriving at this hour would invariably feel like invaders, strangers in a closed circle. The darkness and the fugitives' lack of confidence added more anguish to their already disheartened poise.

The vestibule of the small wooden church could not offer shelter from the crisp cold, but it provided a much-needed sense of security. It offered no place to sit down other than on the concrete floor or a minute table scattered with religious pamphlets. Unable to rest, with innumerable and undefined feelings racing through their tired minds, the couple had to result to pacing about the confined area. Tension would have prevented either of them from sitting anyway; so much depended on the hours to come.

Five steps, and back. Five steps, and back.

Penskie blessed himself for purchasing a flask of cherry vodka and two large chocolate bars from the train station kiosk—supplies he never ventured into the mountains without. Munching on the hard, sweet bars and washing them down with liqueur—on the one hand fooling the body to stay warm and bringing the anxiety level down, and on the other keeping the necessary energy afloat—they gradually slowed to a snail's pace, their legs mechanically following a circular route.

"What are you thinking about?" Penskie asked when soothing effects of vodka spread through his veins.

"A really hot bath," answered Banks, and handed over the bottle.

They continued to pace in silence, each one preoccupied with his own thoughts. It was not till the chocolate bars were eaten that they felt comfortable enough to halt and lean back against the thick wooden doors. The vestibule effectively muted the dog's continuous barking and occasional sounds of cars passing along the distant highway. The only other sound that could be heard was that of their own breath.

"I still can't believe he turned . . . Ed, I mean." Stan shook his head, only the rustle of his collar indicating the motion.

"Were you friends?"

"Our kind tends to keep together. You probably know it, too. The sort of work we do seals relationships, but I wouldn't say we were friends. Powell kept a distance, something that became clear to me only after all that happened."

"I can't believe the extent to which Balcer was able to infiltrate the intel community. Have to give him credit for it."

"I don't know. The more I think about it the more it looks like his part was made easier by the resources he controlled. I mean . . . perhaps he didn't have to infiltrate? It seems everyone joined in willingly and knowingly. It's as if it was the Fifth that was penetrated only to extract the information or whatever else was of use to—"

"Are you thinking about your father?"

Penskie did not reply. He had not given it enough thought yet. The shock of being deceived by his own father was too great; anger was still permeating his mind. It physically pained him to think that Zbigniew worked with Robert's killer. Sasha's presence at the gas station could not be construed otherwise. Whatever the terms of their cooperation, Stan's own father was responsible for the death of Stan's friend and Margaret's fiancé. Unthinkable! Yet it was true. Zbigniew had tried to stop Penskie from shooting Robert's killer. It explained the peculiar look in Sasha's eyes at the stadium: He did not shoot at Stan despite a clear line of fire. How could he have? Kill the son of his employer? And Urbaniak? It was unlikely that the director chased the killer. It was staged. He was there as part of the operation to kill Małpa. Madness!

Penskie shared his thoughts and doubts with Mollie.

"Do you realize what you're saying?" she replied with reproach.

"Zbigniew isn't here to stop the CIA. They not only work together, but the DCI himself is very much a part of it."

"That's preposterous!"

"Why?"

Banks had no answer.

"What makes you believe *your* director is clear?" she asked in defiance.

Treason had not spared the Federal Bureau of Investigation in the past; no government entity was foolproof, no personal screening and profiling could ever estimate the full specter of an individual's susceptibility to temptations. Everyone had a weakness. To a prospective recruiter it meant everyone has a price. The trouble with the American intelligence where the Fifth Internationale was concerned, as Penskie realized with dismay, was that its aim to seize control might be construed as a patriotic move, or as part of a routine process to neutralize the opponent. Knowing about the true motives driving the community to a takeover put one in a difficult moral position. When an operation had all the signs of a legitimate process, though terribly if not intentionally flawed, one must choose between right and wrong. Penskie did not consider for a moment that the director could be supporting the CIA in the race to incorporate the Fifth Internationale's resources into its own. Unless the CIA planned to release the information concerning counterintelligence matters to the FBI, namely all the Fifth's operatives working on American soil—and Penskie had yet to be convinced of that—there could not be any possible cooperation between the two agencies. On the contrary: The Bureau would start the biggest mole hunt since the McCarthy era, the entire CIA being suspect.

Mollie Banks was not happy to hear his conjectures. His words put the CIA in a decisively negative light. The Company, a conspirator and a lawbreaker? Possessing the key to the information that could have prevented the loss of thousands of lives at the World Trade Center and continuing to withhold the information made the CIA the enemy of the American people. To believe that the CIA would clean itself was not possible. She felt compelled to object. Quietly. She believed the Central Intelligence Agency should be allowed the time and chance to repair any damage it, the government, and above all the American people had suffered as a result of the misjudgments of a few. Any outside intervention could destroy it.

Penskie was firm. Balcer's disks and the laptop computer would be delivered to the director of the FBI. No one else.

"You know what this'll mean to the Company, don't you?" She raised her voice, alcohol triggering her agitation. "A dissemination and complete breakup!"

"For one thing, I think you're being too biased for someone who's supposed to be impartial. Isn't your office independent? Oh, I'm sorry . . . I forgot you were recruited from the CIA!" Even with the last word still in the air, Penskie regretted having said it. Mollie Banks was the last person he wanted to offend.

"Corruption in the law enforcement and intel communities has always existed and will continue to exist," she replied calmly, seemingly unmoved by his last comment. "No amount of cleaning can successfully deter an existing or a potential traitor from conducting his disloyal activities. The Fifth's database gives the Company the upper hand. Knowing who's who, not only within its own ranks but within intel organizations around the world, will—"

"This isn't the Cold War! These treacherous bastards within our government can't even justify their motives ideologically. They are criminals supporting terrorism against their own people! What profit can there be from turning them over? And anyway, how do you turn someone who has not crossed the line but is in fact following sanctioned duties, who's working on orders from the very top of our government ladder?"

"There's no need to be so emotional about it, Stan. Treason has always existed and will never be eradicated. It's a historical process. Whether it's the Soviets, the Iraqis or the Fifth, or whoever comes next, it will always be with us. There's no way of stopping it, but in the case of the Fifth Internationale we stand a chance to learn something and to gain even more. However you see it, one thing you must agree with—it takes considerable genius to accomplish what neither of the superpowers could do during decades of conflict: Create an paninternational organization with a common goal, despite ideological differences, political systems, or religions."

"Balcer told me that the biggest obstacle to true globalization of the organization is its bloody side, those links with terrorist networks, the use of force to accomplish its goals. That he had tried to sever those links but that Central Intelligence already—"

"Oh, stop it! The Company may have been in the position

to know a thing or two, but you can't seriously suggest it supports terrorists!" Mollie caught the look in his eyes and added, "Not *those* terrorists."

"Balcer confirmed it!"

"Of course he confirmed it. You said it yourself: The Company is on his heels. He will stop at nothing to break free."

"The CIA is not *on to* him; it's a *part* of the Fifth. The CIA knew about the organization since the beginning, when it used its own operatives from the Eastern Bloc to penetrate it. Their appetites grew bigger and eventually they wanted to seize complete control. That's what created the rift. That's why we're here tonight."

"You seem to be putting a lot of trust in what Balcer told you."

"I have yet to be convinced that it isn't true! So far all I'm seeing is that most everyone wants the Fifth. Not to terminate it, to persecute its members, or to seek justice to its victims, but to use it for its own profit."

Mollie went out of the vestibule.

Penskie followed her.

They stood in silence, suddenly realizing the barking had stopped, and even the distant sounds of the highway had weakened and disappeared in the night. They looked up into the clear sky. A myriad of tiny flickering stars hung in the dark, infinite blanket. The might of the universe seemed to have centered above their heads. It did not feel so cold anymore. The alcohol worked, and its warm haze had spread into their brain cells; problems and differences became distant and less important. Darkness, loneliness, and the stress of days past and the uncertainty of days to follow drew them closer together. They returned to the vestibule.

Exhaustion and insecurity played a key role in diminishing the tension. They sat on the small and wobbly table, shoulder to shoulder, feeling every breath of their warm bodies. They were not a man and a woman. Lost, tired, scared, and desperate, they were two fugitives thrown on their own resources.

Chapter Thirty-two

The Morskie Oko pond was one of the most popular destinations in the High Tatras. Tourists visiting Zakopane, whether individually or as part of an organized group, and regardless of the amount of time at their disposal, would not miss this natural wonder. Year round the trails around the pond were filled with laughter and youthful enthusiasm. Morskie Oko, or the Eye of the Sea, a name derived from a legend, which described a subterranean passage linking the pond with the Baltic Sea, was a starting point for some of the most beautiful and exciting hiking trails in the Carpathians. From here one had a choice of crossing the ridges of some of the highest peaks, sunbathing in the breathtaking Valley of the Five Ponds, or, when higher aspirations called for it, climbing Poland's highest peak, Rysy. With a paved road linking Morskie Oko with Zakopane, the area, with its easy paths nearby, as well as challenging trails to farther parts of the mountain range, attracted both city slickers and seasoned mountain climbers. In effect the hut built on the edge of the pond was perhaps the only mountain hut in the Tatras where the presence of high-heeled and necktied city folk did not draw immediate attention, for they were perhaps most prevalent here.

When a couple dressed in city clothes walked into the restaurant in the Morskie Oko hut they raised no particular attention from a cheery crowd. The place was chosen ideally, for the newcomers were virtually indistinguishable in a similarly dressed mass of thrill seekers. Even so, both had scanned the room with caution. Apparently satisfied, they chose the corner of a long wooden table someone had just vacated, and the man walked to the bar to order hot raspberry juice. In an effort to absorb the heat they drank the juice while holding tightly to their glasses. The large windows offered spectacular views of the surrounding peaks sparkling in the rays of the morning sun. A continuous flow of tourists passed through the doors, those coming in breathing heavily, their eyes invariably smiling. The weather forecast called for one of those dream days that sometimes descend on the mountains: sunshine and calm that allow for sunbathing while surrounded by a blanket of fresh snow. A winter holiday's dream come true.

It was on a day such as this that even the slouchiest of couch potatoes felt driven to undertake the four-hour trek up the Rysy Mountain, a favorable circumstance for the couple who wanted to blend in. Rysy stood on the border with Slovakia. From the peak the red trail wound its way down to Chata Pod Rysami hut and farther to the Strbske Pleso mountain resort, the Slovak equivalent of Zakopane in its popularity. With the introduction of the passport-free travel within the border zone, one could sneak outside of the country without much ado. That was precisely what the couple was hoping to achieve. They exchanged silent glances and headed toward the doors.

Two beaten trails led from the hut; the third one, less popular, disappeared under the deep snow. The male led the way along the trail also used by the majority of the visitors, who were lured by the charm of the largest of the ponds in the Tatras. It resembled a main walking promenade in any popular tourist resort: Colorful crowds rushed or shuffled along, depending on physical condition, some for the sole purpose of displaying their latest ski equipment or garments.

Shortly after the couple left the hut, a young woman approached them on the narrow trail. She was equally ill prepared for the mountain hike, wearing running shoes and a short suede jacket. Soft-heeled shoes were poor match for sharp ridges that lay ahead, but they were not destined to meet the challenge, for apparently the woman did not come to mountain climb.

"Make no sudden movement, *Panie* Penskie." She spoke English with a very strong accent. "We have you covered, and it would be a real shame to put these families at risk of being caught in a cross-fire."

The abruptness of the woman's approach stunned Mollie and Stan. Scanning the surrounding area they noticed two pairs of eyes focused on them. Two men, some twenty feet apart, were partly visible from behind the trees. How many more were out of sight, hiding behind the snowcapped spruces?

"Just hand over the disks and it will be like we never met," the woman continued, and pointed at the small knapsack hanging over Penskie's shoulder.

"Who are you?" Banks asked icily.

"Do not make this any more unpleasant than it has to be. The disks!"

Penskie looked around again, panic growing in his eyes. *Not now . . . we're this close . . . there must be a way out.* He noticed with angst that one pair of eyes was no longer where he saw them moments earlier. At the same time he felt rather than saw that Mollie Banks, who stood one step behind him, had tensed. He glanced at the strange woman, her right hand holding a small gun partly hidden in her coat pocket. By the time he could reach his weapon the woman would empty half a magazine in his body, and the unseen enemy would riddle Mollie with bullets and perhaps kill innocent bystanders too. It was hopeless!

The trail was narrow to the point that Penskie and Banks had to stand aside to let other tourists pass. A family of four, slipping in the snow, tried to push through in between the fugitives and the stranger. The woman stepped forward to close the gap, and found herself within arm's reach of Penskie. She turned her head slightly to assess the newcomers.

This was the time.

Without thinking Penskie swooped onto the woman, his arms hitting her chest. Immobilized, she struggled to withdraw the pistol from her pocket and to free herself in complete silence. They fell. Mollie grasped the gun out of the stranger's hand and shoved it into her own pocket. The incident escaped the passersby; it was nothing more than a slip in the snow. Some of the younger hikers in climbing gear projected wide smiles, giving looks that said they were clearly amused by the city folk's shoes and clothes—*cepry!*

Penskie stood up and pulled the woman to her feet. Moving behind her, he looked where the prying eyes hid behind the trees. There were none.

Suddenly the woman screamed in Polish: "Leave me alone! Pervert!"

The scream brought the attention of the closest tourists but none intervened. Somewhat surprised by the outburst, Penskie loosened his grip, and the woman pulled away. She walked rapidly uphill, slipping in the snow.

"Crazy!" she cried, her eyes frantically searching for her backup team.

Flabbergasted by the lack of any response from the woman's partners, Mollie pulled Stan's shoulder. They retreated quickly, examining every face, tree, and larger snow mounds.

"Agent Penskie!" a voice called in English from behind a thicket of young spruces, where a pair of eyes had stood before. A middle-aged man, who might have appeared to have walked off the trail in response to the call of nature, was gesticulating toward them. "Quickly. Here!"

An escape was not possible. They could either return back up the trail onto Rysy, following the strange woman, or run past the man toward the hut. In either case they could not dodge the bullets that would inevitably follow. They stood still in hesitation. Why was the man not firing? Where was his weapon? His hands were free. Was the weapon on the snow next to his legs and at arm's length? Was there another man behind the tree?

"I'm on your side! I've come from Hungary with Director Weber."

The world spun in front of Stan's eyes. Impossible! Overwhelmed with rage, Penskie covered the distance of some ten feet in a deep snow in just three large leaps. He fell on the man like an eagle on a chamois. He would have killed him with his bare hands had the man's head not been covered with a thick fur hat. Penskie knocked the breath out of the man with a powerful blow in the solar plexus and knocked him off his feet with a hook in the jaw.

He sat on the man's chest, hitting at random, until Mollie managed to pull him off.

"Stan! Stan! He's telling the truth! Look!"

Two bodies lay in the snow, only short steps away, hidden behind a large snow mound. Thin white mists coming from their mouths with every breath suggested they were alive.

Michael Gaertner was the Federal Bureau of Investigation's special agent whose duties revolved around countless cases involving Eastern European organized crime groups. His job required his presence and insight throughout the region, from one legal attaché office to another, and where none existed as well. In one way or another most countries had some sort of liaison between their police agencies and the FBI. Wherever offices were not present, agents such as Gaertner traveled to deliver their hands-on experience and exchange information. Gaertner knew every corner of the continent and problems police agencies were grappling with. He stayed in direct contact with the director, and in addition to his official duties carried the task of overseeing legal attachés' operations. Only a handful of people in the FBI knew the true reason behind Gaertner's frequent visits to the United States diplomatic missions: a series of irregularities discovered in some of the legat offices. Suspicions of corruption led to shattering discoveries of possible treason. For a long time the news was discarded, as particular cases lacked probable cause. The privileged information in the legats' possession could undoubtedly benefit the underworld, but the line linking corruption with treason could not be established. Through a series of controlled operations it was further discovered out of which offices the volatile information was leaking. Among them was Warsaw. Legal attachés there were put under scrutiny, their every move monitored, communications recorded. The findings were stunning and received with the greatest awe. The recipient of the information gathered by the legats in Warsaw, Moscow, Rome, and around the world was traced to the FBI headquarters. Certain particulars of the case, such as the elaborate mode of acquiring information, which turned out to be available to law enforcement agencies by means of the National Crime Information Center anyway, made the investigators scratch their heads in utter confusion. Why steal—and steal so obviously as to be quickly discovered—information that was available to the very suspect through legal channels? The conclusion was drawn, therefore, that the operation was a decoy, its purpose to confuse and tie up the Bureau's resources. It was not until much later that the truth became obvious. It cleared the legal attachés but shattered the United States intelligence community. It was proven beyond any doubt that the Central Intelligence Agency had been spying on the Federal Bureau of Investigation. The confusing transfer of information was a lead planted by someone who wanted the FBI to learn what the CIA was up to. Someone who knew. Someone who wanted to be found out: the Fifth Internationale.

Penskie vaguely recognized Gaertner from his visits to the embassy, though the two men had never met face-to-face before. The information the special agent had just related did not have as big an effect as he had expected. Penskie listened with a stoic expression. Little, he thought, was left out there to surprise him where the Fifth Internationale was concerned. Everything agreed with what he had learned so far. Moreover, it satisfied him as to the Bureau's position. The Federal Bureau of Investigation was not implicated in the race for takeover. To the contrary: It was in position to thwart the CIA's plans.

"How did you know where to find us?" Banks asked matter-of-factly as soon as Gaertner finished his story.

They left the two unconscious bodies in the snow and walked toward the hut, taking a left turn to the Valley of the Five Ponds, a less-traveled trail that allowed for great deal of privacy. With no one in immediate sight they spoke with confidence, their voices drowning in the snow-covered surroundings.

"The director's presence in Europe, in Budapest, is no coincidence. We've been negotiating with Tadeusz Balcer for some time now. He's in a delicate situation surrounded by hard-liners who believe in fist law. I trust you're fully aware of the volatility of the information he's offering the USG. . . ."

"Balcer is selling out his organization?"

"He believes he can save it."

"Why bother talking to him at all? The president made it clear that whoever's behind the September eleventh attacks, directly or indirectly by harboring the terrorists or extending any kind of help to them, will pay for their part!"

"I'm afraid it just not that simple. The Fifth Internationale is not a terrorist organization per se, though they do have extensive links to that side of the underworld. We prefer to treat them as an intelligence organization, with resources equal to or greater than those available to USINTEL. They are, however, guilty of terrorism by association, as much as we are in so many parts of the world where various factions build bombs financed by American taxpayers. The Fifth's mistake was to withhold information that could have prevented Nine-eleven. Of course, we cannot rule out that the Fifth, or at least some of its people, knew what was coming, and frankly we think that with the level of reach they had, they must have known. Combine it with the CIA's strong position in the organization and you'll come to a staggering conclusion: We did it ourselves. It's preposterous! I know. But, the fact remains that our government wants the Fifth Internationale. We've . . . shit, what am I saying, *they*, the CIA, have been trying to seize control for years. They are guilty of negligence. They overlooked the danger. Nine-eleven was a sign for them to back off. Whether they did it or not is a different matter. We, the FBI, have one duty: to bring justice to those who lost their families and the truth to the nation. Just how do we retaliate against someone with deep roots in the heart of American intelligence? We take them out one by one; we pluck 'em like fleas off a stray dog, and crush them. We'll find those bastards, and if we can bring down the Fifth Internationale in the process, so much the better. Rest assured, in one way or another we will. Balcer's been trying to save his organization, but we are not the CIA. We don't deal."

"You haven't answered the question," Banks reminded him, unmoved.

"I was supposed to do the job Balcer trusted to you." Gaertner glanced at Stan. "The database—I was supposed to do it, take it to the director. This route through the mountains would have been my choice too."

Penskie looked at him in shock. So it was true, then?

"But how did you . . . ?" Banks raised her voice impatiently.

"Balcer's satellite phone and the Palm Pilot. They're equipped with tracking devices. We monitor them. By the by, thanks for not separating them, not leaving one of them behind—would have had our heads scratching. I followed you. I thought it better not to show myself. With all that happened there was no saying what your reaction might be. Well, we've seen it now."

They walked in silence. The sun was now fully above the ridges, its warm and blinding rays sparkling in the melting snow. The continuous uphill walk became more strenuous as it turned steeper. It was becoming hot. The blue trail to the Valley of the Five Ponds was not as challenging as that to Rysy, and more visitors opted for the one-and-a-half-hour trek as the weather turned warmer. Their unintelligible voices could be heard somewhere behind.

Gaertner's plan was to cross the border, not at Rysy, which was crawling with undercover agents, but somewhere else where they would not be expected. On the other side, in Slovakia, a car was waiting to take them to the director. Gaertner's plans ended there; he did not know how to cross the border. It was therefore Penskie's task to choose the route.

The legal attaché assessed the clothes the three of them were wearing and shook his head disapprovingly. As nice as the day had turned out to be, the mountains were not for city folks wearing slippery boots and cotton coats that soaked up the snow like sponges. There were easier trails in the western Tatras, some of them passable even in the winter, but having been detected they had to cross the border quickly. The closest were the Gładka and Sucha passes, both difficult even for well-equipped and experienced mountain climbers. Penskie knew that so much as reaching either of them would border on miraculous. He said so. Gaertner was eager to climb the highest peaks—so far the climb was nothing more than a little sweat. Mollie was more skeptical. Seeing worry in Stan's eyes she had to force herself to keep her keen composure. They all understood one thing: There was no turning back. They had to take the chance.

They passed the invitingly smoking chimney of the Valley of the Five Ponds hut without a word. The weather was excellent, the walk, which in any other circumstance might have been considered a pleasure, was not as difficult as Stan had painted it. The valley opened its magnificent panoramas. The smooth sheet of black water underneath a layer of crystal-clear ice contrasted with the snowy slopes topped with sharp ridges; Poland's highest peaks were breathtaking. The views stirred energy in their young bodies. They walked with vigor, Penskie, his coat wrapped around his waist, leading the way. Tourists became scarcer as the three of them approached the Wielki Staw pond, and soon all that lay ahead was snow and rock glistening in the sun. As the trail ascended, walking becoming more strenuous, Penskie and Gaertner pulled off their sweaters and continued along wearing only T-shirts.

It was almost two and a half hours after they left Morskie Oko when the trail reached the steepest part, the final ascent to the Zawrat Pass. Once there, they would turn onto another trail leading to still another one, which would take them to Slovakia. With Zawrat visible in the distance, the party, although tired from the exhaustive pace imposed by

Penskie, were rejuvenated by seeing the majestic vastness of the unattainable peaks that stood ahead.

Once they were on top, the sight of the descent from Zawrat sent shivers down Stan's back. The upper part of the steep slope was covered in ice. Numerous trekkers had trodden down the snow; the hot sun had melted the top layer and at night the dry, cold weather created what resembled a slide. Attempting to cross the slippery surface could turn into disaster.

Banks and Gaertner sat on an exposed rock, breathless. They received Penskie's mention of the hard bit yet to come with bemused expressions. They had climbed what seemed sky-high, and they made it with little trouble! There simply was no mountain they could not conquer. A quick glance at the ridge of Świnica, the next peak, showed an easy hike from their vantage point. They were ready for it. It was Penskie's estimate of about a three-hour steep climb to the Slovak trail that momentarily shook their confidence, but the marvelous vistas, the warm sun, and the deafening calm brought peace to their minds.

The world was theirs to conquer!

The world shattered as quickly as it raised its beautiful prospects.

Four snowmobiles roared on their way up from the Valley of the Five Ponds.

Chapter Thirty-three

Three figures stood hopelessly on the crescent of the mountain pass as the snowmobiles approached. The two men and the woman awaited the unknown with their weapons drawn. They had no place to run to for cover. The two options at their disposal: Surrender or fight. Both meant defeat.

One civilian and three WOP border guards in white suits came to a halt some fifteen meters below the pass. The civilian stepped forward while the guards remained behind, no apparent hostility in their behavior, automatic rifles strapped over their shoulders.

To his amazement Penskie recognized the civilian. It was Ed Powell.

"Drop your weapons, Stan, and come down. You're confused and tired."

"Back off, Eddie! I'm in no mood for a chitchat!"

"Stan, you should've been told from the start. We all should've been told, but someone fucked up and things got bad. It's over, though. Come down and we can forget all about it!"

"No, you're wrong, Eddie; we can't forget! And it won't be over until the director has the information."

"That's right, Stan, you can deliver it to the director yourself. Now, come down and we'll go back together."

"What? Where?"

"To the consulate. To the director."

"The director's in Kraków?" Penskie asked in astonishment. "But how?"

"It's a long story."

"Well, find the time, goddamn it!"

Powell looked over his shoulder at the soldiers and drove the snowmobile closer to the pass. He stopped two meters from Penskie, turned off the engine, and lowered his voice.

"The director's been negotiating with Balcer for the release of his databases, at least those pertaining to the bombing of the World Trade Center and the Pentagon and the whereabouts of the Al Qaeda members. Balcer's got contacts in places no one else can dream of: People, organizations, he knows their modus operandi . . . everything needed to put an end to terrorism. What's more, he knows what Iraq is hiding and where. He sells weapons to Iraq. Now he's willing to sell Saddam to us. The director was scheduled to meet with Balcer in Budapest. The Bureau is the only organization that can make responsible use out of this information. Unfortunately some people didn't agree with Balcer's cooperation. They fought back. The director learned about the opposition and came to Poland."

"Who are *you* siding with, Eddie?"

"Look, I know what you're thinking: Who knows who's who? Right? The deception's been going on for over a decade. Everybody profits from Balcer's resources; that's why he was able to flourish. Everybody *but* the FBI."

"Oh, but we do! Balcer's database would be a giant leap forward for our counterintelligence!"

"We've never been a part of it. You've got to believe it, Stan. Had the Bureau known about Balcer and had access to his databases, the September eleventh attacks would not have happened!"

"What were you doing in Nowa Wieś?"

The legal attaché hesitated.

"I was ordered by the director to secure the exchange place."

"Nowa Wieś? That's not what you told me before."

"I know. . . . It was strictly on a need-to-know basis. The Poles . . . I phoned to warn you. Urbaniak answered the phone. I knew he was on our side; at least, the director thought so. Urbaniak said that Balcer changed his mind and that he held you hostage. We called GROM and . . . and . . ."

"What about the INR?"

"I don't know, Stan! The deception reaches very deep. I don't think it had anything to do with Hank anymore, as much as I'd like to. That's why we need this information! We need Balcer's database!"

"Why didn't you ask him yourself? That was quite a show you two put up in Nowa Wieś."

"Balcer's dead, Stan. When I came to I found him with his throat slit. The GROM soldier who was watching the helipad was dead. The Fifth's comm center, the entire underground complex of Nowa Wieś where the Fifth ran its worldwide operations from, was blown out! Apparently self-destructed. By the way, thanks for leaving me in the freezing cold!"

"You told me there is no Fifth Internationale! No conspiracy . . . remember?"

"I told you: need—"

"Need-to-know. I know," Penskie interjected doubtfully.

"I was under direct orders. Look, Stan, Nowa Wieś may be destroyed, but there are still forces out there who want a piece of the organization. The Fifth was highly compartmentalized. Its hundreds, if not thousands of cells worked independently, often without any contact with the rest of the organization, without even knowing they were a part of it. Even if the databases were destroyed in the explosion, someone might have slipped through the blockade Urbaniak's people imposed, someone with copies, perhaps only partial. They might pose a great risk. The Fifth will be rebuilt! We need the disks you took from Balcer."

"How do I know you're telling the truth?"

"Stan, we've been friends for a long time."

"Need-to-know basis . . ."

"All right. Call the consulate . . . speak with the director." Powell reached inside his coat and retrieved a cellular telephone. He threw it to Stan. "Two, two . . ."

Penskie switched on the telephone and waited for signal. There was none.

"Sorry, Eddie."

"Oh, for crying out loud, Stan! I'm telling the truth!"

Penskie turned to Gaertner.

"If he is telling the truth, then who the hell are you?"

No one had paid any attention to the special agent. No one had noticed him withdraw backward toward the side of Zawrat Pass, where the trail continued down through

Hala Gąsienicowa to Zakopane. He was ten feet away from the edge.

"There was a traitor at the embassy," Gaertner replied. "The legats' office was investigated for leaking vital information."

"What? Who is that?" Powell asked in bewilderment. He appeared to have noticed the stranger only now.

The tension grew high. Gaertner appeared calm. He took another step back in order to have the entire group in sight.

Banks was standing on the eastern flank, listening intently, her weapon drawn and pointing in the direction of the special agent.

"You must've met Special Agent Michael Gaertner," Penskie spoke to the legal attaché. He then turned to Gaertner. "You also told us that someone with ties to the legats' offices was the suspect. Perhaps it was not someone inside the embassy? Perhaps it was someone who visits embassies frequently? Someone like yourself?"

Gaertner took another step backward, and another. . . .

Suddenly a distant noise from the other side of Zawrat could be heard. It grew louder and louder until a helicopter appeared from behind Zawratowa Turnia. Gaertner turned abruptly to face the new surprise and he slipped on the icy surface. Struggling to regain balance, he shot his arms up, his weapon flew into the air, and he fell onto his back. Banks screamed out, and Penskie made a step forward in an attempt to grab the man's arm. It was too late. Gaertner slid down the steep slope of Zawrat, his body hitting an exposed razor-sharp rock twenty meters below. It bounced off of it and continued farther, rolling, bouncing, and breaking bones until it landed in the soft snow barely visible in the distance.

Chapter Thirty-four

Three border guards from *Wojska Ochrony Pogranicza*, WOP, anxiously looked out for the approaching helicopter, their position below the ridge of the pass making it impossible to see what lay on the other side. The group leader radioed the base, while the two others stood by, uncertain and astounded by, the events that unfolded above them. They did not see Gaertner fall; the woman's scream was lost in the aircraft's thundering noise. It was the unusual commotion and tension among the foreigners that drew their attention. While the diplomat from the embassy whom they escorted stood quietly and in anticipation of the helicopter, the man and the woman appeared very worried.

The Sokół helicopter with its checkered military insignia ascended and leveled itself with the Zawrat pass, some thirty meters away. It turned sideways, and a man appeared in the door.

It was Zbigniew Penskie. Headphones over his head, he adjusted a microphone at his mouth.

"Stan, use the telephone," his voice shot out from the powerful speakers.

Penskie did not understand.

Someone inside the helicopter passed a mobile phone to Zbigniew. The old man held it out and placed it to his ear.

Penskie took off the knapsack and retrieved Balcer's satellite telephone. It was vibrating. He switched it on and listened. Nothing. He gestured to his father and shook his head.

Zbigniew spoke to the microphone; the pilot nodded, and the helicopter moved slowly away from the pass then hovered a distance away. It was still very loud, but far enough for Stan to hear his father's voice in the headset.

"Stan, I spoke with Gosia," Zbigniew said. "She's worried about you."

He's got the copies, the thought shot through Penskie's head.

"She'd worry about you too if she only knew what you've been up to," he replied.

Zbigniew ignored the comment.

"I had no idea she and this Officer . . . Sito . . . Poor Gosia. I'm worried about her, all alone in that empty apartment. I asked her to move to Wola; you know, the house is empty most of the year, but at least now, when I'm in Poland . . . Well, you know her, the always independent Gosia. She refused."

Something did not add up, Penskie realized. He could not tell what made him feel this way; perhaps the words were not what he had expected.

"How did you find her?" he asked.

"Like I said, she was very upset." Zbigniew appeared puzzled by the question.

"No, I meant . . ." Penskie started, then bit his tongue.

He suddenly understood. Margaret had returned home. Of course! It was just like her. She always disregarded danger, never considering the state department's warnings when choosing travel destinations—a constant bone of contention between the siblings. Disregarding Stan's advice not to return home, she did the exact opposite. Penskie did not anticipate it and did not realize that it was not his sister's stubborn nature that drove her home despite his warning. Margaret wanted to return to all the mementos of her fiancé that her apartment was filled with: the photographs, the letters, and the little things he touched.

Margaret did not know he had made copies of Balcer's disks. She did not know they lay under the clutter of her friend's study; therefore she could not have told. Perhaps not everything was lost yet.

"What do you want, Dad?"

"I've always strived to seed a sense of patriotism in you, son. I hope you can find it in your heart now—"

"What do you want?"

"The same thing you do. Make the terrorists pay for what they did to us. To accomplish that, we need the database. Having it will help us go much farther than punishing only the trigger pushers. If we go after the top we can prevent any such actions in the future. The world will be better off with the United States having complete—"

"Control? Is that what you want to say?" Penskie interjected impatiently.

"Well, yes, but let's not argue over semantics. Control . . . access to information . . . The bottom line is that the USINTEL failed us. We cannot let this happen again. It is worth the price, Stan, and the price isn't even that great. It would be a big mistake to bring this into public scrutiny. What the eyes can't see the heart does not long for, as the Polish proverb goes. Let the people, the media, get a hint of it and they'll tear it apart. We can do more good if the information contained on these disks is kept from the public."

"I'm not a politician, Dad. I'm a cop. I can't see anything good coming out of burying the fact that the U.S. intelligence did not just fail, but was in fact partly responsible for what happened!"

Zbigniew flinched. The move was barely perceptible from a distance, but the momentary silence and a cold response assured Stan that his eyes did not deceive him.

"We did not have full access to the Fifth Internationale's resources then. If we had, we would have been able to put the pieces together and prevent the terrorists from taking innocent lives."

"It is precisely the innocent lives I worry about! As long as this organization exists there will be more blood. Did you even know what my colleagues and I have been through in the past two days? What about Robert, Officer Sito? Was he not innocent? I'm sorry, Dad. I will hand the disks over to the director of the FBI only."

"Director Weber is here with me, Stan."

It was as if the surrounding peaks had crumbled on Penskie's head. He watched as his father gave way and another man appeared in the door. Even from the distance Penskie recognized the characteristic bearing of the tall and slightly hunched director Weber. He could see Zbigniew pass the satellite telephone over to the director; he could see and hear the Director speak into the receiver, but he could not understand the words.

It was all over.

Someone touched his arm. Ed Powell was staring at the helicopter, just as shocked to see his director. He could not hear the conversation, but from Penskie's body language and the expression on his face he understood that the two of them were but a small link in a big chain whose ends were tightly held by forces beyond their ability to keep hold of.

Distant noises from below drew the attention of the people standing on the Zawrat Pass. Four more snowmobiles were nearing from the direction of the Valley of the Five Ponds.

"Do not panic," Zbigniew Penskie's voice shot out from the helicopter's speakers. "Those men you are seeing right now are the INR agents. Do not make any sudden movements and you will be all right."

The snowmobiles stopped in front of the flabbergasted WOP soldiers. The INR men proceeded to disarm the stunned soldiers at gunpoint and sent them off to the nearest hut at the Valley of the Five Ponds.

Mollie Banks was the only one who kept her wits about her during the standoff. While the INR agents were preoccupied with the WOP soldiers, she managed to withdraw from the pass without drawing attention to herself. Unseen from the helicopter she started the snowmobile Powell had used and drove it up the slope to the pass. She appeared next to Stan, causing the two men inside the helicopter's door to fall still in anticipation. She picked up Penskie's knapsack, strapped it to the handlebar and over the fuel tank, and pushed the snowmobile toward the icy edge of Zawrat. All eyes followed the vehicle as it slowly gained momentum and slid down the long and steep slope.

Whether it was the impact of the snowmobile hitting the same sharp rock that had mutilated Michael Gaertner's body, or the blasts from the machine gun Mollie fired was not important. The effect was that a large fireball bounced and rolled down the long slope until it landed in the soft snow some hundred meters below, where it finally exploded, sending deafening shock waves through the surrounding peaks.

Epilogue

"The good thing, Mr. President, is that no one will be able to tie the American intelligence to the September eleventh terrorist attacks," said the old man.

"I don't like the way it sounds! It wasn't involvement, just the frailty of our intelligence and defense networks," replied the president of the United States.

"It could be read either way. The fact remains that our intelligence was hands-on in the largest enemy organization in the world since the end of World War Two. We failed twice, Mr. President—we failed to gain control of the Fifth, and now the attack on the headquarters failed to secure its database. I suppose the good thing is that no one else will be able to get hold of it."

"We have no way of knowing it for sure. The flip side of dealing with digital technology is the ease of making copies.

Therefore, it would be prudent to assume that there could be additional copies somewhere."

"With our position, with what we *did* get hold of, we are bound to find and collect the rest sooner or later," said the secretary of state.

"I hope to God it happens soon. If even the slightest hint of what happened finds its way to the media, it might be the end of our government!"

"Everyone who had even the remotest contact with the takeover process of the Fifth Internationale's leadership was either eliminated or turned to our side." The old man gazed at the director of Central Intelligence.

"Everyone but your son!" scoffed the president.

"Stan will never know what *really* happened. All he faced was confusion, everyone running after some elusive information that drew a lot of blood and vanished in a big flame. He may suspect many things, but he'll never know the truth. Anyway, he's resigned from the FBI. He's on his own, with no resources and no friends. He's utterly disillusioned with the Bureau."

"You're an old friend, and I take your word for it, Zibi. You know as well as I do that if any of it should ever surface we will both be skinned alive, but it's not me I worry about. It's our great country and the American people and their futures that I have to regard."

"It is only a matter of time before we re-create most of the database. Once we have it, there is nothing anyone can do to stop us. For now, the handful of people who know what really happened are here." Zbigniew Penskie looked around the Oval Office, where five men sat quietly, their heads drooping under the burden of their involvement. "We are all ready to give our lives to protect this great country of ours. You know us all, Mr. President. We stand by you all the way."

"It was the best, the only thing to do to protect our country, Mr. President." The secretary of defense raised his head and looked into his president's eyes. "The only way to win the war against the scum of the world is to hold the strings that strap them. We have them now, or at least the ends of them, and so help me God, we won't rest until the world is ours . . . clean of them. The only thing I personally regret is that we did not get to it sooner, before the tragedy fell upon New York City, and indeed on our entire nation."

"The world was different then," said the director of Central Intelligence. "The Company was badly crippled by regulations and restrictions. Had we the privileges you and Congress bestowed on us after Nine-eleven we would have been able to act before the hyena had a chance to show its ugly fangs."

"It is a terrible thing that we humans have to learn the most valuable lessons from our failures," said the director of the Federal Bureau of Investigation. "One good thing that came out of this terrible time, lest we forget it, was that it brought us together."

"Hear, hear," said the attorney general. "Under Zbigniew's . . . Alpha's leadership, and with the resources of the Fifth Internationale, for the first time in history the world can sleep in peace. For the first time we can be sure that nothing like September eleventh will happen again, certainly not without our prior knowledge."

"Director Weber said it right," said Zbigniew Penskie. "It is truly the legacy of all generations to learn from their predecessors' dark mistakes."

"Then our thoughts are unified on the subject. Thank you

all, gentlemen." The president stood up. After the dignitaries left the Oval Office he spoke to Zbigniew. "I never doubted your ability to seize control of the situation. And I'm glad you did not need to sacrifice your son for the greater good."

"I assure you that Stan poses no danger. If he did, I would not hesitate to . . . As a father my heart would weep, but there are hundreds and thousands of parents, wives, and children whose loved ones died in the quest for the freedom and democracy we all so cherish. I promise you, Stan is as much a patriot as I am, but if I should ever doubt it, if there should ever be a hint of his noncompliance, we'll know immediately. We have a perfect warden, someone who breathes his every breath, knows his every thought."

The Renault convertible glided through the narrow curves of the coastal road in western Italy, on one side a steep rocky formation, on the other the calm waters of an azure lagoon. The sun was rising, casting long, soft shadows on the waking earth. A refreshing early-morning breeze blew through the driver's hair. He shook his head and caught the look on the woman's face. She smiled, but a distant shadow of concern remained deep in her eyes. She had to close them when sunrays shot out from around the narrow curve of the road.

The man looked ahead. Another sunrise, another day. Days were like people one encountered during the course of one's life: They came and went, sometimes leaving a deep impact on one's life, sometimes disappearing without a trace, without so much as a faint memory. A new day came every day, just as new people appeared on one's life's path, bringing new opportunities and new hopes.

Such a day will come, the man thought and smiled. *People change, new ideas sweep through administrations. Someday the truth will be told.*

He slowed down before a narrow hairpin curve. As he turned the steering wheel a compact disk attached by fishing line to the inside mirror swung and threw blinding reflections off the bright Mediterranean sun.